AMERICUS

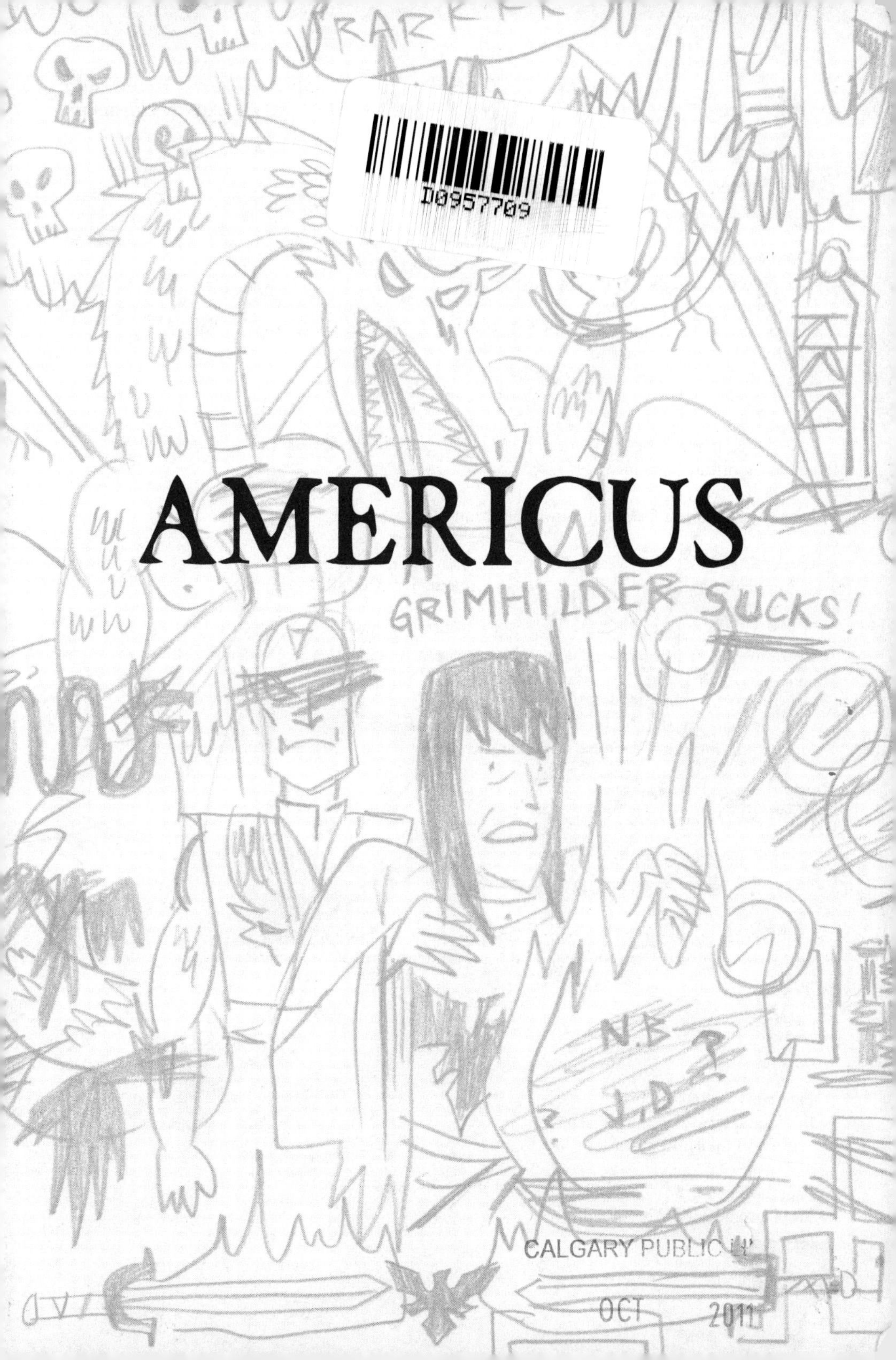

GRIMHILDER SUCKS!
N.B
J.D

:01

First Second

Thanks to Galen Longstreth, Greg Means, and Jason Rainey for their parts in making this book.

First Second
New York & London

Text copyright © 2011 by MK Reed
Illustrations copyright © 2011 by Jonathan Hill
Published by First Second
First Second is an imprint of Roaring Brook Press, a division of Holtzbrinck Publishing
Holdings Limited Partnership
175 Fifth Avenue, New York, New York 10010

Distributed in the United Kingdom by Macmillan Children's Books,
a division of Pan Macmillan.

Library of Congress Cataloging-in-Publication Data

Reed, M. K.
   Americus / MK Reed ; [illustrations by] Jonathan David Hill.—1st ed.
      p. cm.
   Summary: Oklahoma teen Neil Barton stands up for his favorite fantasy series, The
Chronicles of Apathea Ravenchilde, when conservative Christians try to bully the town of
Americus into banning it from the public library.
   ISBN 978-1-59643-601-5
   1. Graphic novels. [1. Graphic novels. 2. Books and reading—Fiction. 3. Censorship—
Fiction. 4. Libraries—Fiction. 5. Fundamentalism—Fiction.] I. Hill, Jonathan David, ill.
II. Title.
   PZ7.7.R42Ame 2011
   741.5'973—dc22

                                                                    2010051586

Hardcover ISBN: 978-1-59643-768-5

First Second books are available for special promotions and premiums.
For details, contact: Director of Special Markets, Holtzbrinck Publishers.

FIRST
EDITION

First edition 2011
Book design by Colleen AF Venable
Printed in the United States of America

Paperback: 10 9 8 7 6 5 4 3 2 1
Hardcover: 10 9 8 7 6 5 4 3 2 1

BY ART
WE LIVE

AMERICUS

Written by MK REED
Art by JONATHAN HILL

First Second
New York & London

CHAPTER 1

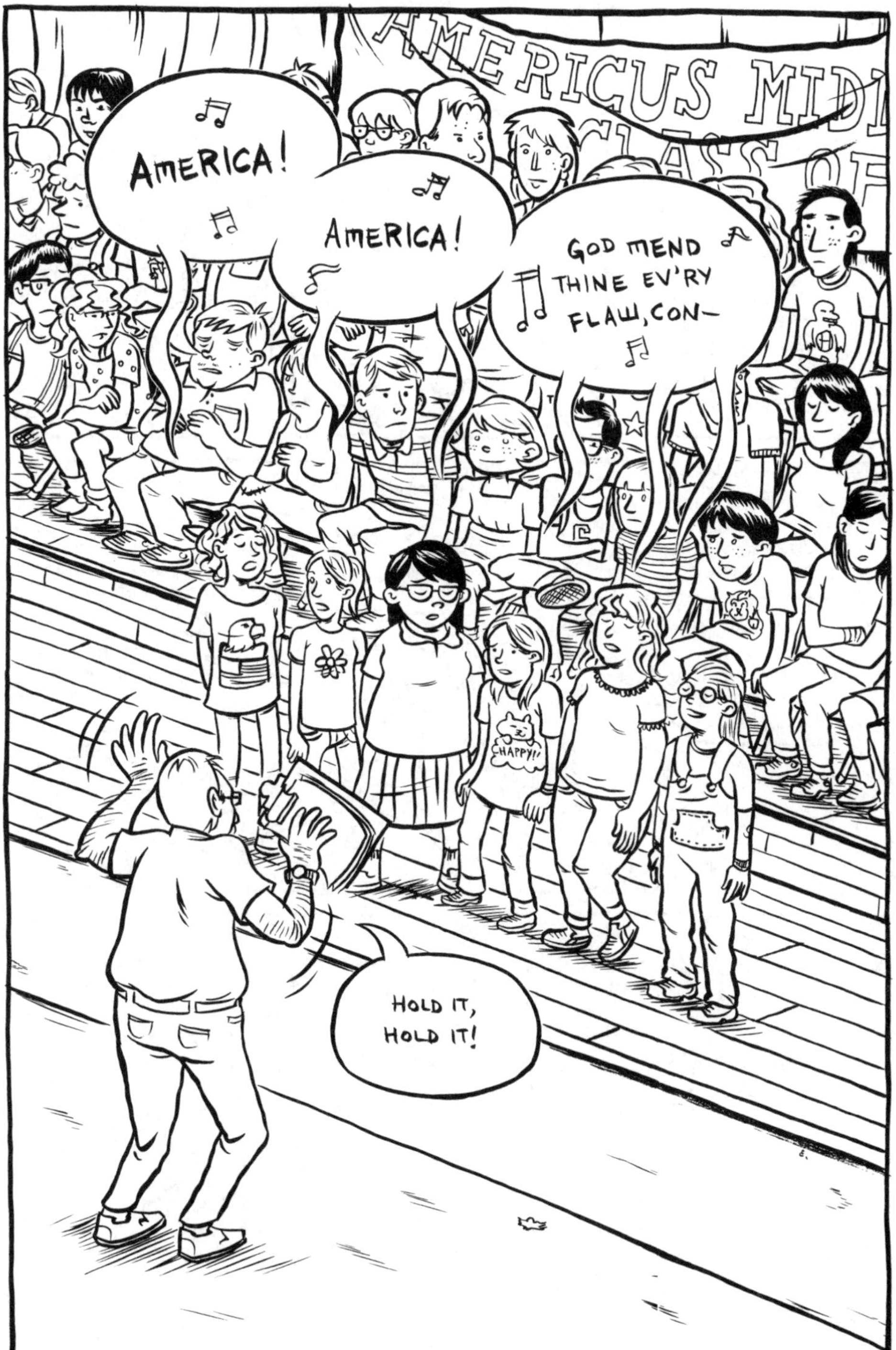
AMERICUS MIDI
CLASS OF
AMERICA!
AMERICA!
GOD MEND THINE EV'RY FLAW, CON–
HAPPY!!
HOLD IT, HOLD IT!

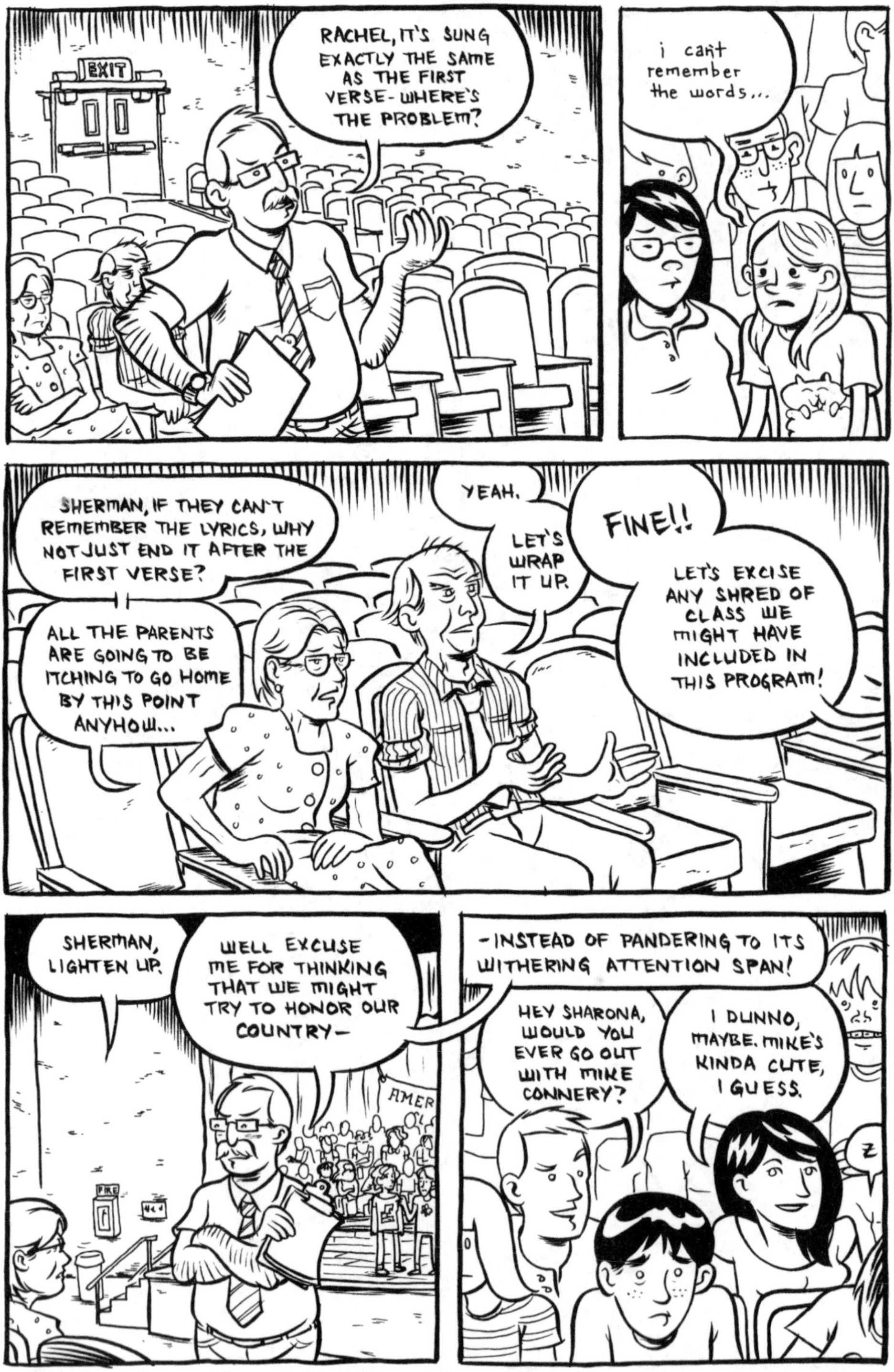
RACHEL, IT'S SUNG EXACTLY THE SAME AS THE FIRST VERSE- WHERE'S THE PROBLEM?
EXIT
i can't remember the words...
SHERMAN, IF THEY CAN'T REMEMBER THE LYRICS, WHY NOT JUST END IT AFTER THE FIRST VERSE?
ALL THE PARENTS ARE GOING TO BE ITCHING TO GO HOME BY THIS POINT ANYHOW...
YEAH.
LET'S WRAP IT UP.
FINE!!
LET'S EXCISE ANY SHRED OF CLASS WE MIGHT HAVE INCLUDED IN THIS PROGRAM!
SHERMAN, LIGHTEN UP.
WELL EXCUSE ME FOR THINKING THAT WE MIGHT TRY TO HONOR OUR COUNTRY—
—INSTEAD OF PANDERING TO ITS WITHERING ATTENTION SPAN!
FIRE
HEY SHARONA, WOULD YOU EVER GO OUT WITH MIKE CONNERY?
I DUNNO, MAYBE. MIKE'S KINDA CUTE, I GUESS.
Z

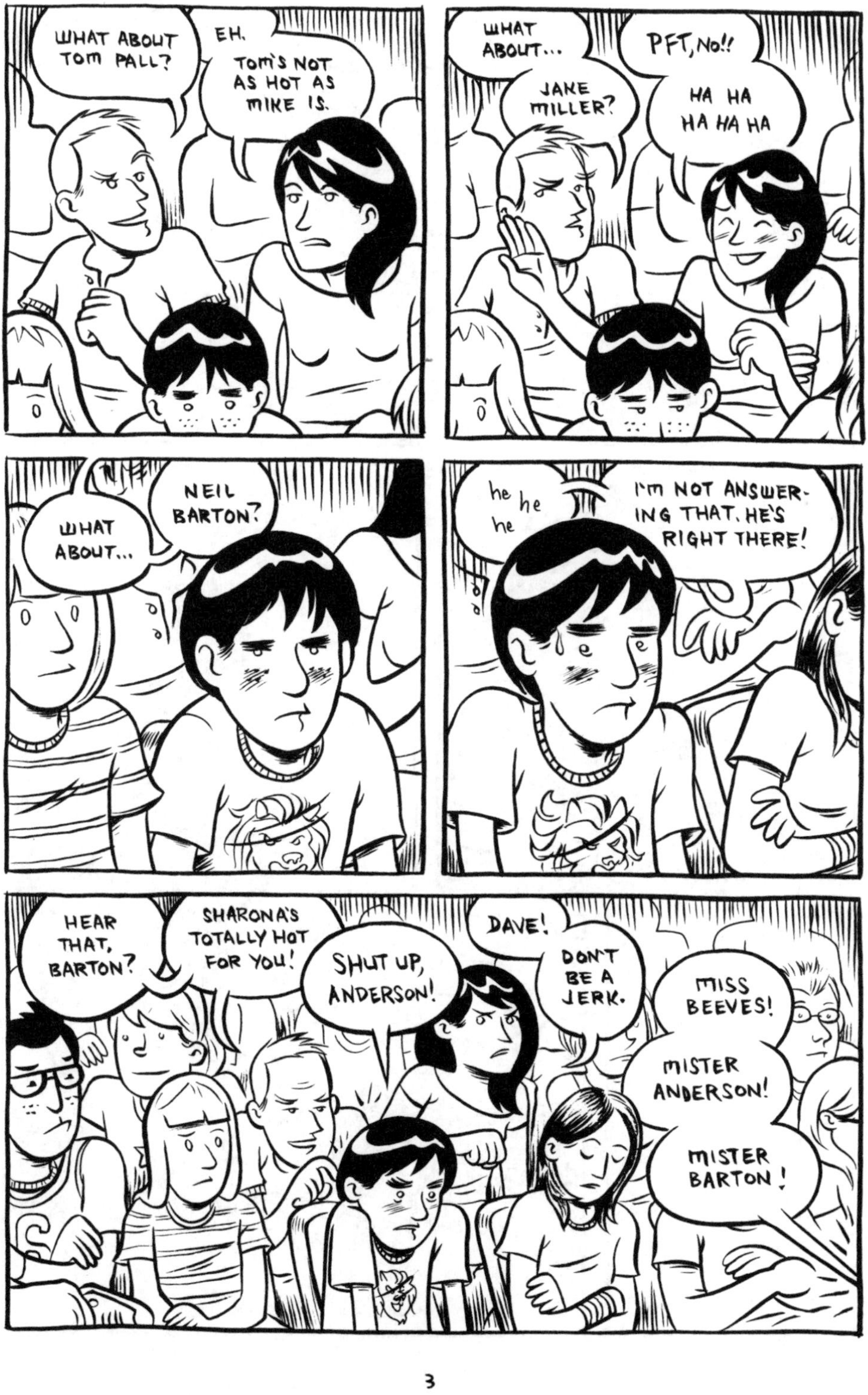
WHAT ABOUT TOM PALL?
EH.
TOM'S NOT AS HOT AS MIKE IS.
WHAT ABOUT...
JAKE MILLER?
PFT, NO!!
HA HA HA HA HA
WHAT ABOUT...
NEIL BARTON?
he he he
I'M NOT ANSWERING THAT. HE'S RIGHT THERE!
HEAR THAT, BARTON?
SHARONA'S TOTALLY HOT FOR YOU!
SHUT UP, ANDERSON!
DAVE!
DON'T BE A JERK.
MISS BEEVES!
MISTER ANDERSON!
MISTER BARTON!

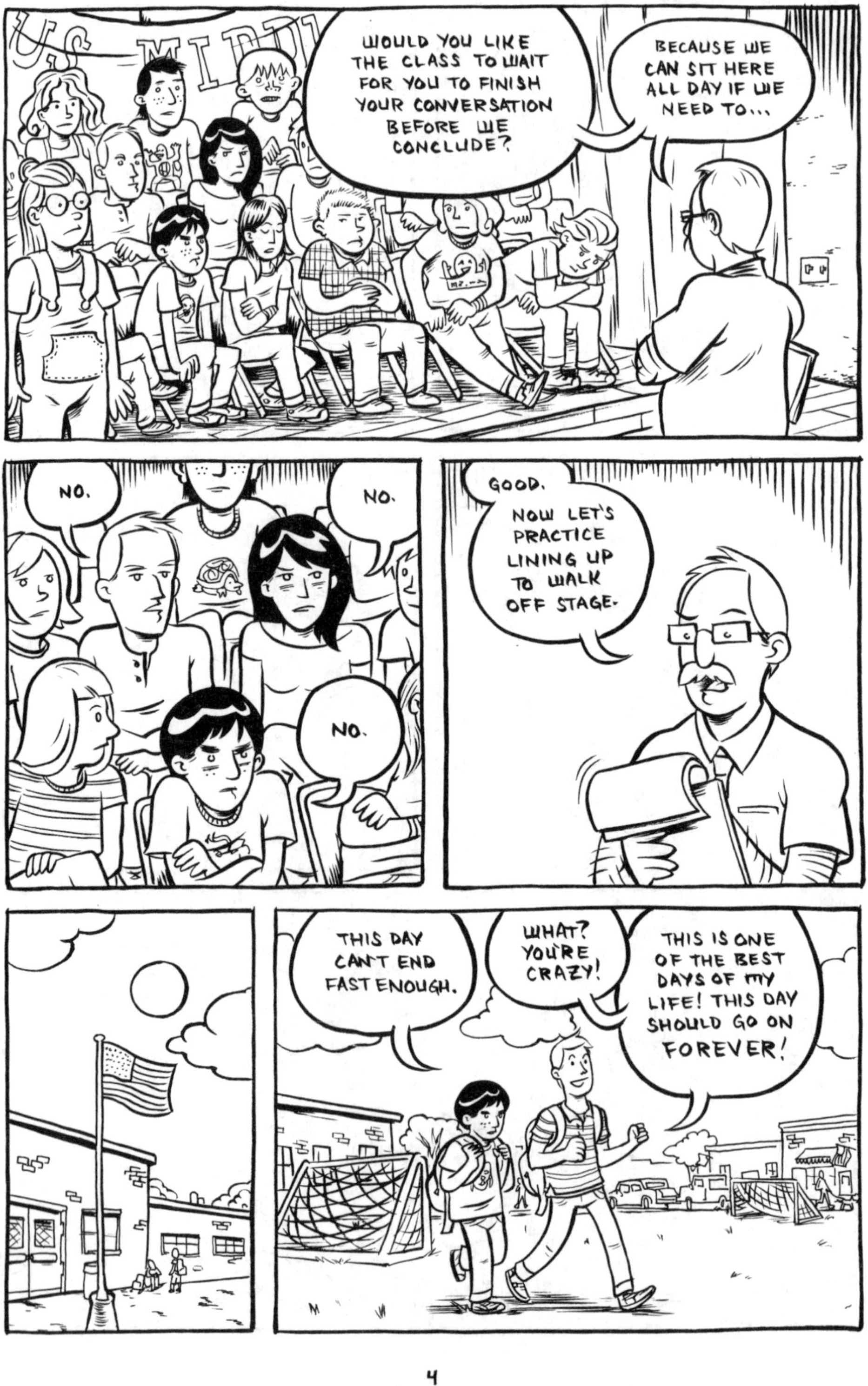
WOULD YOU LIKE THE CLASS TO WAIT FOR YOU TO FINISH YOUR CONVERSATION BEFORE WE CONCLUDE?
BECAUSE WE CAN SIT HERE ALL DAY IF WE NEED TO...
NO.
NO.
NO.
GOOD.
NOW LET'S PRACTICE LINING UP TO WALK OFF STAGE.
THIS DAY CAN'T END FAST ENOUGH.
WHAT? YOU'RE CRAZY!
THIS IS ONE OF THE BEST DAYS OF MY LIFE! THIS DAY SHOULD GO ON FOREVER!

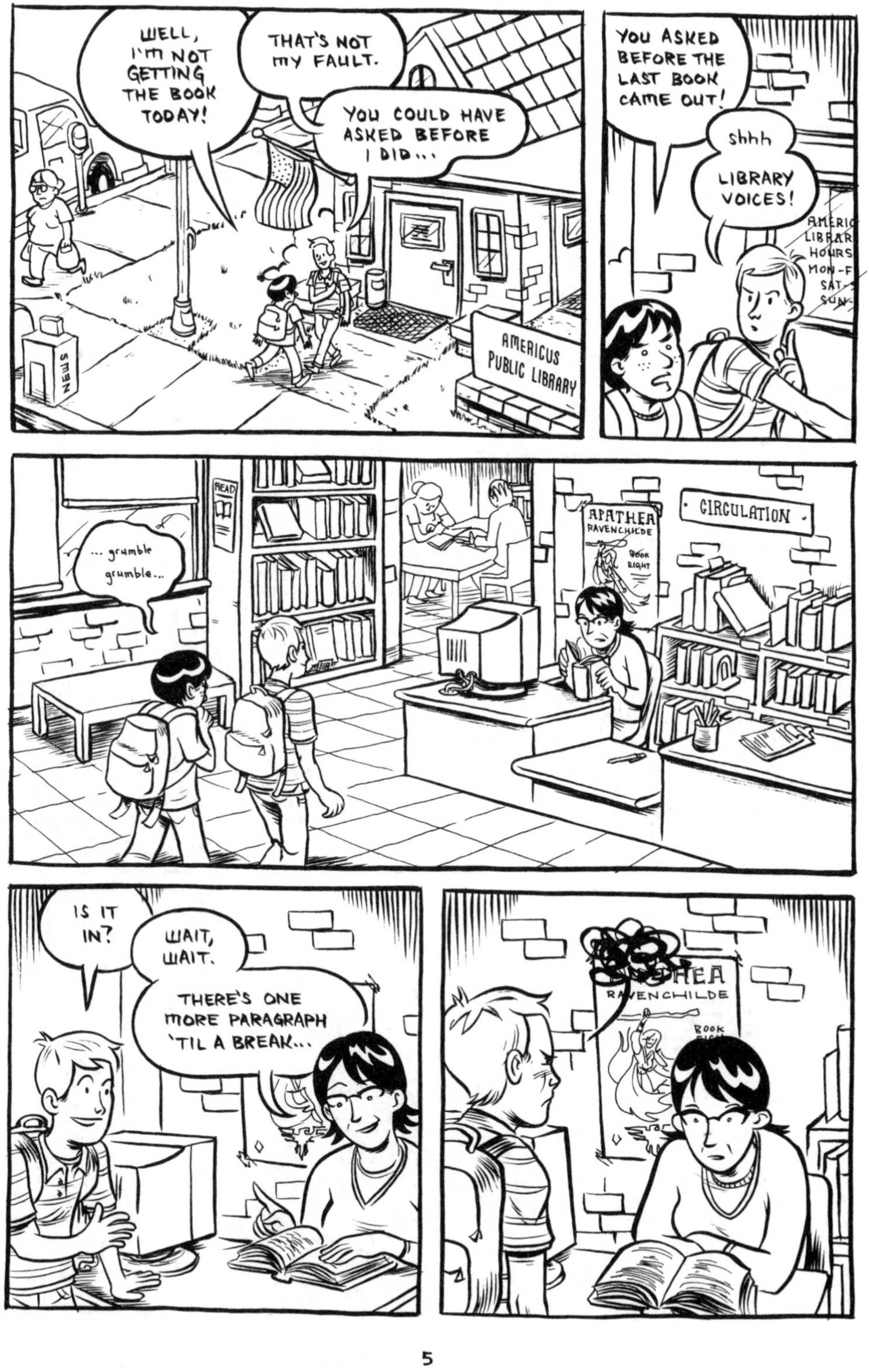
WELL, I'M NOT GETTING THE BOOK TODAY!
THAT'S NOT MY FAULT.
YOU COULD HAVE ASKED BEFORE I DID...
NEWS
AMERICUS PUBLIC LIBRARY
YOU ASKED BEFORE THE LAST BOOK CAME OUT!
shhh
LIBRARY VOICES!
HOURS
READ
... grumble grumble...
APATHEA RAVENCHILDE
BOOK EIGHT
CIRCULATION
IS IT IN?
WAIT, WAIT.
THERE'S ONE MORE PARAGRAPH 'TIL A BREAK...
RAVENCHILDE

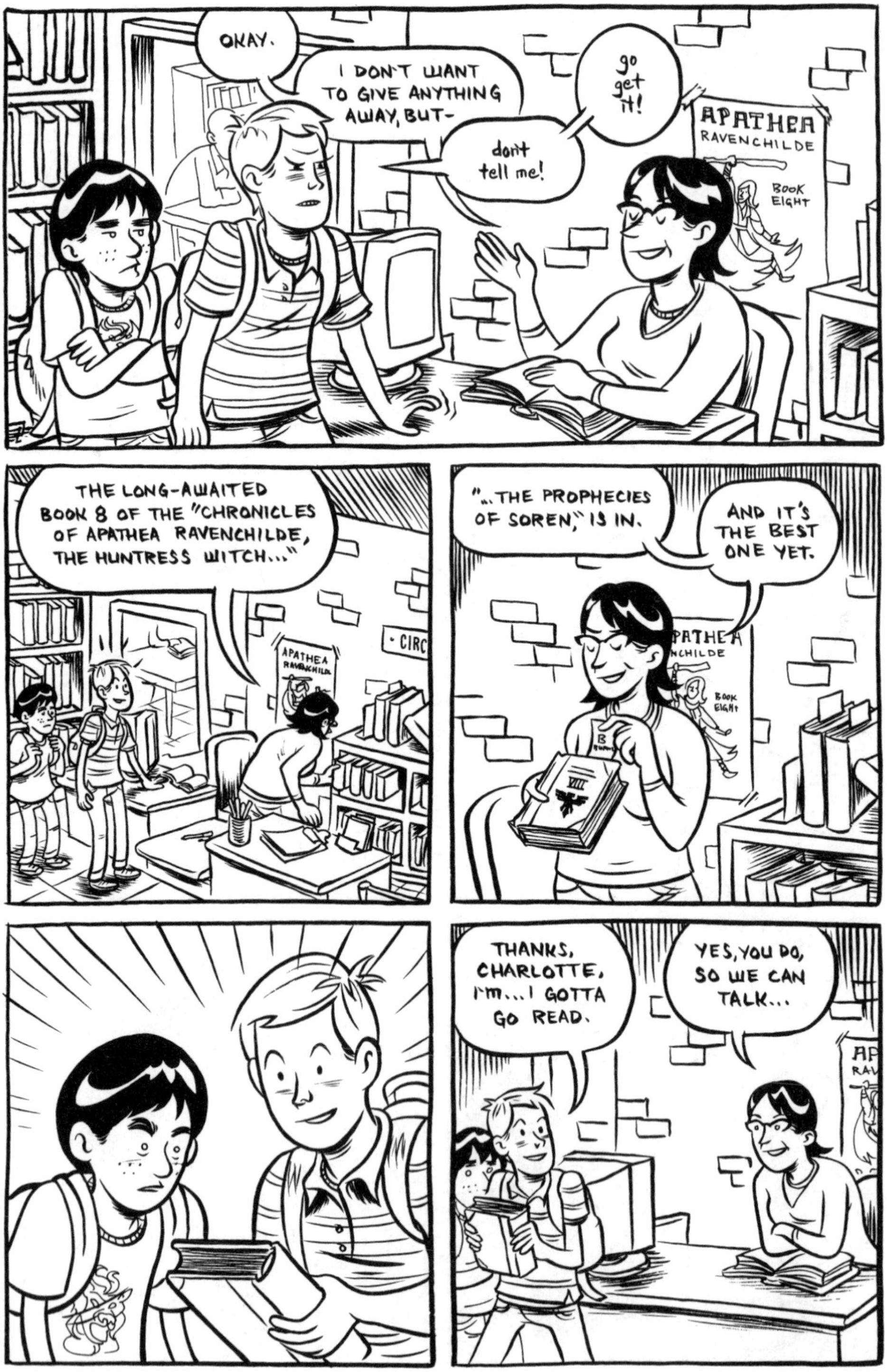

OKAY.
I DON'T WANT TO GIVE ANYTHING AWAY, BUT-
don't tell me!
go get it!
APATHEA RAVENCHILDE
BOOK EIGHT
THE LONG-AWAITED BOOK 8 OF THE "CHRONICLES OF APATHEA RAVENCHILDE, THE HUNTRESS WITCH..."
APATHEA RAVENCHILDE
CIRC
"...THE PROPHECIES OF SOREN," IS IN.
AND IT'S THE BEST ONE YET.
BOOK EIGHT
VIII
THANKS, CHARLOTTE, I'M... I GOTTA GO READ.
YES, YOU DO, SO WE CAN TALK...

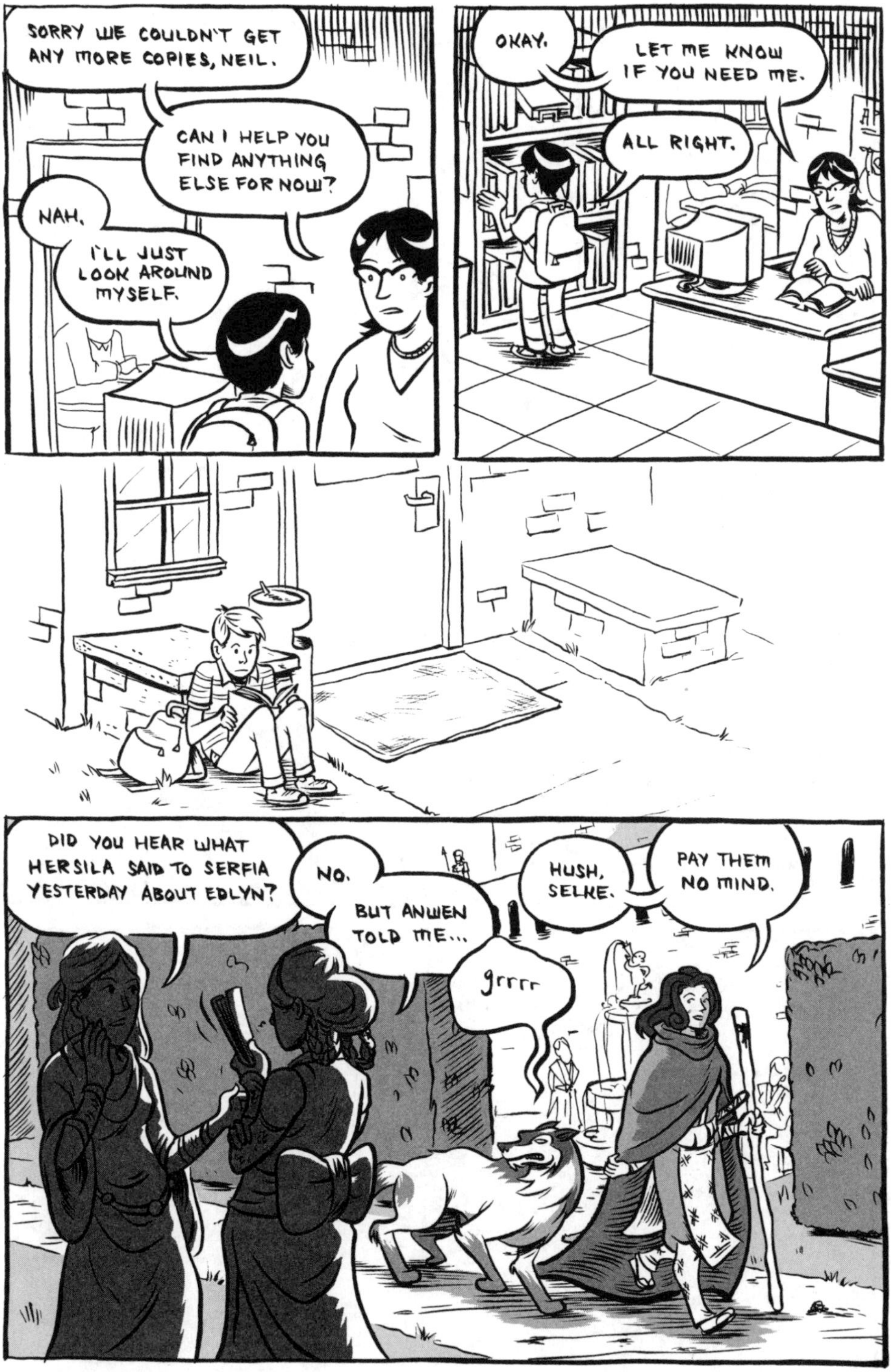
SORRY WE COULDN'T GET ANY MORE COPIES, NEIL.
CAN I HELP YOU FIND ANYTHING ELSE FOR NOW?
NAH.
I'LL JUST LOOK AROUND MYSELF.
OKAY.
LET ME KNOW IF YOU NEED ME.
ALL RIGHT.
DID YOU HEAR WHAT HERSILA SAID TO SERFIA YESTERDAY ABOUT EDLYN?
NO.
BUT ANWEN TOLD ME...
grrrr
HUSH, SELKE.
PAY THEM NO MIND.

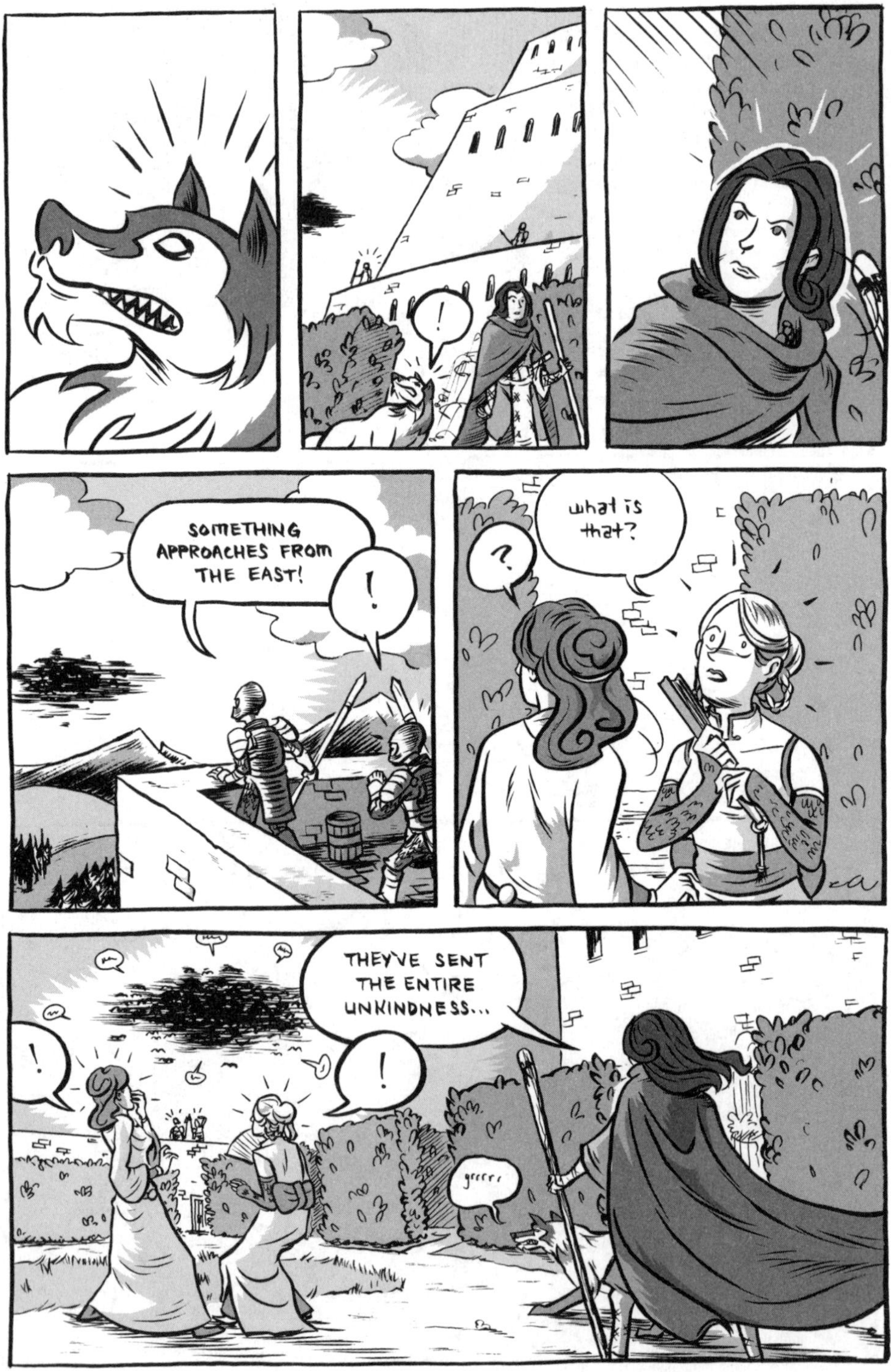
!
SOMETHING APPROACHES FROM THE EAST!
!
?
what is that?
!
THEY'VE SENT THE ENTIRE UNKINDNESS...
!
grrrr

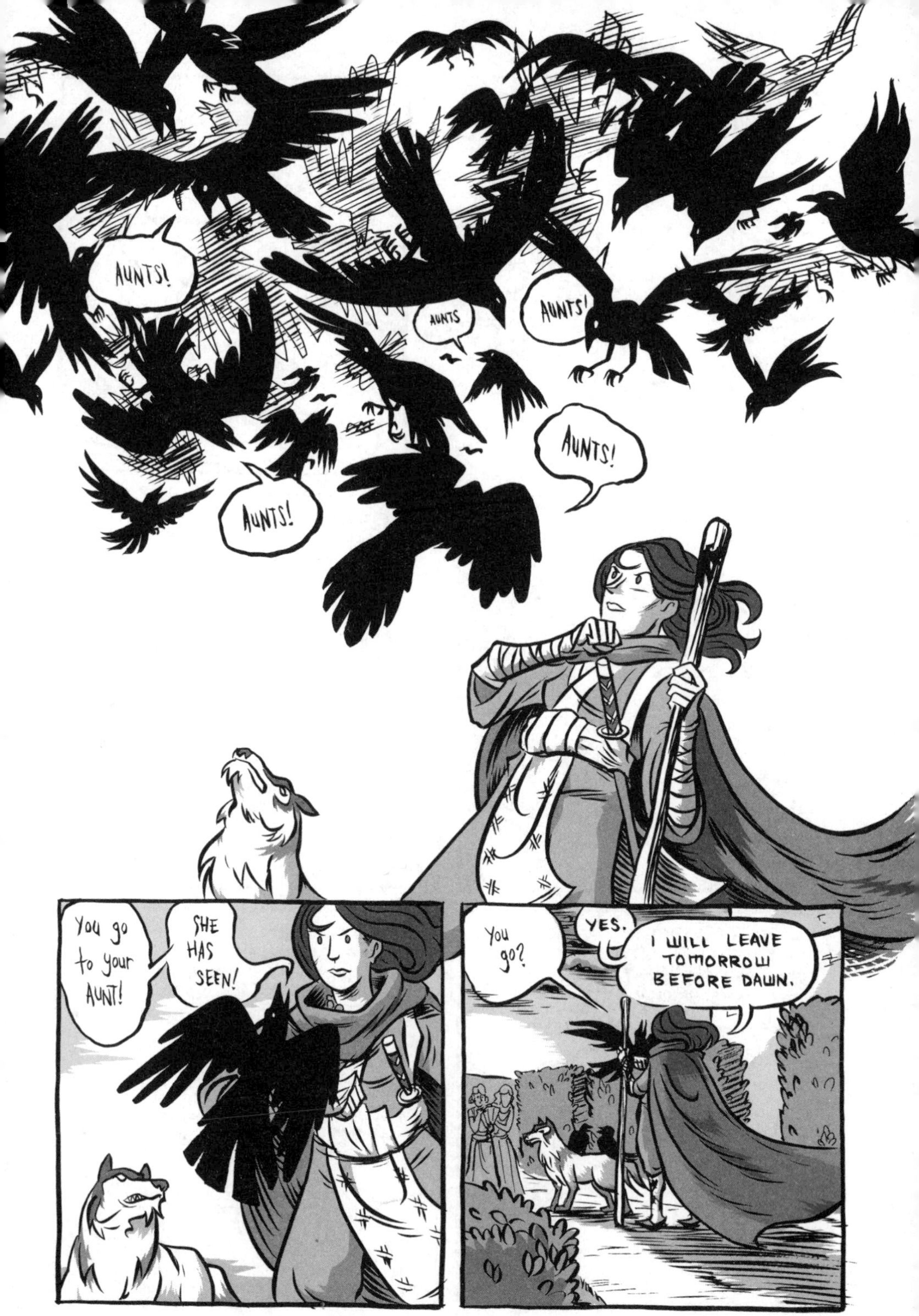
AUNTS!
AUNTS
AUNTS!
AUNTS!
AUNTS!
You go to your AUNT!
SHE HAS SEEN!
You go?
YES.
I WILL LEAVE TOMORROW BEFORE DAWN.

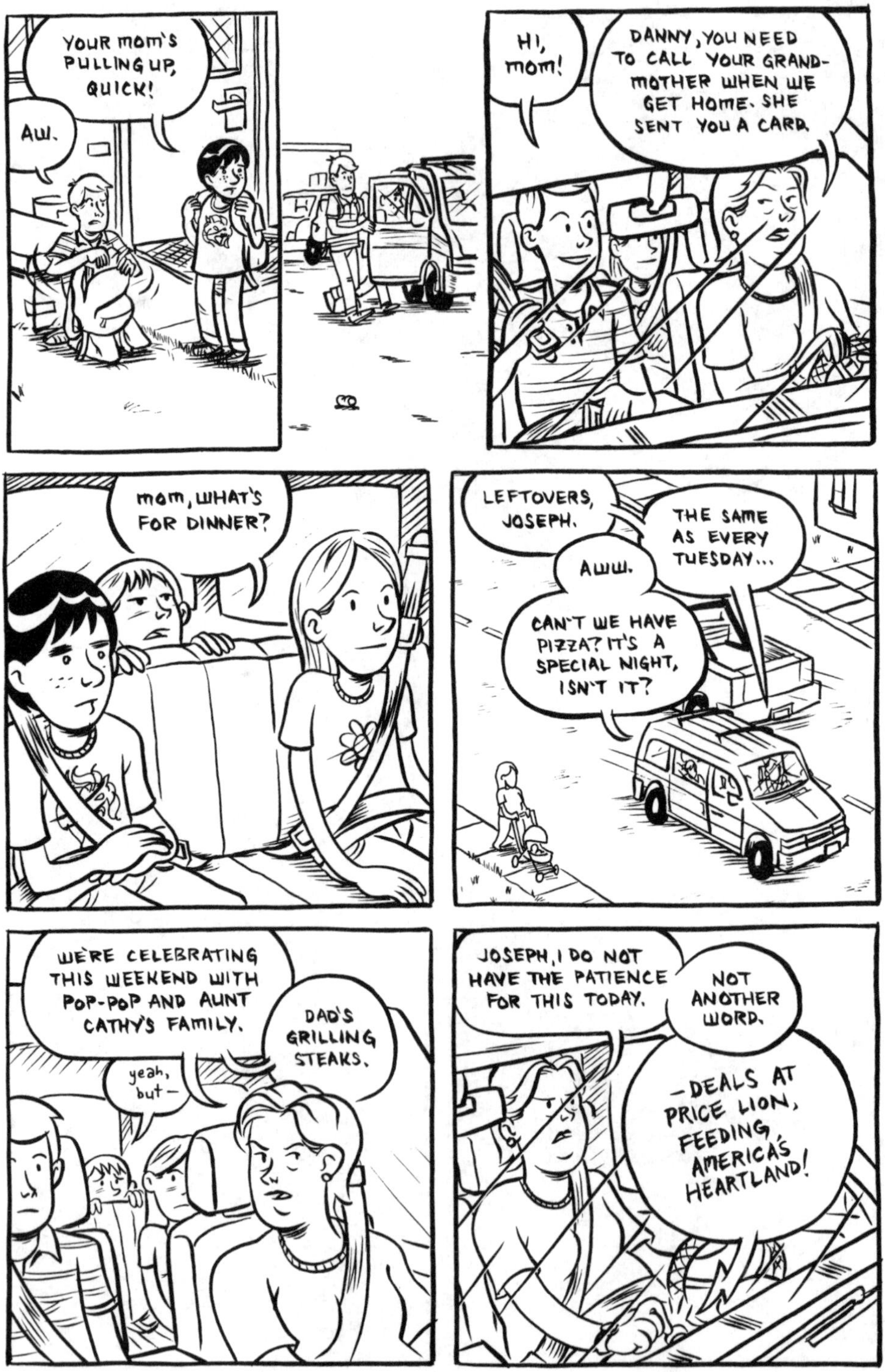
YOUR MOM'S PULLING UP, QUICK!
AW.
HI, MOM!
DANNY, YOU NEED TO CALL YOUR GRANDMOTHER WHEN WE GET HOME. SHE SENT YOU A CARD.
MOM, WHAT'S FOR DINNER?
LEFTOVERS, JOSEPH.
THE SAME AS EVERY TUESDAY...
AWW.
CAN'T WE HAVE PIZZA? IT'S A SPECIAL NIGHT, ISN'T IT?
WE'RE CELEBRATING THIS WEEKEND WITH POP-POP AND AUNT CATHY'S FAMILY.
DAD'S GRILLING STEAKS.
yeah, but—
JOSEPH, I DO NOT HAVE THE PATIENCE FOR THIS TODAY.
NOT ANOTHER WORD.
—DEALS AT PRICE LION, FEEDING AMERICA'S HEARTLAND!

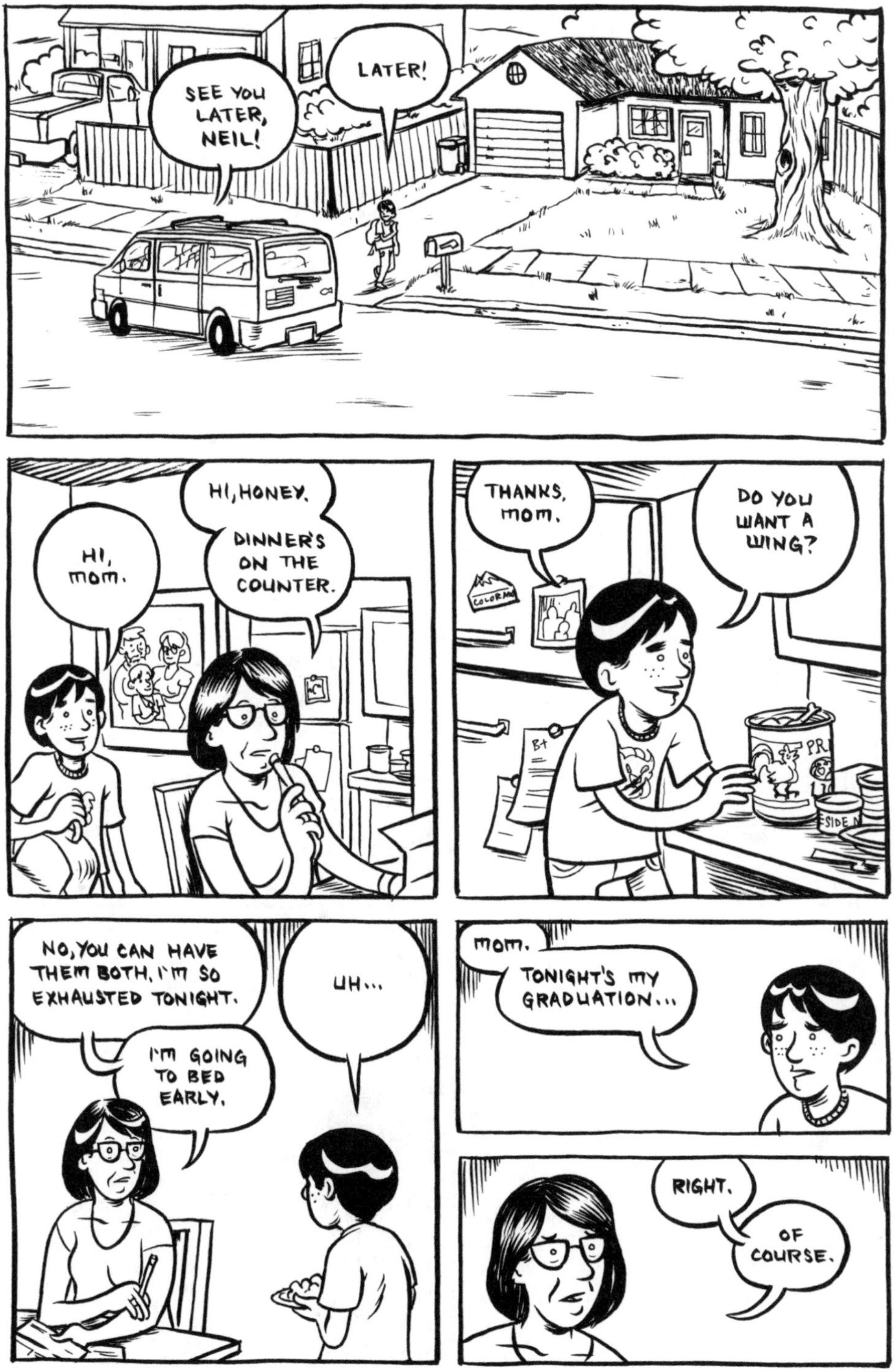

SEE YOU LATER, NEIL!
LATER!
HI, MOM.
HI, HONEY.
DINNER'S ON THE COUNTER.
THANKS, MOM.
DO YOU WANT A WING?
NO, YOU CAN HAVE THEM BOTH, I'M SO EXHAUSTED TONIGHT.
I'M GOING TO BED EARLY.
UH...
MOM.
TONIGHT'S MY GRADUATION...
RIGHT.
OF COURSE.

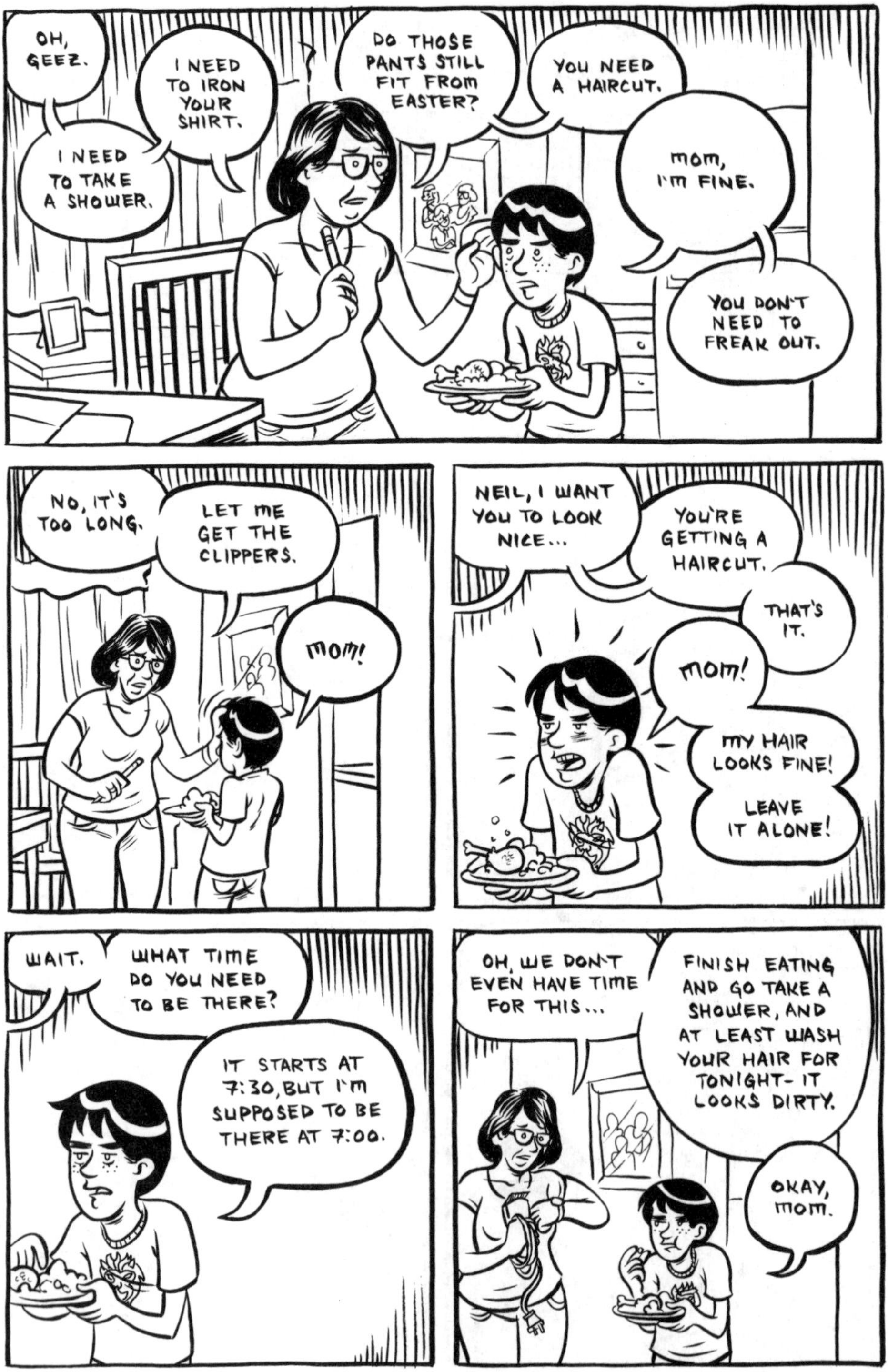
OH, GEEZ.
I NEED TO TAKE A SHOWER.
I NEED TO IRON YOUR SHIRT.
DO THOSE PANTS STILL FIT FROM EASTER?
YOU NEED A HAIRCUT.
MOM, I'M FINE.
YOU DON'T NEED TO FREAK OUT.
NO, IT'S TOO LONG.
LET ME GET THE CLIPPERS.
MOM!
NEIL, I WANT YOU TO LOOK NICE...
YOU'RE GETTING A HAIRCUT.
THAT'S IT.
MOM!
MY HAIR LOOKS FINE!
LEAVE IT ALONE!
WAIT.
WHAT TIME DO YOU NEED TO BE THERE?
IT STARTS AT 7:30, BUT I'M SUPPOSED TO BE THERE AT 7:00.
OH, WE DON'T EVEN HAVE TIME FOR THIS...
FINISH EATING AND GO TAKE A SHOWER, AND AT LEAST WASH YOUR HAIR FOR TONIGHT- IT LOOKS DIRTY.
OKAY, MOM.

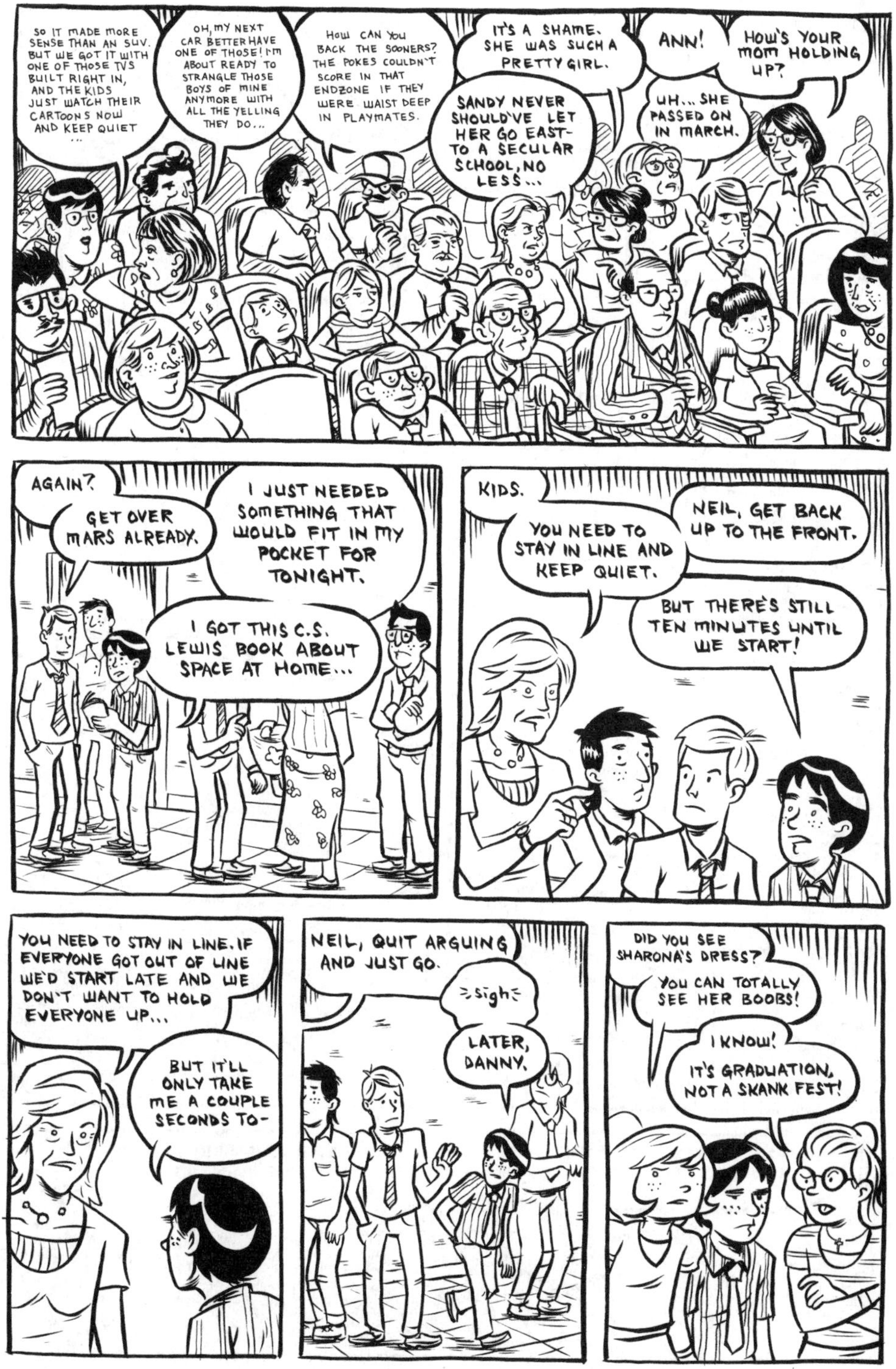
SO IT MADE MORE SENSE THAN AN SUV. BUT WE GOT IT WITH ONE OF THOSE TVS BUILT RIGHT IN, AND THE KIDS JUST WATCH THEIR CARTOONS NOW AND KEEP QUIET ...
OH, MY NEXT CAR BETTER HAVE ONE OF THOSE! I'M ABOUT READY TO STRANGLE THOSE BOYS OF MINE ANYMORE WITH ALL THE YELLING THEY DO...
HOW CAN YOU BACK THE SOONERS? THE POKES COULDN'T SCORE IN THAT ENDZONE IF THEY WERE WAIST DEEP IN PLAYMATES.
IT'S A SHAME. SHE WAS SUCH A PRETTY GIRL.
SANDY NEVER SHOULD'VE LET HER GO EAST- TO A SECULAR SCHOOL, NO LESS...
ANN!
HOW'S YOUR MOM HOLDING UP?
UH... SHE PASSED ON IN MARCH.
AGAIN?
GET OVER MARS ALREADY.
I JUST NEEDED SOMETHING THAT WOULD FIT IN MY POCKET FOR TONIGHT.
I GOT THIS C.S. LEWIS BOOK ABOUT SPACE AT HOME...
KIDS.
YOU NEED TO STAY IN LINE AND KEEP QUIET.
NEIL, GET BACK UP TO THE FRONT.
BUT THERE'S STILL TEN MINUTES UNTIL WE START!
YOU NEED TO STAY IN LINE. IF EVERYONE GOT OUT OF LINE WE'D START LATE AND WE DON'T WANT TO HOLD EVERYONE UP...
BUT IT'LL ONLY TAKE ME A COUPLE SECONDS TO-
NEIL, QUIT ARGUING AND JUST GO.
sigh
LATER, DANNY.
DID YOU SEE SHARONA'S DRESS?
YOU CAN TOTALLY SEE HER BOOBS!
I KNOW!
IT'S GRADUATION, NOT A SKANK FEST!

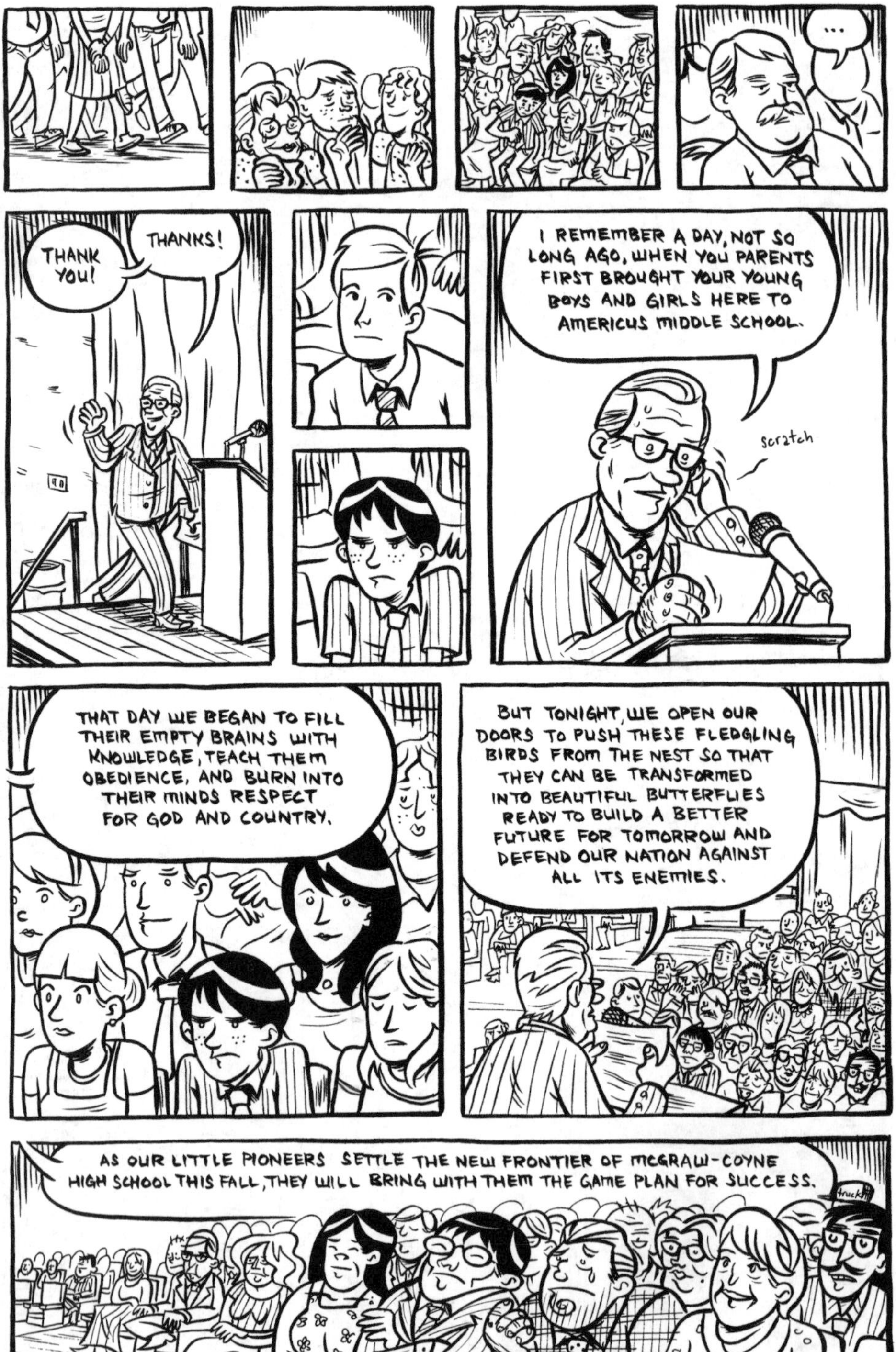
...
THANK YOU!
THANKS!
I REMEMBER A DAY, NOT SO LONG AGO, WHEN YOU PARENTS FIRST BROUGHT YOUR YOUNG BOYS AND GIRLS HERE TO AMERICUS MIDDLE SCHOOL.
scratch
THAT DAY WE BEGAN TO FILL THEIR EMPTY BRAINS WITH KNOWLEDGE, TEACH THEM OBEDIENCE, AND BURN INTO THEIR MINDS RESPECT FOR GOD AND COUNTRY.
BUT TONIGHT, WE OPEN OUR DOORS TO PUSH THESE FLEDGLING BIRDS FROM THE NEST SO THAT THEY CAN BE TRANSFORMED INTO BEAUTIFUL BUTTERFLIES READY TO BUILD A BETTER FUTURE FOR TOMORROW AND DEFEND OUR NATION AGAINST ALL ITS ENEMIES.
AS OUR LITTLE PIONEERS SETTLE THE NEW FRONTIER OF MCGRAW-COYNE HIGH SCHOOL THIS FALL, THEY WILL BRING WITH THEM THE GAME PLAN FOR SUCCESS.

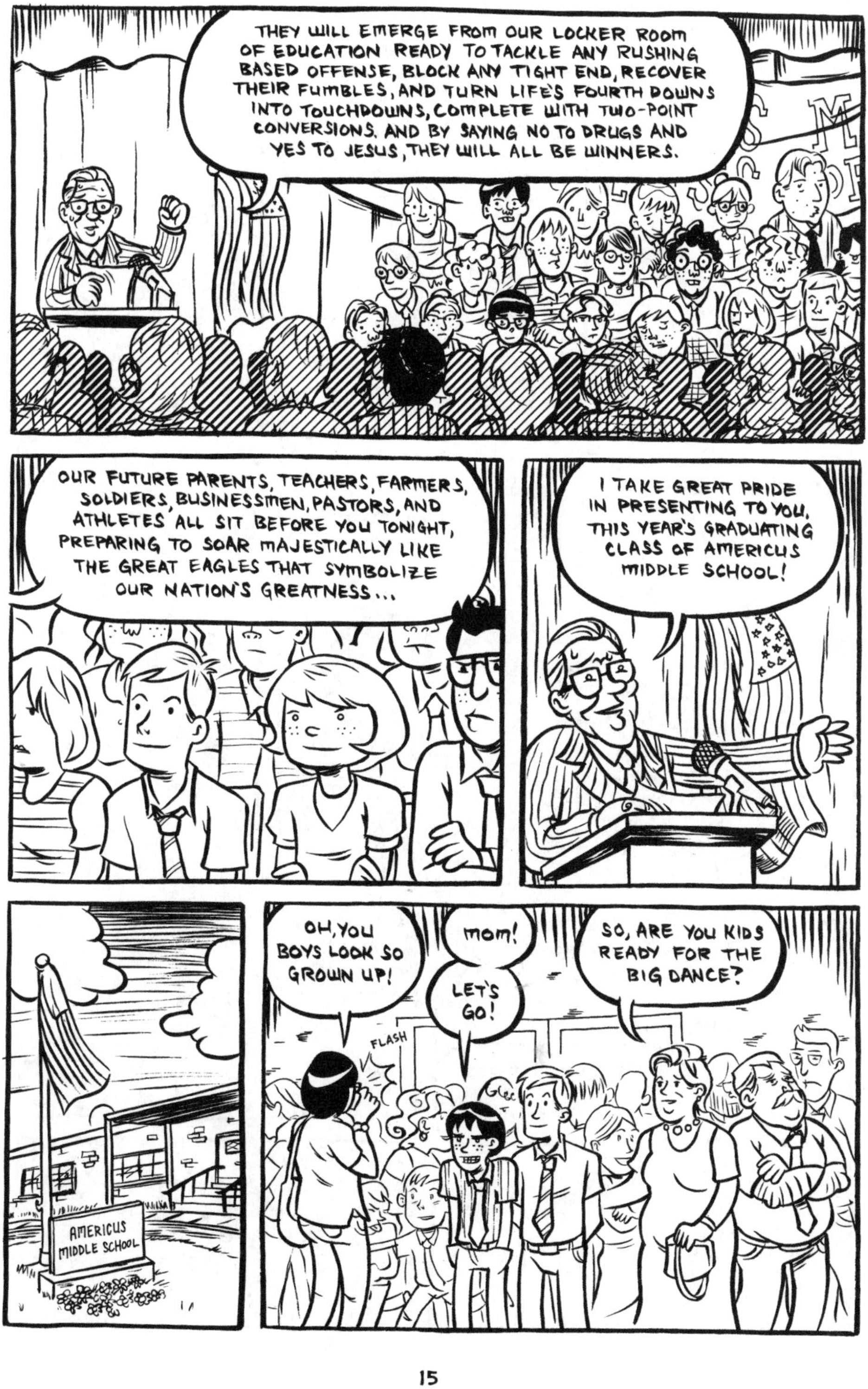
THEY WILL EMERGE FROM OUR LOCKER ROOM OF EDUCATION READY TO TACKLE ANY RUSHING BASED OFFENSE, BLOCK ANY TIGHT END, RECOVER THEIR FUMBLES, AND TURN LIFE'S FOURTH DOWNS INTO TOUCHDOWNS, COMPLETE WITH TWO-POINT CONVERSIONS. AND BY SAYING NO TO DRUGS AND YES TO JESUS, THEY WILL ALL BE WINNERS.
OUR FUTURE PARENTS, TEACHERS, FARMERS, SOLDIERS, BUSINESSMEN, PASTORS, AND ATHLETES ALL SIT BEFORE YOU TONIGHT, PREPARING TO SOAR MAJESTICALLY LIKE THE GREAT EAGLES THAT SYMBOLIZE OUR NATION'S GREATNESS...
I TAKE GREAT PRIDE IN PRESENTING TO YOU, THIS YEAR'S GRADUATING CLASS OF AMERICUS MIDDLE SCHOOL!
AMERICUS MIDDLE SCHOOL
OH, YOU BOYS LOOK SO GROWN UP!
FLASH
MOM!
LET'S GO!
SO, ARE YOU KIDS READY FOR THE BIG DANCE?

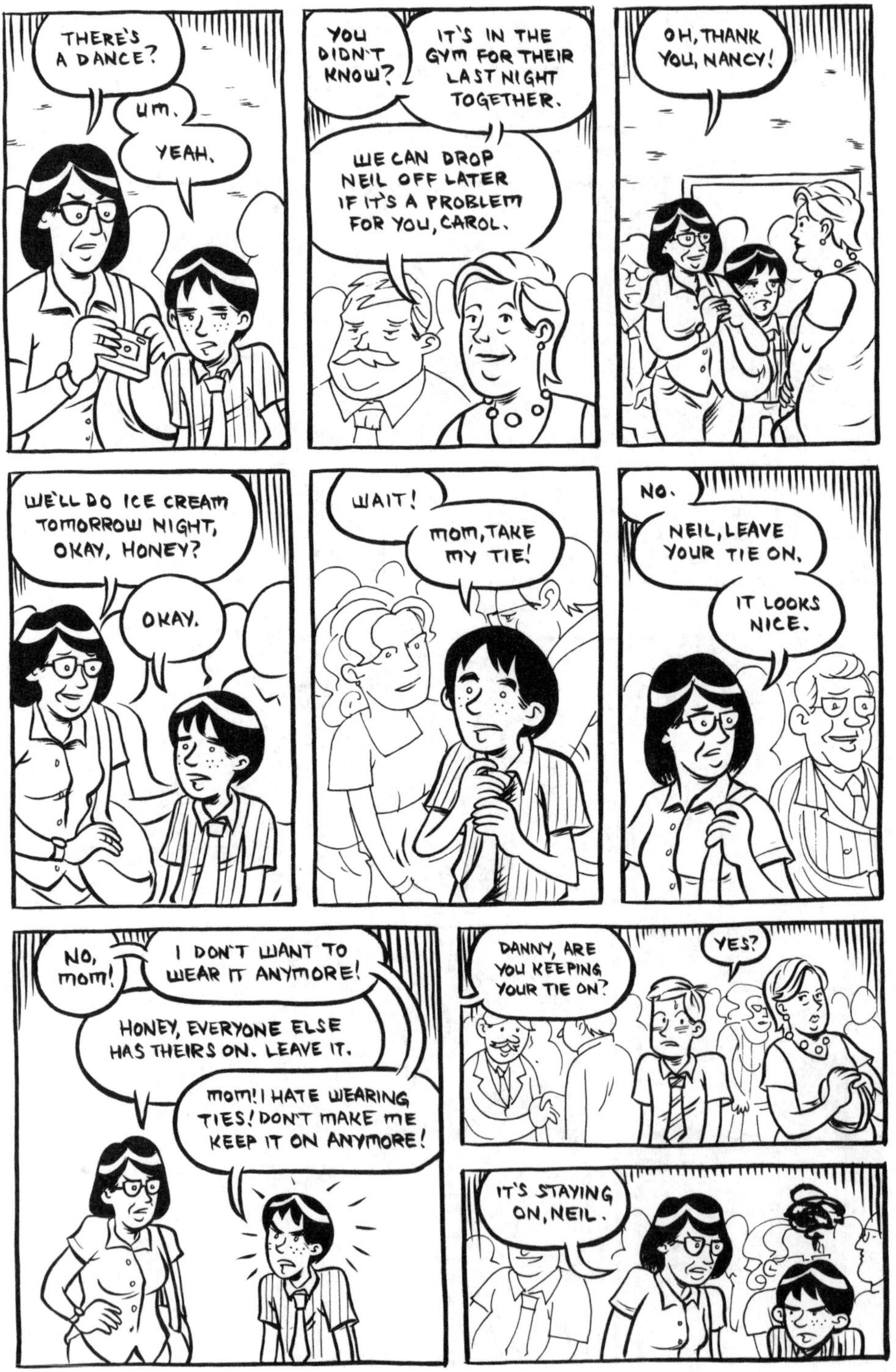
THERE'S A DANCE?
UM.
YEAH.
YOU DIDN'T KNOW?
IT'S IN THE GYM FOR THEIR LAST NIGHT TOGETHER.
WE CAN DROP NEIL OFF LATER IF IT'S A PROBLEM FOR YOU, CAROL.
OH, THANK YOU, NANCY!
WE'LL DO ICE CREAM TOMORROW NIGHT, OKAY, HONEY?
OKAY.
WAIT!
MOM, TAKE MY TIE!
NO.
NEIL, LEAVE YOUR TIE ON.
IT LOOKS NICE.
NO, MOM!
I DON'T WANT TO WEAR IT ANYMORE!
HONEY, EVERYONE ELSE HAS THEIRS ON. LEAVE IT.
MOM! I HATE WEARING TIES! DON'T MAKE ME KEEP IT ON ANYMORE!
DANNY, ARE YOU KEEPING YOUR TIE ON?
YES?
IT'S STAYING ON, NEIL.

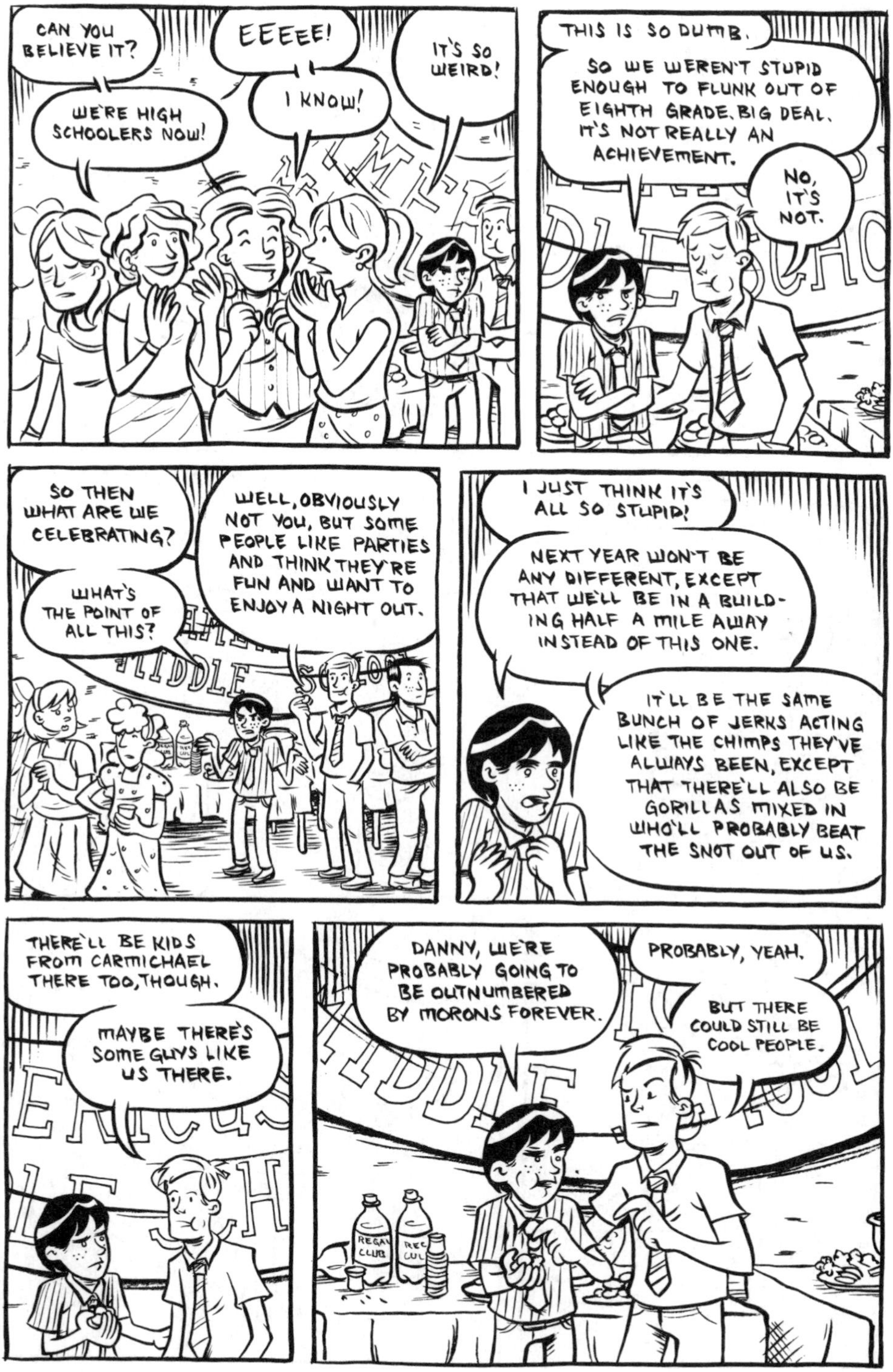
CAN YOU BELIEVE IT?
WE'RE HIGH SCHOOLERS NOW!
EEEEE!
I KNOW!
IT'S SO WEIRD!
THIS IS SO DUMB.
SO WE WEREN'T STUPID ENOUGH TO FLUNK OUT OF EIGHTH GRADE. BIG DEAL. IT'S NOT REALLY AN ACHIEVEMENT.
NO, IT'S NOT.
SO THEN WHAT ARE WE CELEBRATING?
WHAT'S THE POINT OF ALL THIS?
WELL, OBVIOUSLY NOT YOU, BUT SOME PEOPLE LIKE PARTIES AND THINK THEY'RE FUN AND WANT TO ENJOY A NIGHT OUT.
I JUST THINK IT'S ALL SO STUPID!
NEXT YEAR WON'T BE ANY DIFFERENT, EXCEPT THAT WE'LL BE IN A BUILD-ING HALF A MILE AWAY INSTEAD OF THIS ONE.
IT'LL BE THE SAME BUNCH OF JERKS ACTING LIKE THE CHIMPS THEY'VE ALWAYS BEEN, EXCEPT THAT THERE'LL ALSO BE GORILLAS MIXED IN WHO'LL PROBABLY BEAT THE SNOT OUT OF US.
THERE'LL BE KIDS FROM CARMICHAEL THERE TOO, THOUGH.
MAYBE THERE'S SOME GUYS LIKE US THERE.
DANNY, WE'RE PROBABLY GOING TO BE OUTNUMBERED BY MORONS FOREVER.
PROBABLY, YEAH.
BUT THERE COULD STILL BE COOL PEOPLE.

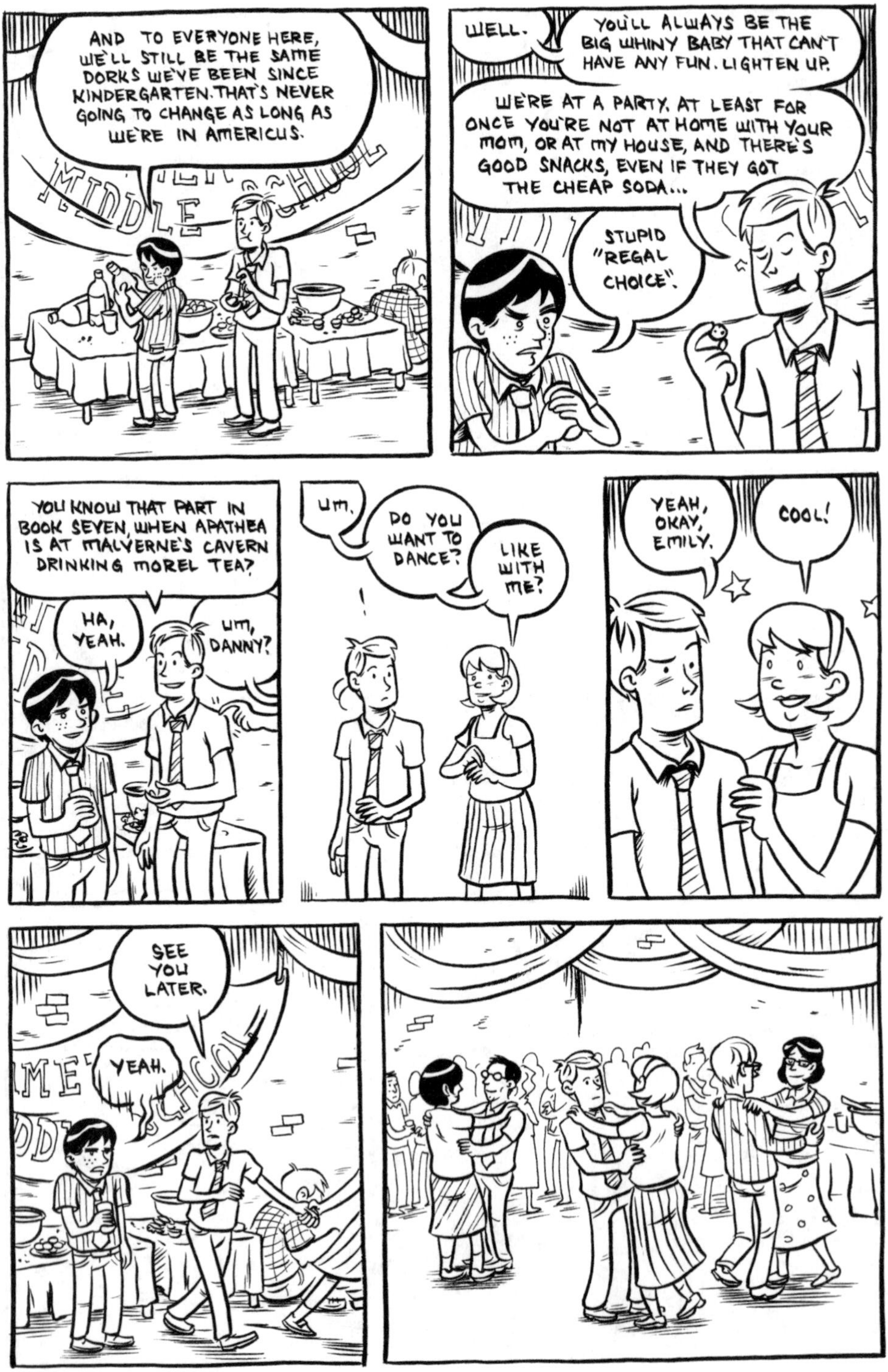
AND TO EVERYONE HERE, WE'LL STILL BE THE SAME DORKS WE'VE BEEN SINCE KINDERGARTEN. THAT'S NEVER GOING TO CHANGE AS LONG AS WE'RE IN AMERICUS.
MIDDLE SCHOOL
WELL.
YOU'LL ALWAYS BE THE BIG WHINY BABY THAT CAN'T HAVE ANY FUN. LIGHTEN UP.
WE'RE AT A PARTY. AT LEAST FOR ONCE YOU'RE NOT AT HOME WITH YOUR MOM, OR AT MY HOUSE, AND THERE'S GOOD SNACKS, EVEN IF THEY GOT THE CHEAP SODA...
STUPID "REGAL CHOICE".
YOU KNOW THAT PART IN BOOK SEVEN, WHEN APATHEA IS AT MALVERNE'S CAVERN DRINKING MOREL TEA?
HA, YEAH.
UM, DANNY?
UM.
DO YOU WANT TO DANCE?
LIKE WITH ME?
!
YEAH, OKAY, EMILY.
COOL!
SEE YOU LATER.
YEAH.

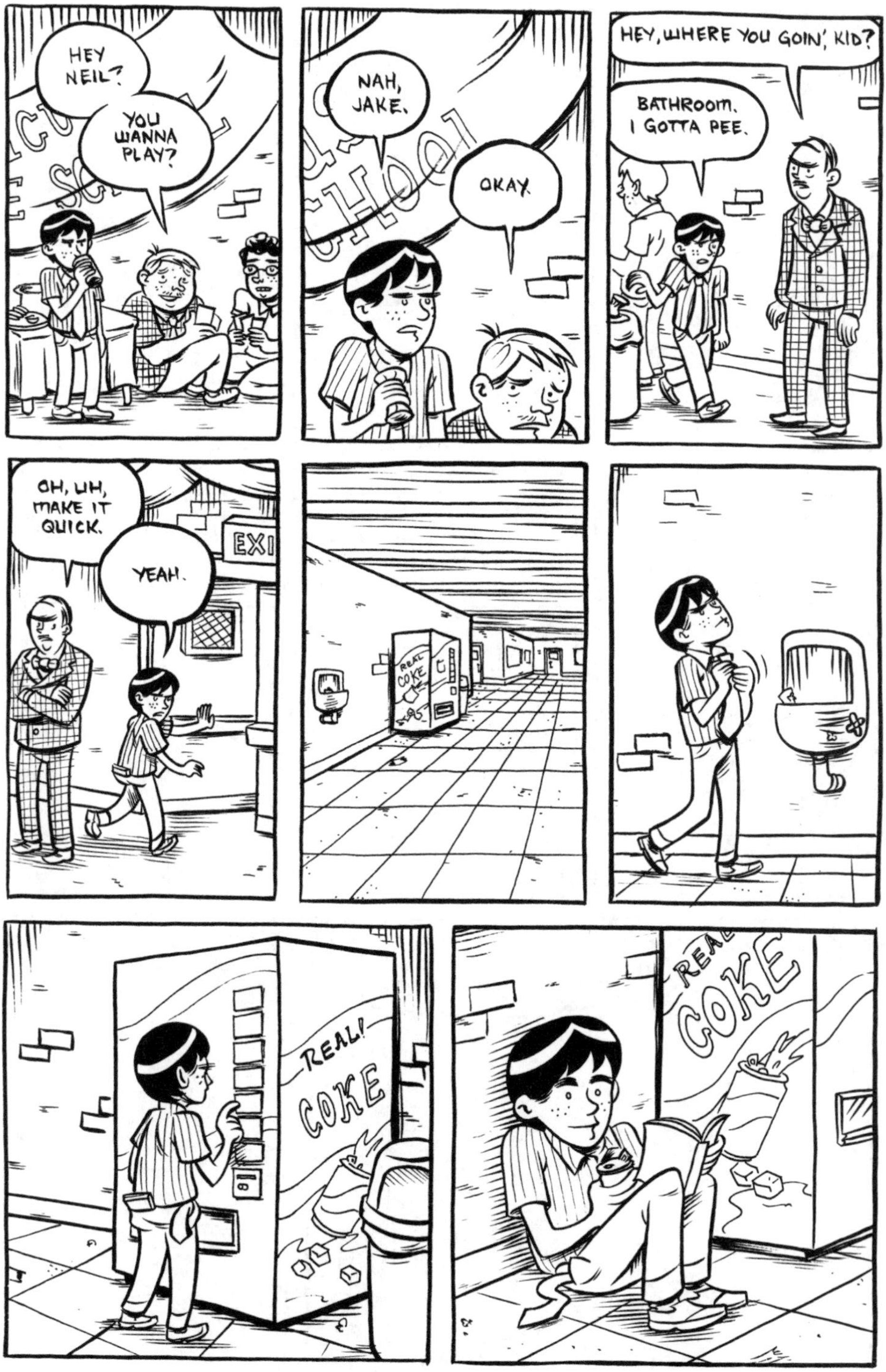
HEY NEIL?
YOU WANNA PLAY?
NAH, JAKE.
OKAY.
HEY, WHERE YOU GOIN', KID?
BATHROOM. I GOTTA PEE.
OH, UH, MAKE IT QUICK.
YEAH.
EXI
REAL COKE
REAL!
COKE
REAL
COKE

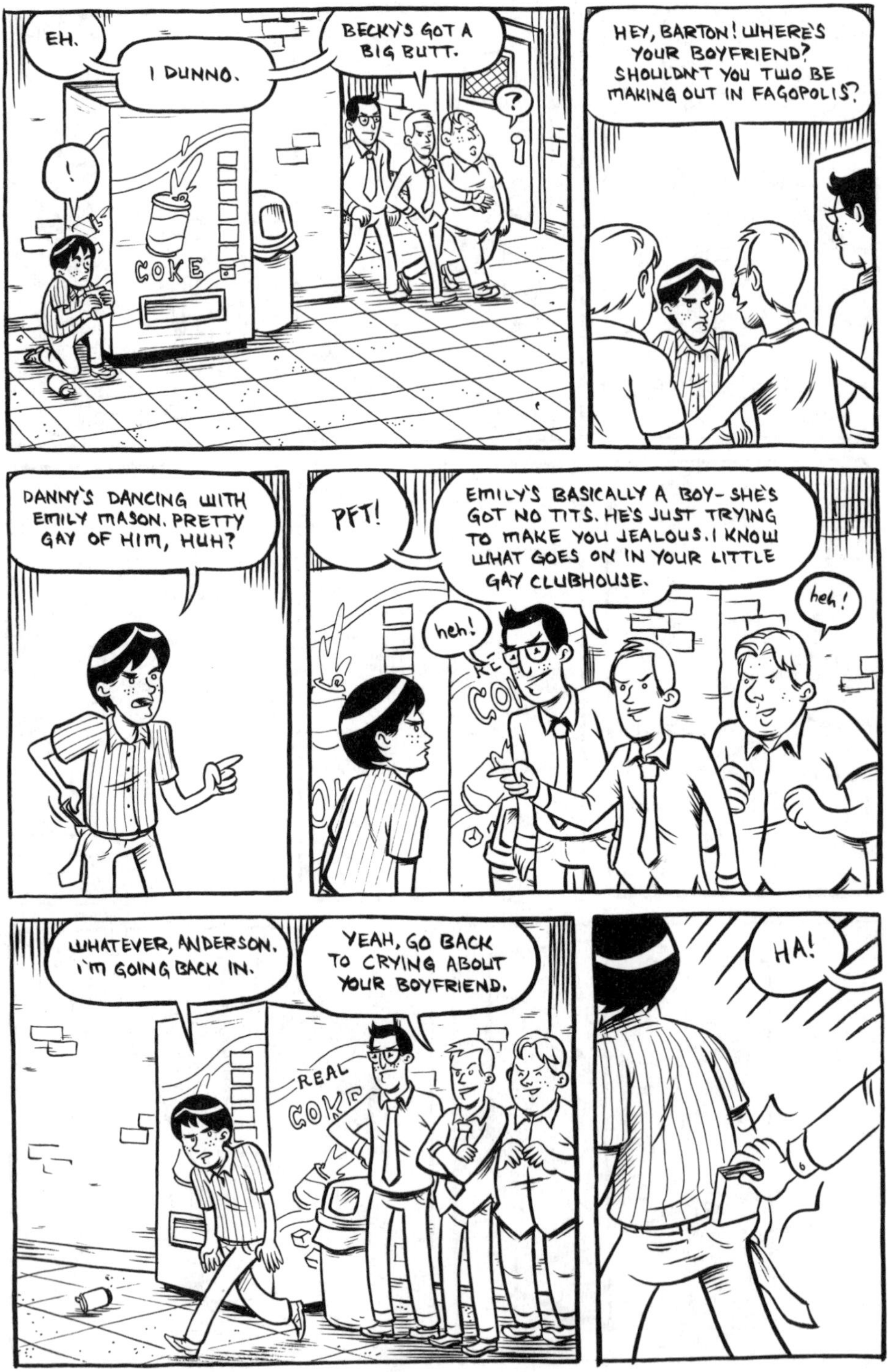
EH.
I DUNNO.
BECKY'S GOT A BIG BUTT.
?
!
COKE
HEY, BARTON! WHERE'S YOUR BOYFRIEND? SHOULDN'T YOU TWO BE MAKING OUT IN FAGOPOLIS?
DANNY'S DANCING WITH EMILY MASON. PRETTY GAY OF HIM, HUH?
PFT!
EMILY'S BASICALLY A BOY- SHE'S GOT NO TITS. HE'S JUST TRYING TO MAKE YOU JEALOUS. I KNOW WHAT GOES ON IN YOUR LITTLE GAY CLUBHOUSE.
heh!
heh!
WHATEVER, ANDERSON. I'M GOING BACK IN.
YEAH, GO BACK TO CRYING ABOUT YOUR BOYFRIEND.
REAL
HA!

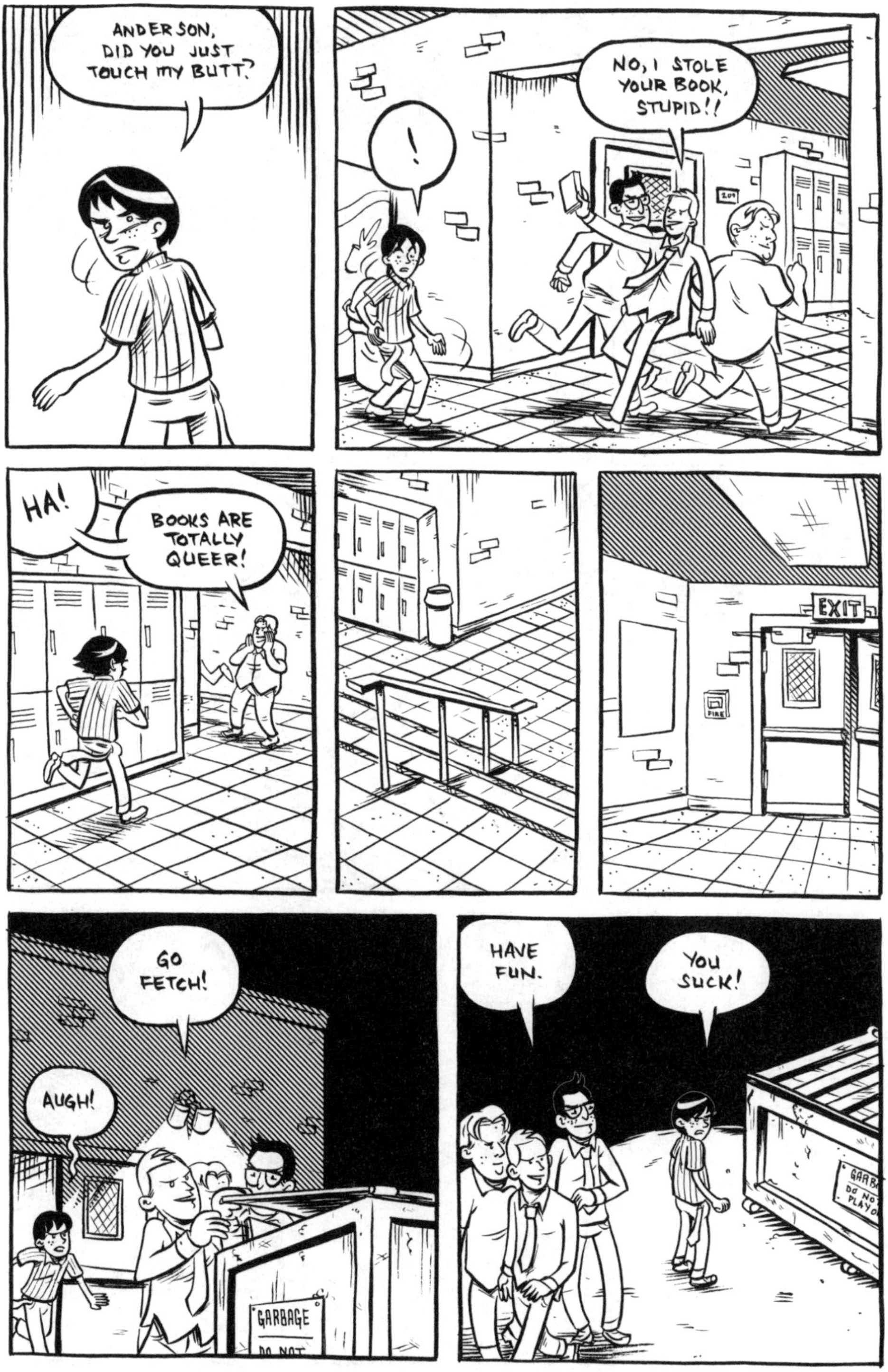
ANDERSON, DID YOU JUST TOUCH MY BUTT?
!
NO, I STOLE YOUR BOOK, STUPID!!
HA!
BOOKS ARE TOTALLY QUEER!
EXIT
GO FETCH!
AUGH!
GARBAGE
HAVE FUN.
YOU SUCK!

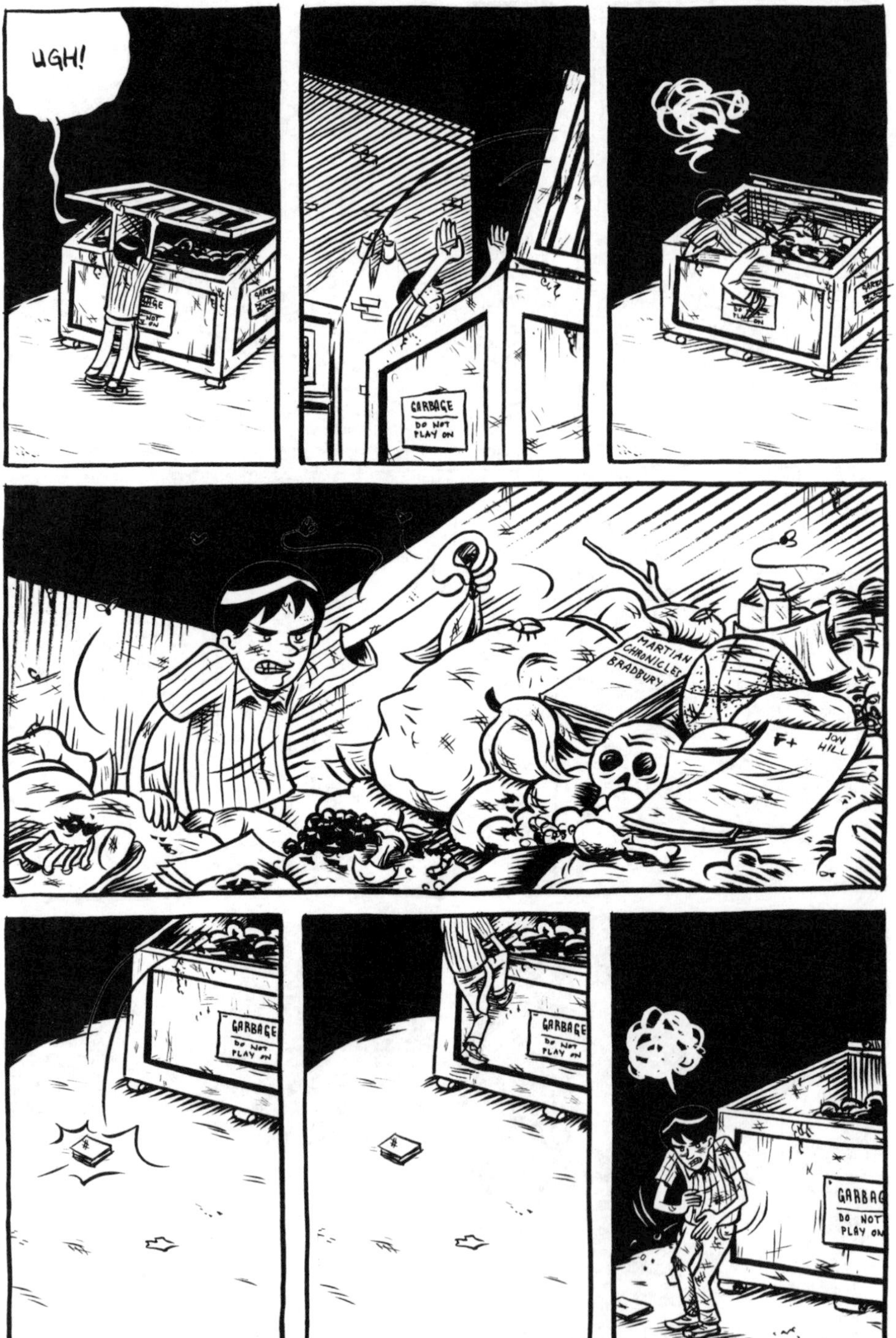
UGH!
GARBAGE
DO NOT PLAY ON
MARTIAN CHRONICLES
BRADBURY
F+
JON HILL
GARBAGE
DO NOT PLAY ON
GARBAGE
DO NOT PLAY ON
GARBAGE
DO NOT PLAY ON

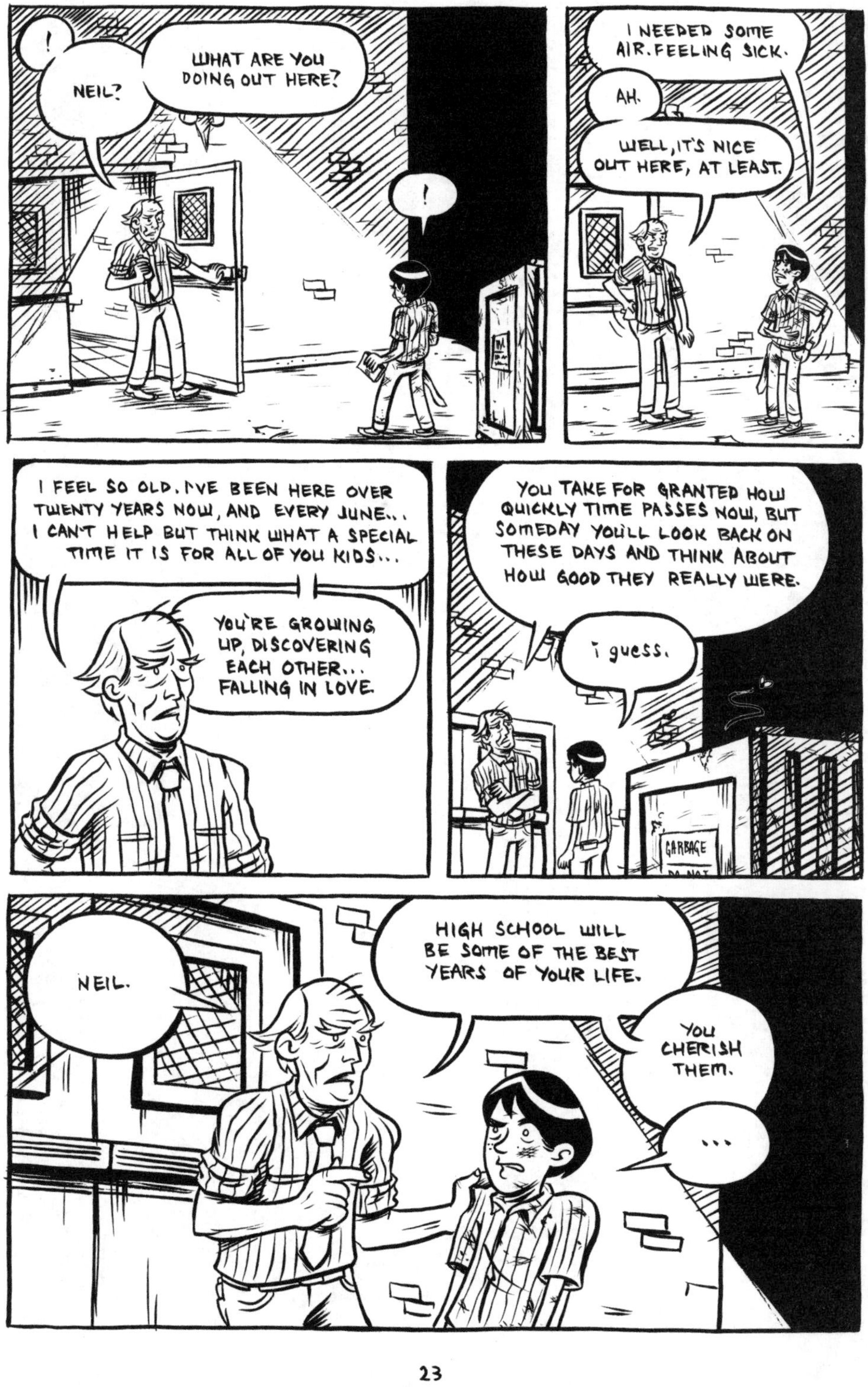
!
NEIL?
WHAT ARE YOU DOING OUT HERE?
!
I NEEDED SOME AIR. FEELING SICK.
AH.
WELL, IT'S NICE OUT HERE, AT LEAST.
I FEEL SO OLD. I'VE BEEN HERE OVER TWENTY YEARS NOW, AND EVERY JUNE... I CAN'T HELP BUT THINK WHAT A SPECIAL TIME IT IS FOR ALL OF YOU KIDS...
YOU'RE GROWING UP, DISCOVERING EACH OTHER... FALLING IN LOVE.
YOU TAKE FOR GRANTED HOW QUICKLY TIME PASSES NOW, BUT SOMEDAY YOU'LL LOOK BACK ON THESE DAYS AND THINK ABOUT HOW GOOD THEY REALLY WERE.
i guess.
GARBAGE
NEIL.
HIGH SCHOOL WILL BE SOME OF THE BEST YEARS OF YOUR LIFE.
YOU CHERISH THEM.
...

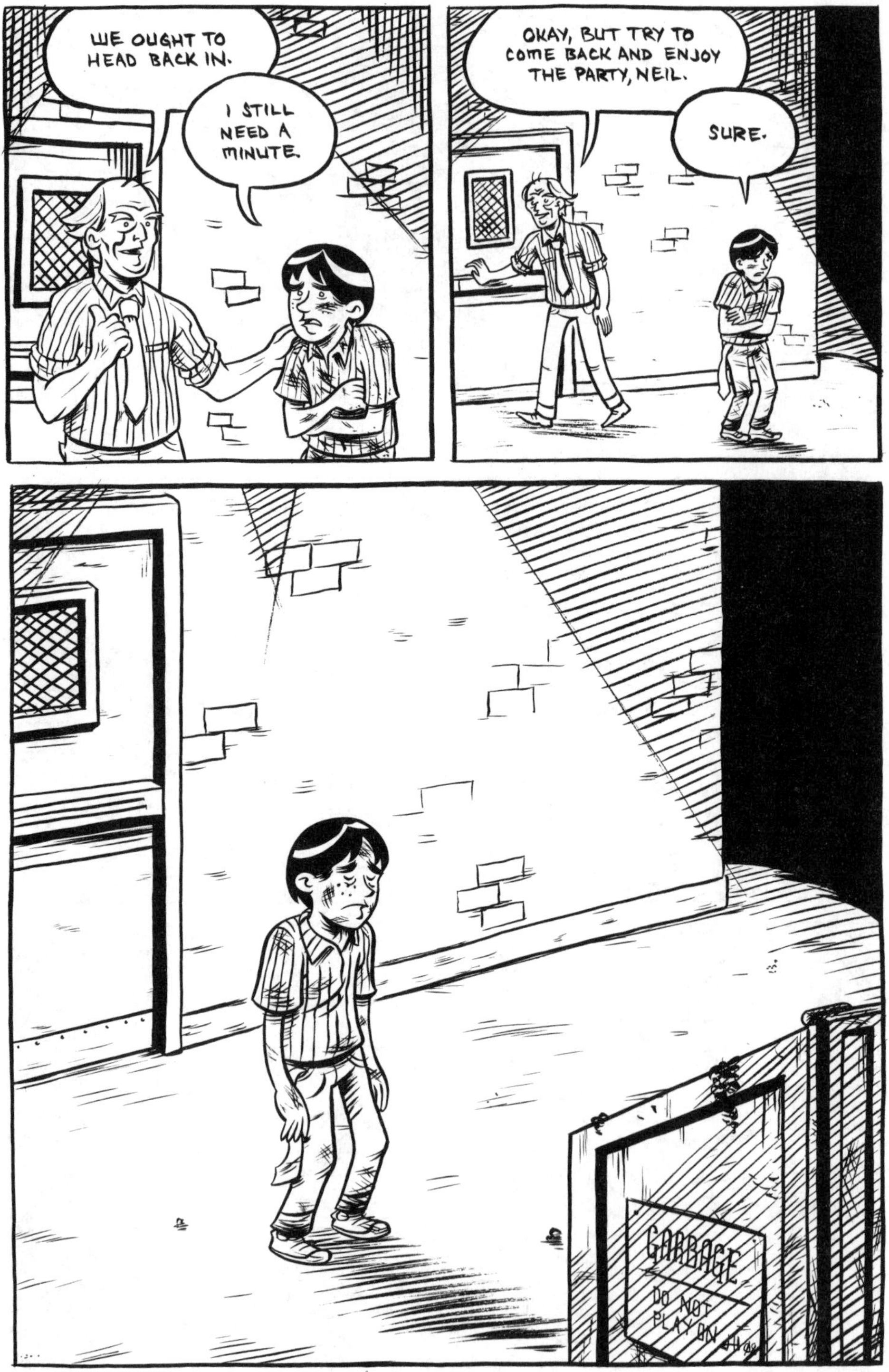
WE OUGHT TO HEAD BACK IN.
I STILL NEED A MINUTE.
OKAY, BUT TRY TO COME BACK AND ENJOY THE PARTY, NEIL.
SURE.
GARBAGE
DO NOT PLAY ON

CHAPTER 2

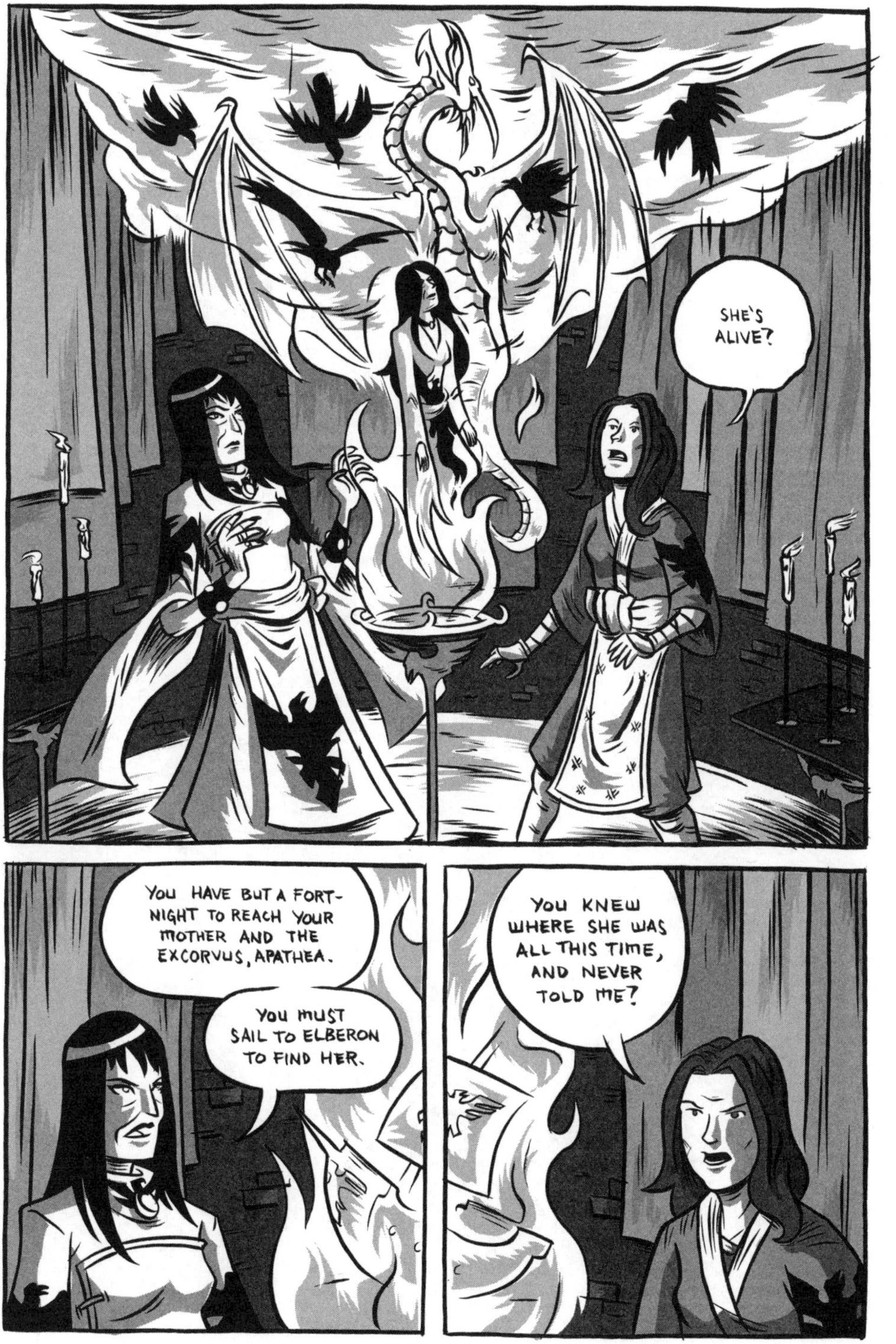
SHE'S ALIVE?
YOU HAVE BUT A FORTNIGHT TO REACH YOUR MOTHER AND THE EXCORVUS, APATHEA.
YOU MUST SAIL TO ELBERON TO FIND HER.
YOU KNEW WHERE SHE WAS ALL THIS TIME, AND NEVER TOLD ME?

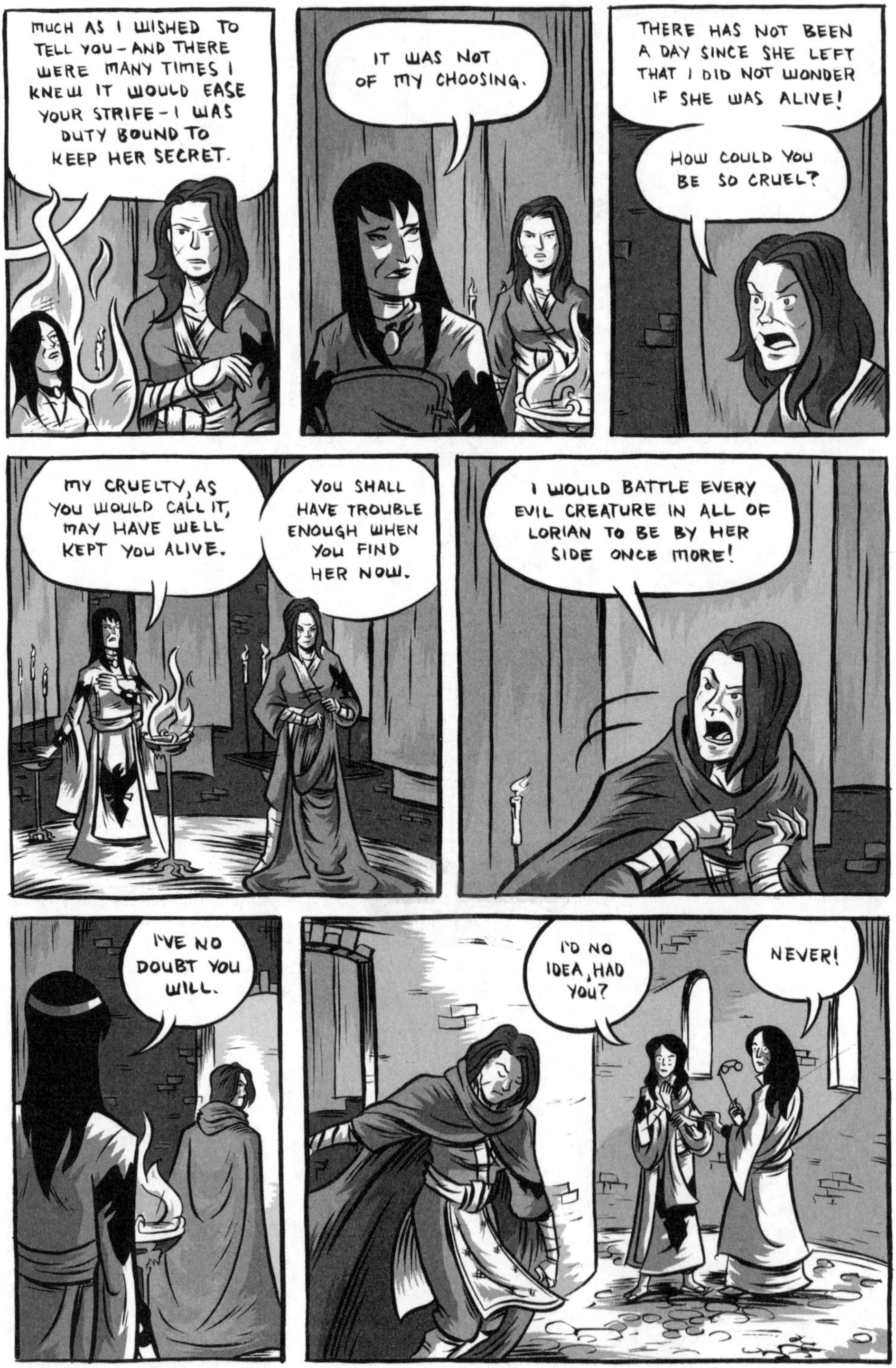
MUCH AS I WISHED TO TELL YOU - AND THERE WERE MANY TIMES I KNEW IT WOULD EASE YOUR STRIFE - I WAS DUTY BOUND TO KEEP HER SECRET.
IT WAS NOT OF MY CHOOSING.
THERE HAS NOT BEEN A DAY SINCE SHE LEFT THAT I DID NOT WONDER IF SHE WAS ALIVE!
HOW COULD YOU BE SO CRUEL?
MY CRUELTY, AS YOU WOULD CALL IT, MAY HAVE WELL KEPT YOU ALIVE.
YOU SHALL HAVE TROUBLE ENOUGH WHEN YOU FIND HER NOW.
I WOULD BATTLE EVERY EVIL CREATURE IN ALL OF LORIAN TO BE BY HER SIDE ONCE MORE!
I'VE NO DOUBT YOU WILL.
I'D NO IDEA, HAD YOU?
NEVER!

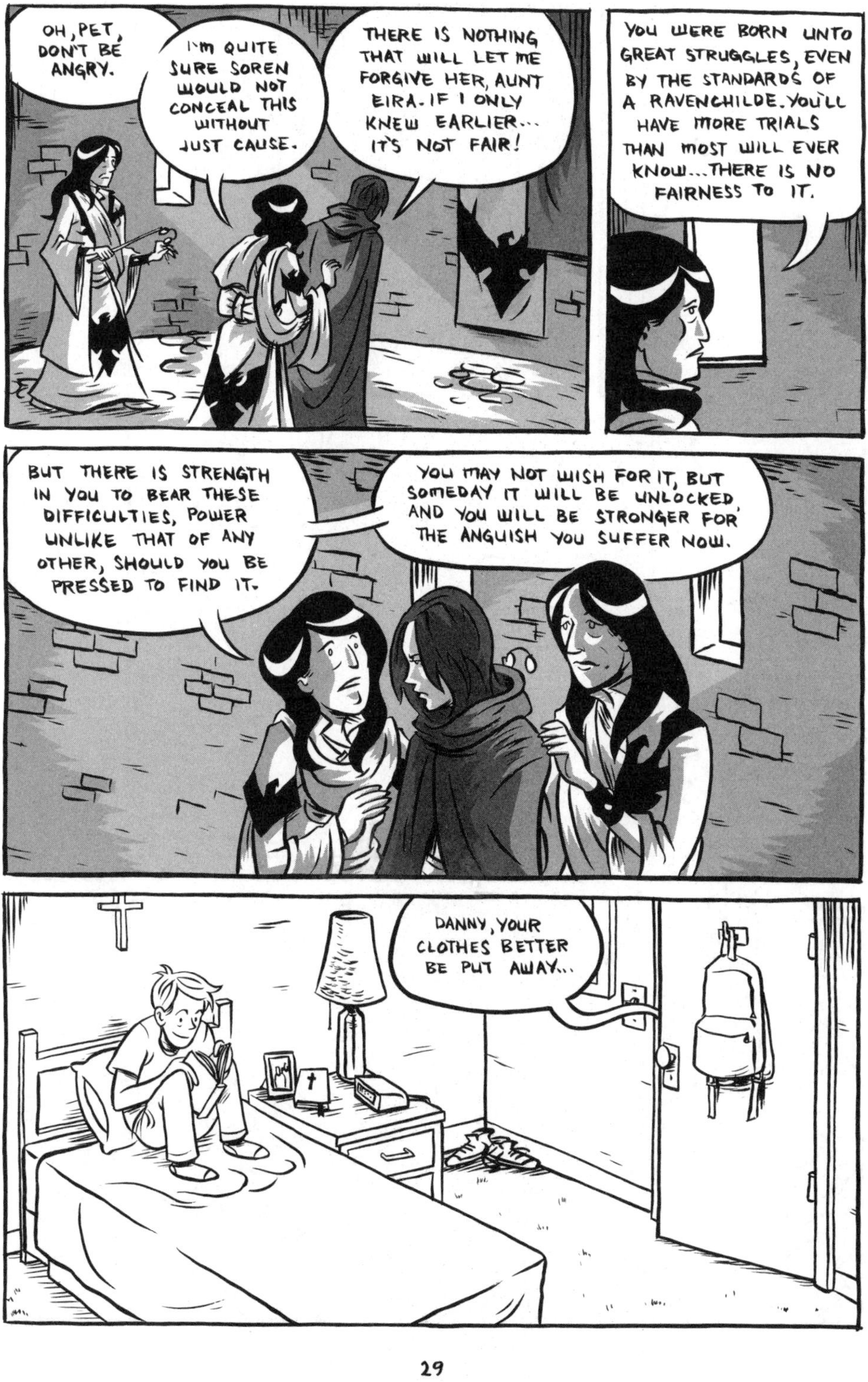
OH, PET, DON'T BE ANGRY.
I'M QUITE SURE SOREN WOULD NOT CONCEAL THIS WITHOUT JUST CAUSE.
THERE IS NOTHING THAT WILL LET ME FORGIVE HER, AUNT EIRA. IF I ONLY KNEW EARLIER... IT'S NOT FAIR!
YOU WERE BORN UNTO GREAT STRUGGLES, EVEN BY THE STANDARDS OF A RAVENCHILDE. YOU'LL HAVE MORE TRIALS THAN MOST WILL EVER KNOW... THERE IS NO FAIRNESS TO IT.
BUT THERE IS STRENGTH IN YOU TO BEAR THESE DIFFICULTIES, POWER UNLIKE THAT OF ANY OTHER, SHOULD YOU BE PRESSED TO FIND IT.
YOU MAY NOT WISH FOR IT, BUT SOMEDAY IT WILL BE UNLOCKED, AND YOU WILL BE STRONGER FOR THE ANGUISH YOU SUFFER NOW.
DANNY, YOUR CLOTHES BETTER BE PUT AWAY...

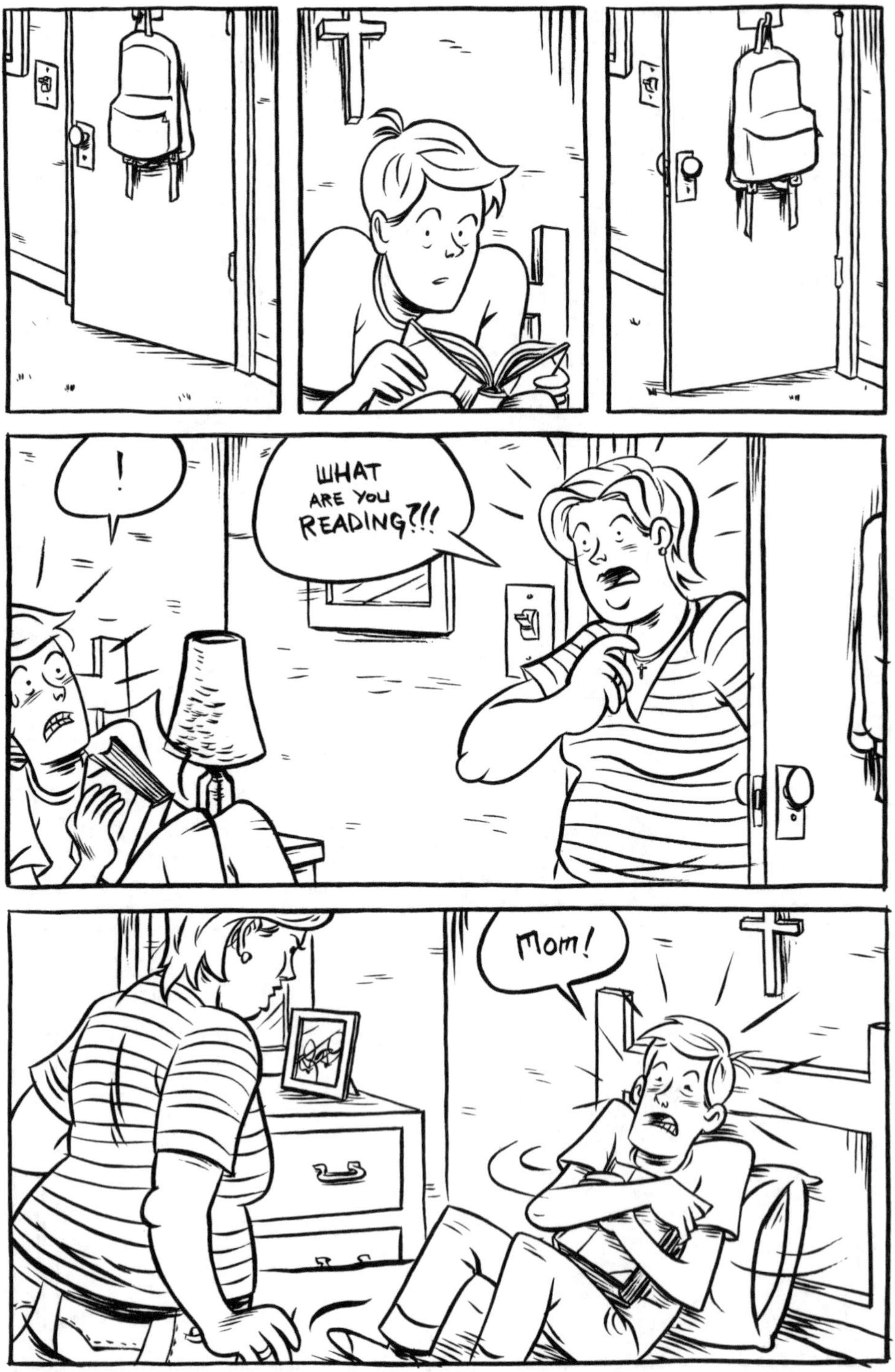
!
WHAT ARE YOU READING?!!
Mom!

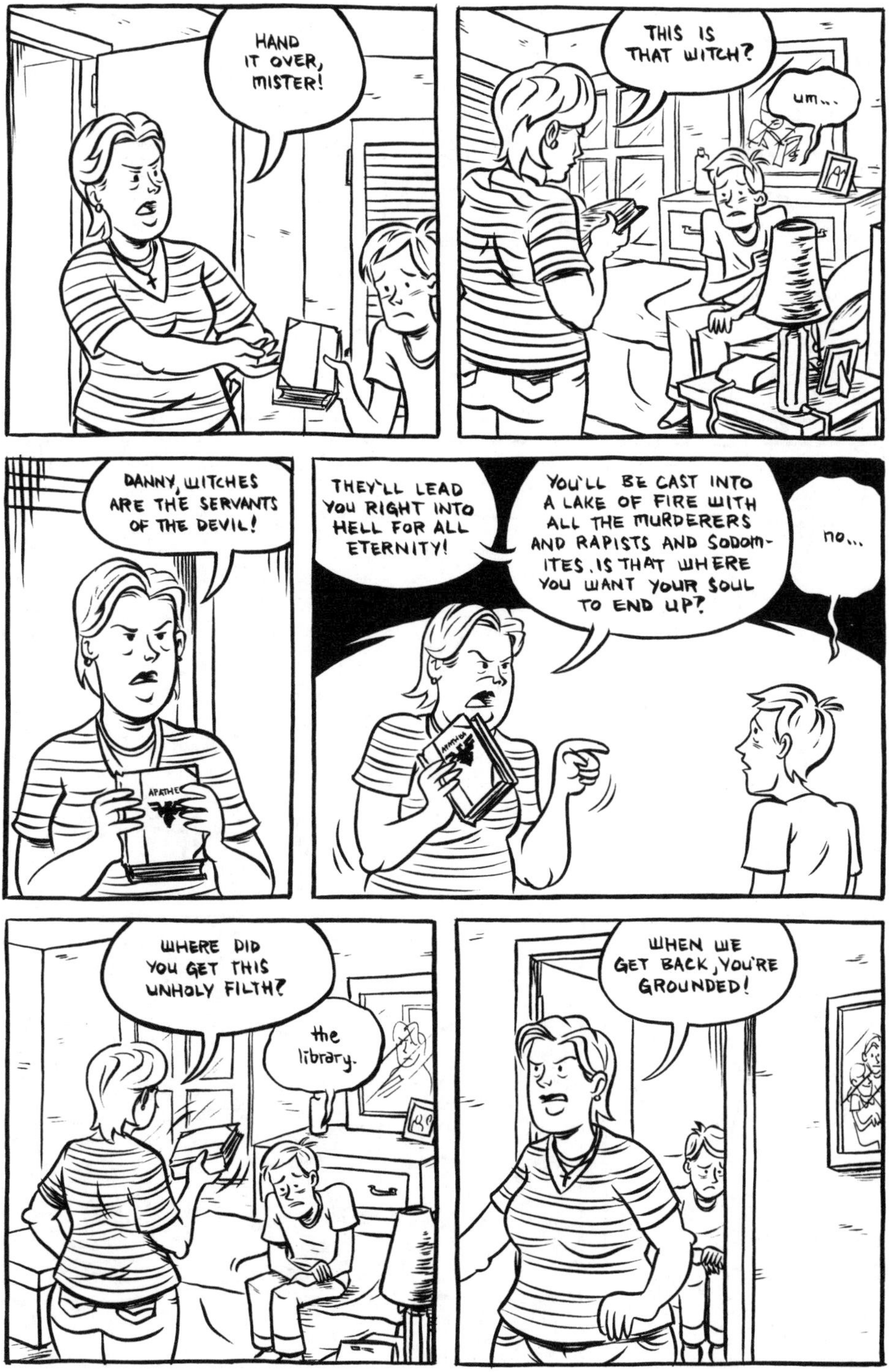
HAND IT OVER, MISTER!
THIS IS THAT WITCH?
um...
DANNY, WITCHES ARE THE SERVANTS OF THE DEVIL!
APATHE
THEY'LL LEAD YOU RIGHT INTO HELL FOR ALL ETERNITY!
YOU'LL BE CAST INTO A LAKE OF FIRE WITH ALL THE MURDERERS AND RAPISTS AND SODOMITES. IS THAT WHERE YOU WANT YOUR SOUL TO END UP?
no...
WHERE DID YOU GET THIS UNHOLY FILTH?
the library.
WHEN WE GET BACK, YOU'RE GROUNDED!

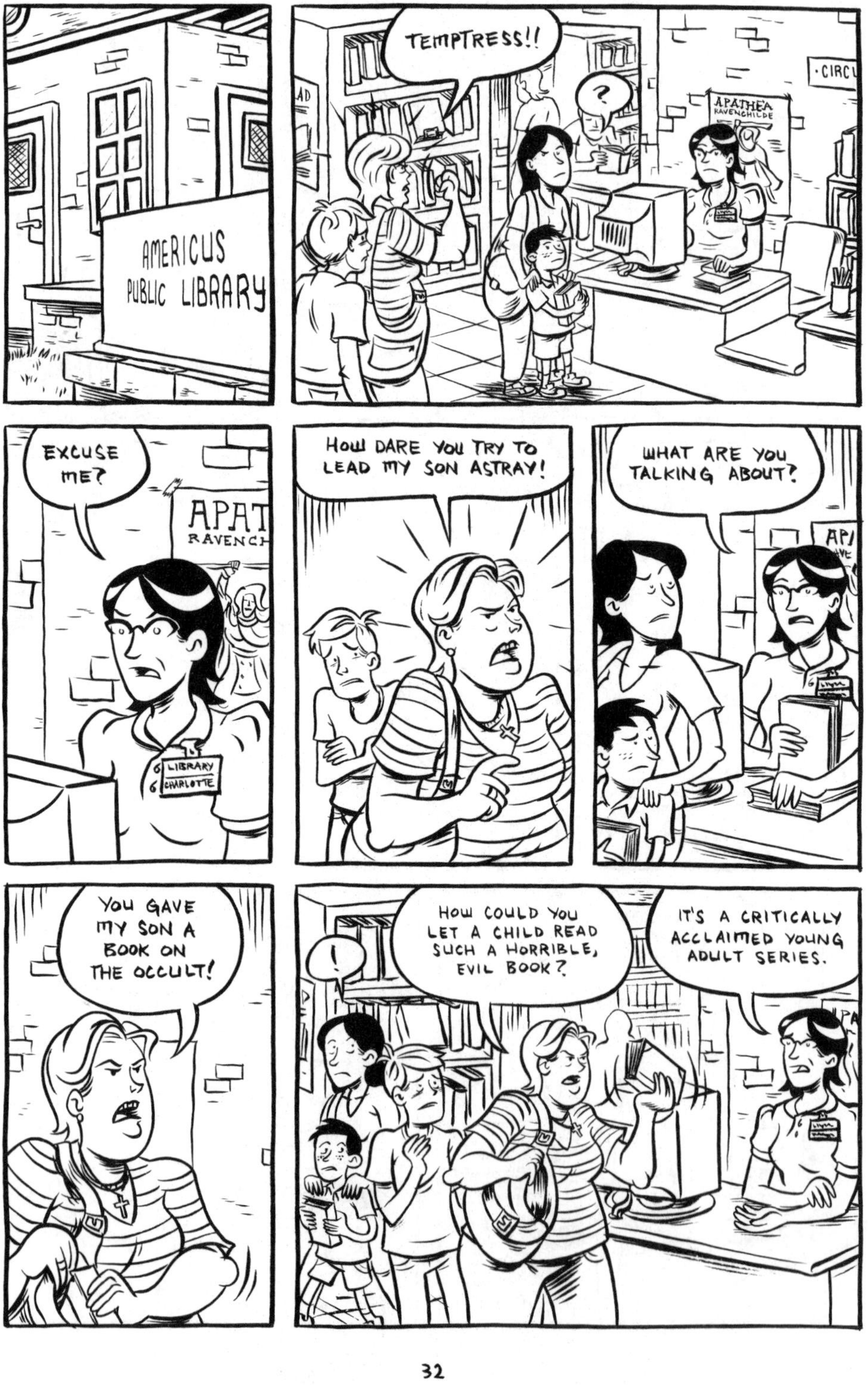
AMERICUS PUBLIC LIBRARY
TEMPTRESS!!
?
APATHEA RAVENCHILDE
·CIRCU
EXCUSE ME?
LIBRARY CHARLOTTE
HOW DARE YOU TRY TO LEAD MY SON ASTRAY!
WHAT ARE YOU TALKING ABOUT?
YOU GAVE MY SON A BOOK ON THE OCCULT!
!
HOW COULD YOU LET A CHILD READ SUCH A HORRIBLE, EVIL BOOK?
IT'S A CRITICALLY ACCLAIMED YOUNG ADULT SERIES.

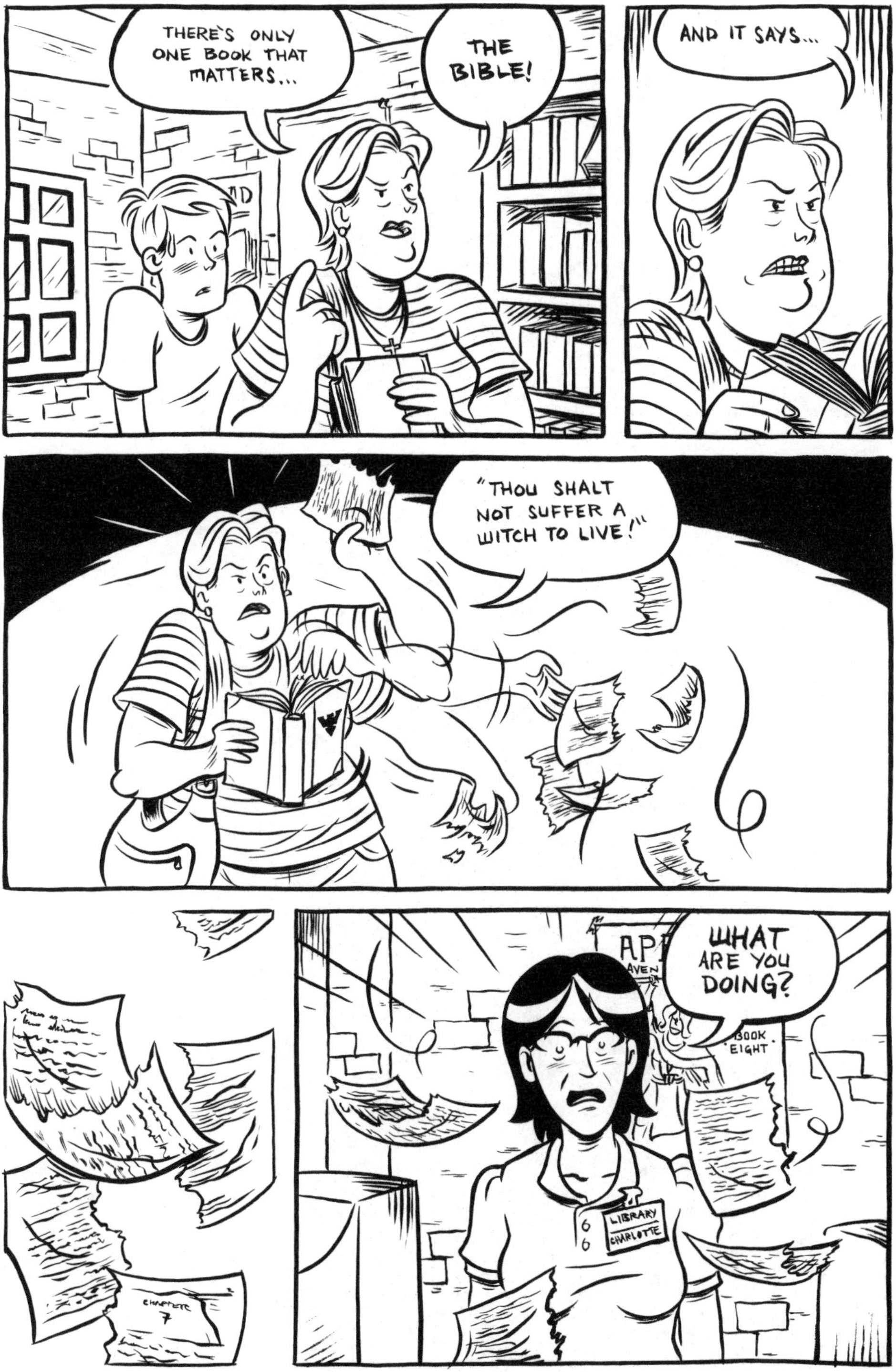
THERE'S ONLY ONE BOOK THAT MATTERS...
THE BIBLE!
AND IT SAYS...
"THOU SHALT NOT SUFFER A WITCH TO LIVE!"
WHAT ARE YOU DOING?
BOOK EIGHT
LIBRARY
CHARLOTTE

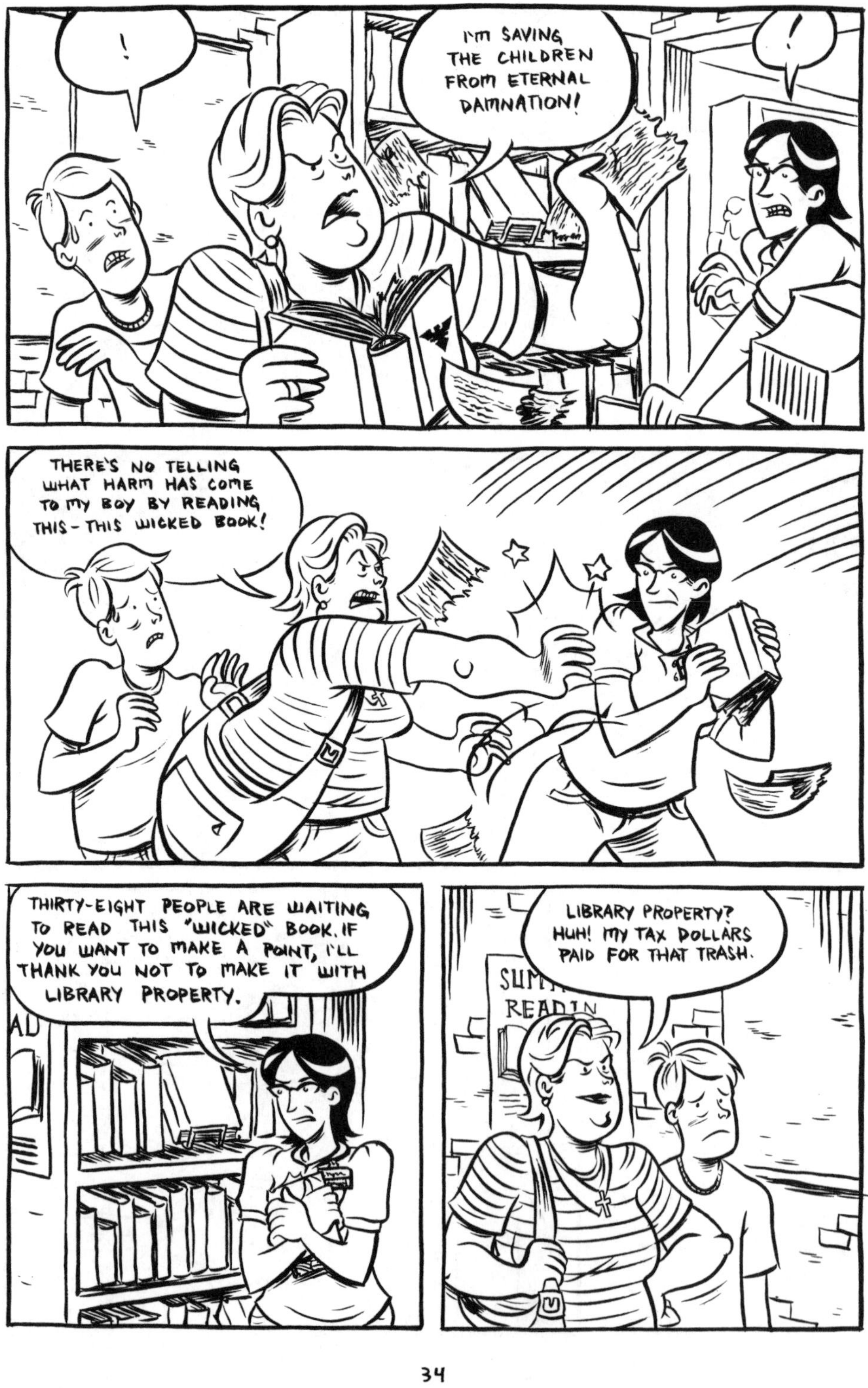
!
I'M SAVING THE CHILDREN FROM ETERNAL DAMNATION!
!
THERE'S NO TELLING WHAT HARM HAS COME TO MY BOY BY READING THIS- THIS WICKED BOOK!
THIRTY-EIGHT PEOPLE ARE WAITING TO READ THIS "WICKED" BOOK. IF YOU WANT TO MAKE A POINT, I'LL THANK YOU NOT TO MAKE IT WITH LIBRARY PROPERTY.
LIBRARY PROPERTY? HUH! MY TAX DOLLARS PAID FOR THAT TRASH.

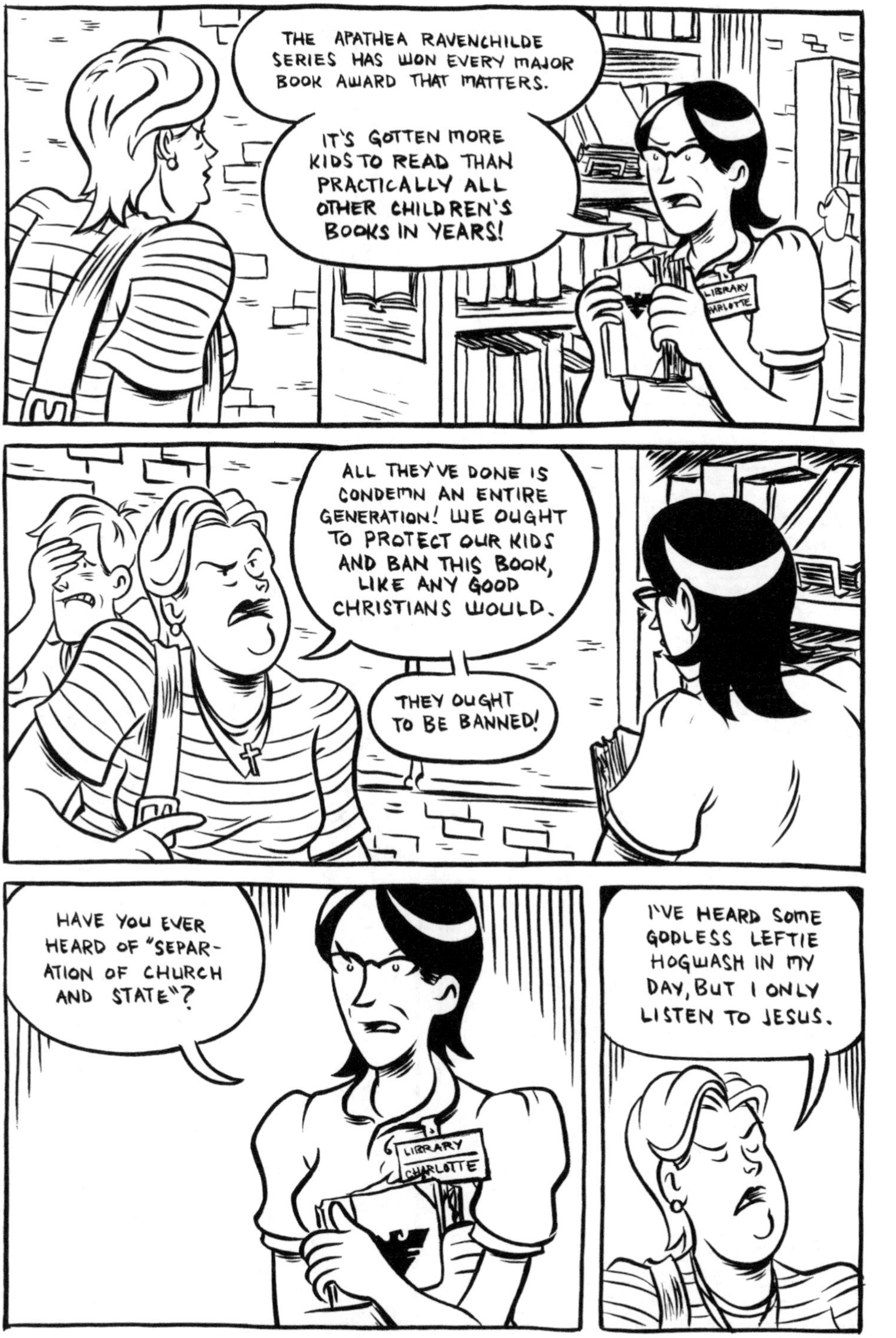
THE APATHEA RAVENCHILDE SERIES HAS WON EVERY MAJOR BOOK AWARD THAT MATTERS.
IT'S GOTTEN MORE KIDS TO READ THAN PRACTICALLY ALL OTHER CHILDREN'S BOOKS IN YEARS!
LIBRARY
CHARLOTTE
ALL THEY'VE DONE IS CONDEMN AN ENTIRE GENERATION! WE OUGHT TO PROTECT OUR KIDS AND BAN THIS BOOK, LIKE ANY GOOD CHRISTIANS WOULD.
THEY OUGHT TO BE BANNED!
HAVE YOU EVER HEARD OF "SEPARATION OF CHURCH AND STATE"?
LIBRARY
CHARLOTTE
I'VE HEARD SOME GODLESS LEFTIE HOGWASH IN MY DAY, BUT I ONLY LISTEN TO JESUS.

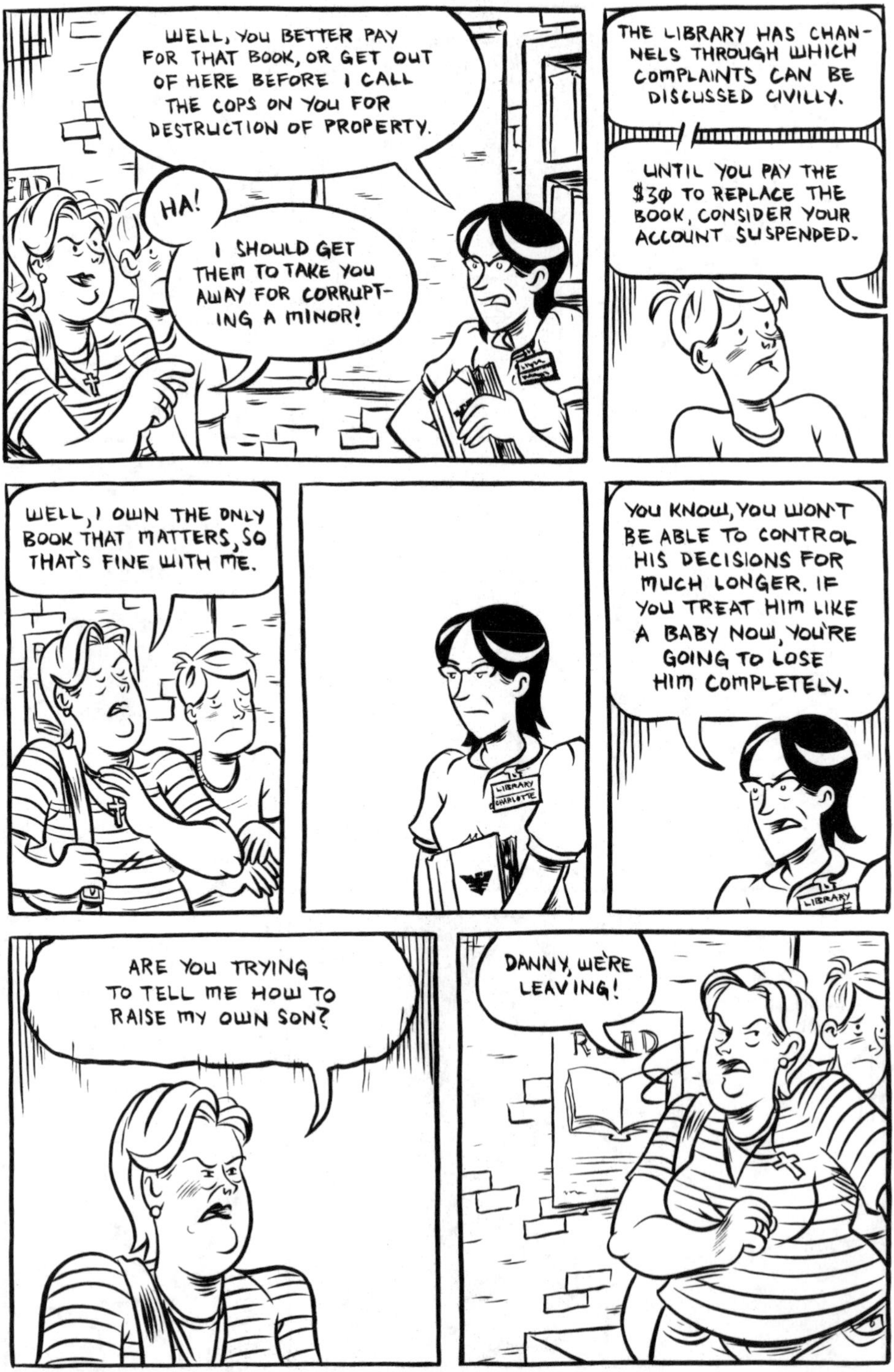
WELL, YOU BETTER PAY FOR THAT BOOK, OR GET OUT OF HERE BEFORE I CALL THE COPS ON YOU FOR DESTRUCTION OF PROPERTY.
HA!
I SHOULD GET THEM TO TAKE YOU AWAY FOR CORRUPTING A MINOR!
THE LIBRARY HAS CHANNELS THROUGH WHICH COMPLAINTS CAN BE DISCUSSED CIVILLY.
UNTIL YOU PAY THE $30 TO REPLACE THE BOOK, CONSIDER YOUR ACCOUNT SUSPENDED.
WELL, I OWN THE ONLY BOOK THAT MATTERS, SO THAT'S FINE WITH ME.
LIBRARY
CHARLOTTE
YOU KNOW, YOU WON'T BE ABLE TO CONTROL HIS DECISIONS FOR MUCH LONGER. IF YOU TREAT HIM LIKE A BABY NOW, YOU'RE GOING TO LOSE HIM COMPLETELY.
LIBRARY
ARE YOU TRYING TO TELL ME HOW TO RAISE MY OWN SON?
DANNY, WE'RE LEAVING!
READ

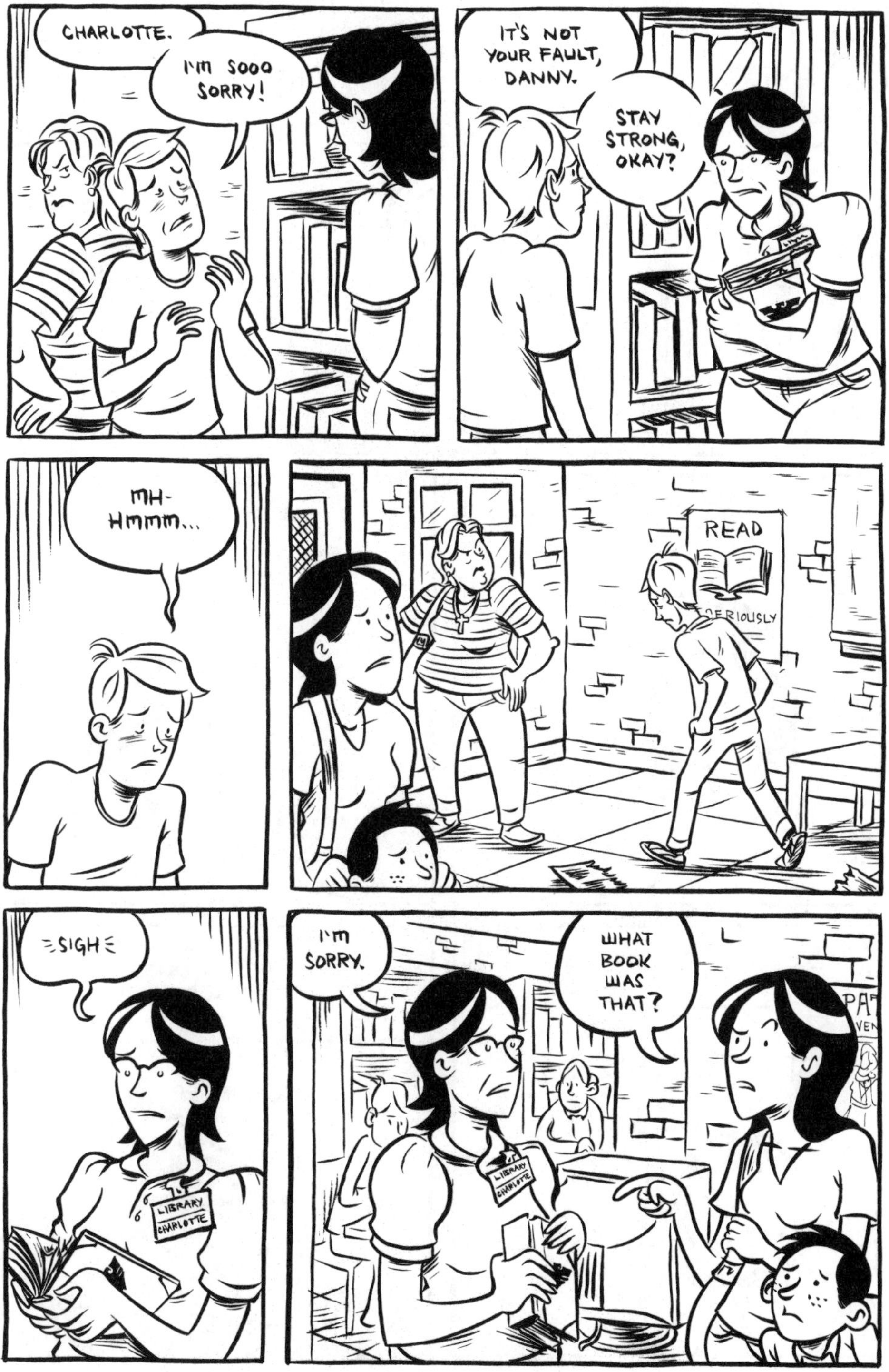
CHARLOTTE.
I'M SOOO SORRY!
IT'S NOT YOUR FAULT, DANNY.
STAY STRONG, OKAY?
MH-HMMM...
READ
SERIOUSLY
SIGH
LIBRARY
CHARLOTTE
I'M SORRY.
WHAT BOOK WAS THAT?

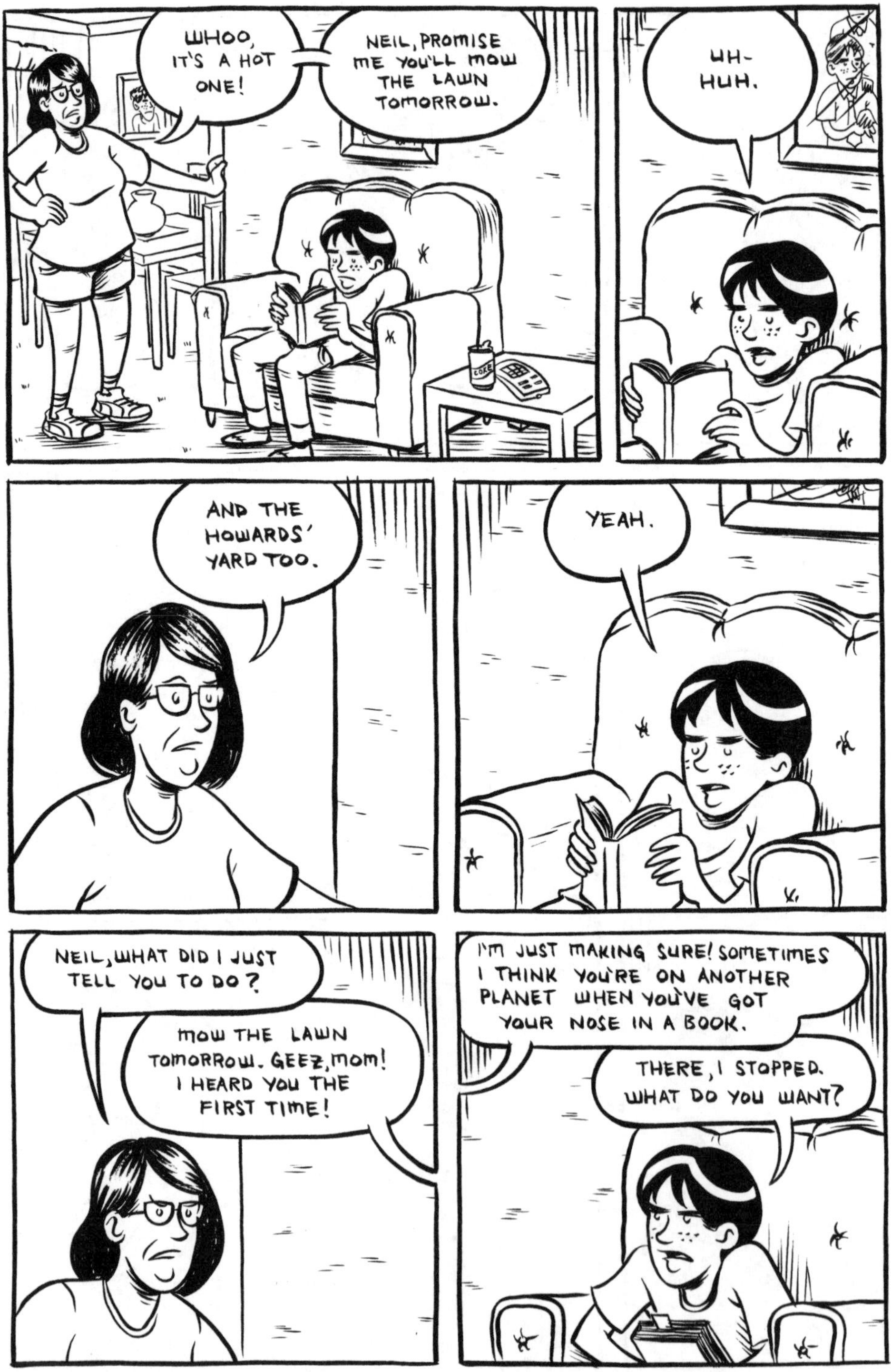
WHOO, IT'S A HOT ONE!
NEIL, PROMISE ME YOU'LL MOW THE LAWN TOMORROW.
UH-HUH.
AND THE HOWARDS' YARD TOO.
YEAH.
NEIL, WHAT DID I JUST TELL YOU TO DO?
MOW THE LAWN TOMORROW. GEEZ, MOM! I HEARD YOU THE FIRST TIME!
I'M JUST MAKING SURE! SOMETIMES I THINK YOU'RE ON ANOTHER PLANET WHEN YOU'VE GOT YOUR NOSE IN A BOOK.
THERE, I STOPPED. WHAT DO YOU WANT?

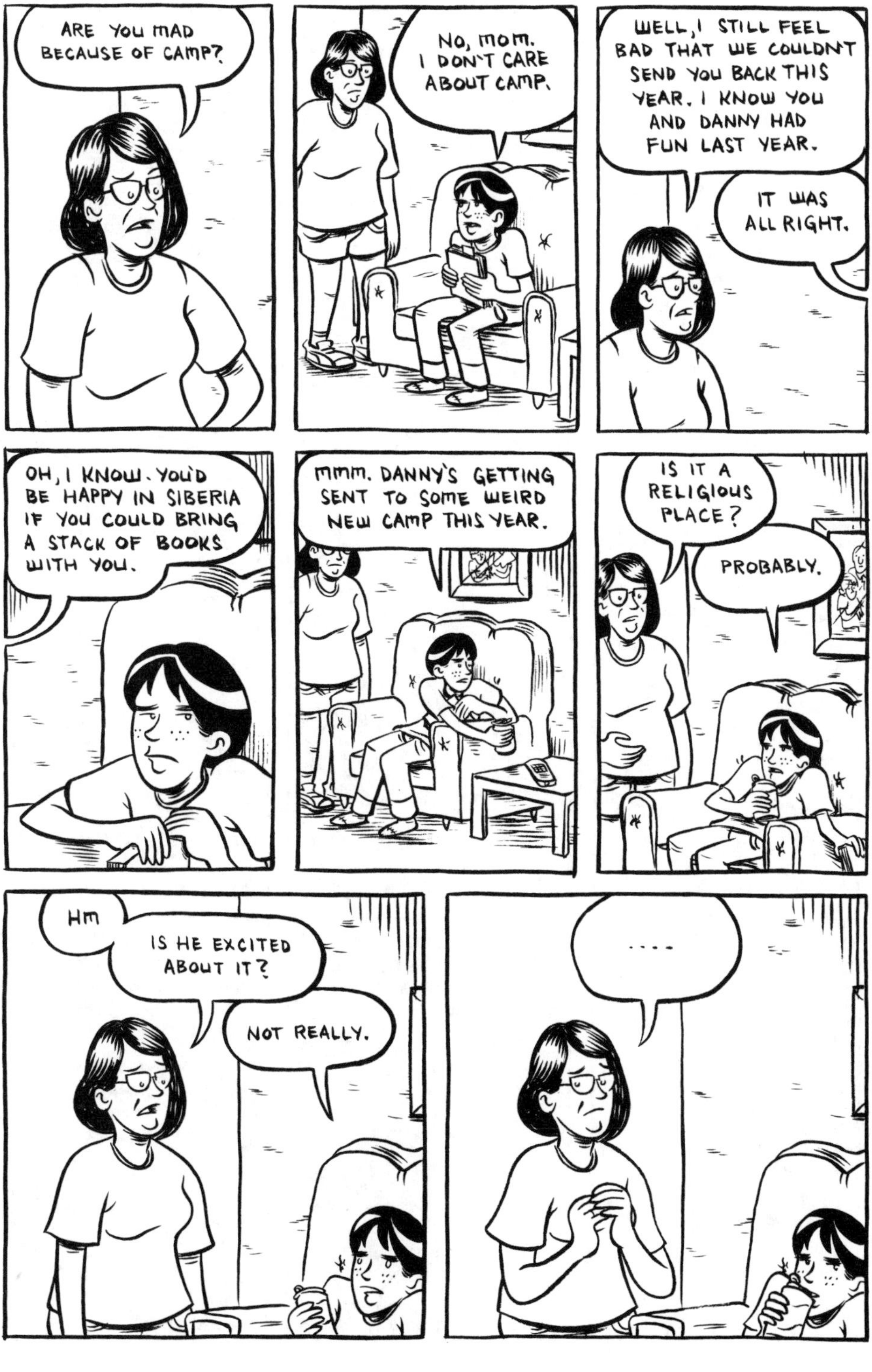
ARE YOU MAD BECAUSE OF CAMP?
NO, MOM. I DON'T CARE ABOUT CAMP.
WELL, I STILL FEEL BAD THAT WE COULDN'T SEND YOU BACK THIS YEAR. I KNOW YOU AND DANNY HAD FUN LAST YEAR.
IT WAS ALL RIGHT.
OH, I KNOW. YOU'D BE HAPPY IN SIBERIA IF YOU COULD BRING A STACK OF BOOKS WITH YOU.
MMM. DANNY'S GETTING SENT TO SOME WEIRD NEW CAMP THIS YEAR.
IS IT A RELIGIOUS PLACE?
PROBABLY.
HM
IS HE EXCITED ABOUT IT?
NOT REALLY.
....

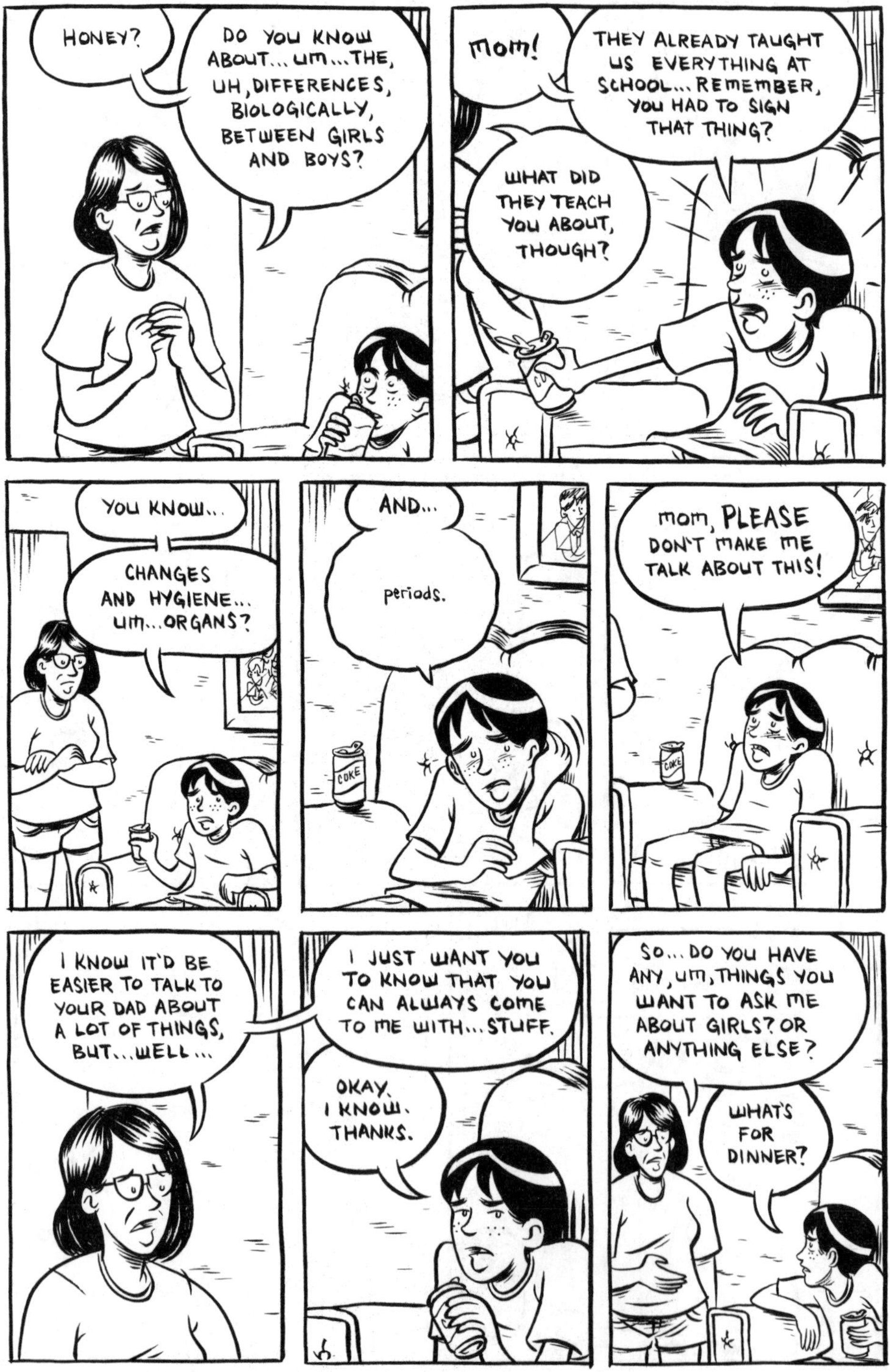

HONEY?
DO YOU KNOW ABOUT... UM... THE, UH, DIFFERENCES, BIOLOGICALLY, BETWEEN GIRLS AND BOYS?
MOM!
THEY ALREADY TAUGHT US EVERYTHING AT SCHOOL... REMEMBER, YOU HAD TO SIGN THAT THING?
WHAT DID THEY TEACH YOU ABOUT, THOUGH?
YOU KNOW...
CHANGES AND HYGIENE... UM... ORGANS?
AND...
periods.
COKE
MOM, PLEASE DON'T MAKE ME TALK ABOUT THIS!
COKE
I KNOW IT'D BE EASIER TO TALK TO YOUR DAD ABOUT A LOT OF THINGS, BUT... WELL...
I JUST WANT YOU TO KNOW THAT YOU CAN ALWAYS COME TO ME WITH... STUFF.
OKAY. I KNOW. THANKS.
SO... DO YOU HAVE ANY, UM, THINGS YOU WANT TO ASK ME ABOUT GIRLS? OR ANYTHING ELSE?
WHAT'S FOR DINNER?

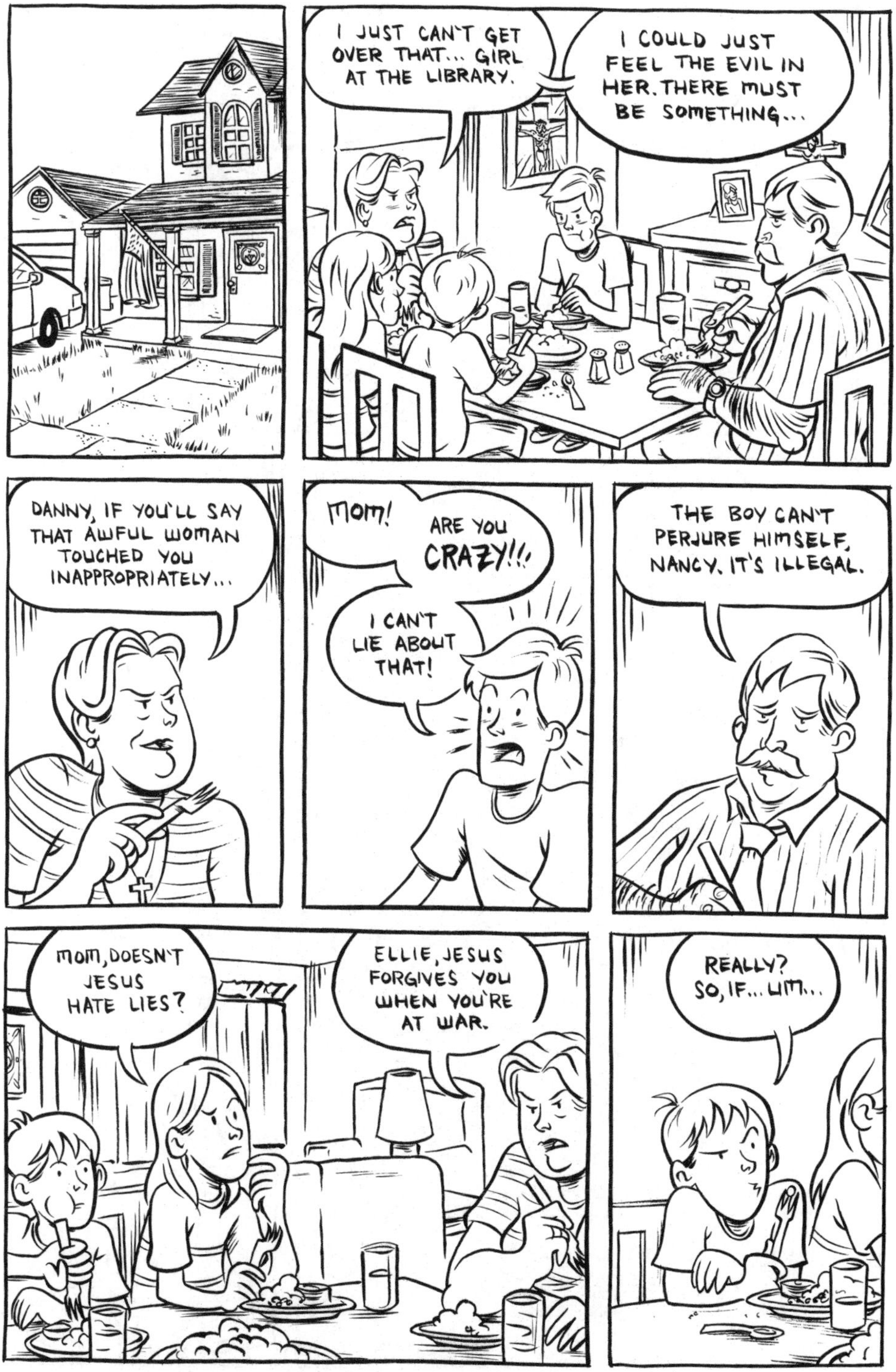
I JUST CAN'T GET OVER THAT... GIRL AT THE LIBRARY.
I COULD JUST FEEL THE EVIL IN HER. THERE MUST BE SOMETHING...
DANNY, IF YOU'LL SAY THAT AWFUL WOMAN TOUCHED YOU INAPPROPRIATELY...
MOM!
ARE YOU CRAZY!!!
I CAN'T LIE ABOUT THAT!
THE BOY CAN'T PERJURE HIMSELF, NANCY. IT'S ILLEGAL.
MOM, DOESN'T JESUS HATE LIES?
ELLIE, JESUS FORGIVES YOU WHEN YOU'RE AT WAR.
REALLY? SO, IF... UM...

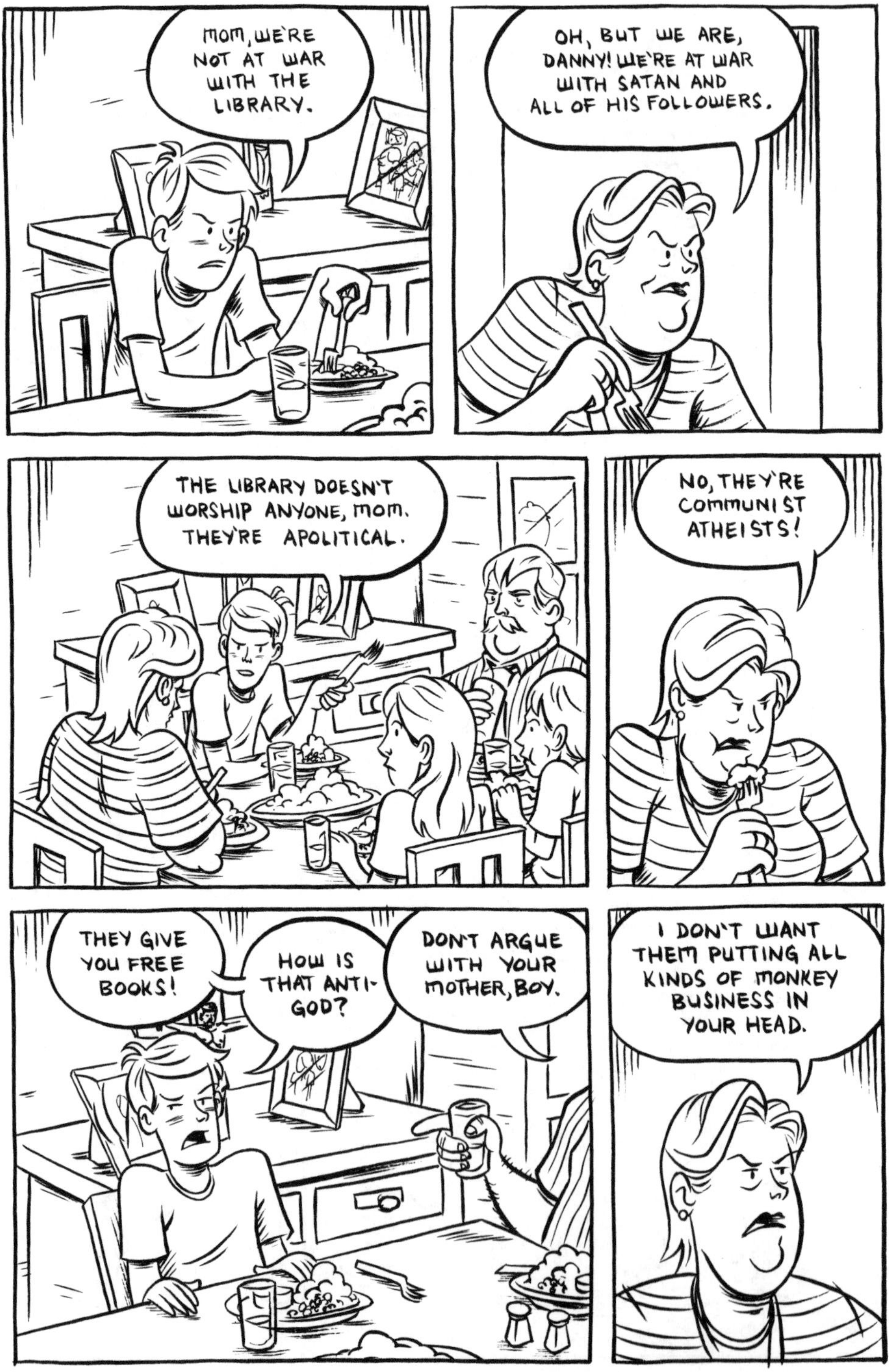
MOM, WE'RE NOT AT WAR WITH THE LIBRARY.
OH, BUT WE ARE, DANNY! WE'RE AT WAR WITH SATAN AND ALL OF HIS FOLLOWERS.
THE LIBRARY DOESN'T WORSHIP ANYONE, MOM. THEY'RE APOLITICAL.
NO, THEY'RE COMMUNIST ATHEISTS!
THEY GIVE YOU FREE BOOKS!
HOW IS THAT ANTI-GOD?
DON'T ARGUE WITH YOUR MOTHER, BOY.
I DON'T WANT THEM PUTTING ALL KINDS OF MONKEY BUSINESS IN YOUR HEAD.

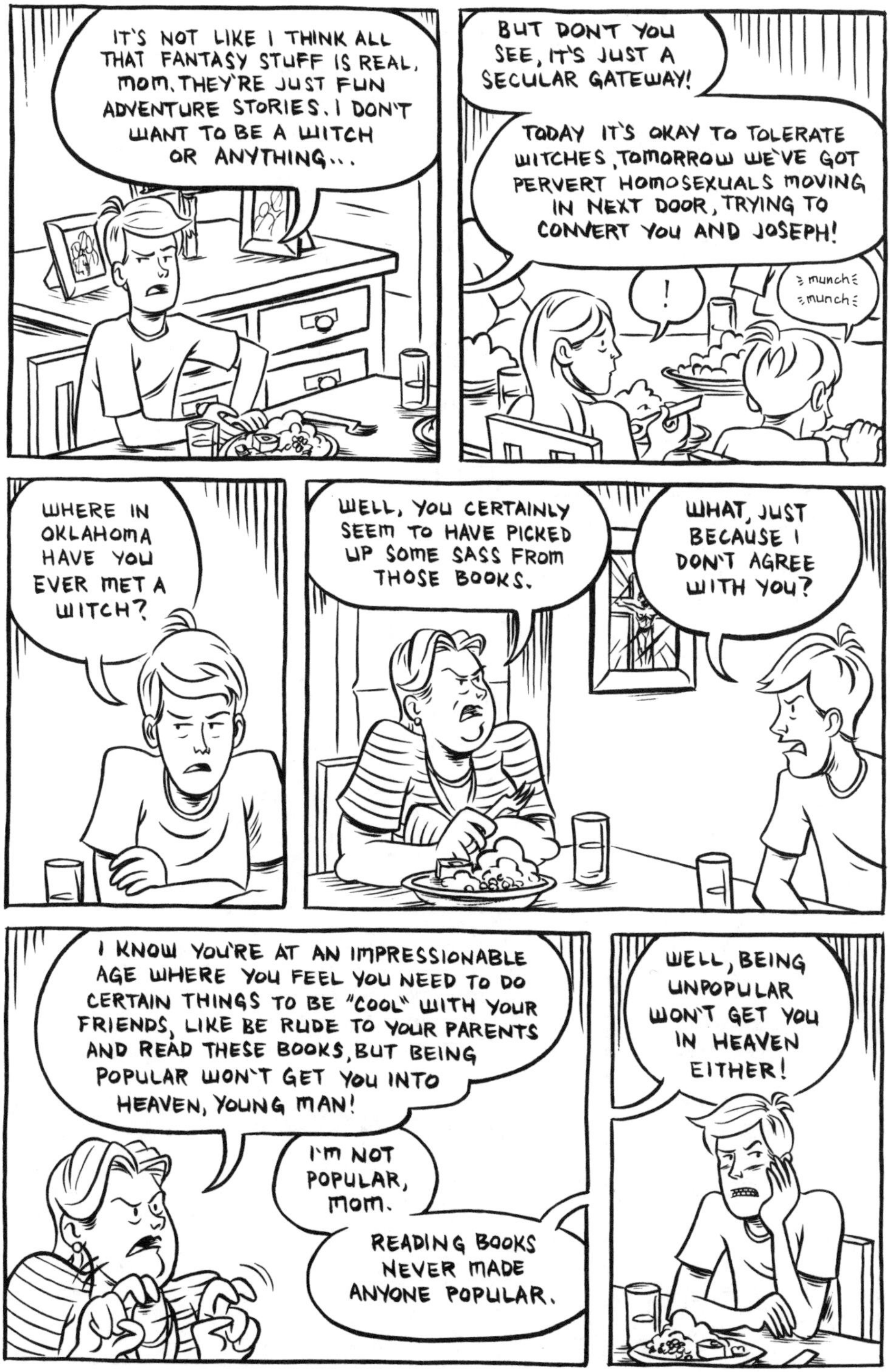
IT'S NOT LIKE I THINK ALL THAT FANTASY STUFF IS REAL, MOM. THEY'RE JUST FUN ADVENTURE STORIES. I DON'T WANT TO BE A WITCH OR ANYTHING...
BUT DON'T YOU SEE, IT'S JUST A SECULAR GATEWAY!
TODAY IT'S OKAY TO TOLERATE WITCHES, TOMORROW WE'VE GOT PERVERT HOMOSEXUALS MOVING IN NEXT DOOR, TRYING TO CONVERT YOU AND JOSEPH!
!
munch munch
WHERE IN OKLAHOMA HAVE YOU EVER MET A WITCH?
WELL, YOU CERTAINLY SEEM TO HAVE PICKED UP SOME SASS FROM THOSE BOOKS.
WHAT, JUST BECAUSE I DON'T AGREE WITH YOU?
I KNOW YOU'RE AT AN IMPRESSIONABLE AGE WHERE YOU FEEL YOU NEED TO DO CERTAIN THINGS TO BE "COOL" WITH YOUR FRIENDS, LIKE BE RUDE TO YOUR PARENTS AND READ THESE BOOKS, BUT BEING POPULAR WON'T GET YOU INTO HEAVEN, YOUNG MAN!
I'M NOT POPULAR, MOM.
READING BOOKS NEVER MADE ANYONE POPULAR.
WELL, BEING UNPOPULAR WON'T GET YOU IN HEAVEN EITHER!

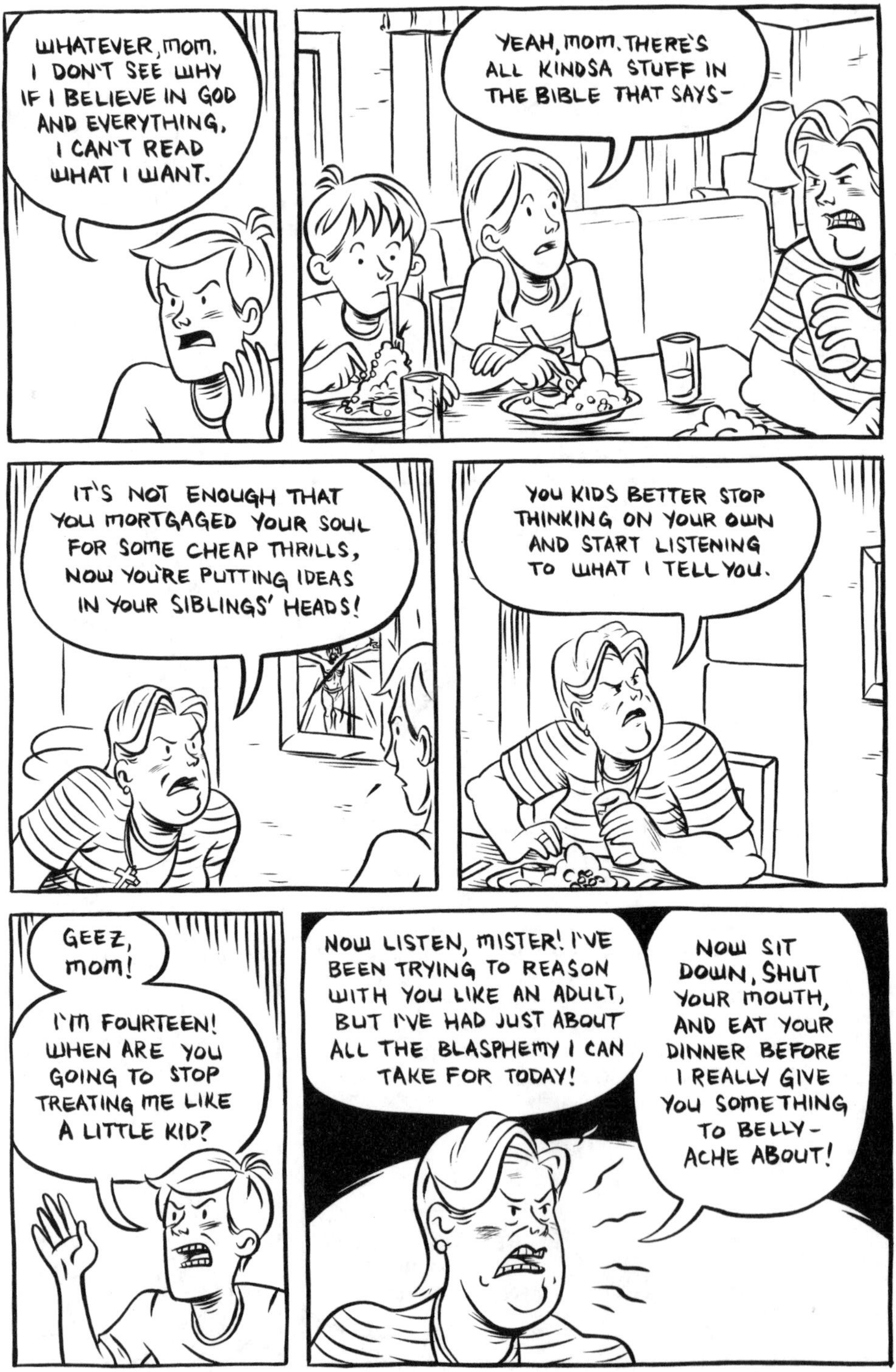
WHATEVER, MOM. I DON'T SEE WHY IF I BELIEVE IN GOD AND EVERYTHING, I CAN'T READ WHAT I WANT.
YEAH, MOM. THERE'S ALL KINDSA STUFF IN THE BIBLE THAT SAYS-
IT'S NOT ENOUGH THAT YOU MORTGAGED YOUR SOUL FOR SOME CHEAP THRILLS, NOW YOU'RE PUTTING IDEAS IN YOUR SIBLINGS' HEADS!
YOU KIDS BETTER STOP THINKING ON YOUR OWN AND START LISTENING TO WHAT I TELL YOU.
GEEZ, MOM!
I'M FOURTEEN! WHEN ARE YOU GOING TO STOP TREATING ME LIKE A LITTLE KID?
NOW LISTEN, MISTER! I'VE BEEN TRYING TO REASON WITH YOU LIKE AN ADULT, BUT I'VE HAD JUST ABOUT ALL THE BLASPHEMY I CAN TAKE FOR TODAY!
NOW SIT DOWN, SHUT YOUR MOUTH, AND EAT YOUR DINNER BEFORE I REALLY GIVE YOU SOMETHING TO BELLY-ACHE ABOUT!

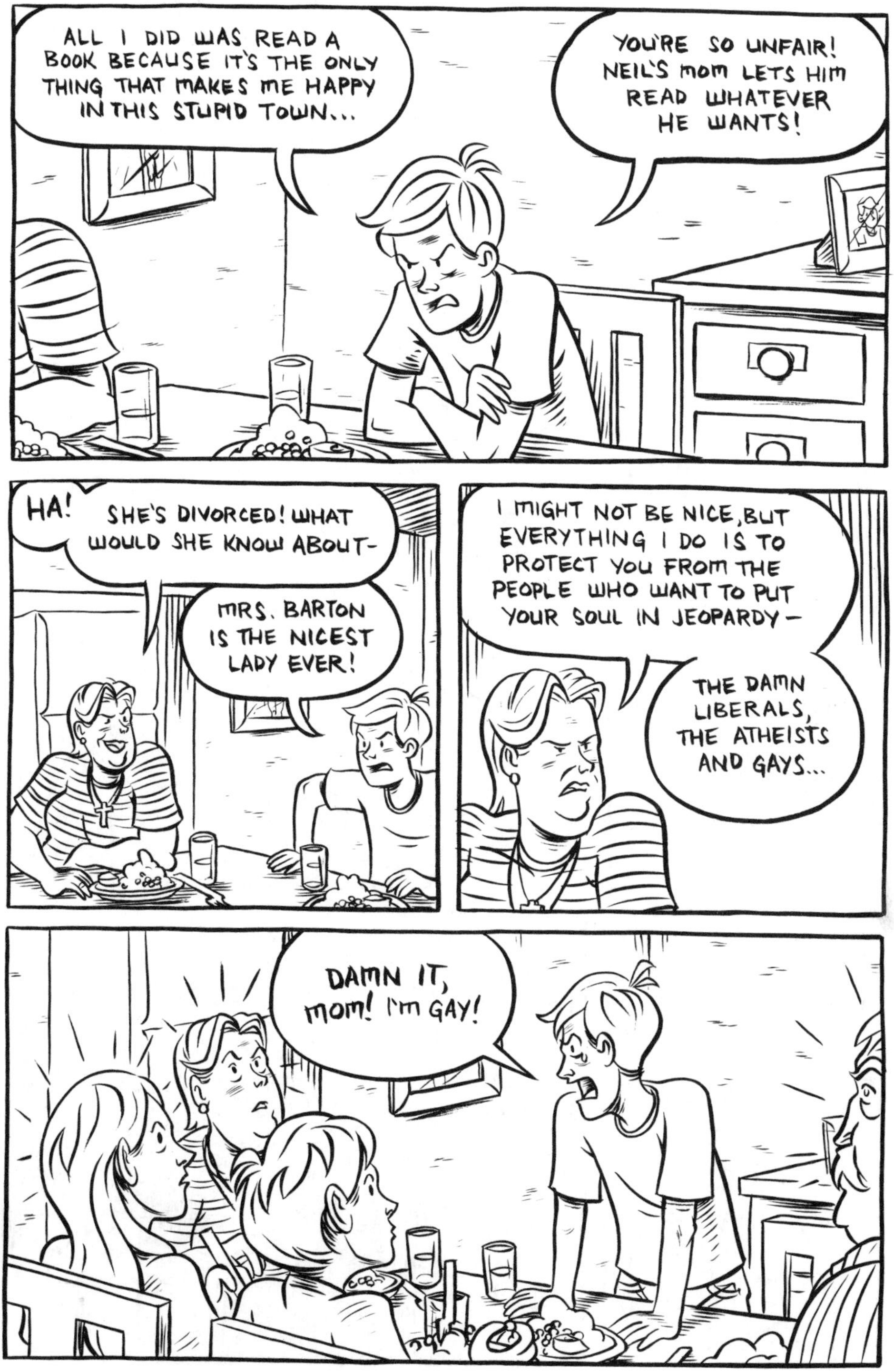
ALL I DID WAS READ A BOOK BECAUSE IT'S THE ONLY THING THAT MAKES ME HAPPY IN THIS STUPID TOWN...
YOU'RE SO UNFAIR! NEIL'S MOM LETS HIM READ WHATEVER HE WANTS!
HA!
SHE'S DIVORCED! WHAT WOULD SHE KNOW ABOUT-
MRS. BARTON IS THE NICEST LADY EVER!
I MIGHT NOT BE NICE, BUT EVERYTHING I DO IS TO PROTECT YOU FROM THE PEOPLE WHO WANT TO PUT YOUR SOUL IN JEOPARDY-
THE DAMN LIBERALS, THE ATHEISTS AND GAYS...
DAMN IT, MOM! I'M GAY!

DANIEL, WE DO NOT CUSS IN THIS HOUSE!

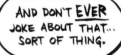

AND DON'T **EVER** JOKE ABOUT THAT... SORT OF THING.

KIDS, TAKE YOUR PLATES TO YOUR ROOMS.

YESSIR.

BUT DAD—

JOSEPH.

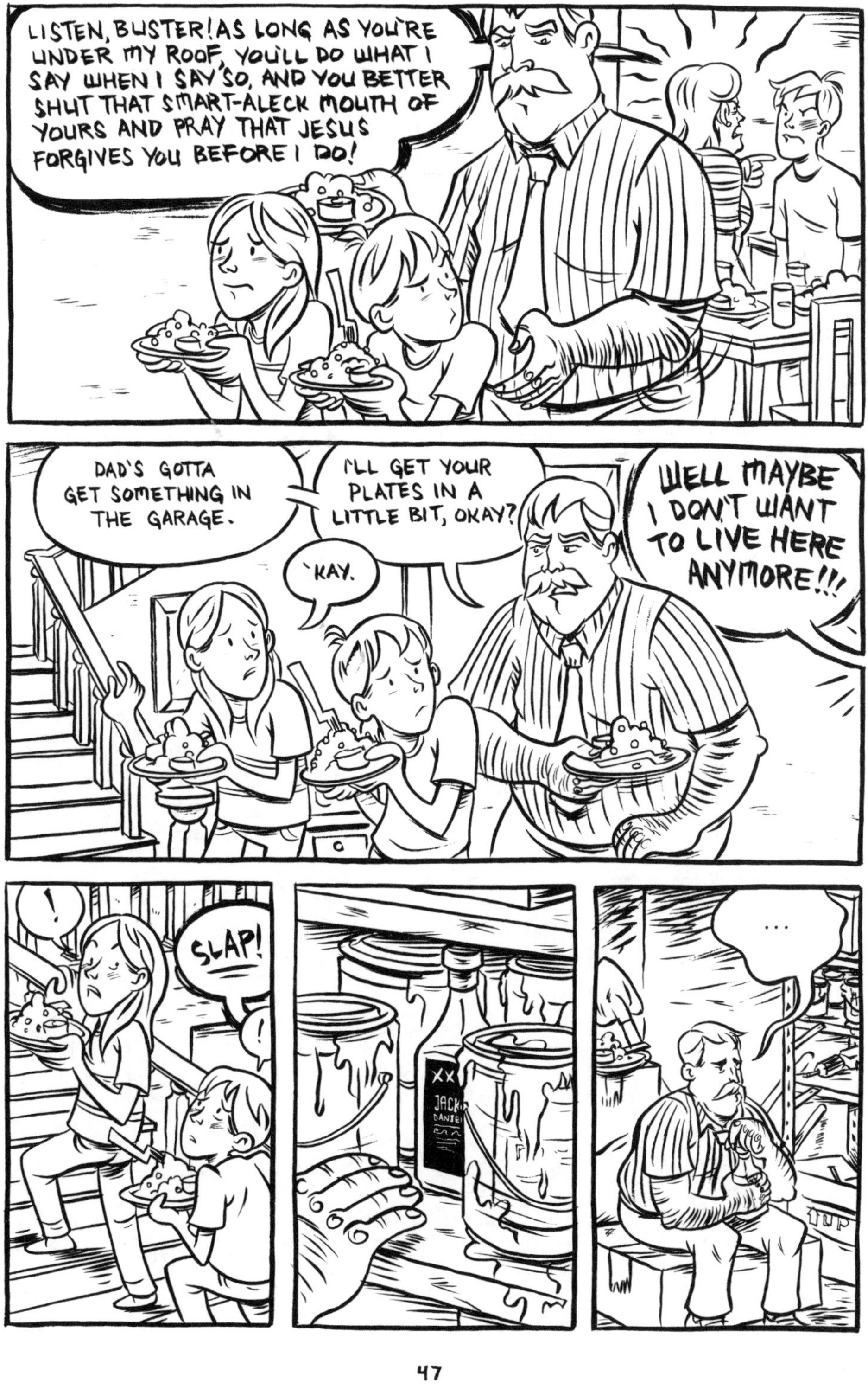
LISTEN, BUSTER! AS LONG AS YOU'RE UNDER MY ROOF, YOU'LL DO WHAT I SAY WHEN I SAY SO, AND YOU BETTER SHUT THAT SMART-ALECK MOUTH OF YOURS AND PRAY THAT JESUS FORGIVES YOU BEFORE I DO!
DAD'S GOTTA GET SOMETHING IN THE GARAGE.
I'LL GET YOUR PLATES IN A LITTLE BIT, OKAY?
`KAY.
WELL MAYBE I DON'T WANT TO LIVE HERE ANYMORE!!!
!
SLAP!
!
...

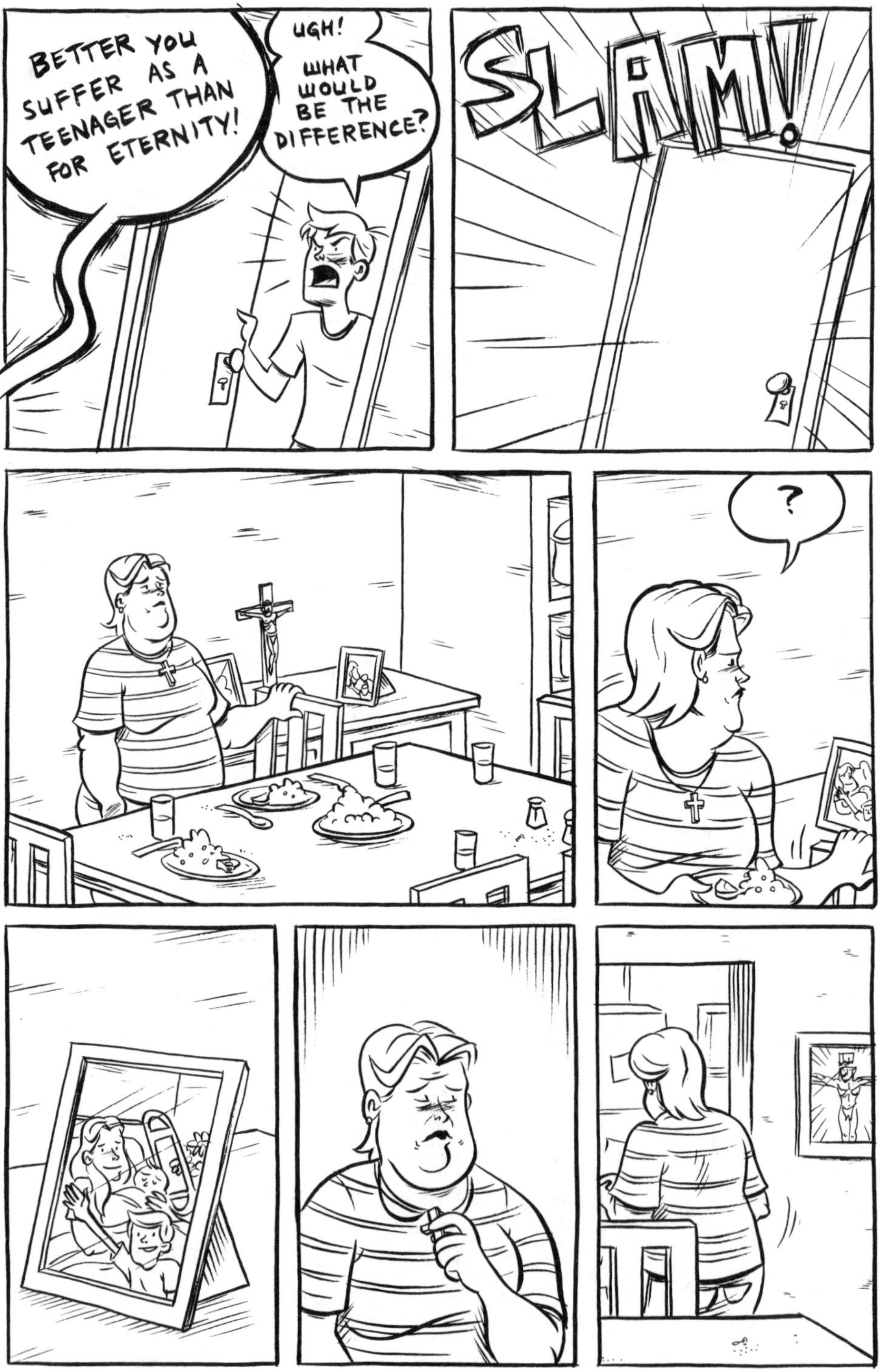

BETTER YOU SUFFER AS A TEENAGER THAN FOR ETERNITY!
UGH!
WHAT WOULD BE THE DIFFERENCE?
SLAM!
?

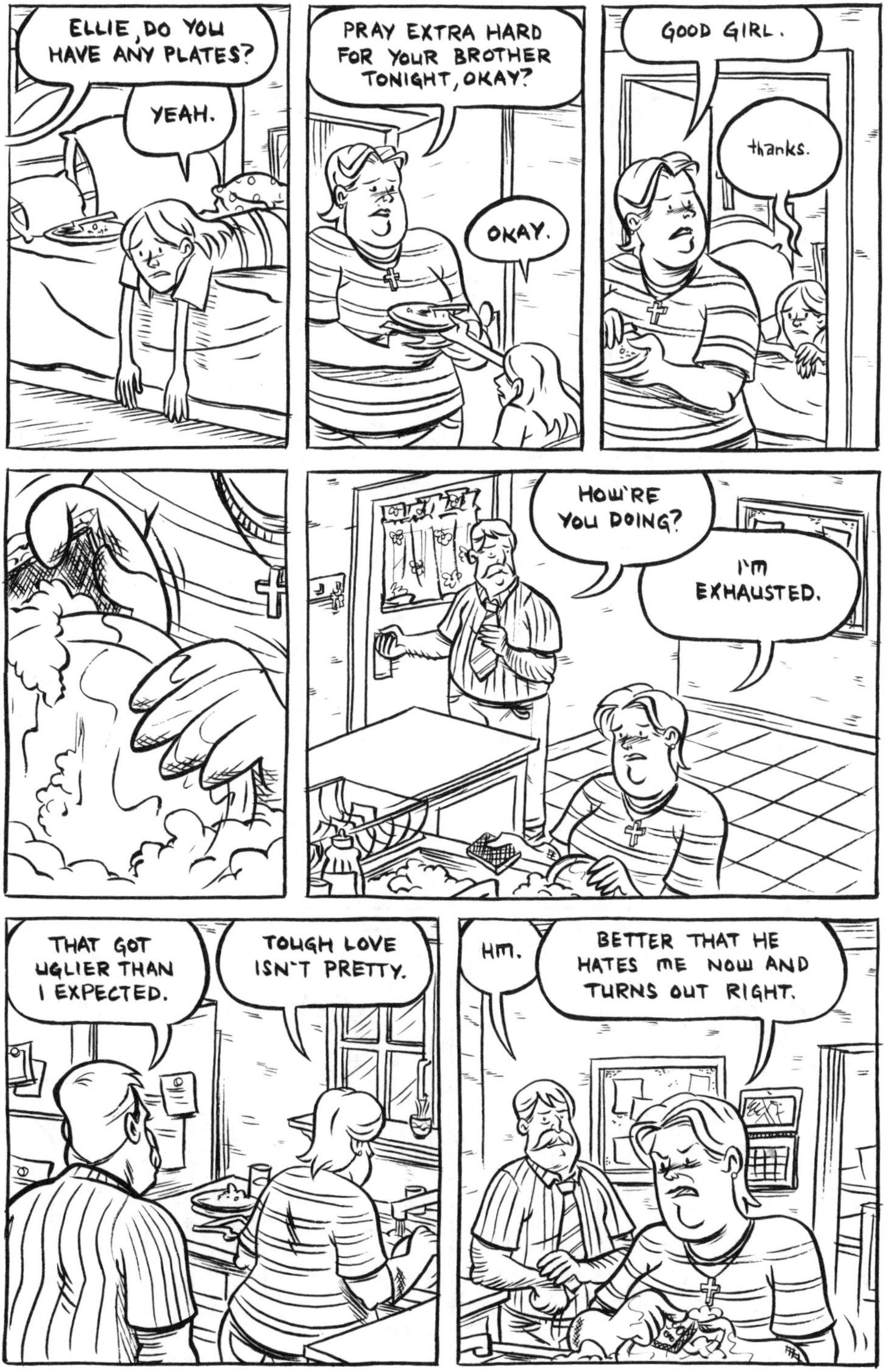
ELLIE, DO YOU HAVE ANY PLATES?
YEAH.
PRAY EXTRA HARD FOR YOUR BROTHER TONIGHT, OKAY?
OKAY.
GOOD GIRL.
thanks.
HOW'RE YOU DOING?
I'M EXHAUSTED.
THAT GOT UGLIER THAN I EXPECTED.
TOUGH LOVE ISN'T PRETTY.
HM.
BETTER THAT HE HATES ME NOW AND TURNS OUT RIGHT.

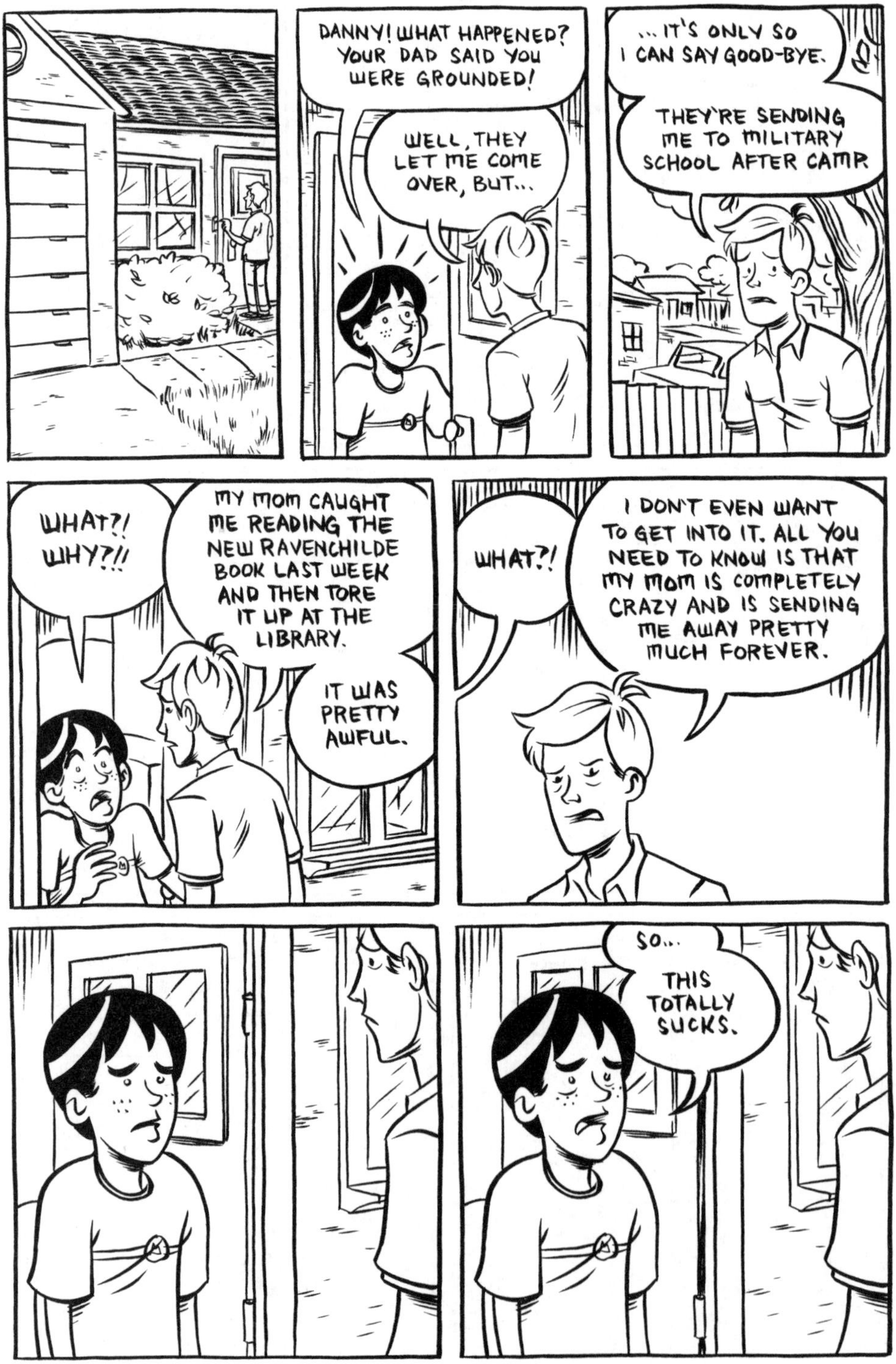
DANNY! WHAT HAPPENED? YOUR DAD SAID YOU WERE GROUNDED!
WELL, THEY LET ME COME OVER, BUT...
... IT'S ONLY SO I CAN SAY GOOD-BYE.
THEY'RE SENDING ME TO MILITARY SCHOOL AFTER CAMP.
WHAT?! WHY?!!
MY MOM CAUGHT ME READING THE NEW RAVENCHILDE BOOK LAST WEEK AND THEN TORE IT UP AT THE LIBRARY.
IT WAS PRETTY AWFUL.
WHAT?!
I DON'T EVEN WANT TO GET INTO IT. ALL YOU NEED TO KNOW IS THAT MY MOM IS COMPLETELY CRAZY AND IS SENDING ME AWAY PRETTY MUCH FOREVER.
SO...
THIS TOTALLY SUCKS.

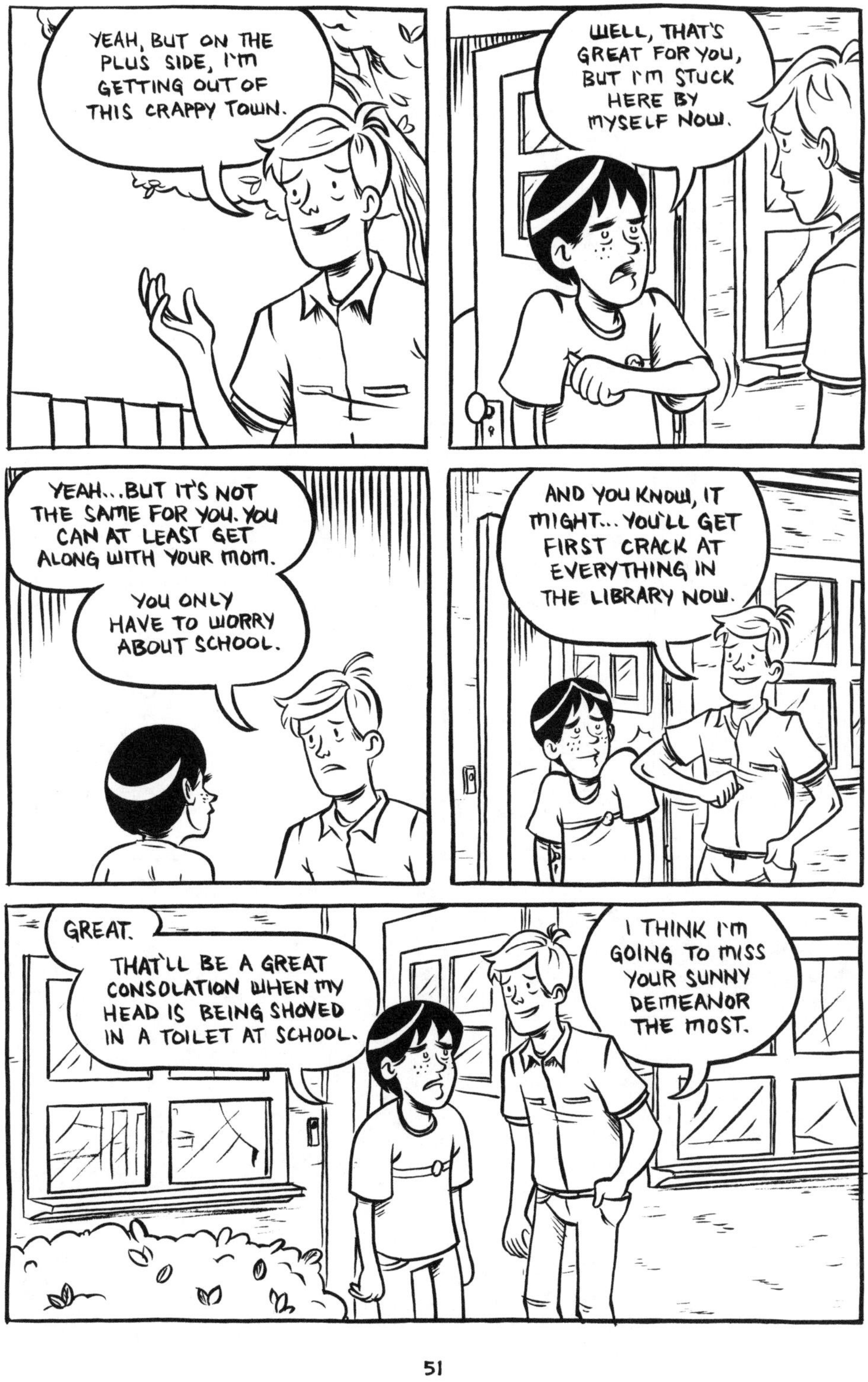
YEAH, BUT ON THE PLUS SIDE, I'M GETTING OUT OF THIS CRAPPY TOWN.
WELL, THAT'S GREAT FOR YOU, BUT I'M STUCK HERE BY MYSELF NOW.
YEAH...BUT IT'S NOT THE SAME FOR YOU. YOU CAN AT LEAST GET ALONG WITH YOUR MOM.
YOU ONLY HAVE TO WORRY ABOUT SCHOOL.
AND YOU KNOW, IT MIGHT... YOU'LL GET FIRST CRACK AT EVERYTHING IN THE LIBRARY NOW.
GREAT.
THAT'LL BE A GREAT CONSOLATION WHEN MY HEAD IS BEING SHOVED IN A TOILET AT SCHOOL.
I THINK I'M GOING TO MISS YOUR SUNNY DEMEANOR THE MOST.

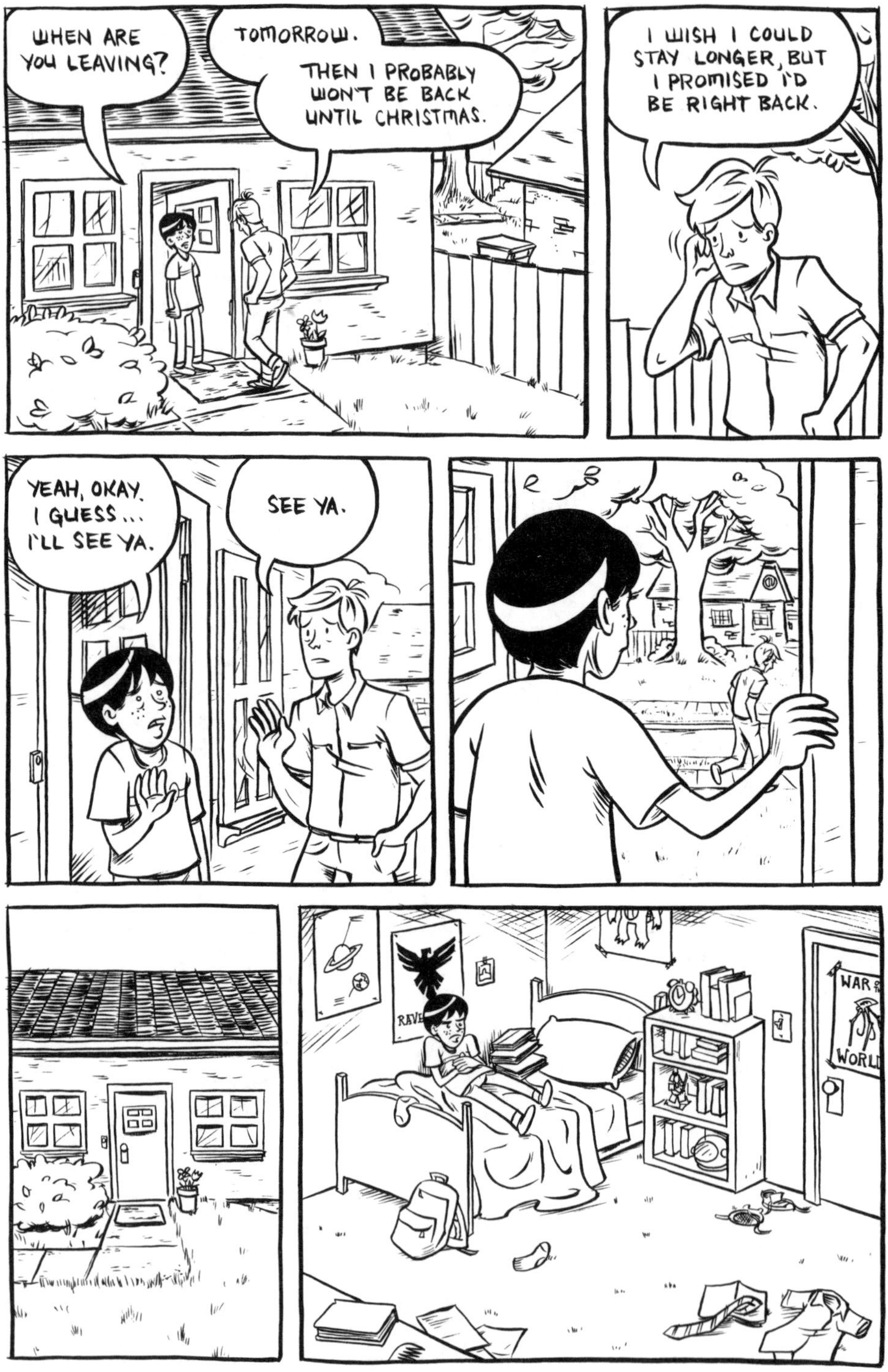
WHEN ARE YOU LEAVING?
TOMORROW.
THEN I PROBABLY WON'T BE BACK UNTIL CHRISTMAS.
I WISH I COULD STAY LONGER, BUT I PROMISED I'D BE RIGHT BACK.
YEAH, OKAY. I GUESS... I'LL SEE YA.
SEE YA.
RAVE
WAR WORLD

CHAPTER 3

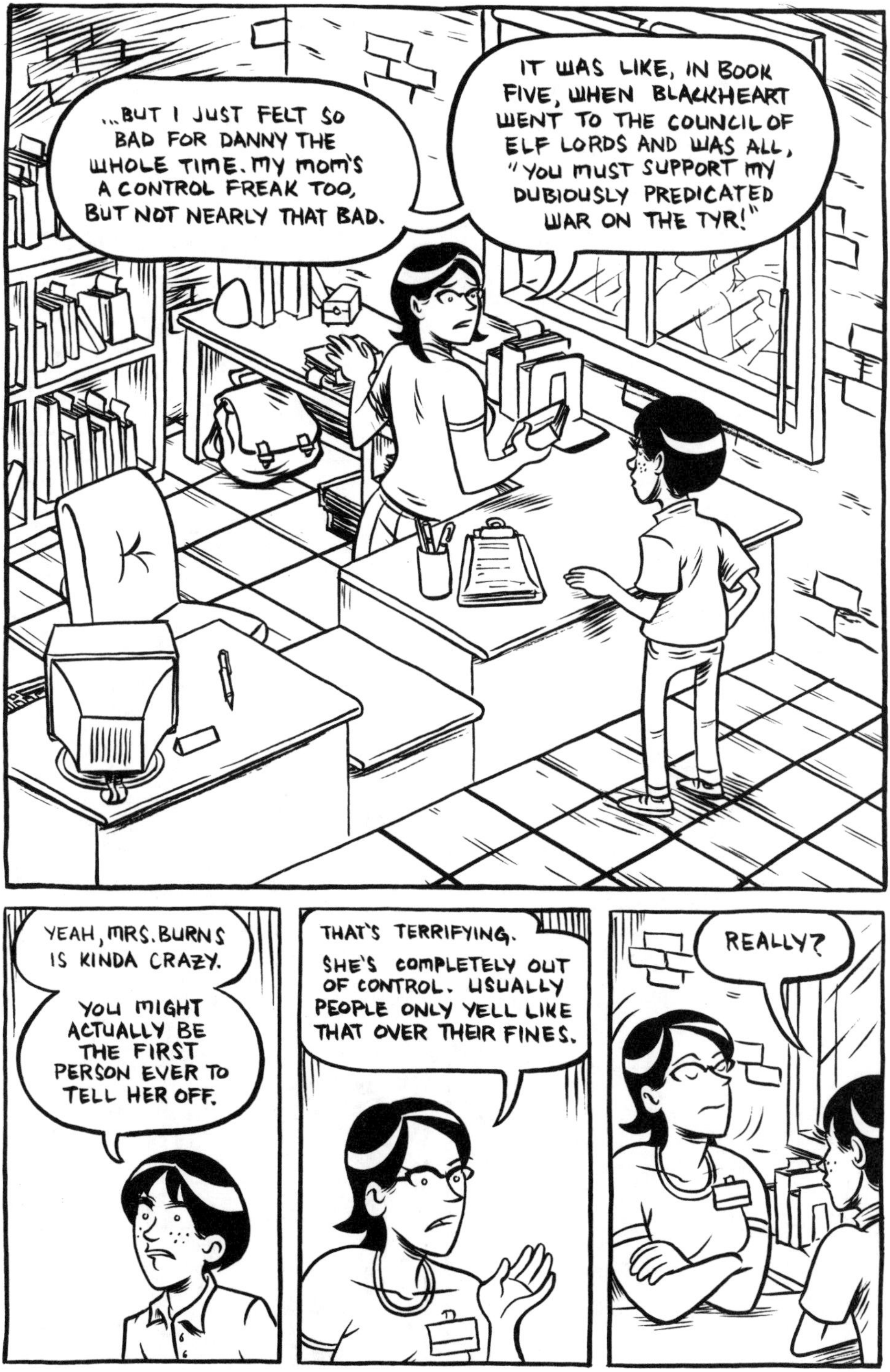
...BUT I JUST FELT SO BAD FOR DANNY THE WHOLE TIME. MY MOM'S A CONTROL FREAK TOO, BUT NOT NEARLY THAT BAD.
IT WAS LIKE, IN BOOK FIVE, WHEN BLACKHEART WENT TO THE COUNCIL OF ELF LORDS AND WAS ALL, "YOU MUST SUPPORT MY DUBIOUSLY PREDICATED WAR ON THE TYR!"
YEAH, MRS. BURNS IS KINDA CRAZY.
YOU MIGHT ACTUALLY BE THE FIRST PERSON EVER TO TELL HER OFF.
THAT'S TERRIFYING.
SHE'S COMPLETELY OUT OF CONTROL. USUALLY PEOPLE ONLY YELL LIKE THAT OVER THEIR FINES.
REALLY?

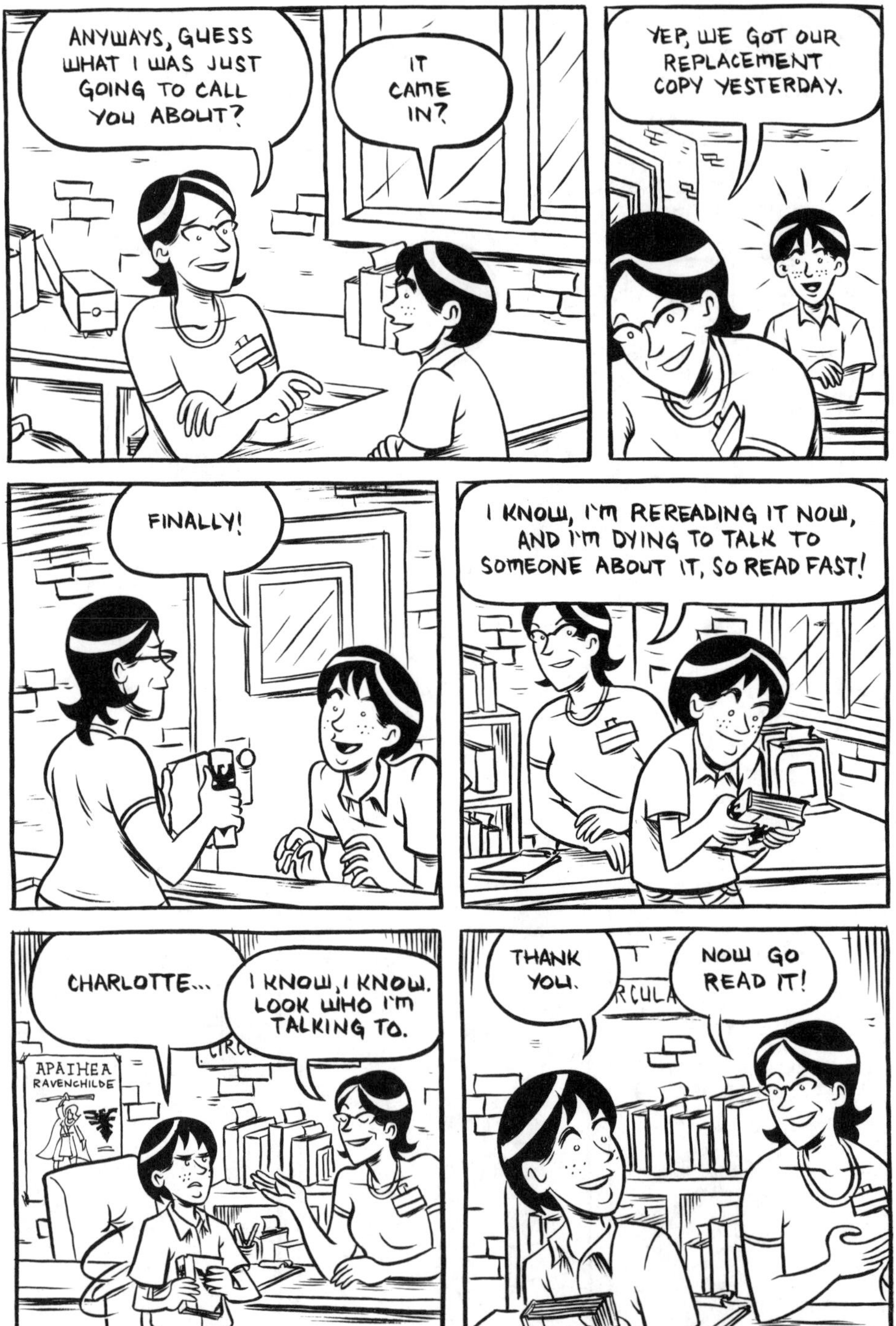
ANYWAYS, GUESS WHAT I WAS JUST GOING TO CALL YOU ABOUT?
IT CAME IN?
YEP, WE GOT OUR REPLACEMENT COPY YESTERDAY.
FINALLY!
I KNOW, I'M REREADING IT NOW, AND I'M DYING TO TALK TO SOMEONE ABOUT IT, SO READ FAST!
CHARLOTTE...
I KNOW, I KNOW. LOOK WHO I'M TALKING TO.
APAIHEA RAVENCHILDE
THANK YOU.
NOW GO READ IT!

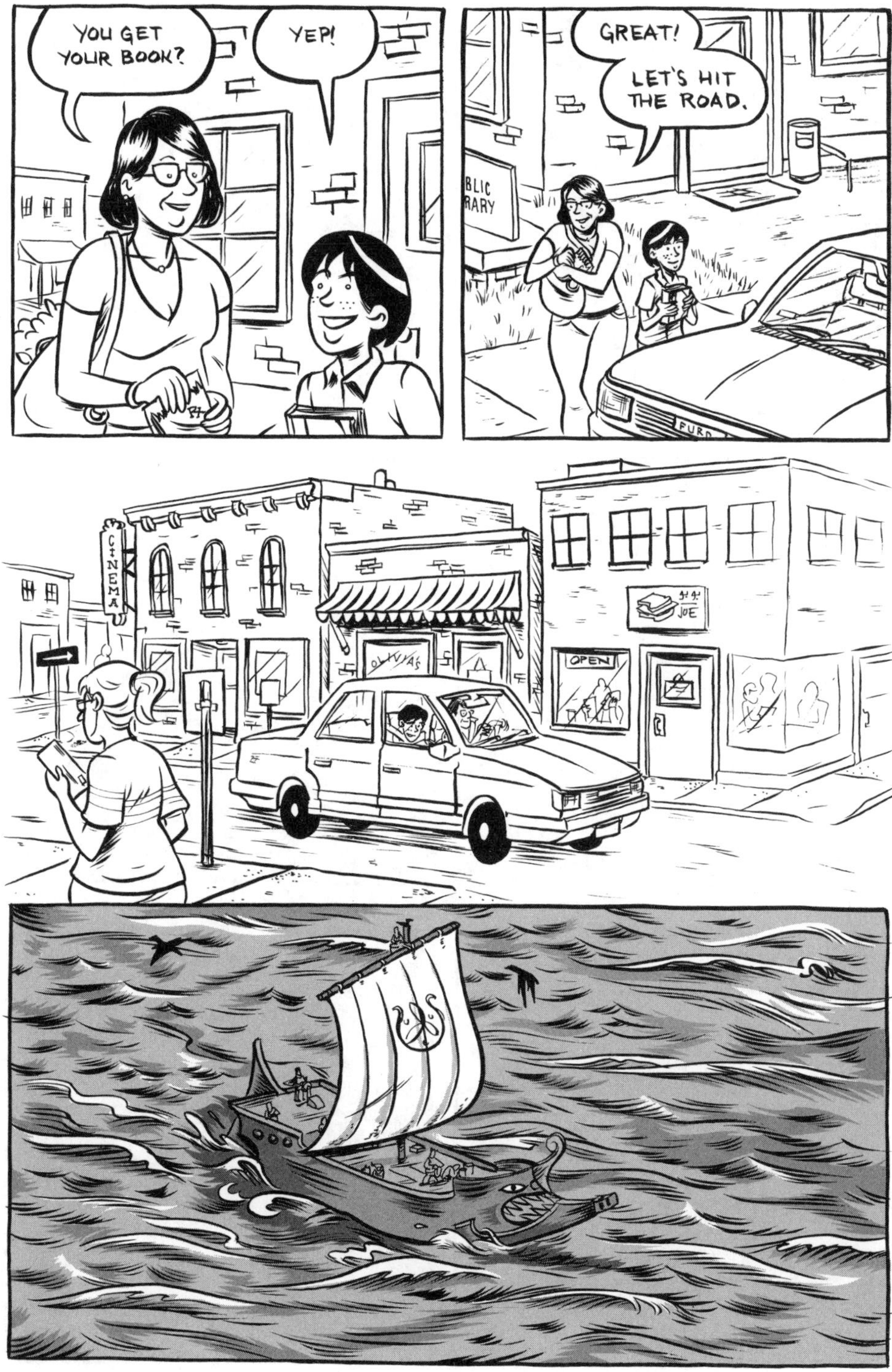

YOU GET YOUR BOOK?
YEP!
GREAT!
LET'S HIT THE ROAD.
BLIC
RARY
CINEMA
OPEN
JOE

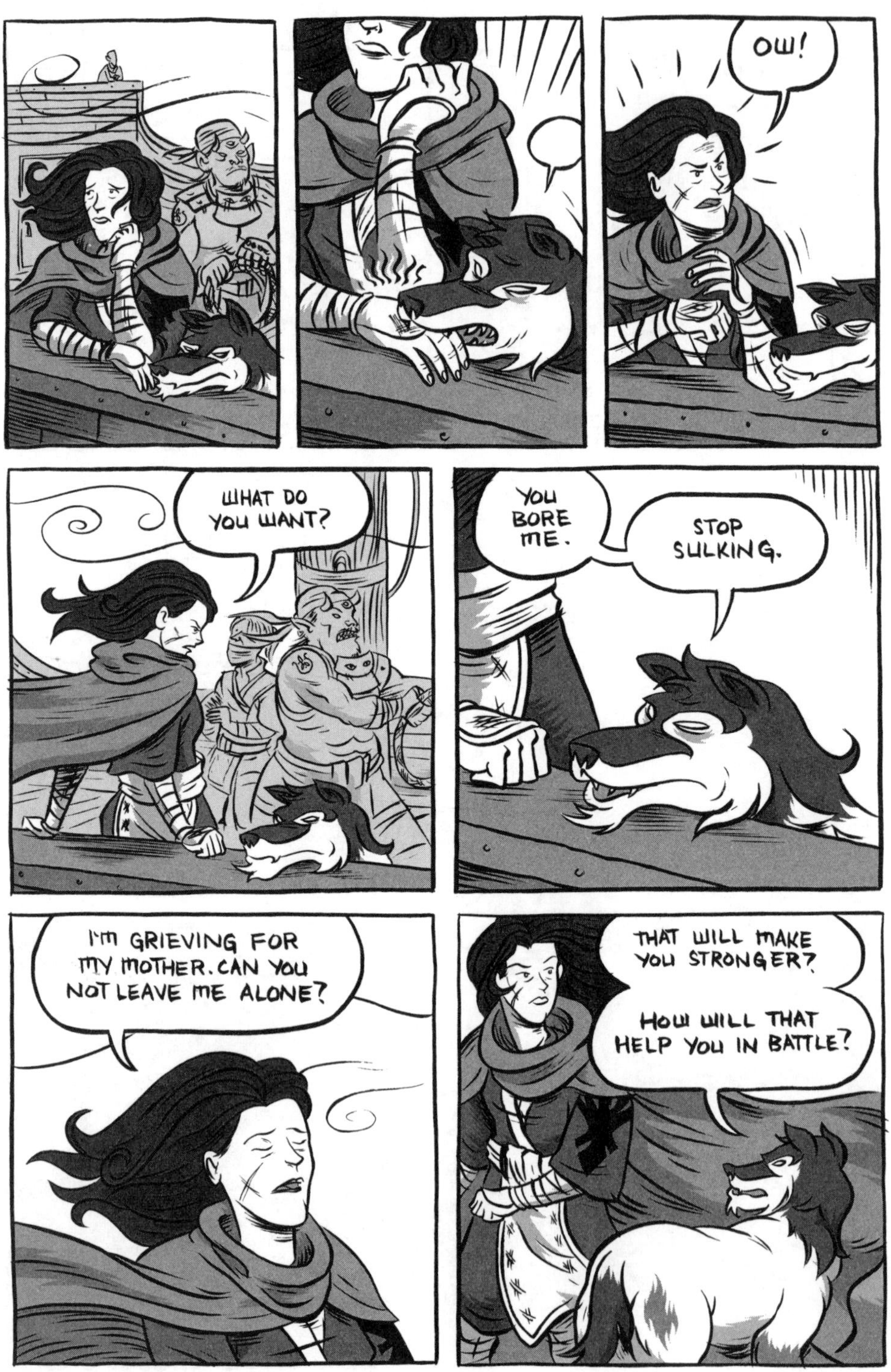
OW!
WHAT DO YOU WANT?
YOU BORE ME.
STOP SULKING.
I'M GRIEVING FOR MY MOTHER. CAN YOU NOT LEAVE ME ALONE?
THAT WILL MAKE YOU STRONGER?
HOW WILL THAT HELP YOU IN BATTLE?

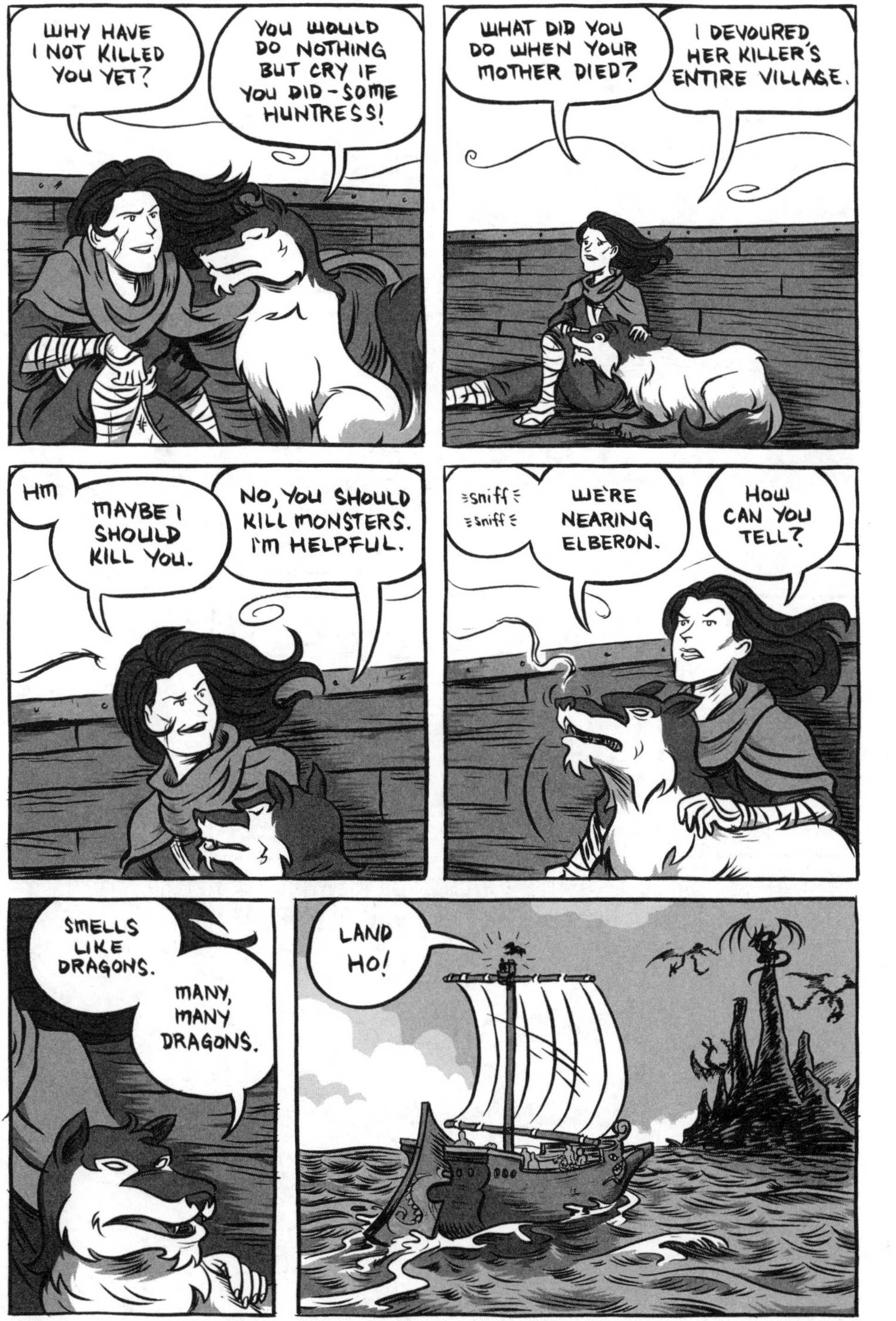
WHY HAVE I NOT KILLED YOU YET?
YOU WOULD DO NOTHING BUT CRY IF YOU DID-SOME HUNTRESS!
WHAT DID YOU DO WHEN YOUR MOTHER DIED?
I DEVOURED HER KILLER'S ENTIRE VILLAGE.
Hm
MAYBE I SHOULD KILL YOU.
NO, YOU SHOULD KILL MONSTERS. I'M HELPFUL.
sniff
sniff
WE'RE NEARING ELBERON.
HOW CAN YOU TELL?
SMELLS LIKE DRAGONS.
MANY, MANY DRAGONS.
LAND HO!

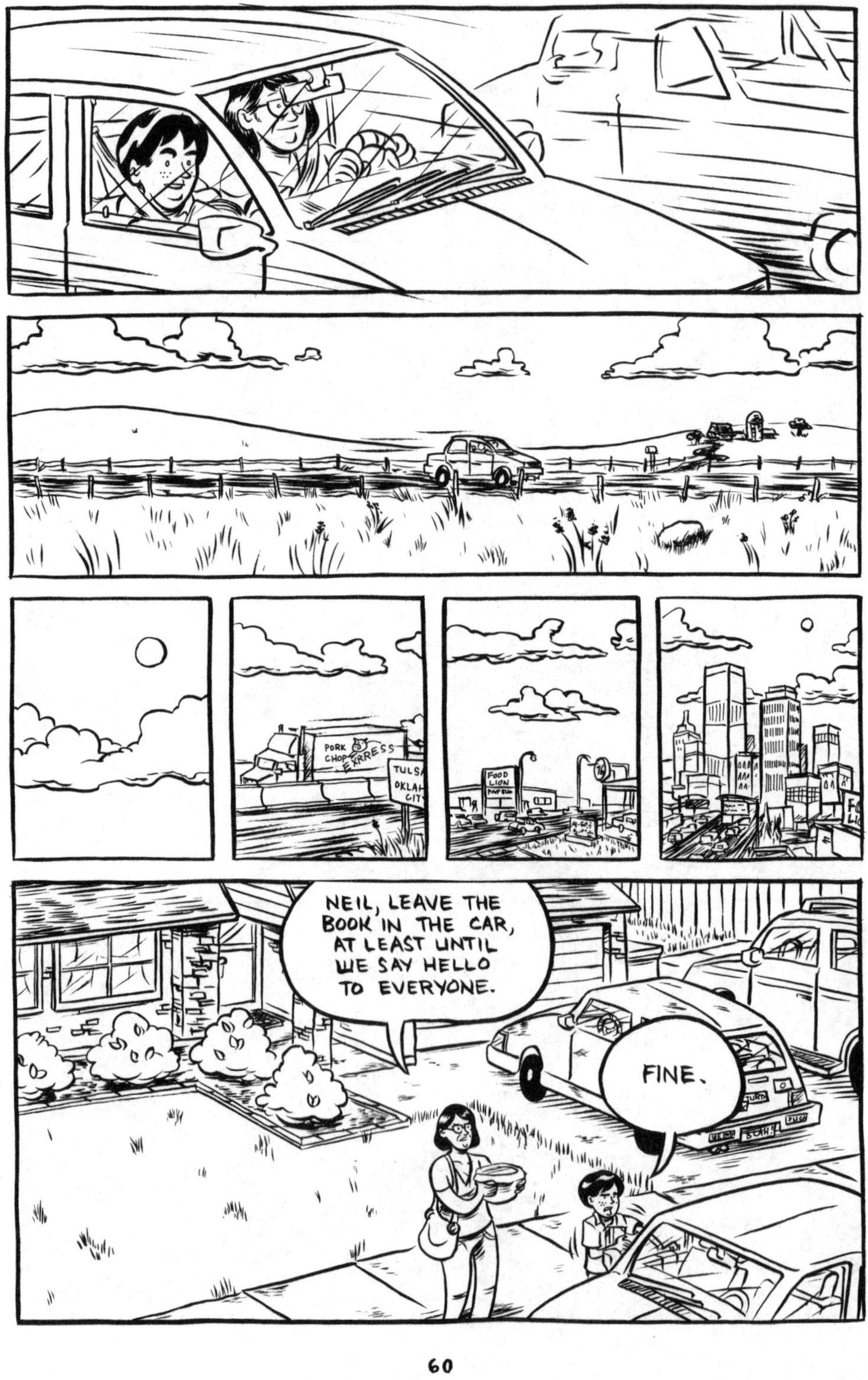
NEIL, LEAVE THE BOOK IN THE CAR, AT LEAST UNTIL WE SAY HELLO TO EVERYONE.
FINE.

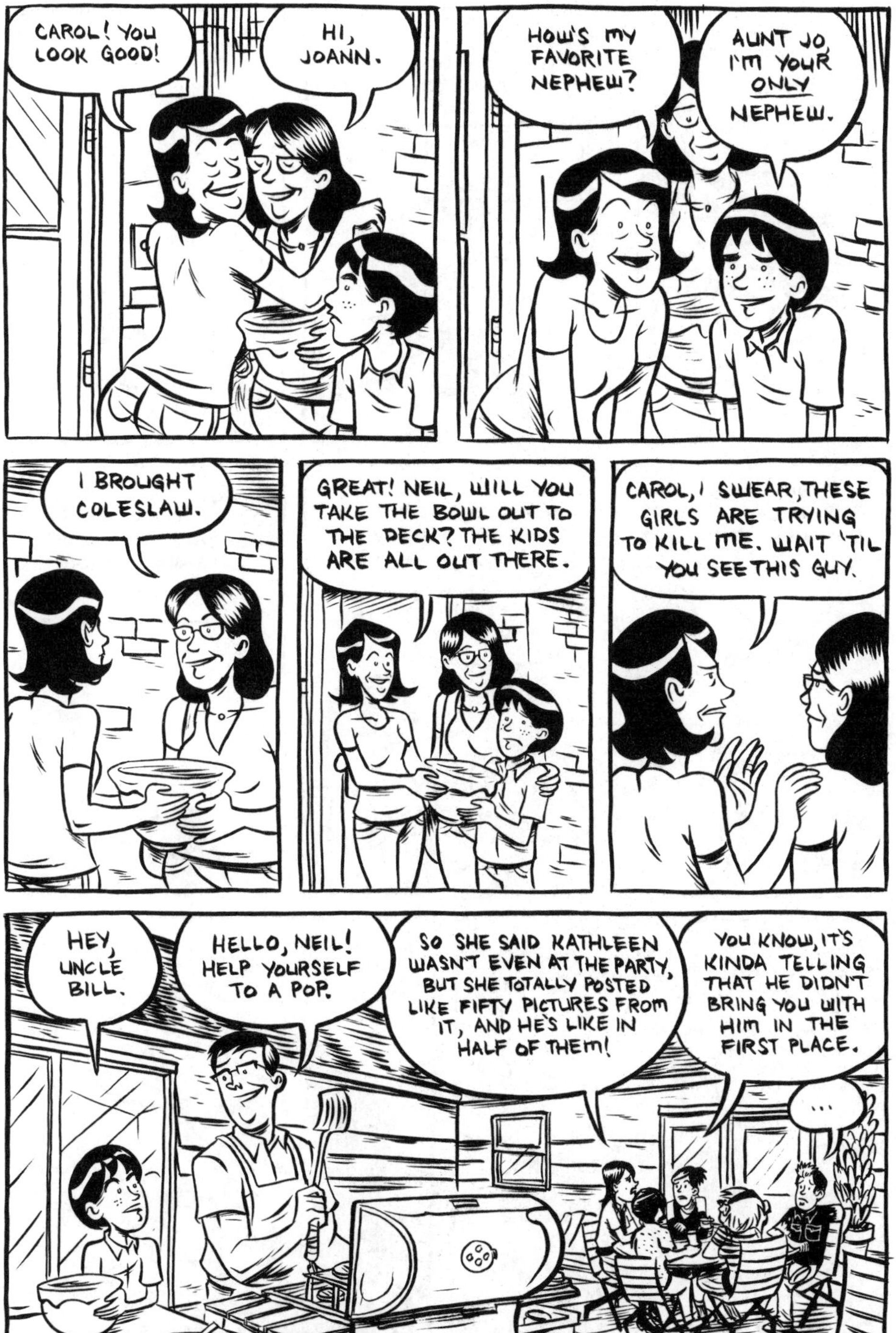
CAROL! YOU LOOK GOOD!
HI, JOANN.
HOW'S MY FAVORITE NEPHEW?
AUNT JO, I'M YOUR ONLY NEPHEW.
I BROUGHT COLESLAW.
GREAT! NEIL, WILL YOU TAKE THE BOWL OUT TO THE DECK? THE KIDS ARE ALL OUT THERE.
CAROL, I SWEAR, THESE GIRLS ARE TRYING TO KILL ME. WAIT 'TIL YOU SEE THIS GUY.
HEY, UNCLE BILL.
HELLO, NEIL! HELP YOURSELF TO A POP.
SO SHE SAID KATHLEEN WASN'T EVEN AT THE PARTY, BUT SHE TOTALLY POSTED LIKE FIFTY PICTURES FROM IT, AND HE'S LIKE IN HALF OF THEM!
YOU KNOW, IT'S KINDA TELLING THAT HE DIDN'T BRING YOU WITH HIM IN THE FIRST PLACE.
...

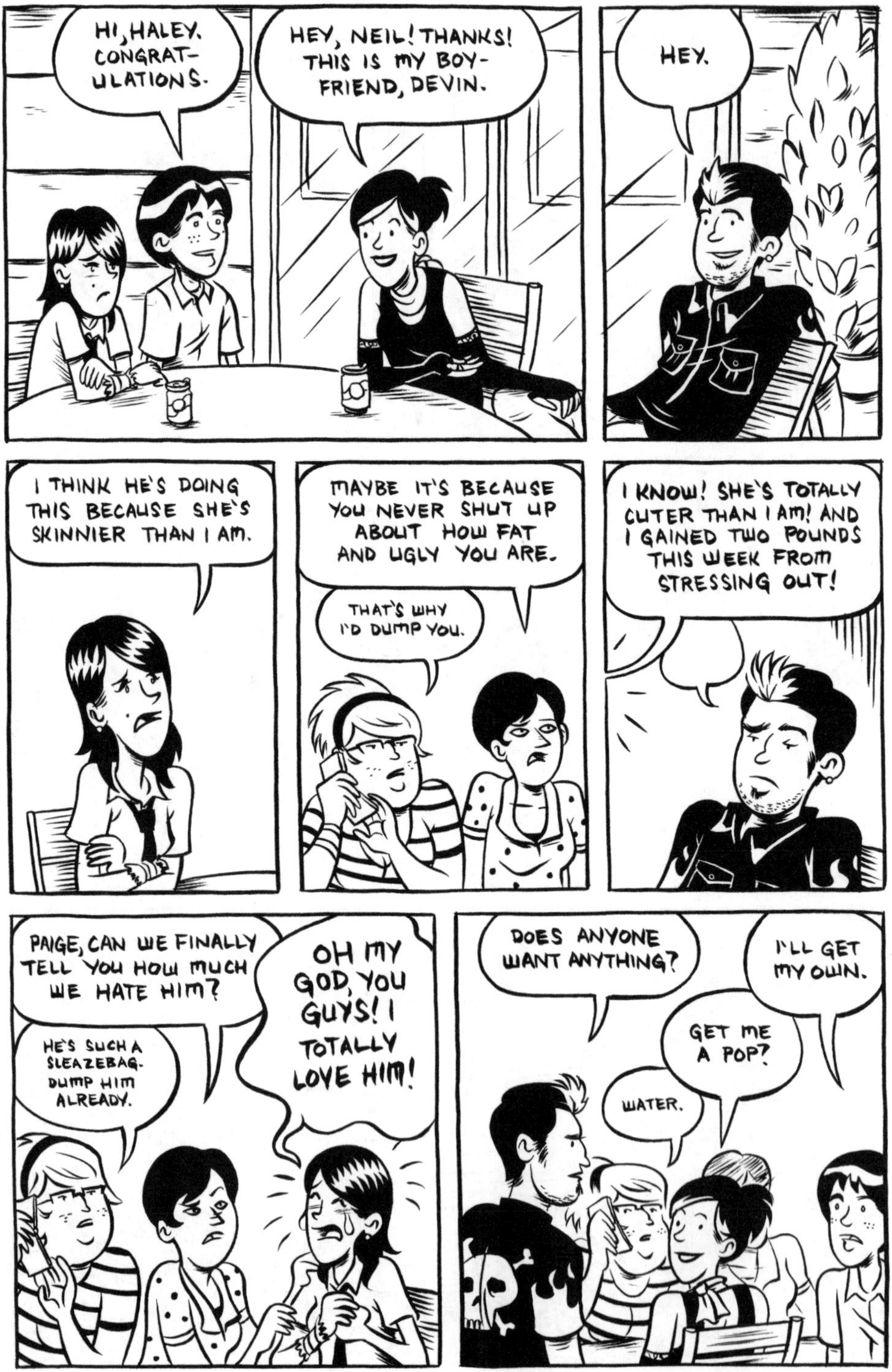
HI, HALEY. CONGRAT-ULATIONS.
HEY, NEIL! THANKS! THIS IS MY BOY-FRIEND, DEVIN.
HEY.
I THINK HE'S DOING THIS BECAUSE SHE'S SKINNIER THAN I AM.
MAYBE IT'S BECAUSE YOU NEVER SHUT UP ABOUT HOW FAT AND UGLY YOU ARE.
THAT'S WHY I'D DUMP YOU.
I KNOW! SHE'S TOTALLY CUTER THAN I AM! AND I GAINED TWO POUNDS THIS WEEK FROM STRESSING OUT!
PAIGE, CAN WE FINALLY TELL YOU HOW MUCH WE HATE HIM?
HE'S SUCH A SLEAZEBAG. DUMP HIM ALREADY.
OH MY GOD, YOU GUYS! I TOTALLY LOVE HIM!
DOES ANYONE WANT ANYTHING?
I'LL GET MY OWN.
GET ME A POP?
WATER.

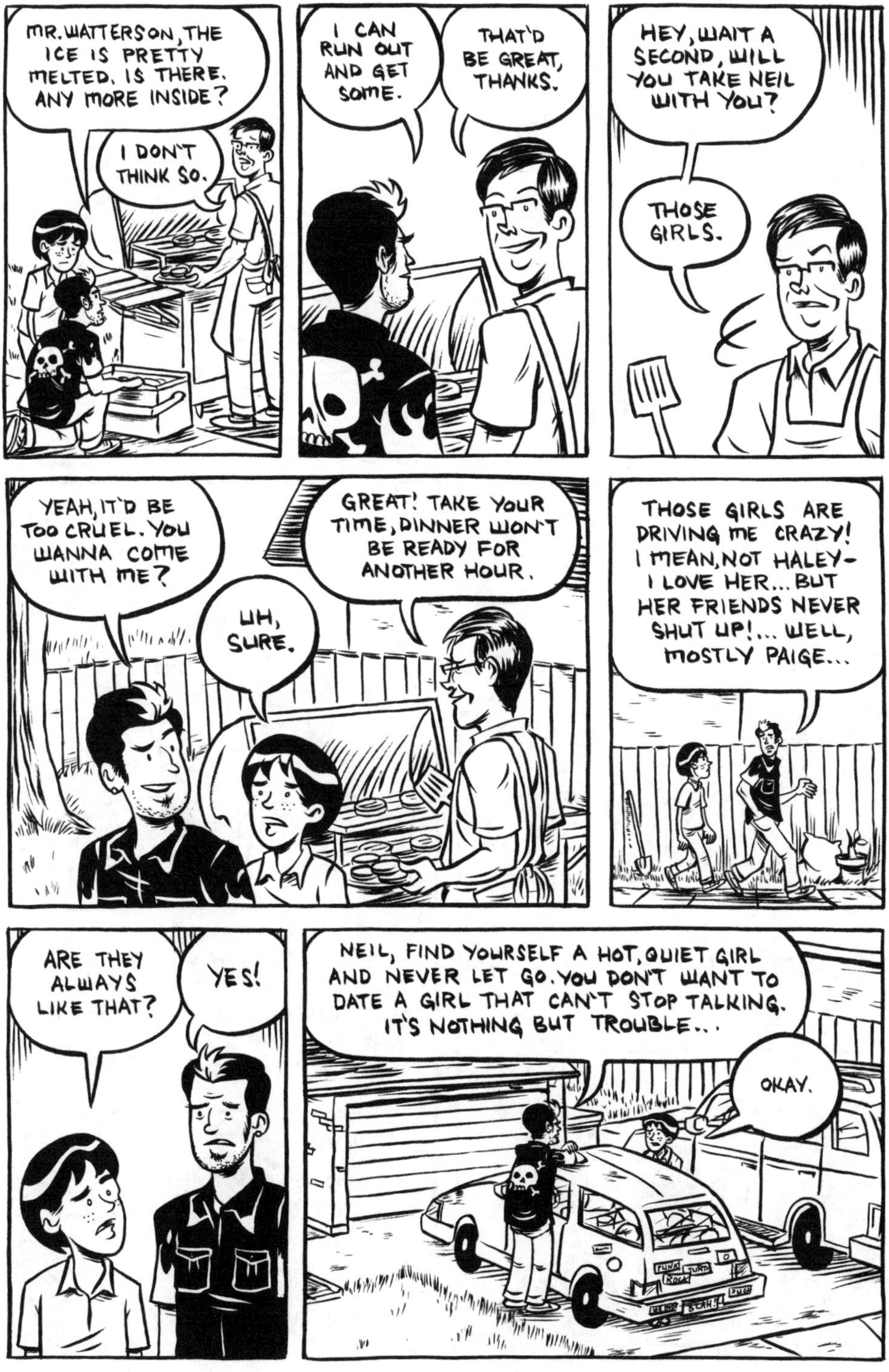
MR. WATTERSON, THE ICE IS PRETTY MELTED. IS THERE ANY MORE INSIDE?
I DON'T THINK SO.
I CAN RUN OUT AND GET SOME.
THAT'D BE GREAT, THANKS.
HEY, WAIT A SECOND, WILL YOU TAKE NEIL WITH YOU?
THOSE GIRLS.
YEAH, IT'D BE TOO CRUEL. YOU WANNA COME WITH ME?
UH, SURE.
GREAT! TAKE YOUR TIME, DINNER WON'T BE READY FOR ANOTHER HOUR.
THOSE GIRLS ARE DRIVING ME CRAZY! I MEAN, NOT HALEY- I LOVE HER... BUT HER FRIENDS NEVER SHUT UP!... WELL, MOSTLY PAIGE...
ARE THEY ALWAYS LIKE THAT?
YES!
NEIL, FIND YOURSELF A HOT, QUIET GIRL AND NEVER LET GO. YOU DON'T WANT TO DATE A GIRL THAT CAN'T STOP TALKING. IT'S NOTHING BUT TROUBLE...
OKAY.

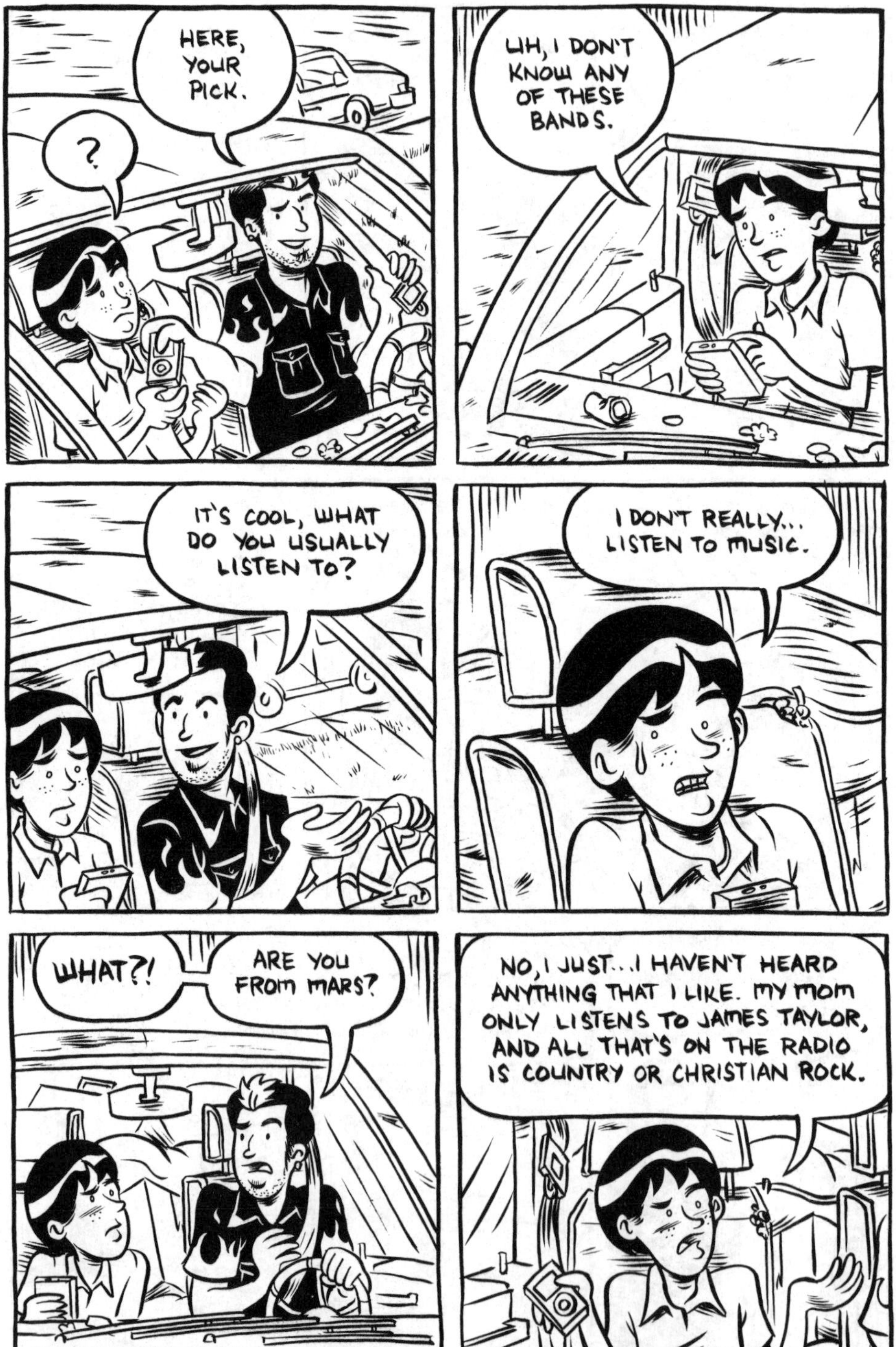
HERE, YOUR PICK.
?
UH, I DON'T KNOW ANY OF THESE BANDS.
IT'S COOL, WHAT DO YOU USUALLY LISTEN TO?
I DON'T REALLY... LISTEN TO MUSIC.
WHAT?!
ARE YOU FROM MARS?
NO, I JUST...I HAVEN'T HEARD ANYTHING THAT I LIKE. MY MOM ONLY LISTENS TO JAMES TAYLOR, AND ALL THAT'S ON THE RADIO IS COUNTRY OR CHRISTIAN ROCK.

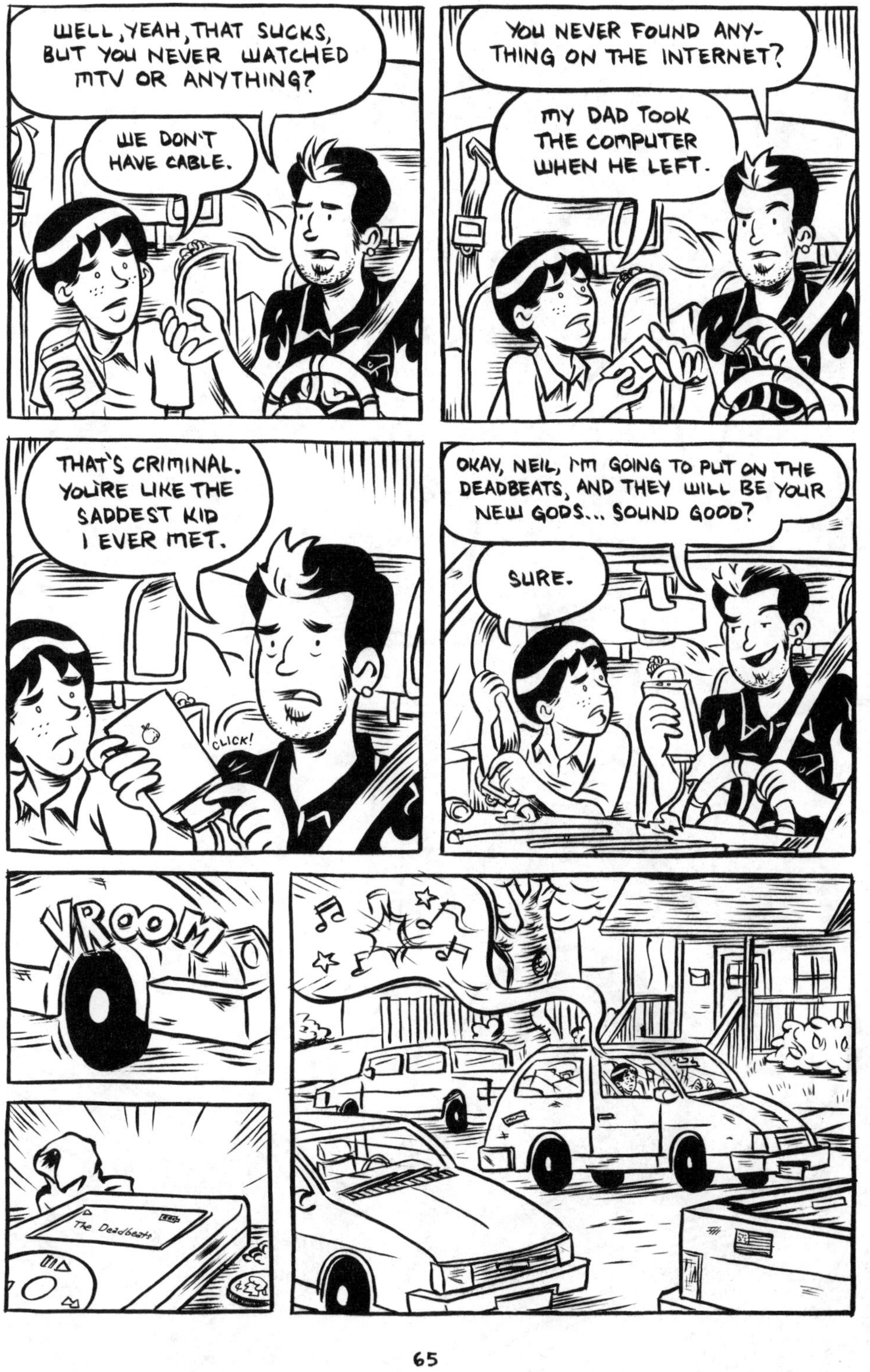
WELL, YEAH, THAT SUCKS, BUT YOU NEVER WATCHED MTV OR ANYTHING?
WE DON'T HAVE CABLE.
YOU NEVER FOUND ANY-THING ON THE INTERNET?
MY DAD TOOK THE COMPUTER WHEN HE LEFT.
THAT'S CRIMINAL. YOU'RE LIKE THE SADDEST KID I EVER MET.
CLICK!
OKAY, NEIL, I'M GOING TO PUT ON THE DEADBEATS, AND THEY WILL BE YOUR NEW GODS... SOUND GOOD?
SURE.
VROOM
The Deadbeats

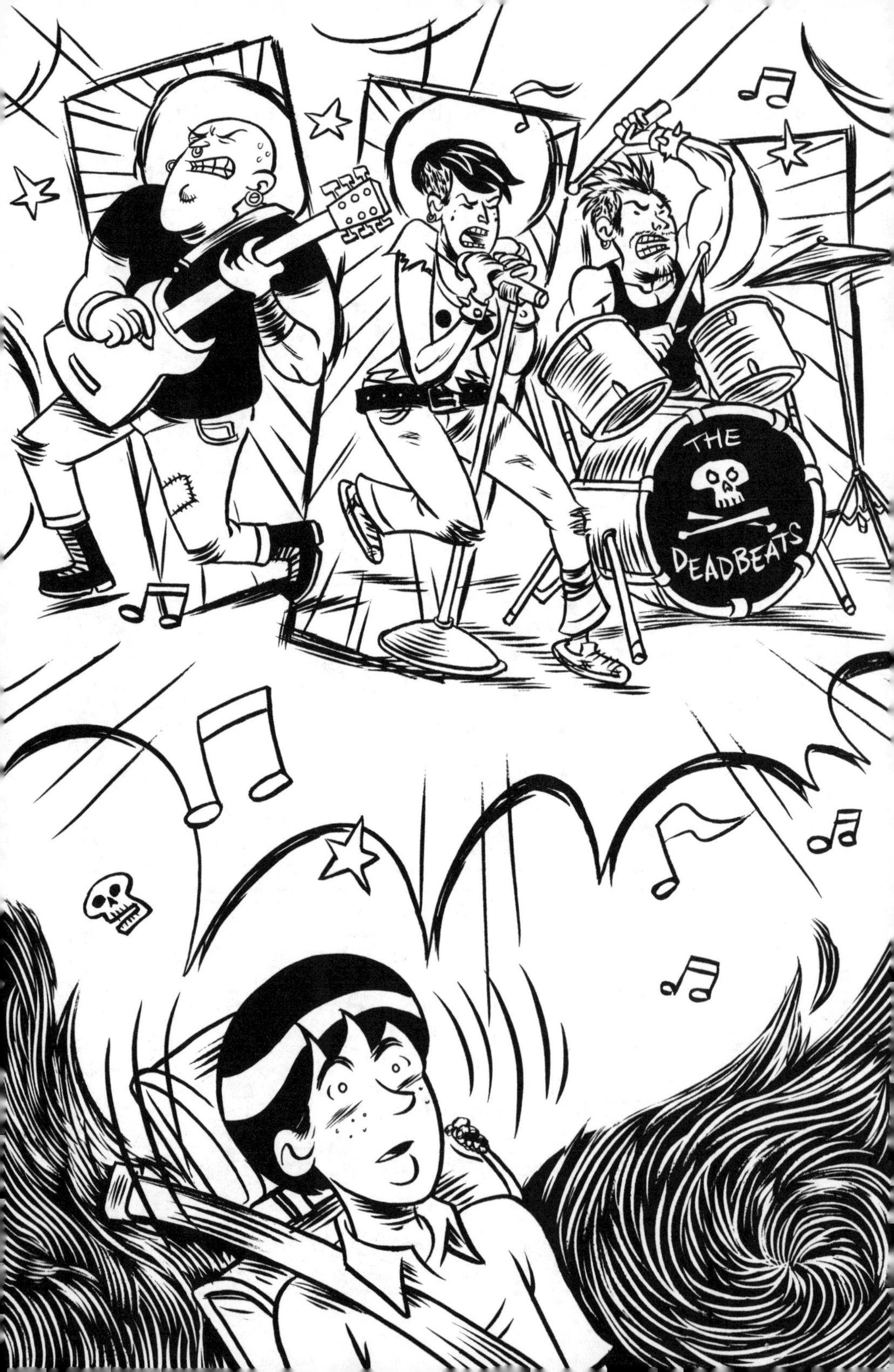
THE
DEADBEATS

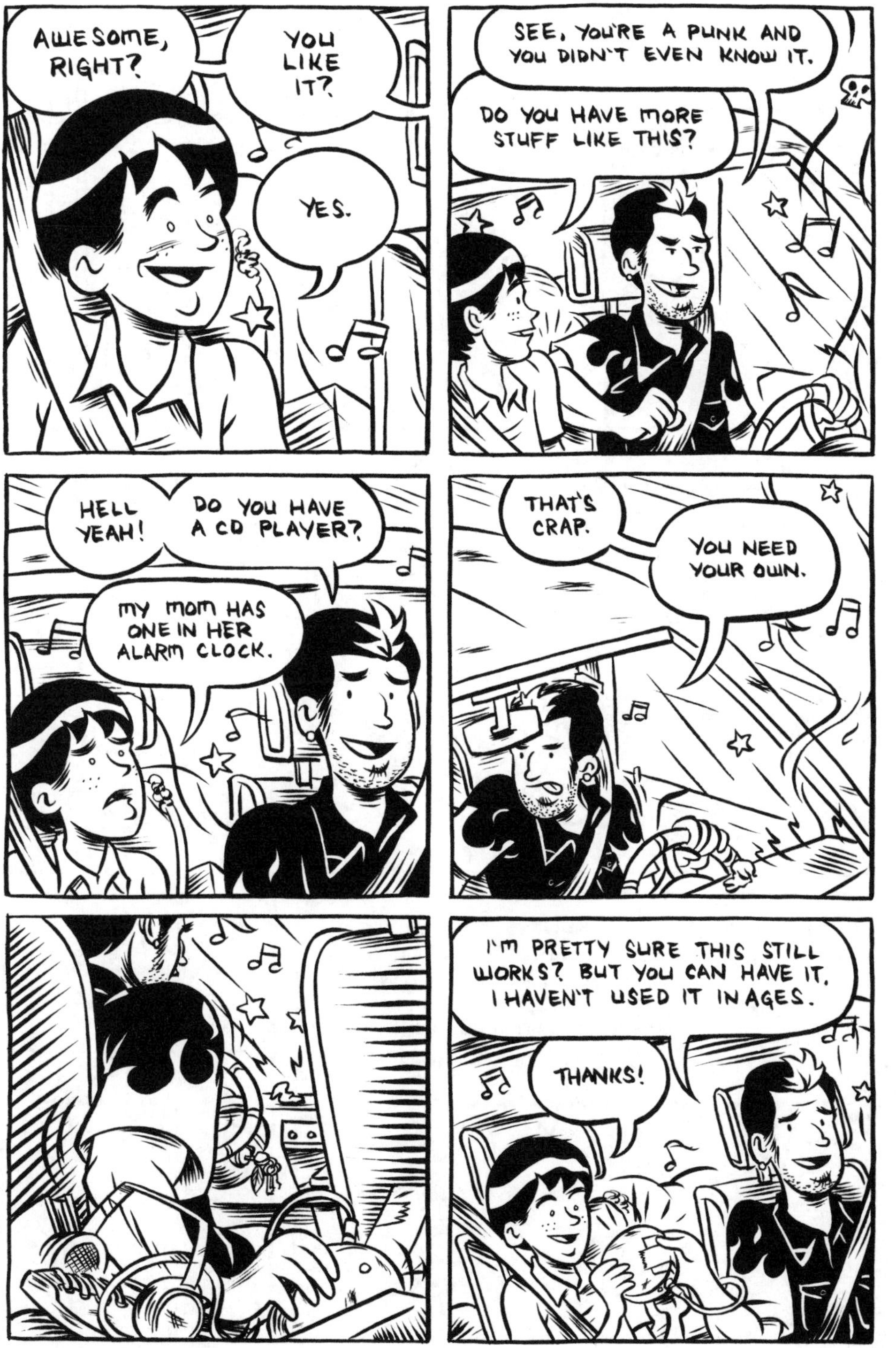
AWESOME, RIGHT?
YOU LIKE IT?
YES.
SEE, YOU'RE A PUNK AND YOU DIDN'T EVEN KNOW IT.
DO YOU HAVE MORE STUFF LIKE THIS?
HELL YEAH!
DO YOU HAVE A CD PLAYER?
MY MOM HAS ONE IN HER ALARM CLOCK.
THAT'S CRAP.
YOU NEED YOUR OWN.
I'M PRETTY SURE THIS STILL WORKS? BUT YOU CAN HAVE IT. I HAVEN'T USED IT IN AGES.
THANKS!

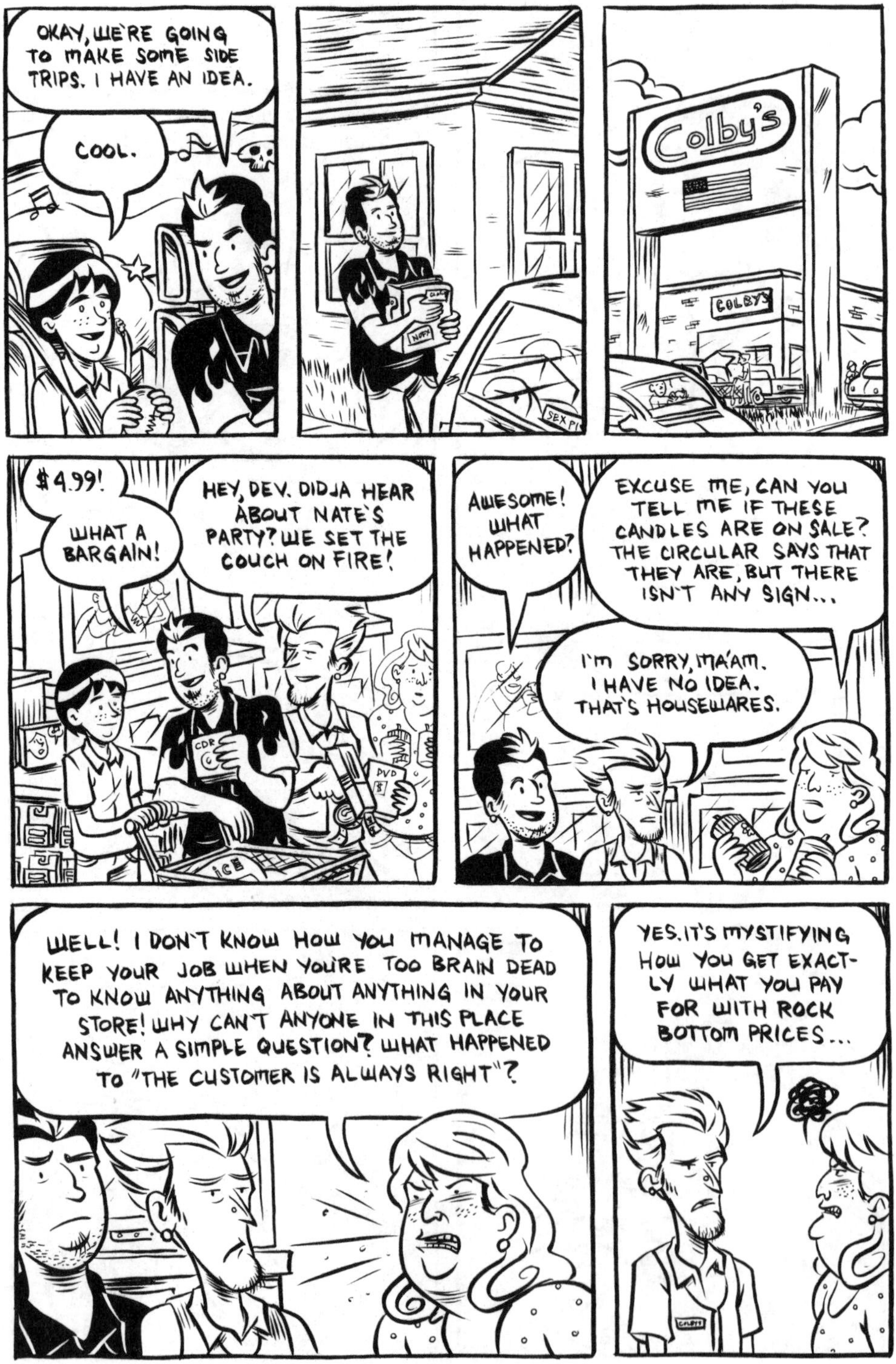
OKAY, WE'RE GOING TO MAKE SOME SIDE TRIPS. I HAVE AN IDEA.
COOL.
Colby's
COLBY'S
$4.99!
WHAT A BARGAIN!
HEY, DEV. DIDJA HEAR ABOUT NATE'S PARTY? WE SET THE COUCH ON FIRE!
ICE
CDR
DVD
AWESOME! WHAT HAPPENED?
EXCUSE ME, CAN YOU TELL ME IF THESE CANDLES ARE ON SALE? THE CIRCULAR SAYS THAT THEY ARE, BUT THERE ISN'T ANY SIGN...
I'M SORRY, MA'AM. I HAVE NO IDEA. THAT'S HOUSEWARES.
WELL! I DON'T KNOW HOW YOU MANAGE TO KEEP YOUR JOB WHEN YOU'RE TOO BRAIN DEAD TO KNOW ANYTHING ABOUT ANYTHING IN YOUR STORE! WHY CAN'T ANYONE IN THIS PLACE ANSWER A SIMPLE QUESTION? WHAT HAPPENED TO "THE CUSTOMER IS ALWAYS RIGHT"?
YES. IT'S MYSTIFYING HOW YOU GET EXACTLY WHAT YOU PAY FOR WITH ROCK BOTTOM PRICES...

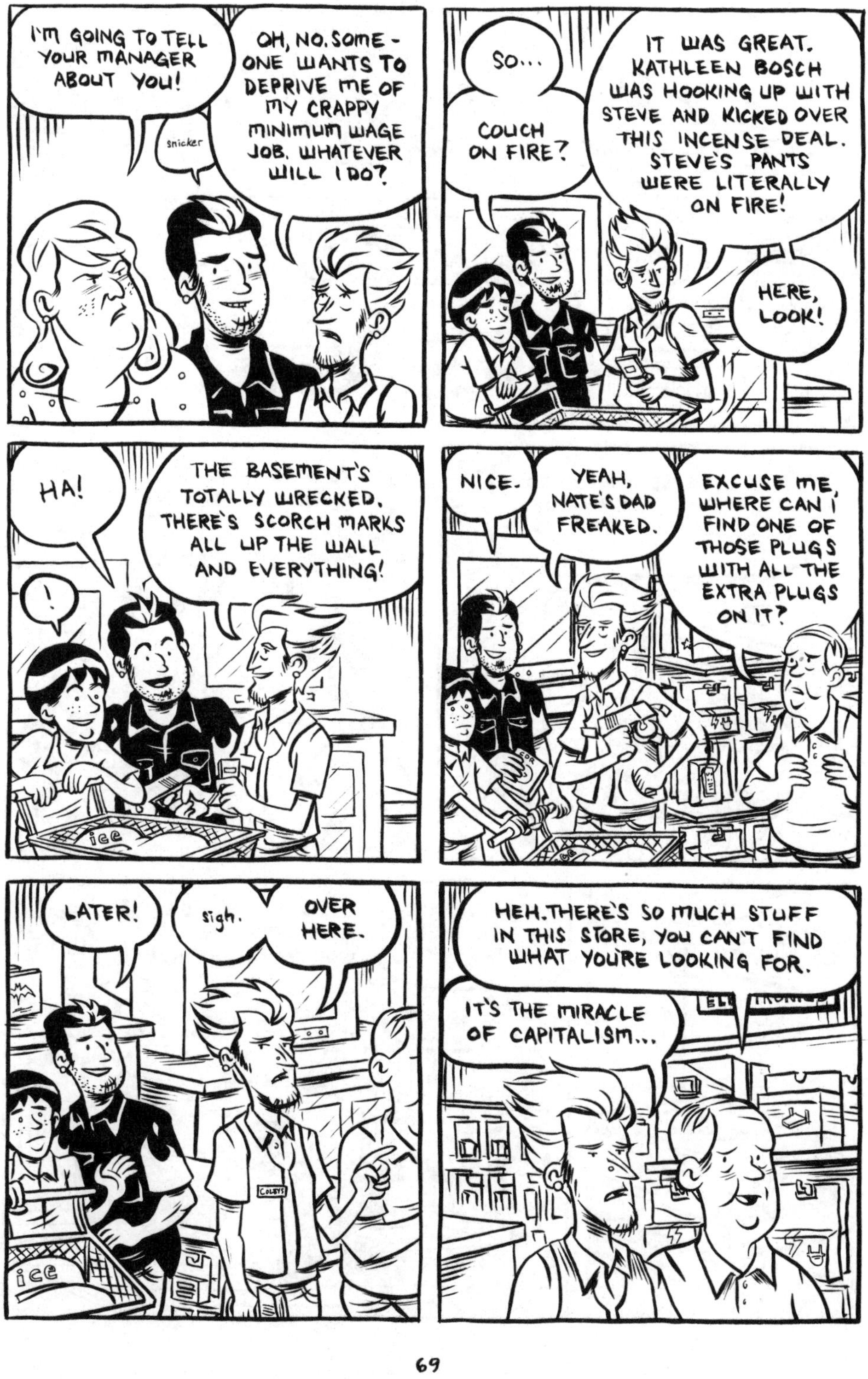
I'M GOING TO TELL YOUR MANAGER ABOUT YOU!
snicker
OH, NO. SOME-ONE WANTS TO DEPRIVE ME OF MY CRAPPY MINIMUM WAGE JOB. WHATEVER WILL I DO?
SO...
COUCH ON FIRE?
IT WAS GREAT. KATHLEEN BOSCH WAS HOOKING UP WITH STEVE AND KICKED OVER THIS INCENSE DEAL. STEVE'S PANTS WERE LITERALLY ON FIRE!
HERE, LOOK!
HA!
THE BASEMENT'S TOTALLY WRECKED. THERE'S SCORCH MARKS ALL UP THE WALL AND EVERYTHING!
!
ice
NICE.
YEAH, NATE'S DAD FREAKED.
EXCUSE ME, WHERE CAN I FIND ONE OF THOSE PLUGS WITH ALL THE EXTRA PLUGS ON IT?
LATER!
sigh.
OVER HERE.
ice
HEH. THERE'S SO MUCH STUFF IN THIS STORE, YOU CAN'T FIND WHAT YOU'RE LOOKING FOR.
IT'S THE MIRACLE OF CAPITALISM...

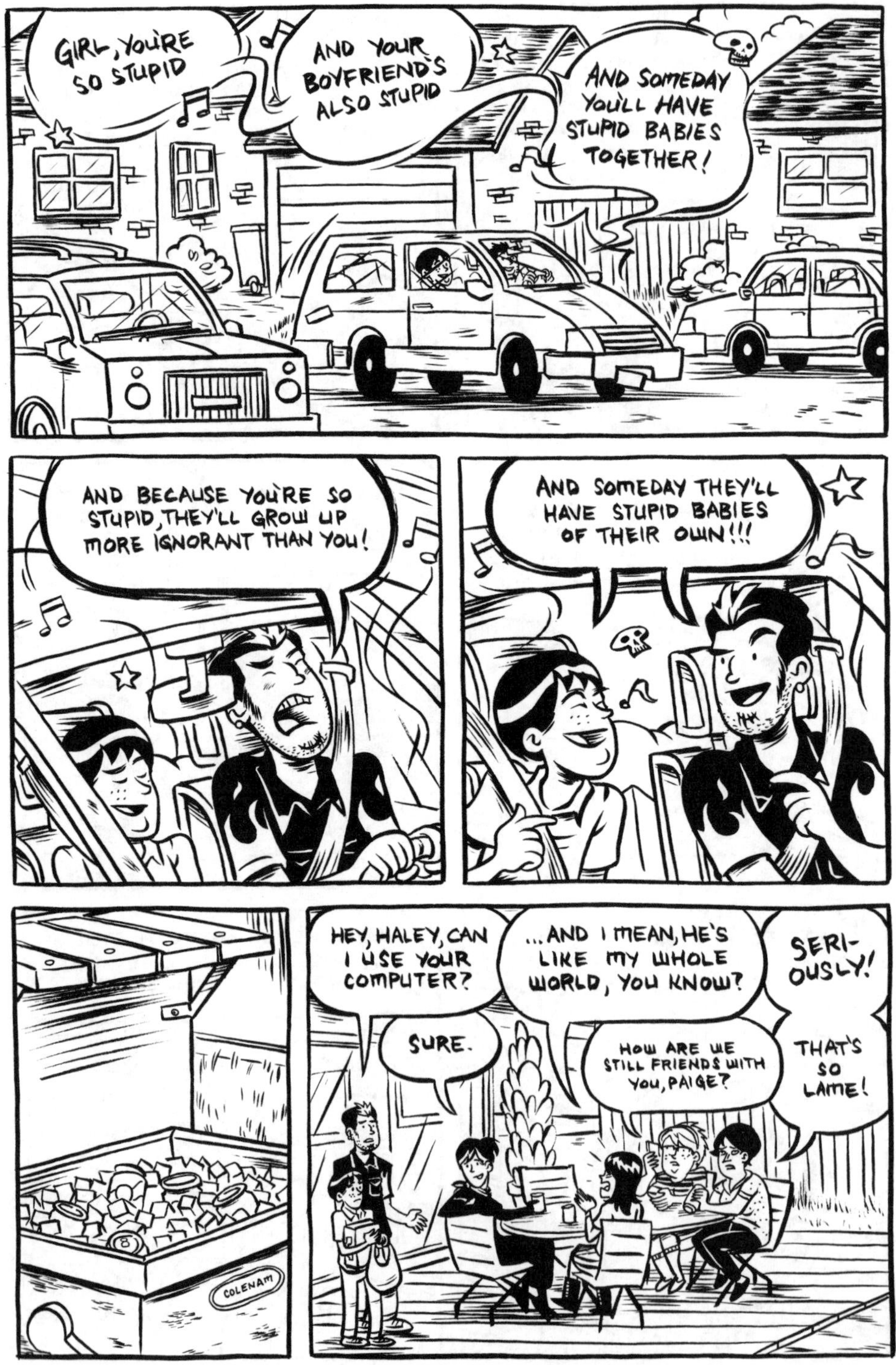
GIRL, YOU'RE SO STUPID
AND YOUR BOYFRIEND'S ALSO STUPID
AND SOMEDAY YOU'LL HAVE STUPID BABIES TOGETHER!
AND BECAUSE YOU'RE SO STUPID, THEY'LL GROW UP MORE IGNORANT THAN YOU!
AND SOMEDAY THEY'LL HAVE STUPID BABIES OF THEIR OWN!!!
COLENAM
HEY, HALEY, CAN I USE YOUR COMPUTER?
SURE.
...AND I MEAN, HE'S LIKE MY WHOLE WORLD, YOU KNOW?
HOW ARE WE STILL FRIENDS WITH YOU, PAIGE?
SERI-OUSLY!
THAT'S SO LAME!

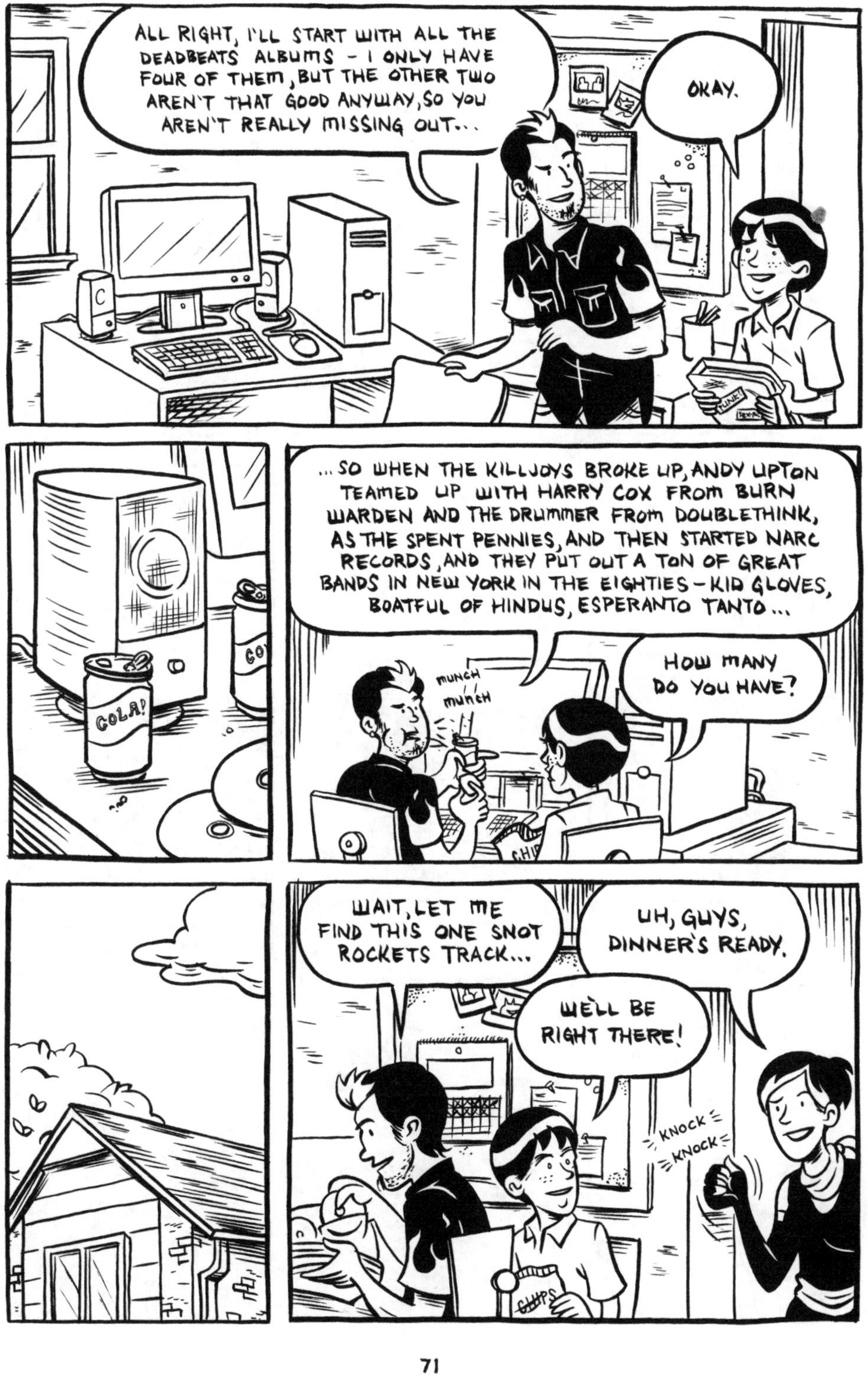
ALL RIGHT, I'LL START WITH ALL THE DEADBEATS ALBUMS - I ONLY HAVE FOUR OF THEM, BUT THE OTHER TWO AREN'T THAT GOOD ANYWAY, SO YOU AREN'T REALLY MISSING OUT...
OKAY.
COLA!
...SO WHEN THE KILLJOYS BROKE UP, ANDY UPTON TEAMED UP WITH HARRY COX FROM BURN WARDEN AND THE DRUMMER FROM DOUBLETHINK, AS THE SPENT PENNIES, AND THEN STARTED NARC RECORDS, AND THEY PUT OUT A TON OF GREAT BANDS IN NEW YORK IN THE EIGHTIES - KID GLOVES, BOATFUL OF HINDUS, ESPERANTO TANTO...
MUNCH MUNCH
HOW MANY DO YOU HAVE?
WAIT, LET ME FIND THIS ONE SNOT ROCKETS TRACK...
UH, GUYS, DINNER'S READY.
WE'LL BE RIGHT THERE!
KNOCK KNOCK
CHIPS

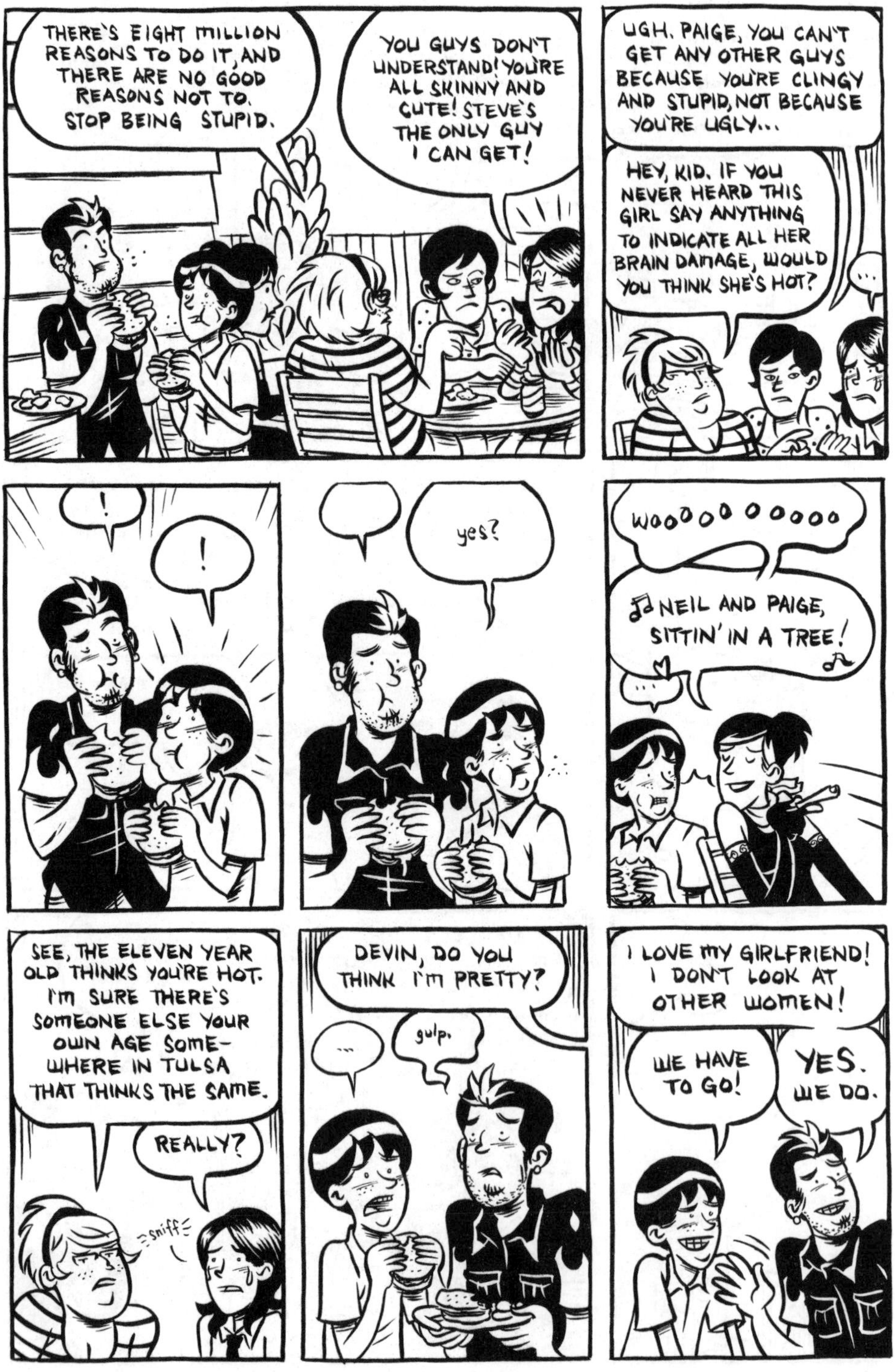
THERE'S EIGHT MILLION REASONS TO DO IT, AND THERE ARE NO GOOD REASONS NOT TO. STOP BEING STUPID.
YOU GUYS DON'T UNDERSTAND! YOU'RE ALL SKINNY AND CUTE! STEVE'S THE ONLY GUY I CAN GET!
UGH. PAIGE, YOU CAN'T GET ANY OTHER GUYS BECAUSE YOU'RE CLINGY AND STUPID, NOT BECAUSE YOU'RE UGLY...
HEY, KID. IF YOU NEVER HEARD THIS GIRL SAY ANYTHING TO INDICATE ALL HER BRAIN DAMAGE, WOULD YOU THINK SHE'S HOT?
...
!
!
yes?
WOOOOOO OOOOO
NEIL AND PAIGE, SITTIN' IN A TREE!
...
SEE, THE ELEVEN YEAR OLD THINKS YOU'RE HOT. I'M SURE THERE'S SOMEONE ELSE YOUR OWN AGE SOMEWHERE IN TULSA THAT THINKS THE SAME.
REALLY?
sniff
DEVIN, DO YOU THINK I'M PRETTY?
...
gulp.
I LOVE MY GIRLFRIEND! I DON'T LOOK AT OTHER WOMEN!
WE HAVE TO GO!
YES. WE DO.

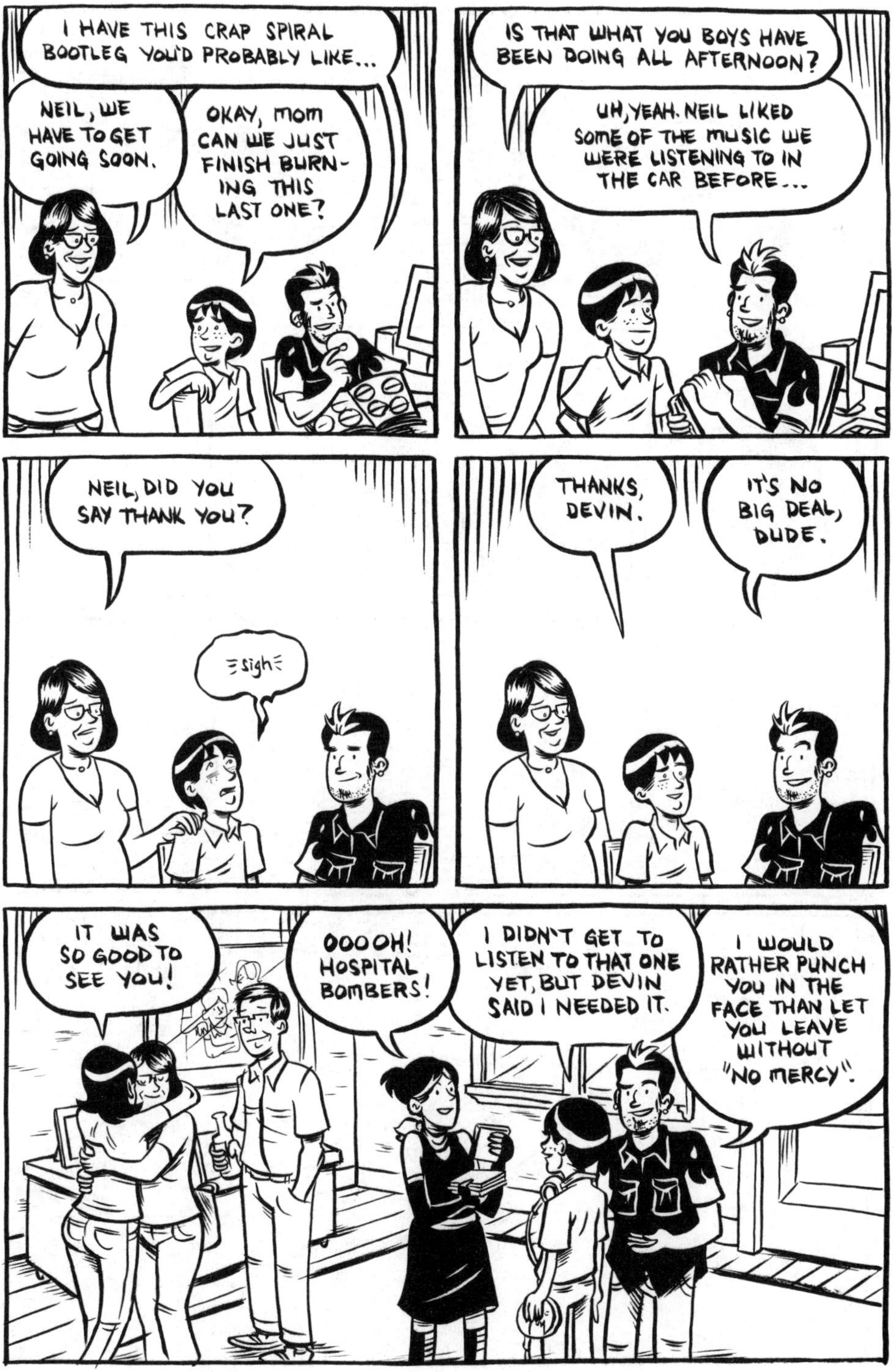
I HAVE THIS CRAP SPIRAL BOOTLEG YOU'D PROBABLY LIKE...
NEIL, WE HAVE TO GET GOING SOON.
OKAY, MOM CAN WE JUST FINISH BURN-ING THIS LAST ONE?
IS THAT WHAT YOU BOYS HAVE BEEN DOING ALL AFTERNOON?
UH, YEAH. NEIL LIKED SOME OF THE MUSIC WE WERE LISTENING TO IN THE CAR BEFORE...
NEIL, DID YOU SAY THANK YOU?
sigh
THANKS, DEVIN.
IT'S NO BIG DEAL, DUDE.
IT WAS SO GOOD TO SEE YOU!
OOOOH! HOSPITAL BOMBERS!
I DIDN'T GET TO LISTEN TO THAT ONE YET, BUT DEVIN SAID I NEEDED IT.
I WOULD RATHER PUNCH YOU IN THE FACE THAN LET YOU LEAVE WITHOUT "NO MERCY".

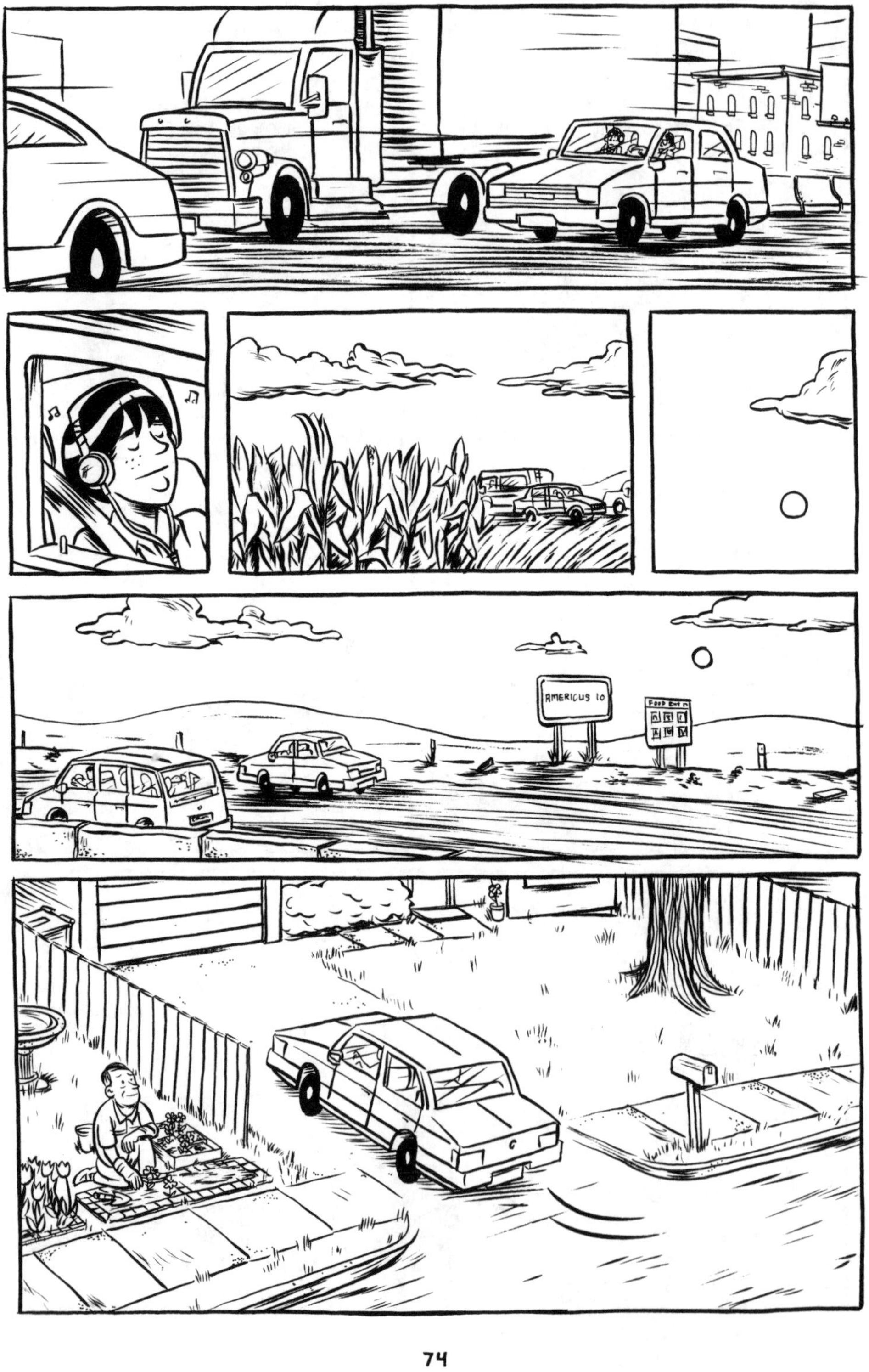
AMERICUS 10
FOOD

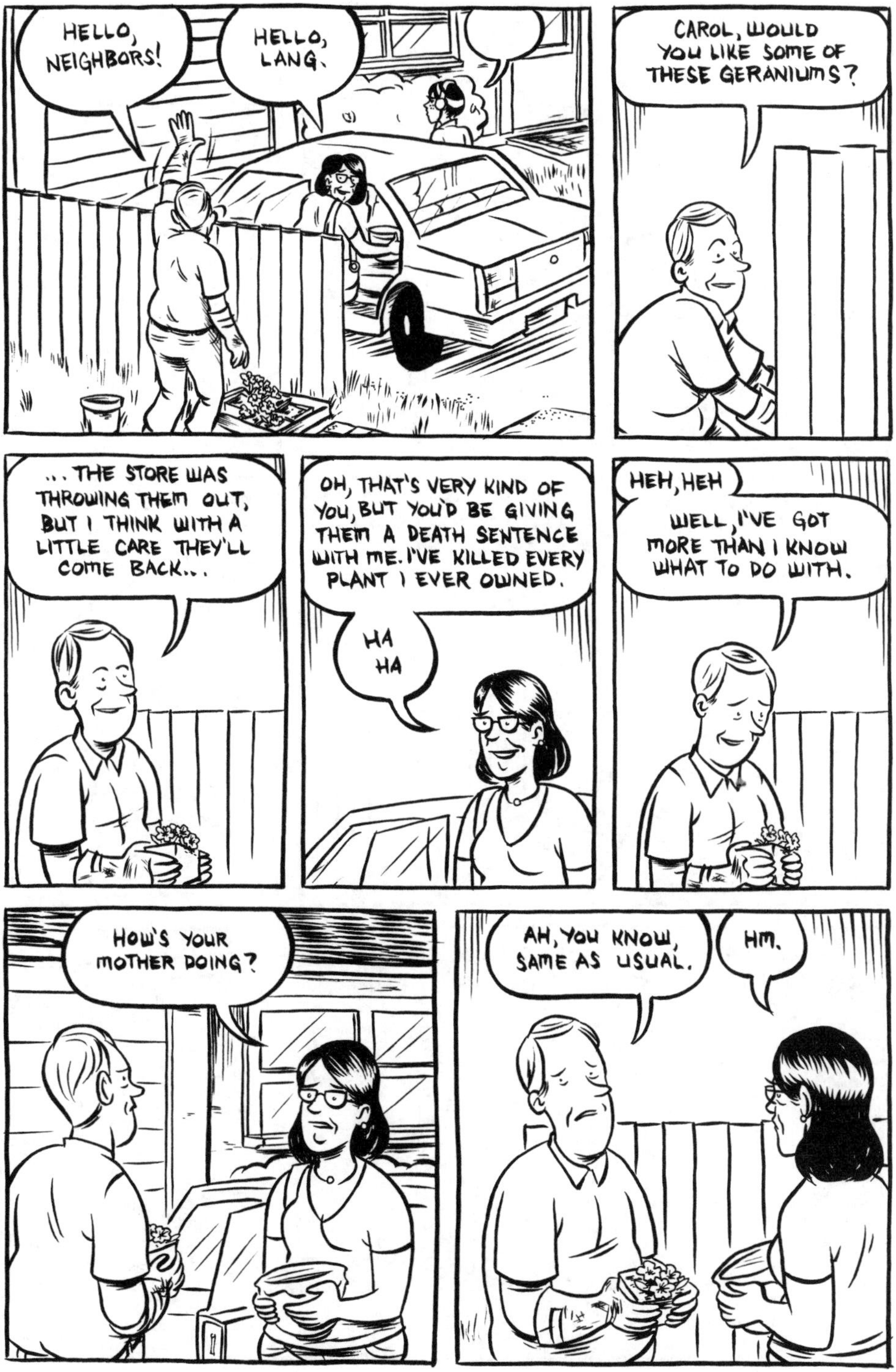
HELLO, NEIGHBORS!
HELLO, LANG.
CAROL, WOULD YOU LIKE SOME OF THESE GERANIUMS?
... THE STORE WAS THROWING THEM OUT, BUT I THINK WITH A LITTLE CARE THEY'LL COME BACK...
OH, THAT'S VERY KIND OF YOU, BUT YOU'D BE GIVING THEM A DEATH SENTENCE WITH ME. I'VE KILLED EVERY PLANT I EVER OWNED.
HA HA
HEH, HEH
WELL, I'VE GOT MORE THAN I KNOW WHAT TO DO WITH.
HOW'S YOUR MOTHER DOING?
AH, YOU KNOW, SAME AS USUAL.
HM.

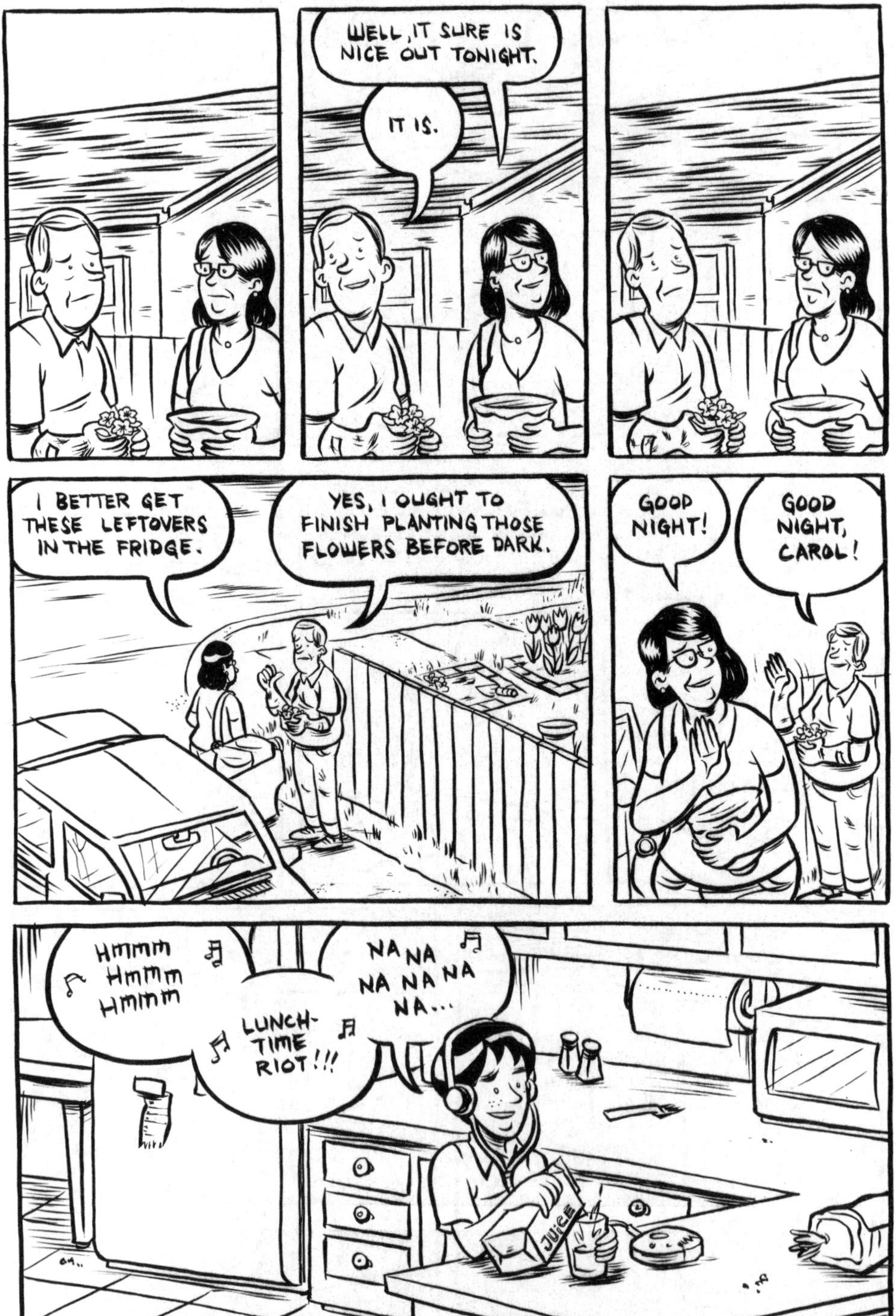
WELL, IT SURE IS NICE OUT TONIGHT.
IT IS.
I BETTER GET THESE LEFTOVERS IN THE FRIDGE.
YES, I OUGHT TO FINISH PLANTING THOSE FLOWERS BEFORE DARK.
GOOD NIGHT!
GOOD NIGHT, CAROL!
HMMM HMMM HMMM
LUNCH-TIME RIOT!!!
NA NA NA NA NA NA...
JUICE

CHAPTER 4

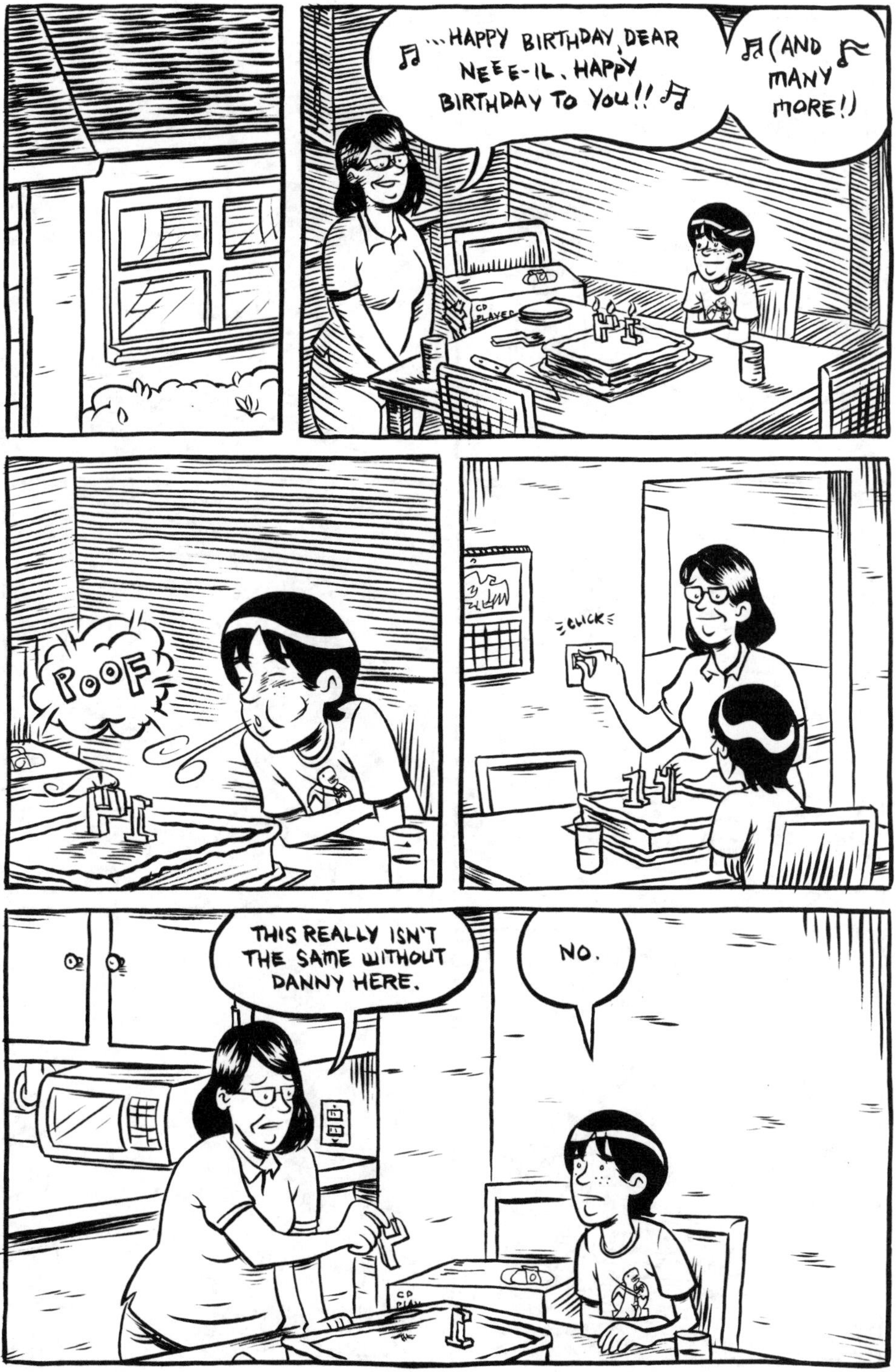
…HAPPY BIRTHDAY, DEAR NEEE-IL. HAPPY BIRTHDAY TO YOU!!
(AND MANY MORE!)
CD PLAYER
POOF
CLICK
THIS REALLY ISN'T THE SAME WITHOUT DANNY HERE.
NO.

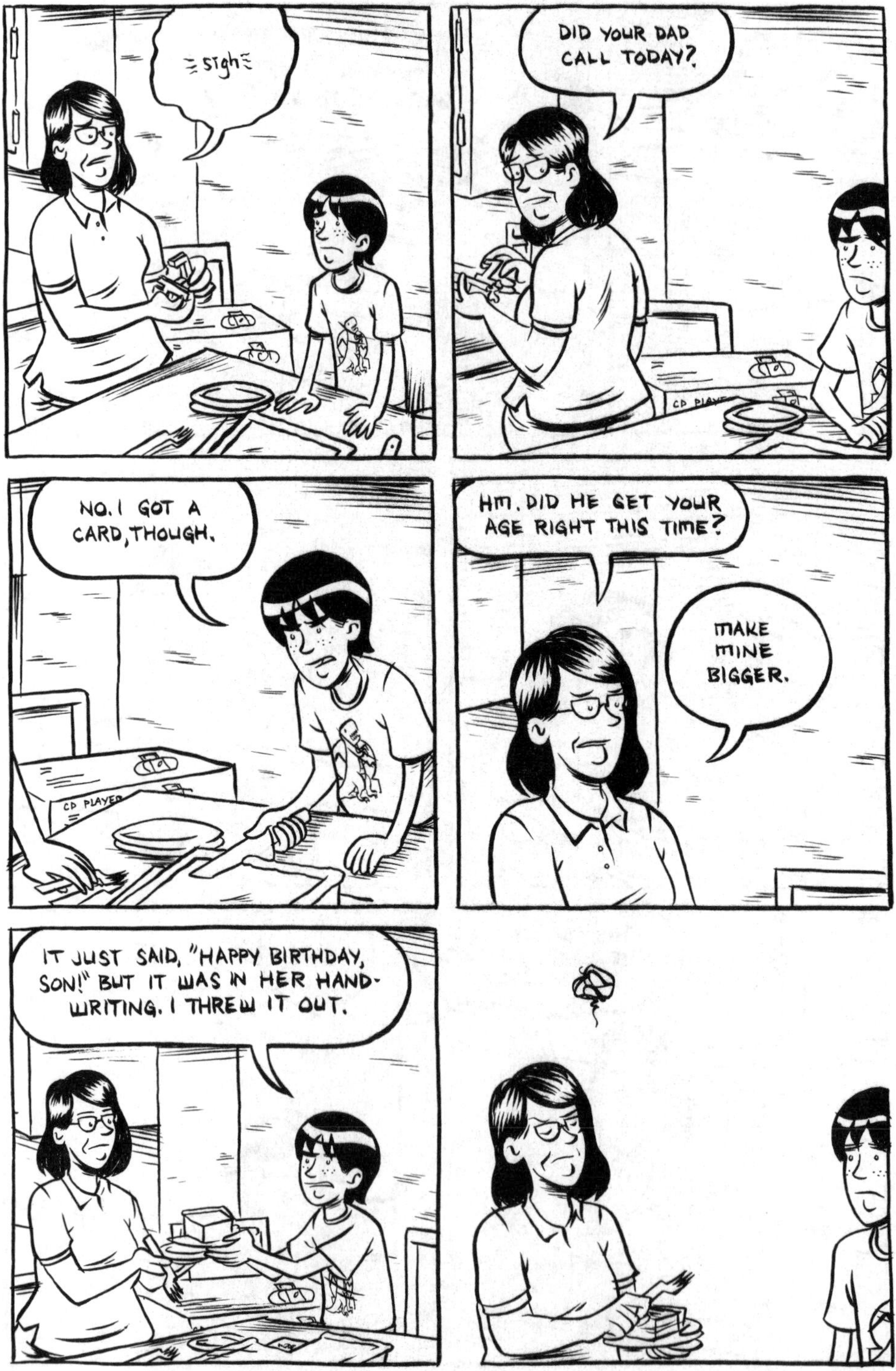
sigh
DID YOUR DAD CALL TODAY?
NO. I GOT A CARD, THOUGH.
CD PLAYER
HM. DID HE GET YOUR AGE RIGHT THIS TIME?
MAKE MINE BIGGER.
IT JUST SAID, "HAPPY BIRTHDAY, SON!" BUT IT WAS IN HER HAND-WRITING. I THREW IT OUT.

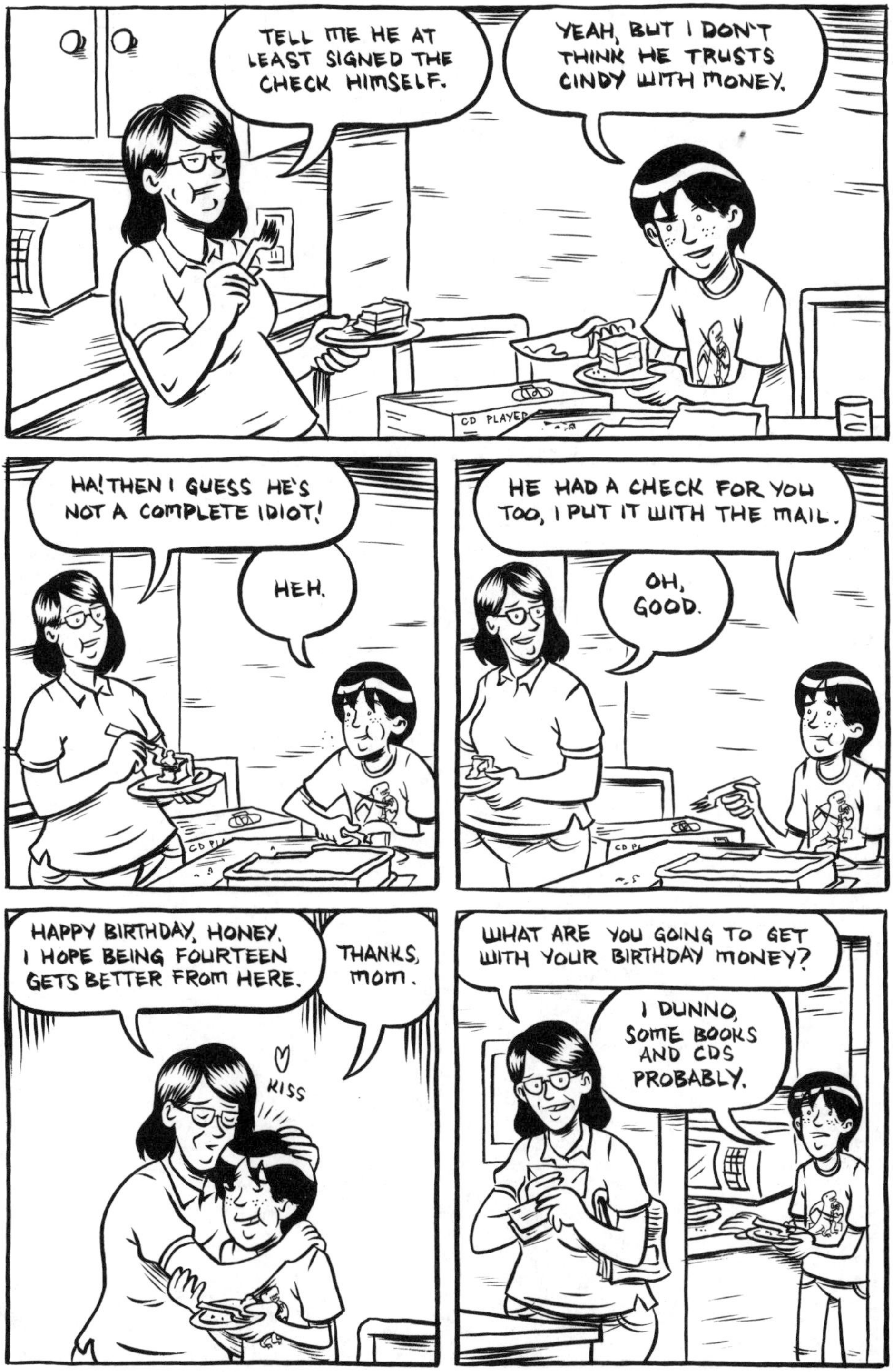
TELL ME HE AT LEAST SIGNED THE CHECK HIMSELF.
YEAH, BUT I DON'T THINK HE TRUSTS CINDY WITH MONEY.
CD PLAYER
HA! THEN I GUESS HE'S NOT A COMPLETE IDIOT!
HEH.
HE HAD A CHECK FOR YOU TOO, I PUT IT WITH THE MAIL.
OH, GOOD.
HAPPY BIRTHDAY, HONEY. I HOPE BEING FOURTEEN GETS BETTER FROM HERE.
THANKS, MOM.
KISS
WHAT ARE YOU GOING TO GET WITH YOUR BIRTHDAY MONEY?
I DUNNO, SOME BOOKS AND CDS PROBABLY.

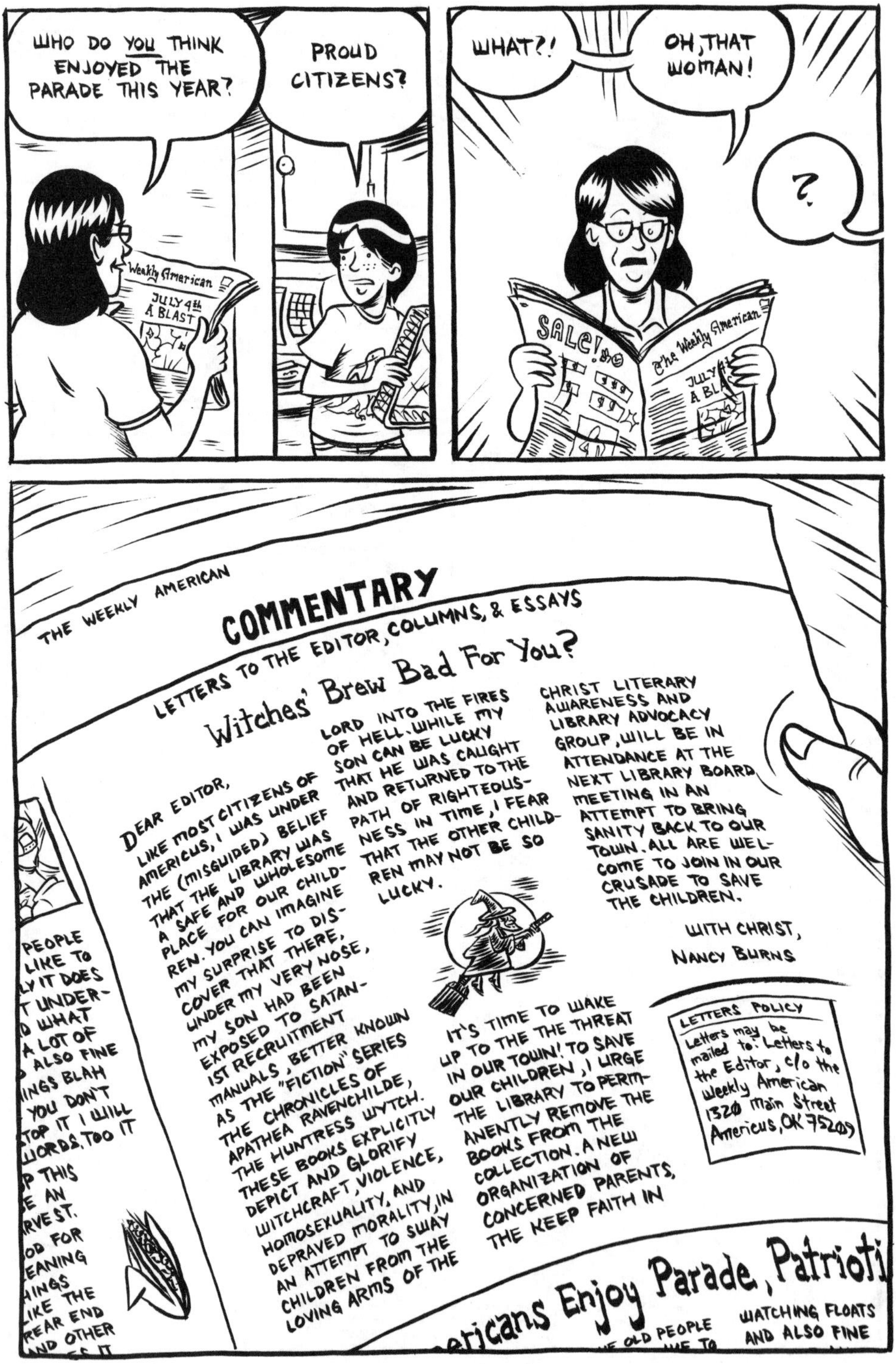
WHO DO YOU THINK ENJOYED THE PARADE THIS YEAR?
Weekly American
JULY 4th A BLAST
PROUD CITIZENS?
WHAT?!
OH, THAT WOMAN!
?
SALE!
The Weekly American
THE WEEKLY AMERICAN
COMMENTARY
LETTERS TO THE EDITOR, COLUMNS, & ESSAYS
Witches' Brew Bad For You?
DEAR EDITOR,
LIKE MOST CITIZENS OF AMERICUS, I WAS UNDER THE (MISGUIDED) BELIEF THAT THE LIBRARY WAS A SAFE AND WHOLESOME PLACE FOR OUR CHILDREN. YOU CAN IMAGINE MY SURPRISE TO DISCOVER THAT THERE, UNDER MY VERY NOSE, MY SON HAD BEEN EXPOSED TO SATANIST RECRUITMENT MANUALS, BETTER KNOWN AS THE "FICTION" SERIES THE CHRONICLES OF APATHEA RAVENCHILDE, THE HUNTRESS WYTCH. THESE BOOKS EXPLICITLY DEPICT AND GLORIFY WITCHCRAFT, VIOLENCE, HOMOSEXUALITY, AND DEPRAVED MORALITY, IN AN ATTEMPT TO SWAY CHILDREN FROM THE LOVING ARMS OF THE LORD INTO THE FIRES OF HELL. WHILE MY SON CAN BE LUCKY THAT HE WAS CAUGHT AND RETURNED TO THE PATH OF RIGHTEOUSNESS IN TIME, I FEAR THAT THE OTHER CHILDREN MAY NOT BE SO LUCKY.
IT'S TIME TO WAKE UP TO THE THE THREAT IN OUR TOWN! TO SAVE OUR CHILDREN, I URGE THE LIBRARY TO PERMANENTLY REMOVE THE BOOKS FROM THE COLLECTION. A NEW ORGANIZATION OF CONCERNED PARENTS, THE KEEP FAITH IN CHRIST LITERARY AWARENESS AND LIBRARY ADVOCACY GROUP, WILL BE IN ATTENDANCE AT THE NEXT LIBRARY BOARD MEETING IN AN ATTEMPT TO BRING SANITY BACK TO OUR TOWN. ALL ARE WELCOME TO JOIN IN OUR CRUSADE TO SAVE THE CHILDREN.
WITH CHRIST,
NANCY BURNS
LETTERS POLICY
Letters may be mailed to: Letters to the Editor, c/o the Weekly American 1320 Main Street Americus, OK 75209
Enjoy Parade,
WATCHING FLOATS AND ALSO FINE

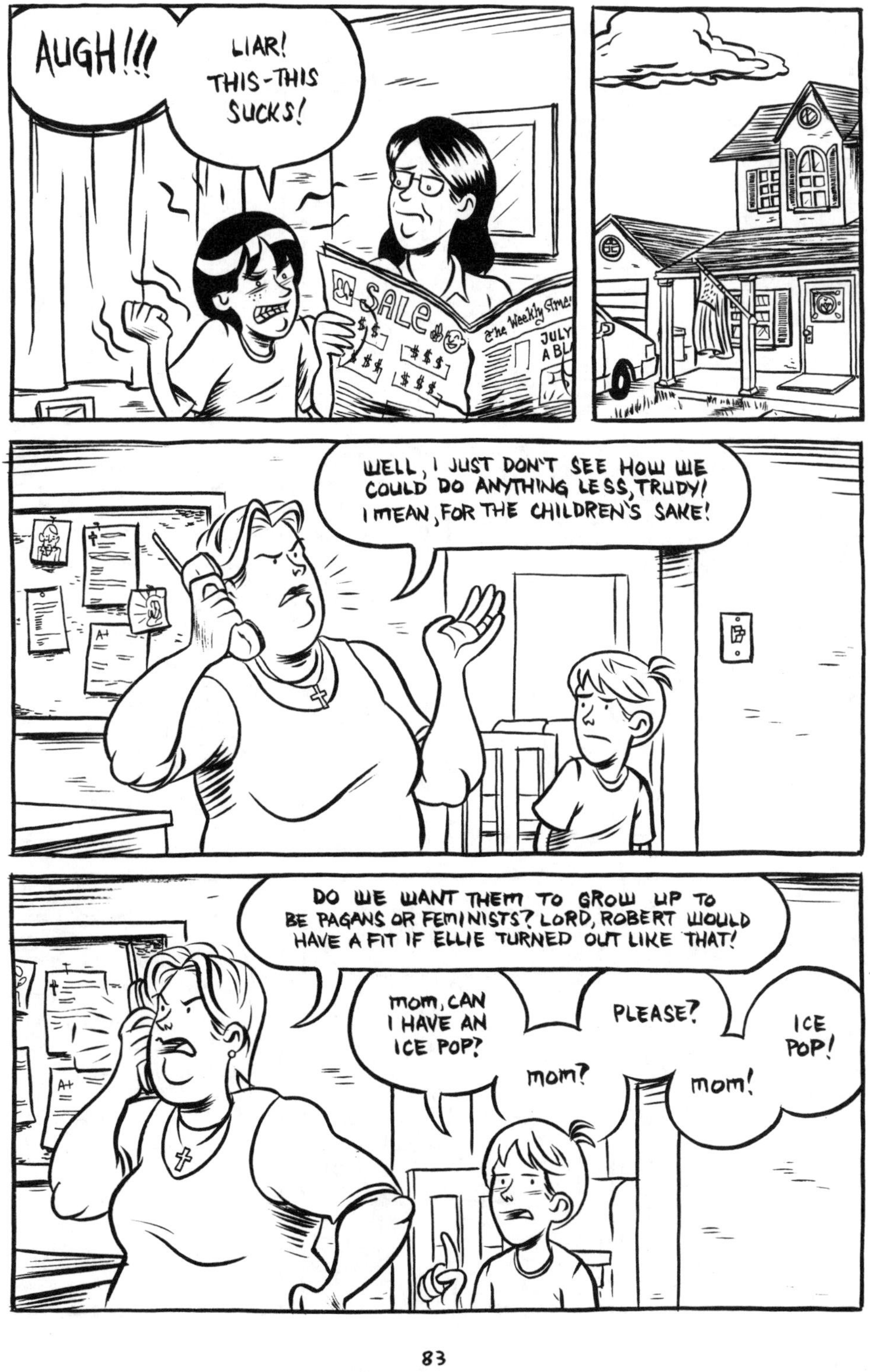
AUGH!!!
LIAR! THIS-THIS SUCKS!
SALE
The Weekly Times
JULY
WELL, I JUST DON'T SEE HOW WE COULD DO ANYTHING LESS, TRUDY! I MEAN, FOR THE CHILDREN'S SAKE!
DO WE WANT THEM TO GROW UP TO BE PAGANS OR FEMINISTS? LORD, ROBERT WOULD HAVE A FIT IF ELLIE TURNED OUT LIKE THAT!
mom, CAN I HAVE AN ICE POP?
mom?
PLEASE?
mom!
ICE POP!

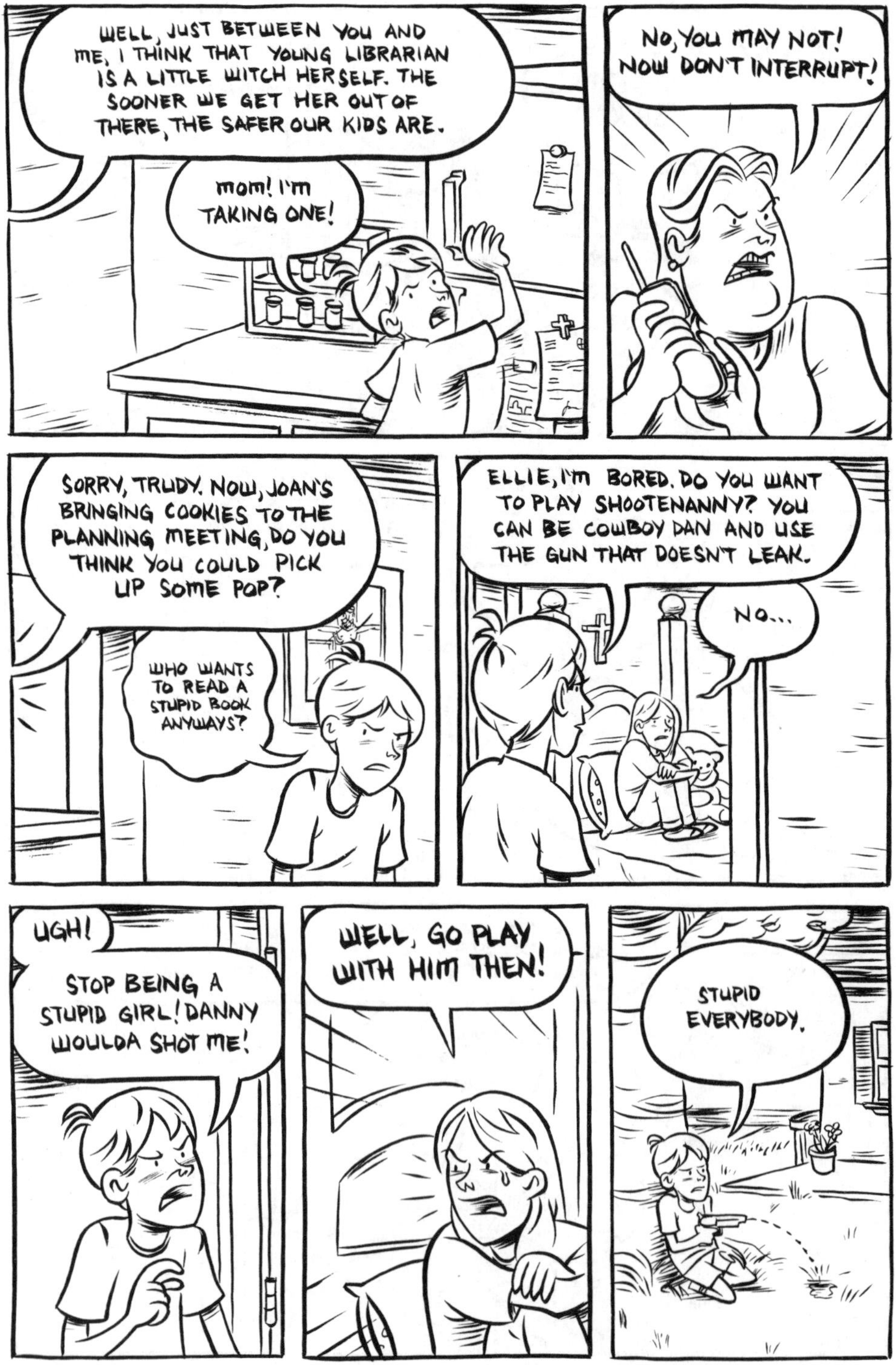
WELL, JUST BETWEEN YOU AND ME, I THINK THAT YOUNG LIBRARIAN IS A LITTLE WITCH HERSELF. THE SOONER WE GET HER OUT OF THERE, THE SAFER OUR KIDS ARE.
MOM! I'M TAKING ONE!
NO, YOU MAY NOT! NOW DON'T INTERRUPT!
SORRY, TRUDY. NOW, JOAN'S BRINGING COOKIES TO THE PLANNING MEETING, DO YOU THINK YOU COULD PICK UP SOME POP?
WHO WANTS TO READ A STUPID BOOK ANYWAYS?
ELLIE, I'M BORED. DO YOU WANT TO PLAY SHOOTENANNY? YOU CAN BE COWBOY DAN AND USE THE GUN THAT DOESN'T LEAK.
NO...
UGH!
STOP BEING A STUPID GIRL! DANNY WOULDA SHOT ME!
WELL, GO PLAY WITH HIM THEN!
STUPID EVERYBODY.

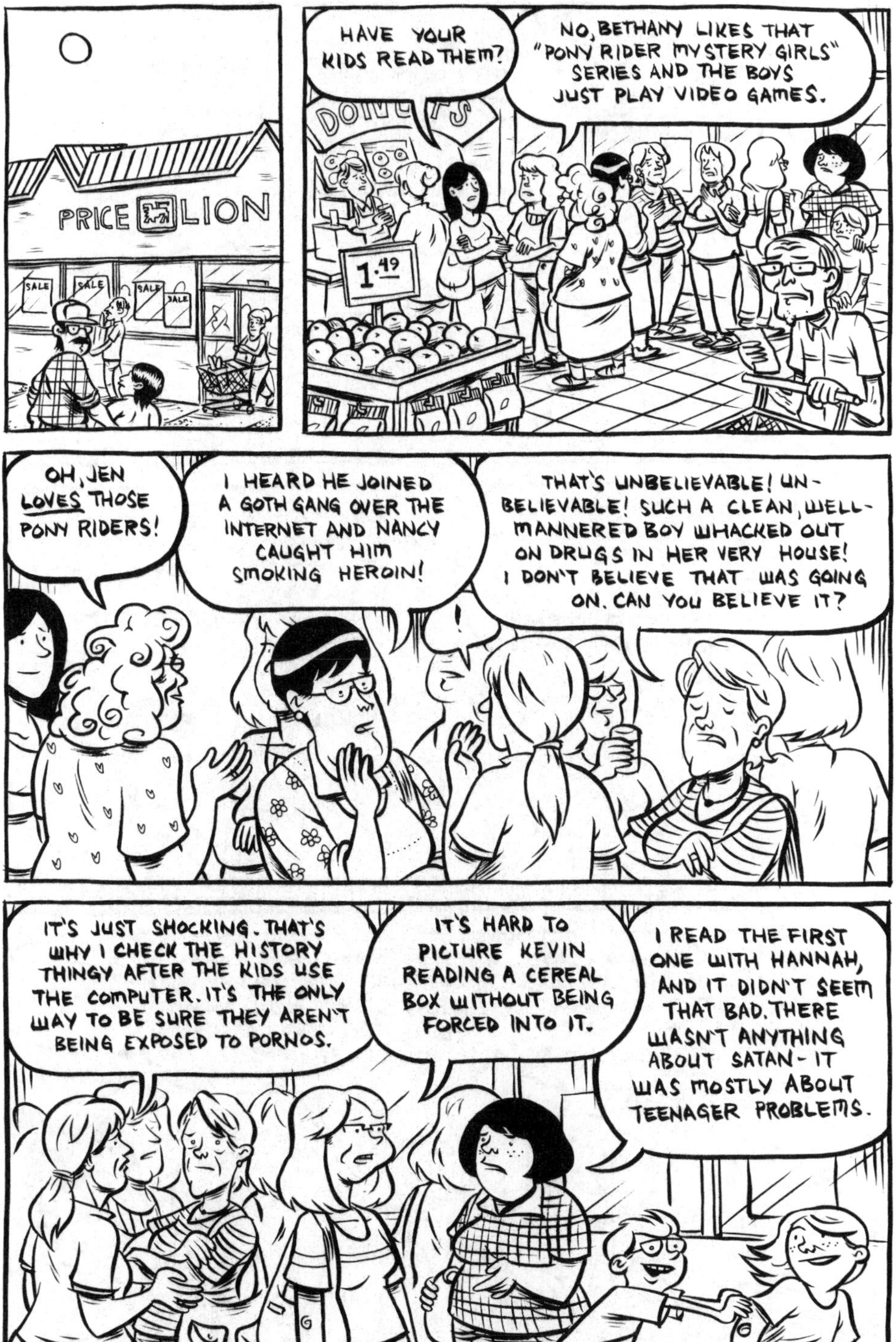
PRICE LION
SALE
SALE
SALE
SALE
HAVE YOUR KIDS READ THEM?
DONUTS
1.49
NO, BETHANY LIKES THAT "PONY RIDER MYSTERY GIRLS" SERIES AND THE BOYS JUST PLAY VIDEO GAMES.
OH, JEN LOVES THOSE PONY RIDERS!
I HEARD HE JOINED A GOTH GANG OVER THE INTERNET AND NANCY CAUGHT HIM SMOKING HEROIN!
!
THAT'S UNBELIEVABLE! UNBELIEVABLE! SUCH A CLEAN, WELL-MANNERED BOY WHACKED OUT ON DRUGS IN HER VERY HOUSE! I DON'T BELIEVE THAT WAS GOING ON. CAN YOU BELIEVE IT?
IT'S JUST SHOCKING. THAT'S WHY I CHECK THE HISTORY THINGY AFTER THE KIDS USE THE COMPUTER. IT'S THE ONLY WAY TO BE SURE THEY AREN'T BEING EXPOSED TO PORNOS.
IT'S HARD TO PICTURE KEVIN READING A CEREAL BOX WITHOUT BEING FORCED INTO IT.
I READ THE FIRST ONE WITH HANNAH, AND IT DIDN'T SEEM THAT BAD. THERE WASN'T ANYTHING ABOUT SATAN- IT WAS MOSTLY ABOUT TEENAGER PROBLEMS.

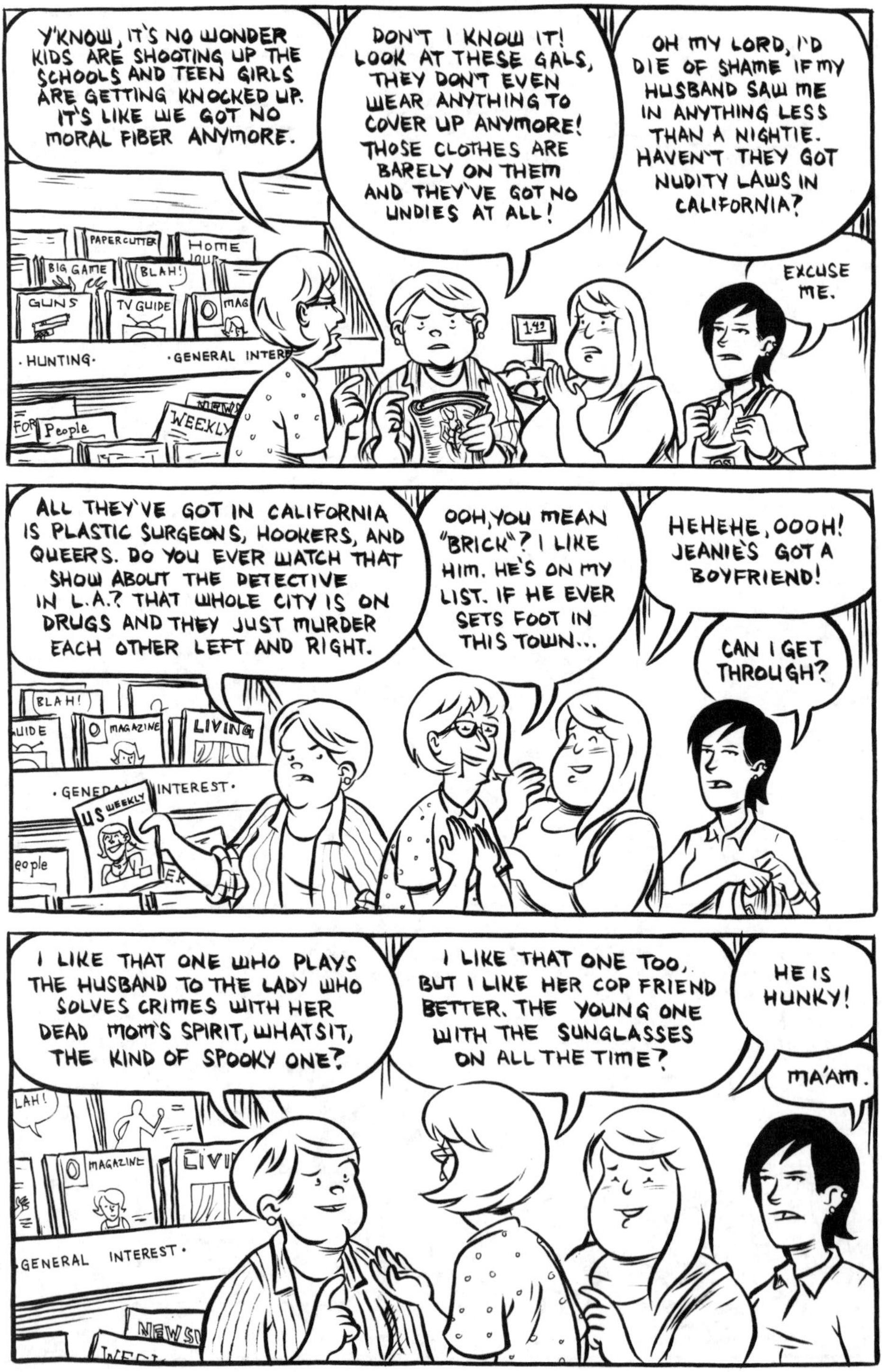
Y'KNOW, IT'S NO WONDER KIDS ARE SHOOTING UP THE SCHOOLS AND TEEN GIRLS ARE GETTING KNOCKED UP. IT'S LIKE WE GOT NO MORAL FIBER ANYMORE.
DON'T I KNOW IT! LOOK AT THESE GALS, THEY DON'T EVEN WEAR ANYTHING TO COVER UP ANYMORE! THOSE CLOTHES ARE BARELY ON THEM AND THEY'VE GOT NO UNDIES AT ALL!
OH MY LORD, I'D DIE OF SHAME IF MY HUSBAND SAW ME IN ANYTHING LESS THAN A NIGHTIE. HAVEN'T THEY GOT NUDITY LAWS IN CALIFORNIA?
EXCUSE ME.
PAPERCUTTER
HOME
BIG GAME
BLAH!
GUNS
TV GUIDE
1.49
·HUNTING·
·GENERAL INTER
People
WEEKLY
ALL THEY'VE GOT IN CALIFORNIA IS PLASTIC SURGEONS, HOOKERS, AND QUEERS. DO YOU EVER WATCH THAT SHOW ABOUT THE DETECTIVE IN L.A.? THAT WHOLE CITY IS ON DRUGS AND THEY JUST MURDER EACH OTHER LEFT AND RIGHT.
OOH, YOU MEAN "BRICK"? I LIKE HIM. HE'S ON MY LIST. IF HE EVER SETS FOOT IN THIS TOWN...
HEHEHE, OOOH! JEANIE'S GOT A BOYFRIEND!
CAN I GET THROUGH?
BLAH!
MAGAZINE
LIVING
·GENERAL INTEREST·
US WEEKLY
I LIKE THAT ONE WHO PLAYS THE HUSBAND TO THE LADY WHO SOLVES CRIMES WITH HER DEAD MOM'S SPIRIT, WHATSIT, THE KIND OF SPOOKY ONE?
I LIKE THAT ONE TOO, BUT I LIKE HER COP FRIEND BETTER. THE YOUNG ONE WITH THE SUNGLASSES ON ALL THE TIME?
HE IS HUNKY!
MA'AM.
MAGAZINE
GENERAL INTEREST·

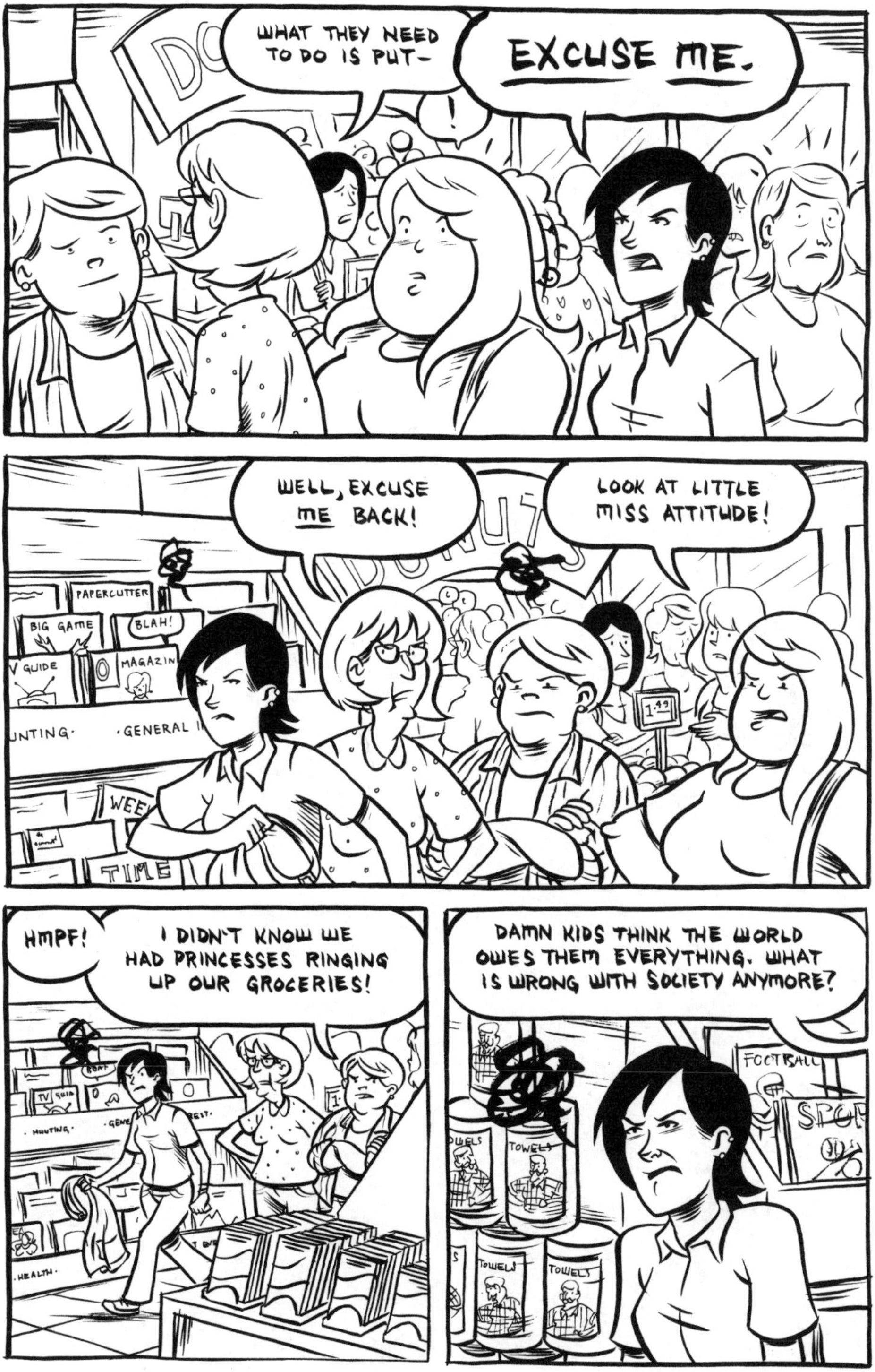

WHAT THEY NEED TO DO IS PUT-
!
EXCUSE ME.
WELL, EXCUSE ME BACK!
LOOK AT LITTLE MISS ATTITUDE!
PAPERCUTTER
BIG GAME
BLAH!
V GUIDE
MAGAZIN
UNTING·
·GENERAL I
TIME
HMPF!
I DIDN'T KNOW WE HAD PRINCESSES RINGING UP OUR GROCERIES!
DAMN KIDS THINK THE WORLD OWES THEM EVERYTHING. WHAT IS WRONG WITH SOCIETY ANYMORE?
FOOTBALL
TOWELS

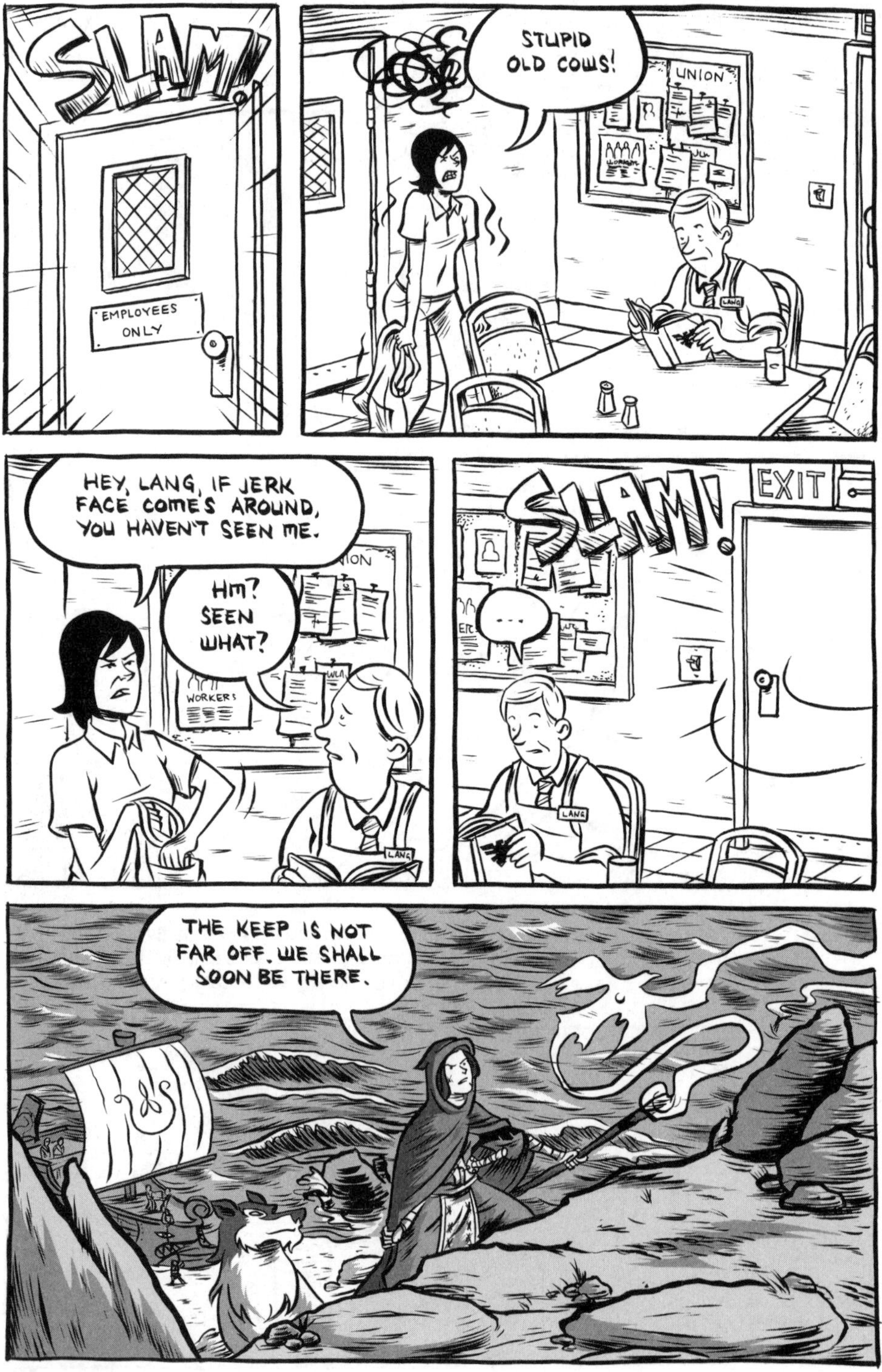
SLAM!
EMPLOYEES ONLY
STUPID OLD COWS!
UNION
HEY, LANG, IF JERK FACE COMES AROUND, YOU HAVEN'T SEEN ME.
HM? SEEN WHAT?
WORKERS
LANG
SLAM!
EXIT
...
LANG
THE KEEP IS NOT FAR OFF. WE SHALL SOON BE THERE.

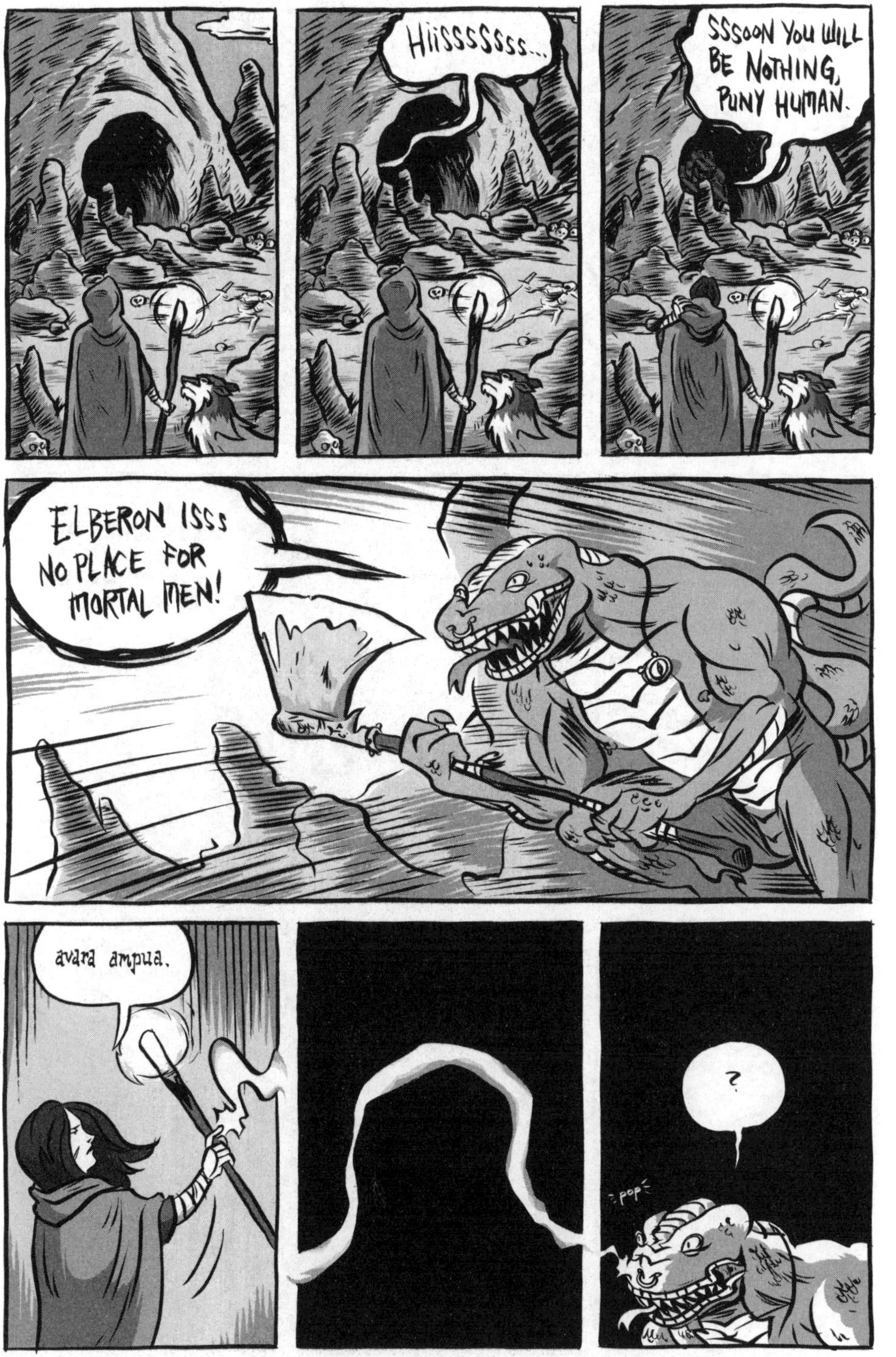
HiiSSSSSSS...
SSSooN YOU WILL BE NOTHING, PUNY HUMAN.
ELBERON ISSS NO PLACE FOR MORTAL MEN!
avara ampua.
?
pop

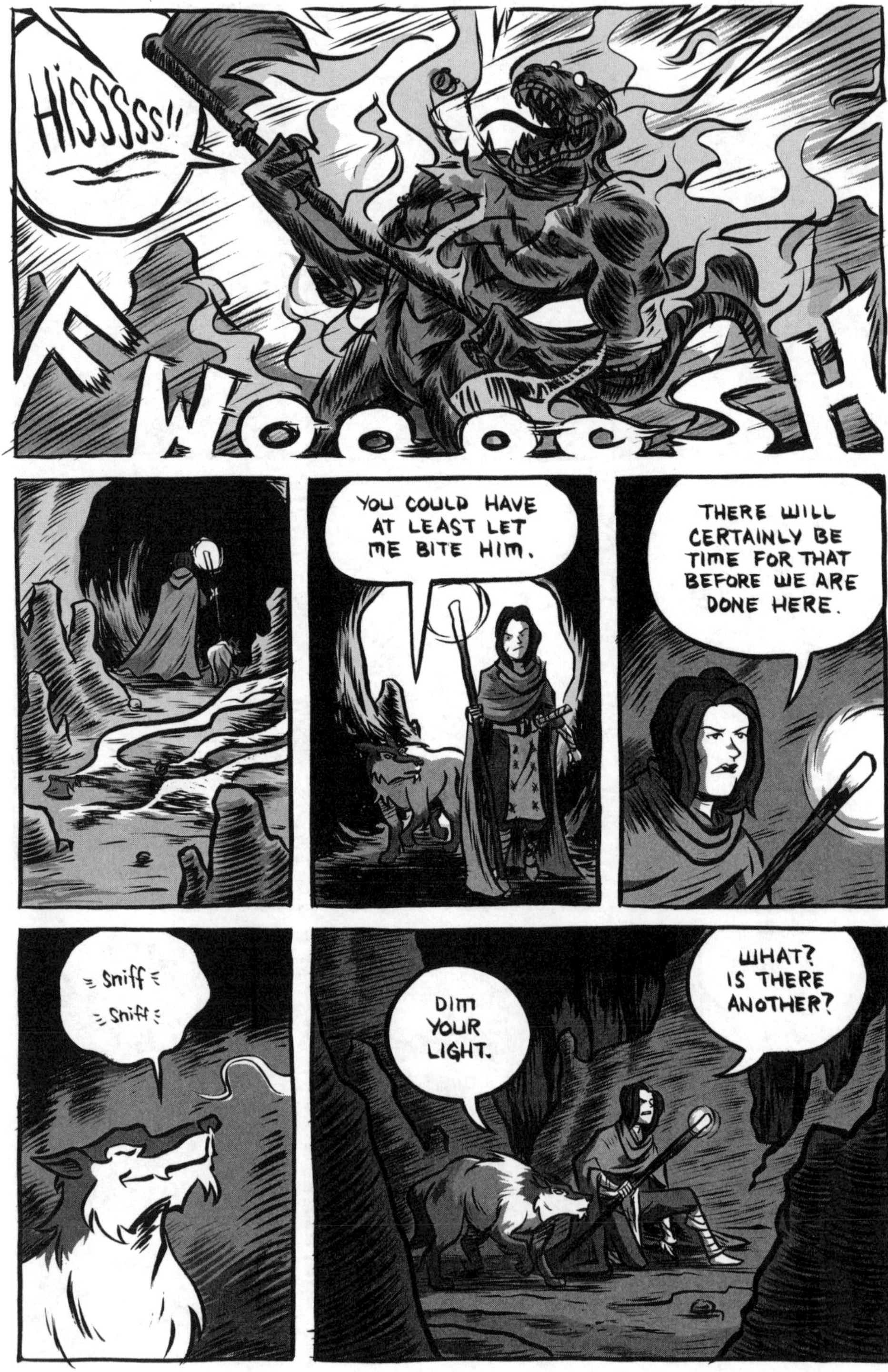
HISSSSS!!
WHOOOOSH!
YOU COULD HAVE AT LEAST LET ME BITE HIM.
THERE WILL CERTAINLY BE TIME FOR THAT BEFORE WE ARE DONE HERE.
Sniff
Sniff
DIM YOUR LIGHT.
WHAT? IS THERE ANOTHER?

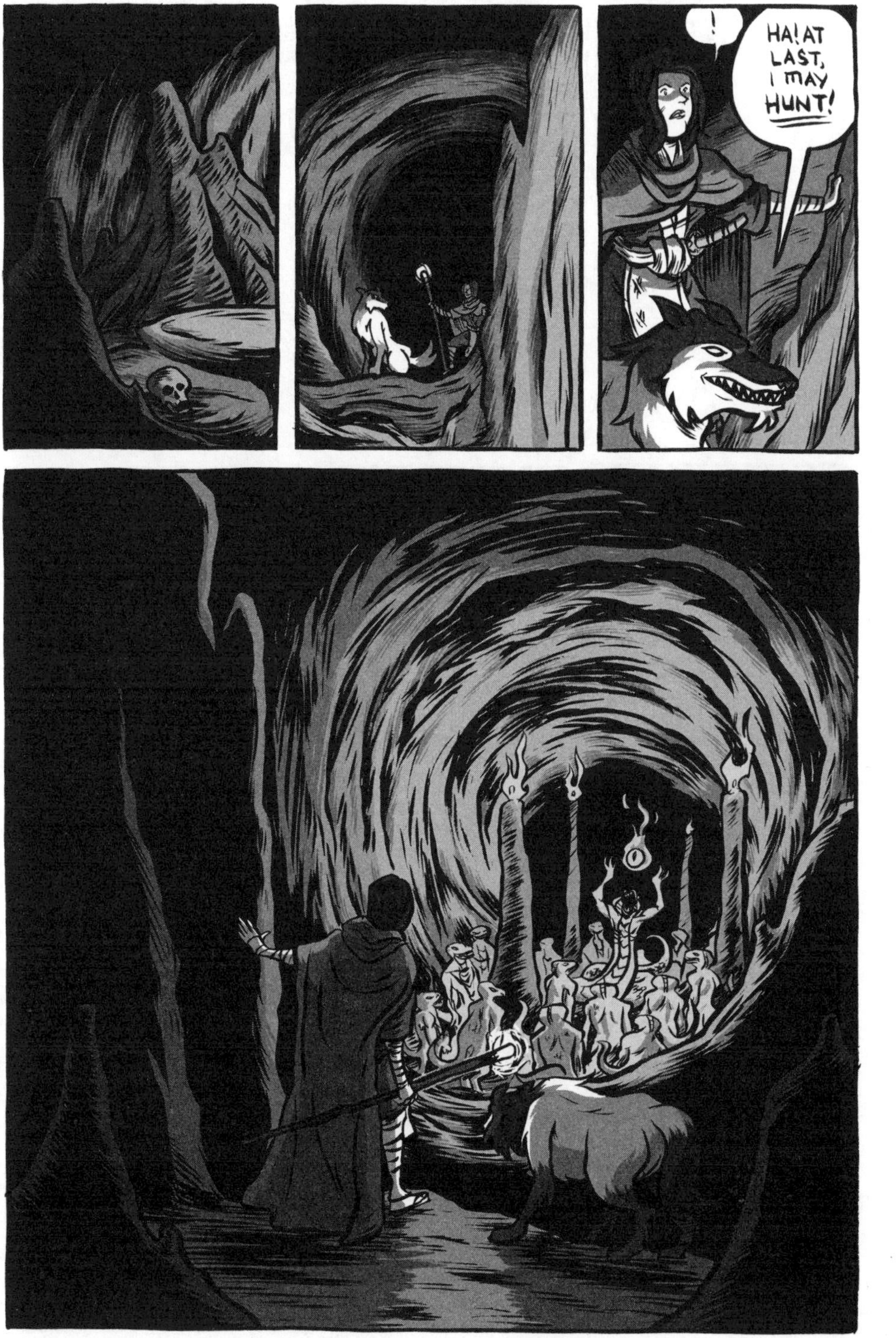
!
HA! AT LAST, I MAY HUNT!

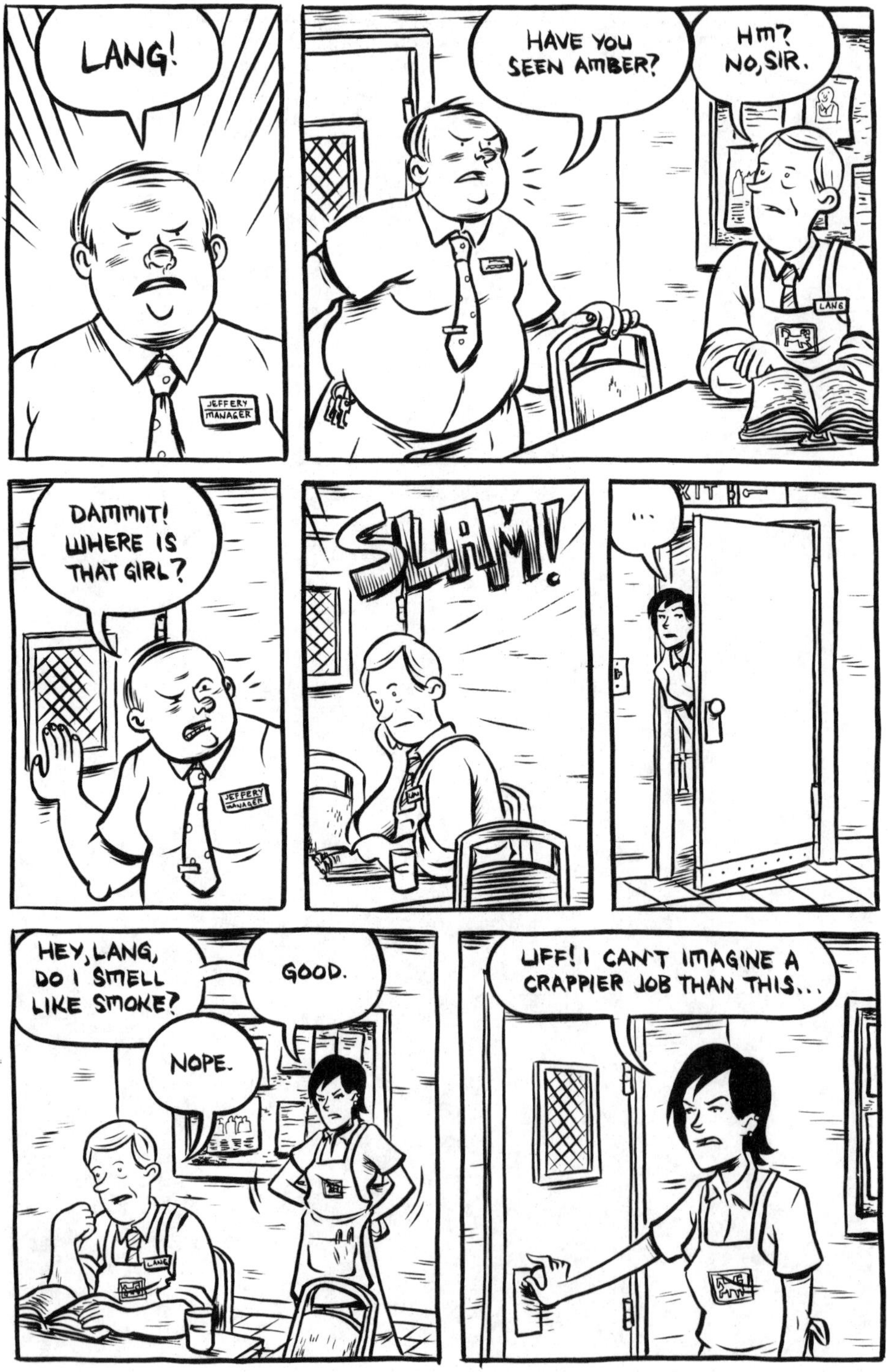
LANG!
JEFFERY MANAGER
HAVE YOU SEEN AMBER?
HM? NO, SIR.
LANG
DAMMIT! WHERE IS THAT GIRL?
JEFFERY MANAGER
SLAM!
...
HEY, LANG, DO I SMELL LIKE SMOKE?
NOPE.
GOOD.
LANG
UFF! I CAN'T IMAGINE A CRAPPIER JOB THAN THIS...

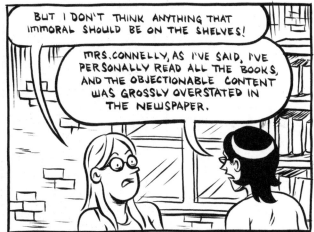

BUT I DON'T THINK ANYTHING THAT IMMORAL SHOULD BE ON THE SHELVES!

MRS. CONNELLY, AS I'VE SAID, I'VE PERSONALLY READ ALL THE BOOKS, AND THE OBJECTIONABLE CONTENT WAS GROSSLY OVERSTATED IN THE NEWSPAPER.

BUT HAVE YOU ACCEPTED JESUS CHRIST INTO YOUR HEART AS YOUR LORD AND SAVIOR?

?

THAT IS TOTALLY IRRELEVANT.

THE BOOKS MEET THE LIBRARY'S GUIDELINES FOR YOUNG ADULTS, AND GIVEN THAT WITCHCRAFT IS FANTASY—

HAVE YOU NOT HEARD OF THESE "WICCANS"? WITCHES ARE REAL AND TRYING TO PERVERT THE MINDS OF CHILDREN! DON'T YOU UNDERSTAND?

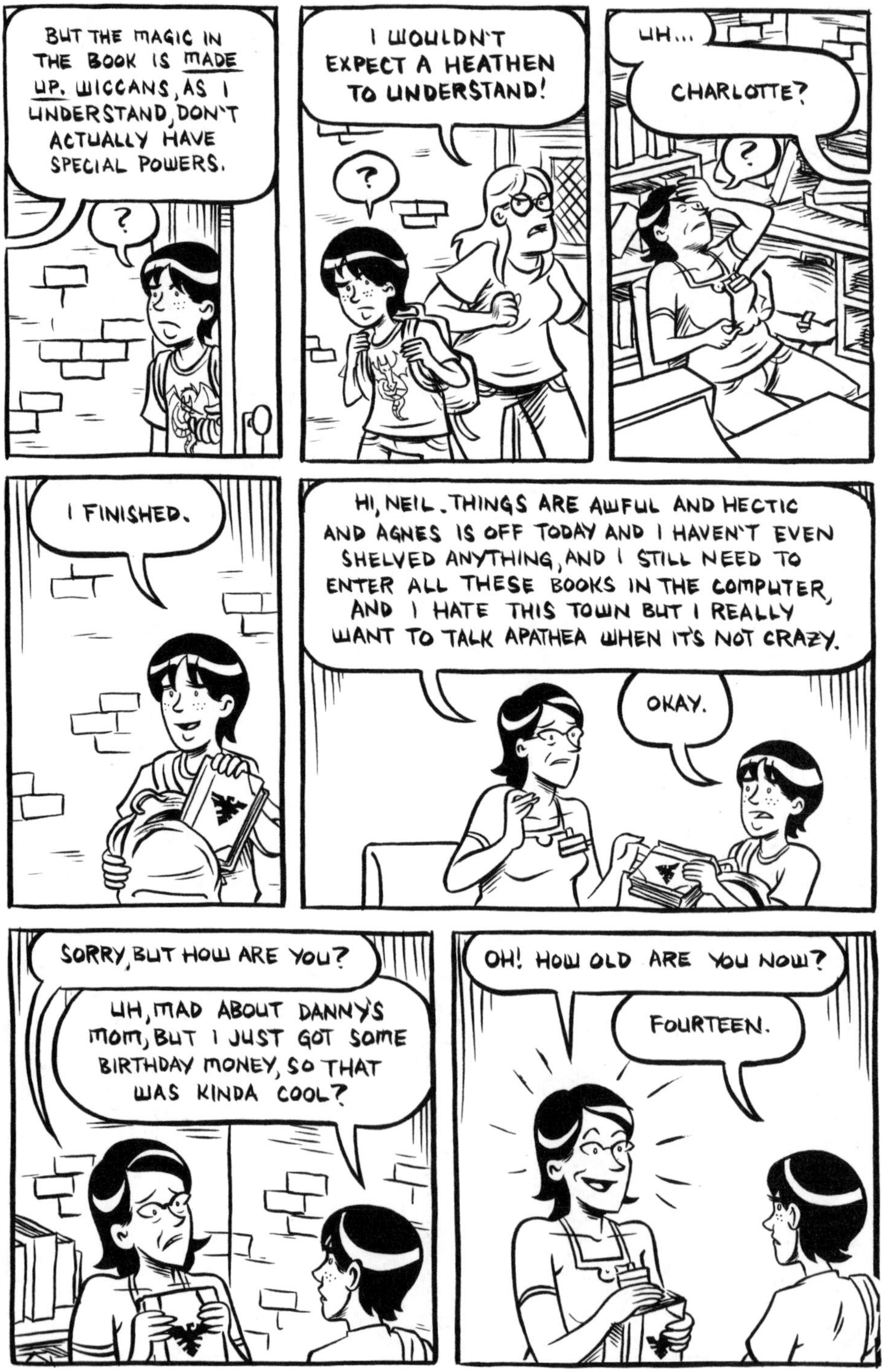
BUT THE MAGIC IN THE BOOK IS MADE UP. WICCANS, AS I UNDERSTAND, DON'T ACTUALLY HAVE SPECIAL POWERS.
?
I WOULDN'T EXPECT A HEATHEN TO UNDERSTAND!
?
UH...
CHARLOTTE?
?
I FINISHED.
HI, NEIL. THINGS ARE AWFUL AND HECTIC AND AGNES IS OFF TODAY AND I HAVEN'T EVEN SHELVED ANYTHING, AND I STILL NEED TO ENTER ALL THESE BOOKS IN THE COMPUTER, AND I HATE THIS TOWN BUT I REALLY WANT TO TALK APATHEA WHEN IT'S NOT CRAZY.
OKAY.
SORRY, BUT HOW ARE YOU?
UH, MAD ABOUT DANNY'S MOM, BUT I JUST GOT SOME BIRTHDAY MONEY, SO THAT WAS KINDA COOL?
OH! HOW OLD ARE YOU NOW?
FOURTEEN.

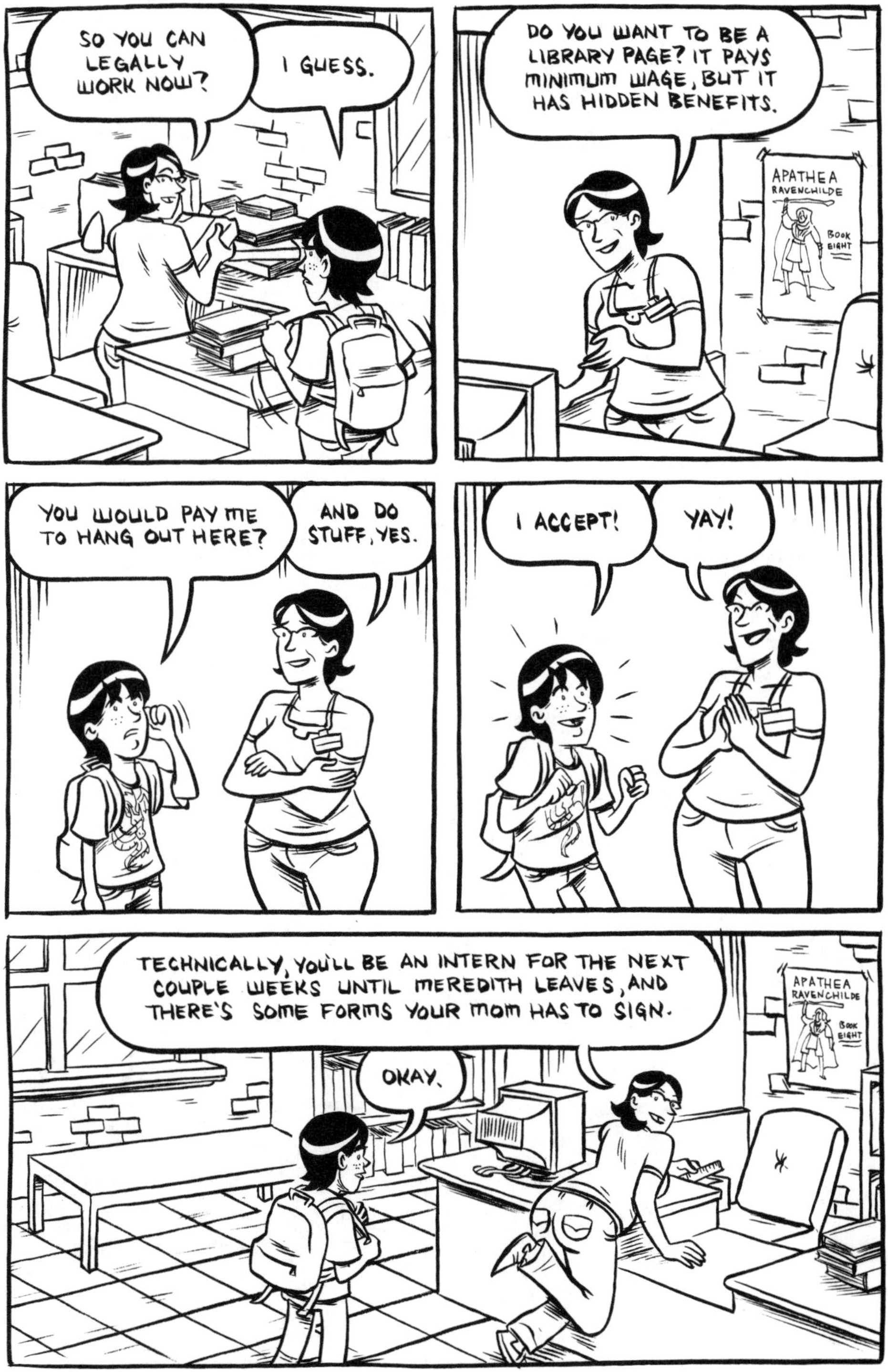
SO YOU CAN LEGALLY WORK NOW?
I GUESS.
DO YOU WANT TO BE A LIBRARY PAGE? IT PAYS MINIMUM WAGE, BUT IT HAS HIDDEN BENEFITS.
APATHEA RAVENCHILDE
BOOK EIGHT
YOU WOULD PAY ME TO HANG OUT HERE?
AND DO STUFF, YES.
I ACCEPT!
YAY!
TECHNICALLY, YOU'LL BE AN INTERN FOR THE NEXT COUPLE WEEKS UNTIL MEREDITH LEAVES, AND THERE'S SOME FORMS YOUR MOM HAS TO SIGN.
APATHEA RAVENCHILDE
BOOK EIGHT
OKAY.

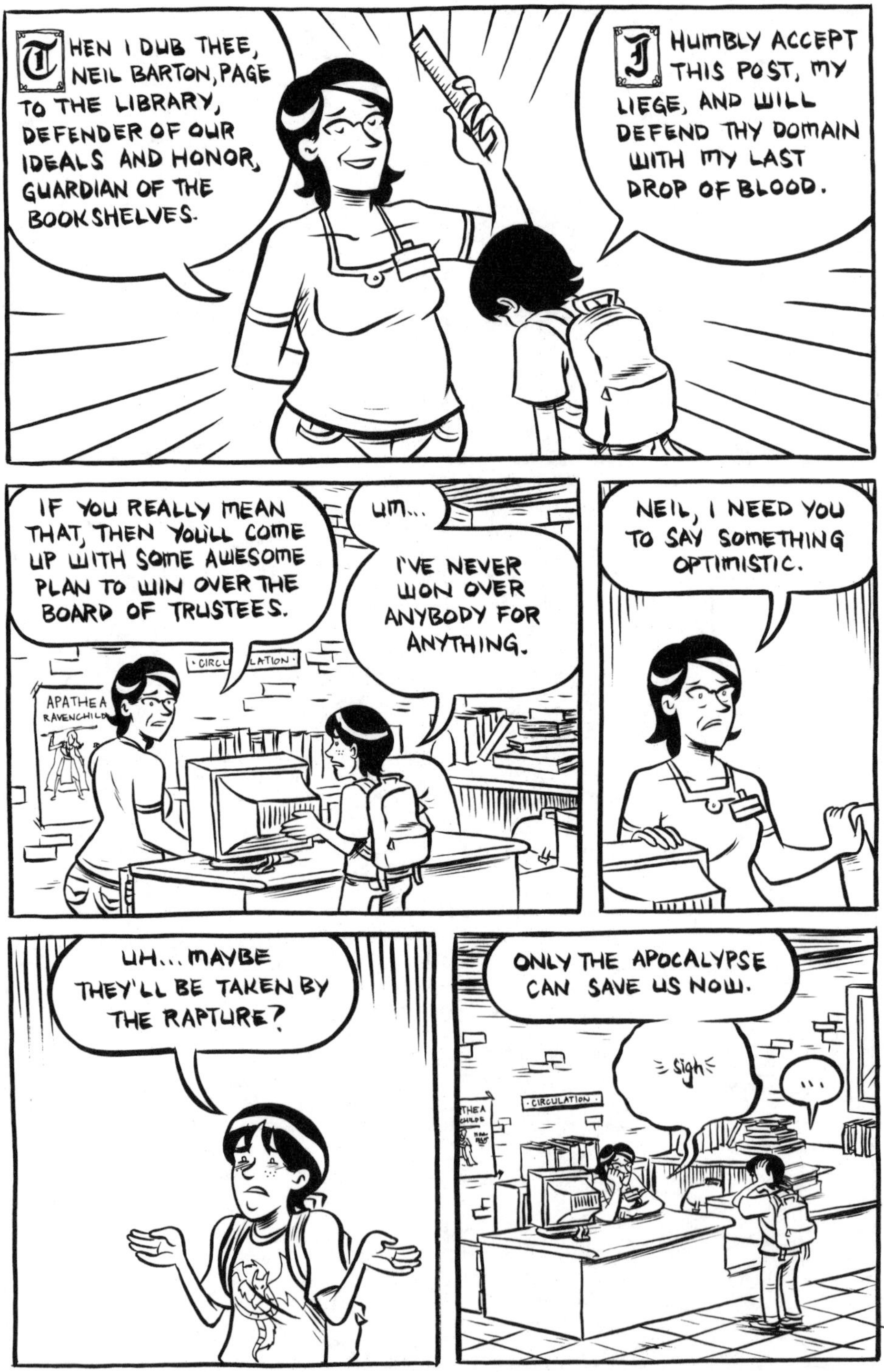
THEN I DUB THEE, NEIL BARTON, PAGE TO THE LIBRARY, DEFENDER OF OUR IDEALS AND HONOR, GUARDIAN OF THE BOOKSHELVES.
I HUMBLY ACCEPT THIS POST, MY LIEGE, AND WILL DEFEND THY DOMAIN WITH MY LAST DROP OF BLOOD.
IF YOU REALLY MEAN THAT, THEN YOU'LL COME UP WITH SOME AWESOME PLAN TO WIN OVER THE BOARD OF TRUSTEES.
UM...
I'VE NEVER WON OVER ANYBODY FOR ANYTHING.
APATHEA RAVENCHILD
·CIRCULATION·
NEIL, I NEED YOU TO SAY SOMETHING OPTIMISTIC.
UH... MAYBE THEY'LL BE TAKEN BY THE RAPTURE?
ONLY THE APOCALYPSE CAN SAVE US NOW.
sigh
...
·CIRCULATION·

CHAPTER 5

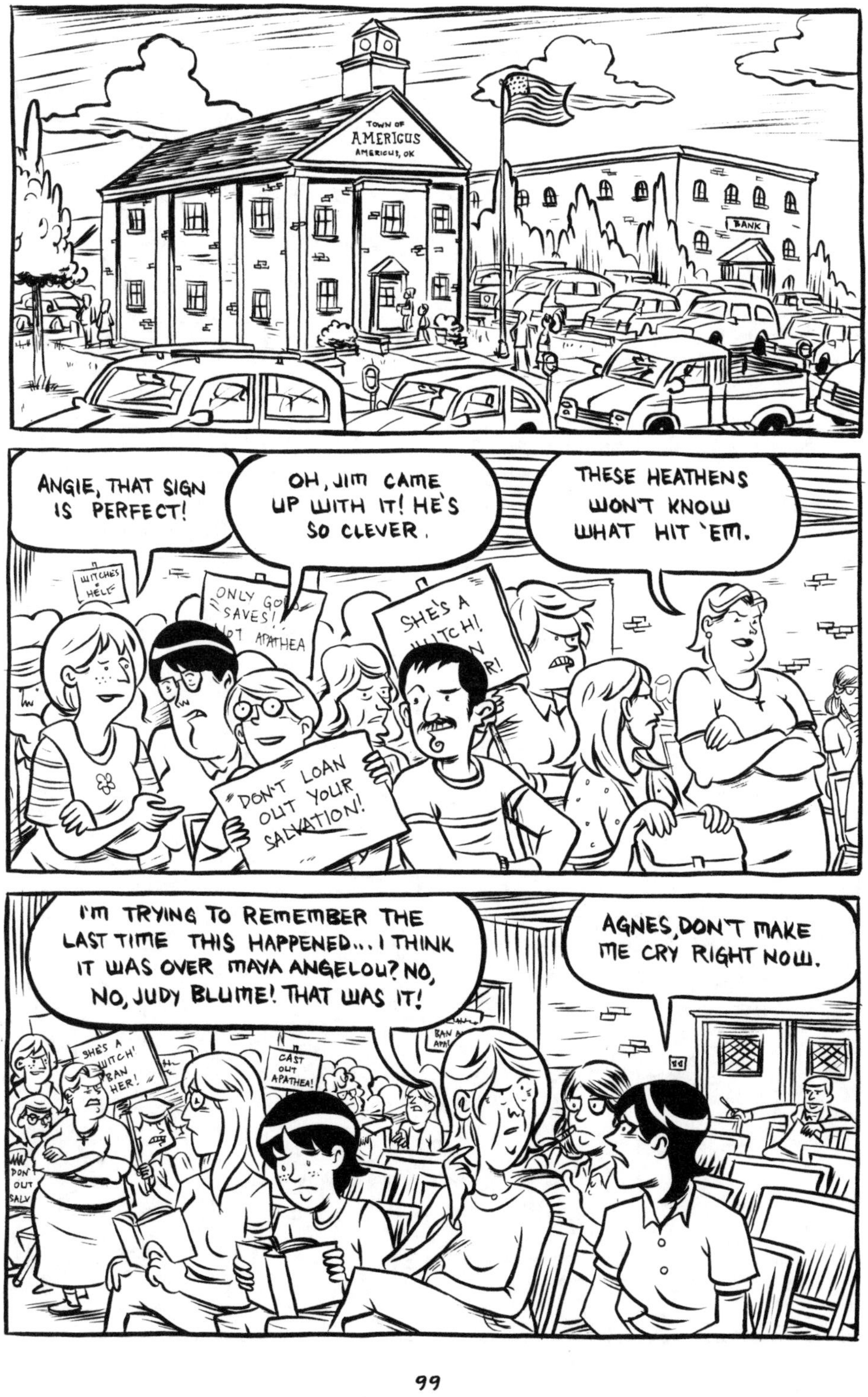
TOWN OF
AMERICUS
AMERICUS, OK
BANK
ANGIE, THAT SIGN IS PERFECT!
OH, JIM CAME UP WITH IT! HE'S SO CLEVER.
THESE HEATHENS WON'T KNOW WHAT HIT 'EM.
DON'T LOAN OUT YOUR SALVATION!
I'M TRYING TO REMEMBER THE LAST TIME THIS HAPPENED... I THINK IT WAS OVER MAYA ANGELOU? NO, NO, JUDY BLUME! THAT WAS IT!
AGNES, DON'T MAKE ME CRY RIGHT NOW.
SHE'S A WITCH! BAN HER!
CAST OUT APATHEA!

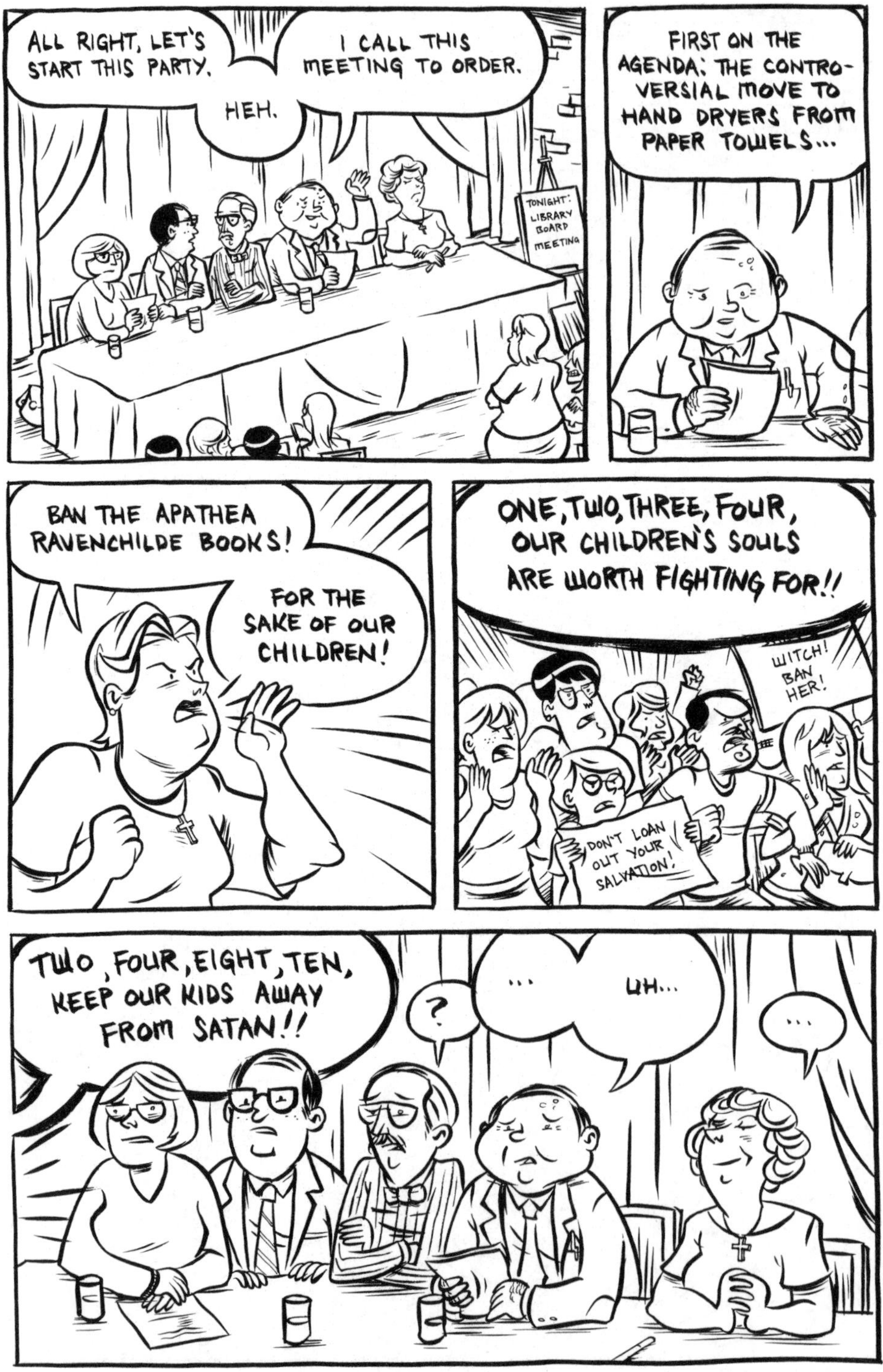
ALL RIGHT, LET'S START THIS PARTY.
I CALL THIS MEETING TO ORDER.
HEH.
TONIGHT: LIBRARY BOARD MEETING
FIRST ON THE AGENDA: THE CONTROVERSIAL MOVE TO HAND DRYERS FROM PAPER TOWELS...
BAN THE APATHEA RAVENCHILDE BOOKS!
FOR THE SAKE OF OUR CHILDREN!
ONE, TWO, THREE, FOUR, OUR CHILDREN'S SOULS ARE WORTH FIGHTING FOR!!
WITCH! BAN HER!
DON'T LOAN OUT YOUR SALVATION!
TWO, FOUR, EIGHT, TEN, KEEP OUR KIDS AWAY FROM SATAN!!
?
...
UH...
...

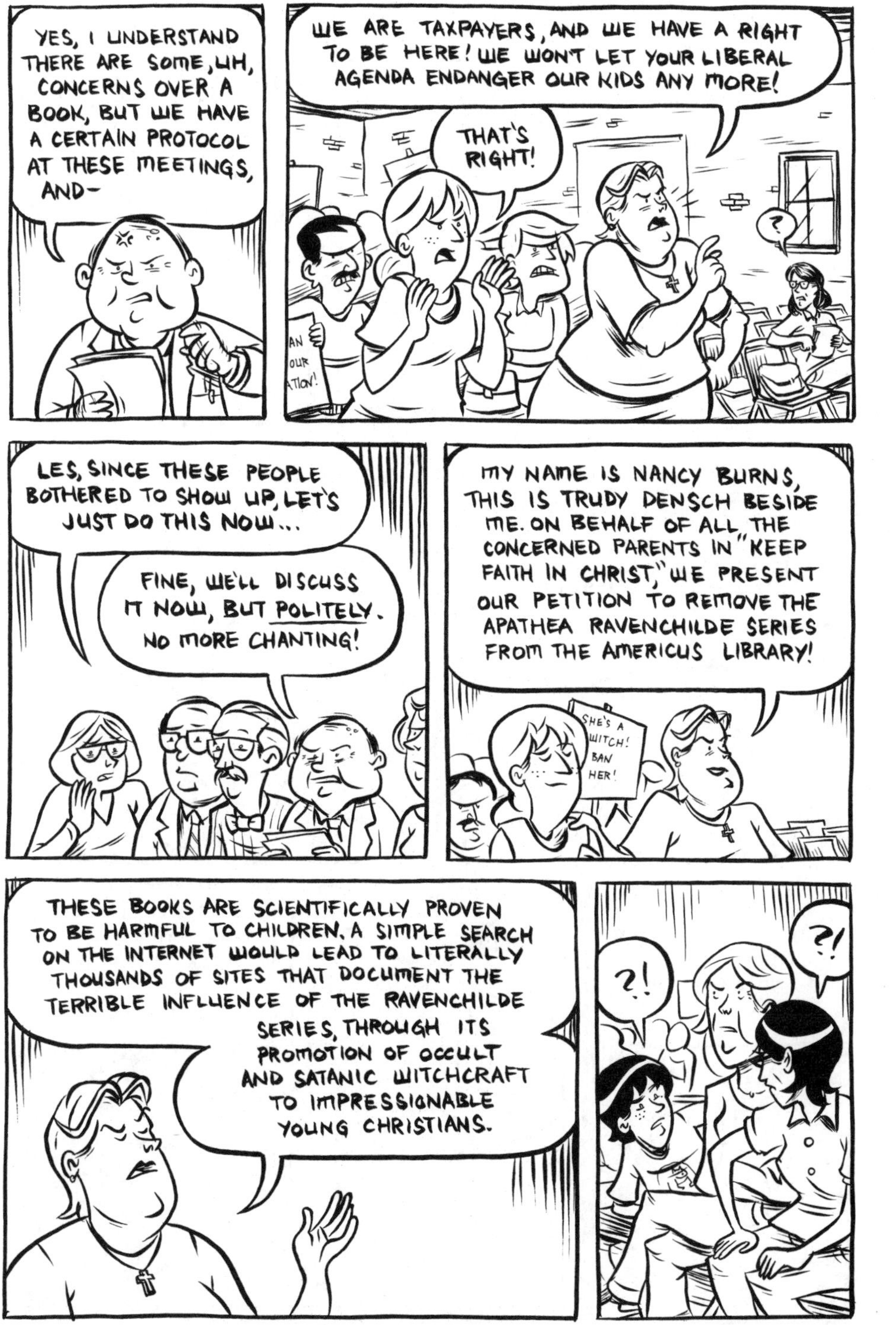
YES, I UNDERSTAND THERE ARE SOME, UH, CONCERNS OVER A BOOK, BUT WE HAVE A CERTAIN PROTOCOL AT THESE MEETINGS, AND-
WE ARE TAXPAYERS, AND WE HAVE A RIGHT TO BE HERE! WE WON'T LET YOUR LIBERAL AGENDA ENDANGER OUR KIDS ANY MORE!
THAT'S RIGHT!
?
LES, SINCE THESE PEOPLE BOTHERED TO SHOW UP, LET'S JUST DO THIS NOW...
FINE, WE'LL DISCUSS IT NOW, BUT POLITELY. NO MORE CHANTING!
MY NAME IS NANCY BURNS, THIS IS TRUDY DENSCH BESIDE ME. ON BEHALF OF ALL THE CONCERNED PARENTS IN "KEEP FAITH IN CHRIST," WE PRESENT OUR PETITION TO REMOVE THE APATHEA RAVENCHILDE SERIES FROM THE AMERICUS LIBRARY!
SHE'S A WITCH! BAN HER!
THESE BOOKS ARE SCIENTIFICALLY PROVEN TO BE HARMFUL TO CHILDREN. A SIMPLE SEARCH ON THE INTERNET WOULD LEAD TO LITERALLY THOUSANDS OF SITES THAT DOCUMENT THE TERRIBLE INFLUENCE OF THE RAVENCHILDE SERIES, THROUGH ITS PROMOTION OF OCCULT AND SATANIC WITCHCRAFT TO IMPRESSIONABLE YOUNG CHRISTIANS.
?!
?!

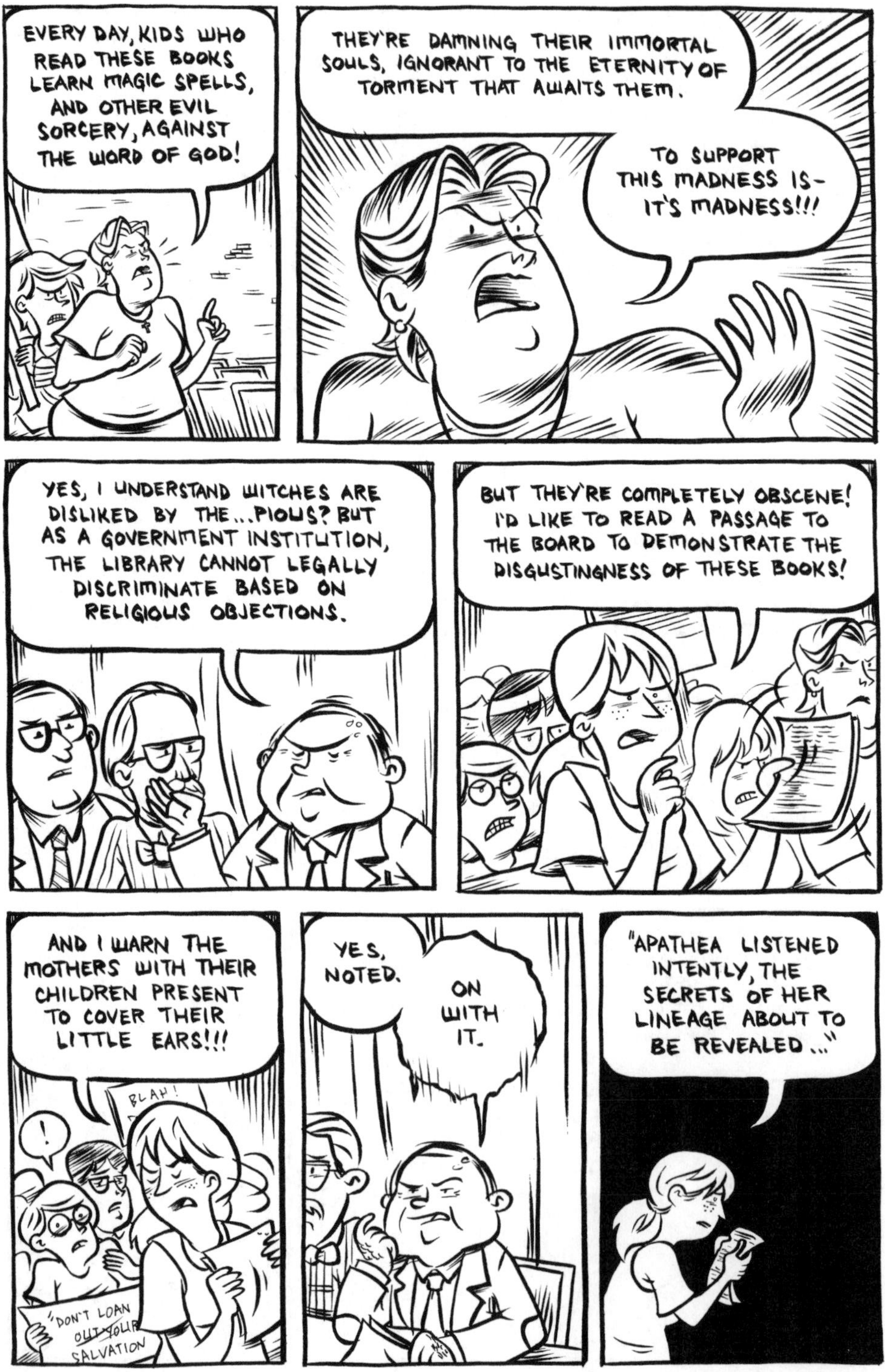
EVERY DAY, KIDS WHO READ THESE BOOKS LEARN MAGIC SPELLS, AND OTHER EVIL SORCERY, AGAINST THE WORD OF GOD!
THEY'RE DAMNING THEIR IMMORTAL SOULS, IGNORANT TO THE ETERNITY OF TORMENT THAT AWAITS THEM.
TO SUPPORT THIS MADNESS IS- IT'S MADNESS!!!
YES, I UNDERSTAND WITCHES ARE DISLIKED BY THE...PIOUS? BUT AS A GOVERNMENT INSTITUTION, THE LIBRARY CANNOT LEGALLY DISCRIMINATE BASED ON RELIGIOUS OBJECTIONS.
BUT THEY'RE COMPLETELY OBSCENE! I'D LIKE TO READ A PASSAGE TO THE BOARD TO DEMONSTRATE THE DISGUSTINGNESS OF THESE BOOKS!
AND I WARN THE MOTHERS WITH THEIR CHILDREN PRESENT TO COVER THEIR LITTLE EARS!!!
BLAH!
!
"DON'T LOAN OUT YOUR SALVATION
YES, NOTED.
ON WITH IT.
"APATHEA LISTENED INTENTLY, THE SECRETS OF HER LINEAGE ABOUT TO BE REVEALED..."

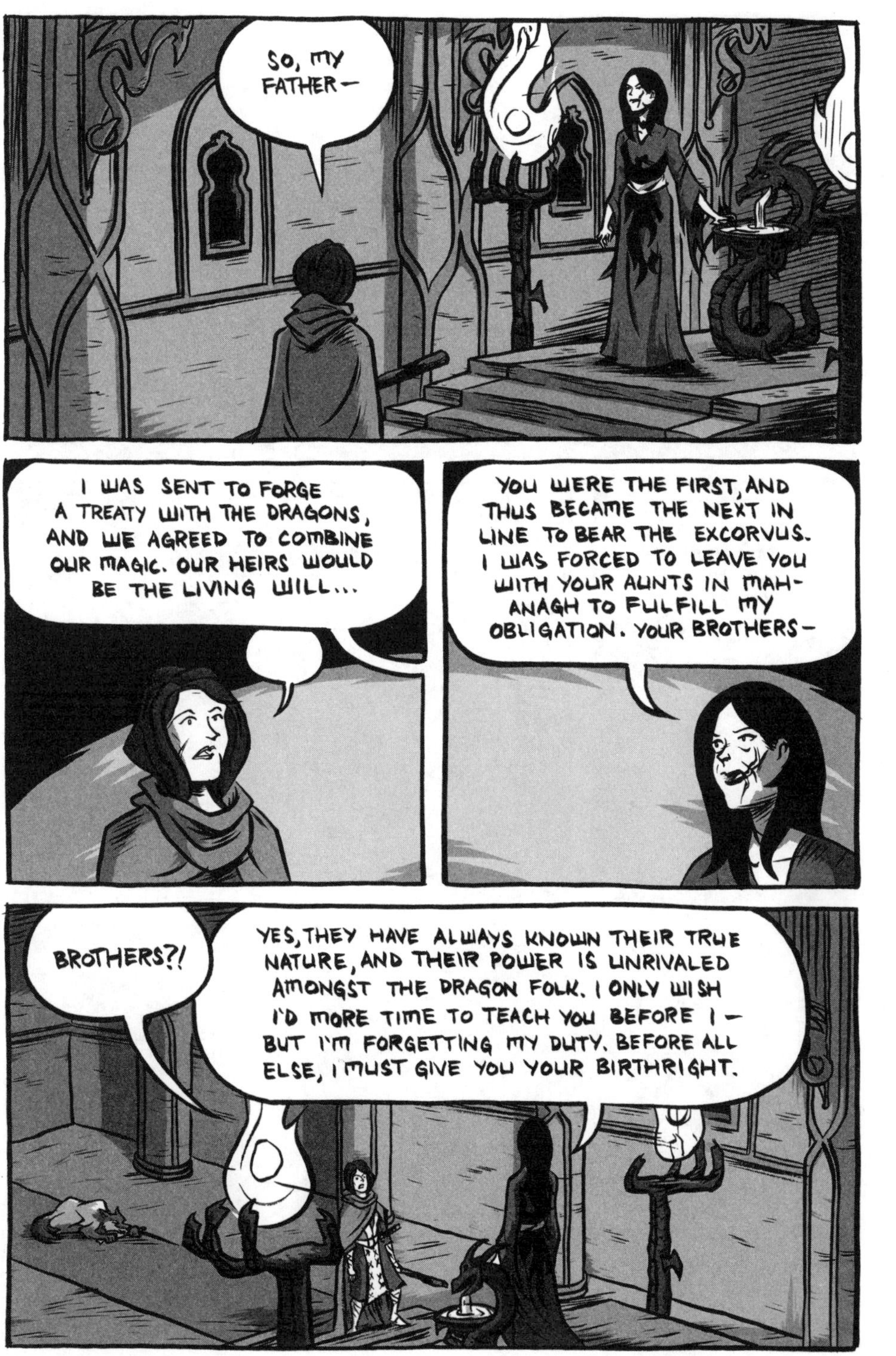
SO, MY FATHER—
I WAS SENT TO FORGE A TREATY WITH THE DRAGONS, AND WE AGREED TO COMBINE OUR MAGIC. OUR HEIRS WOULD BE THE LIVING WILL...
YOU WERE THE FIRST, AND THUS BECAME THE NEXT IN LINE TO BEAR THE EXCORVUS. I WAS FORCED TO LEAVE YOU WITH YOUR AUNTS IN MAH-ANAGH TO FULFILL MY OBLIGATION. YOUR BROTHERS—
BROTHERS?!
YES, THEY HAVE ALWAYS KNOWN THEIR TRUE NATURE, AND THEIR POWER IS UNRIVALED AMONGST THE DRAGON FOLK. I ONLY WISH I'D MORE TIME TO TEACH YOU BEFORE I— BUT I'M FORGETTING MY DUTY. BEFORE ALL ELSE, I MUST GIVE YOU YOUR BIRTHRIGHT.

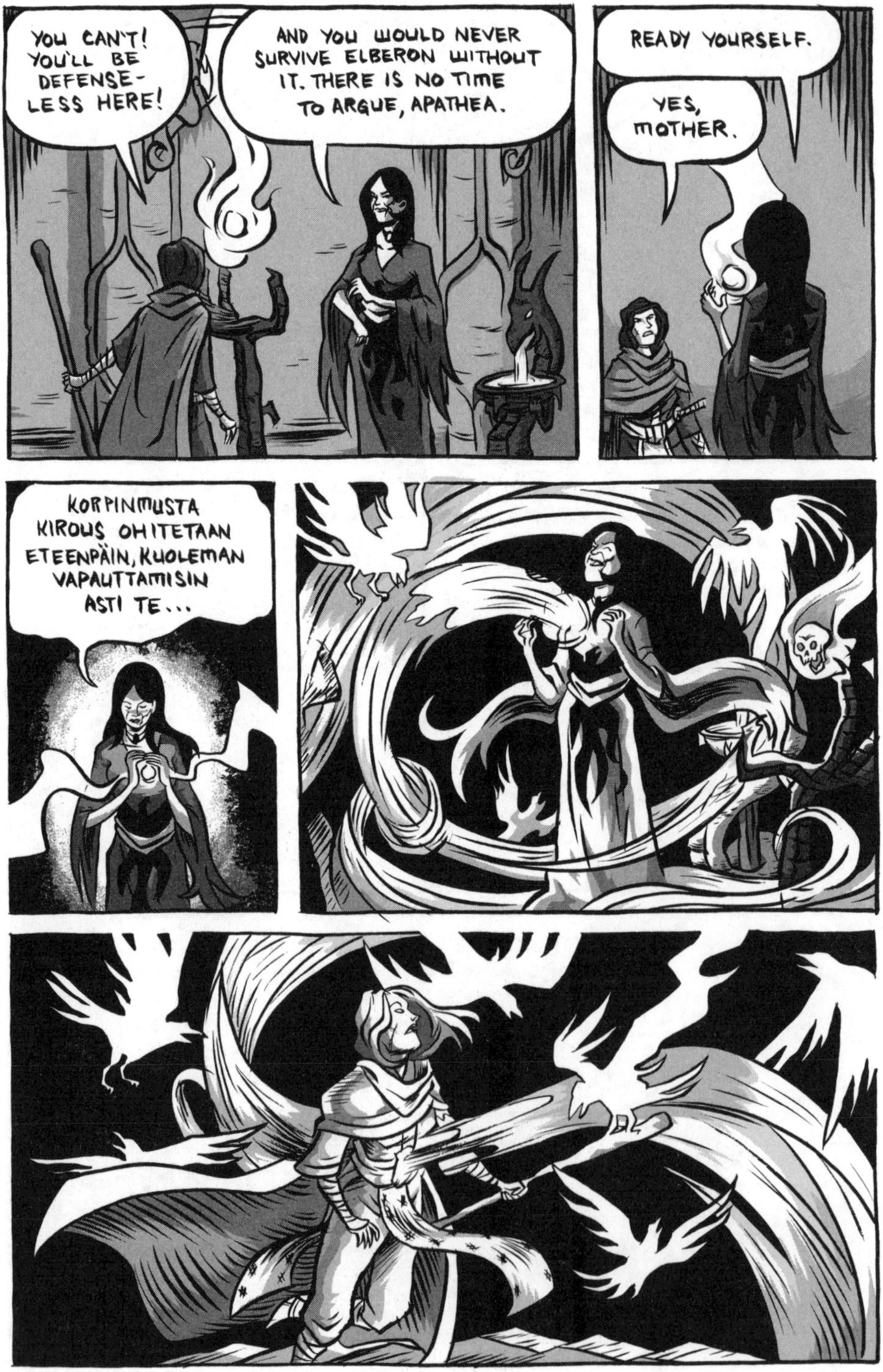
YOU CAN'T! YOU'LL BE DEFENSE-LESS HERE!
AND YOU WOULD NEVER SURVIVE ELBERON WITHOUT IT. THERE IS NO TIME TO ARGUE, APATHEA.
READY YOURSELF.
YES, MOTHER.
KORPINMUSTA KIROUS OHITETAAN ETEENPÄIN, KUOLEMAN VAPAUTTAMISIN ASTI TE...

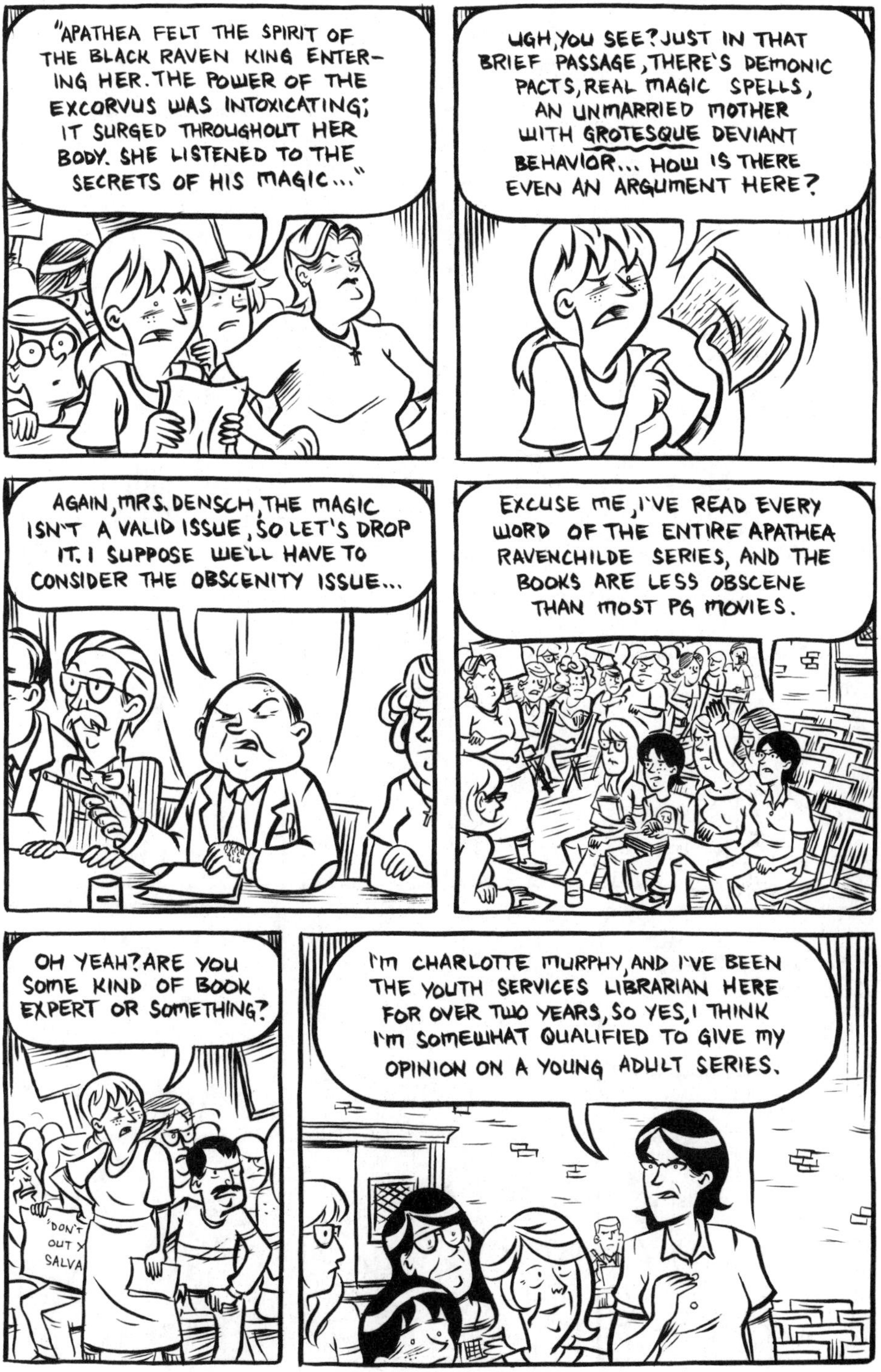
"APATHEA FELT THE SPIRIT OF THE BLACK RAVEN KING ENTERING HER. THE POWER OF THE EXCORVUS WAS INTOXICATING; IT SURGED THROUGHOUT HER BODY. SHE LISTENED TO THE SECRETS OF HIS MAGIC..."
UGH, YOU SEE? JUST IN THAT BRIEF PASSAGE, THERE'S DEMONIC PACTS, REAL MAGIC SPELLS, AN UNMARRIED MOTHER WITH GROTESQUE DEVIANT BEHAVIOR... HOW IS THERE EVEN AN ARGUMENT HERE?
AGAIN, MRS. DENSCH, THE MAGIC ISN'T A VALID ISSUE, SO LET'S DROP IT. I SUPPOSE WE'LL HAVE TO CONSIDER THE OBSCENITY ISSUE...
EXCUSE ME, I'VE READ EVERY WORD OF THE ENTIRE APATHEA RAVENCHILDE SERIES, AND THE BOOKS ARE LESS OBSCENE THAN MOST PG MOVIES.
OH YEAH? ARE YOU SOME KIND OF BOOK EXPERT OR SOMETHING?
I'M CHARLOTTE MURPHY, AND I'VE BEEN THE YOUTH SERVICES LIBRARIAN HERE FOR OVER TWO YEARS, SO YES, I THINK I'M SOMEWHAT QUALIFIED TO GIVE MY OPINION ON A YOUNG ADULT SERIES.

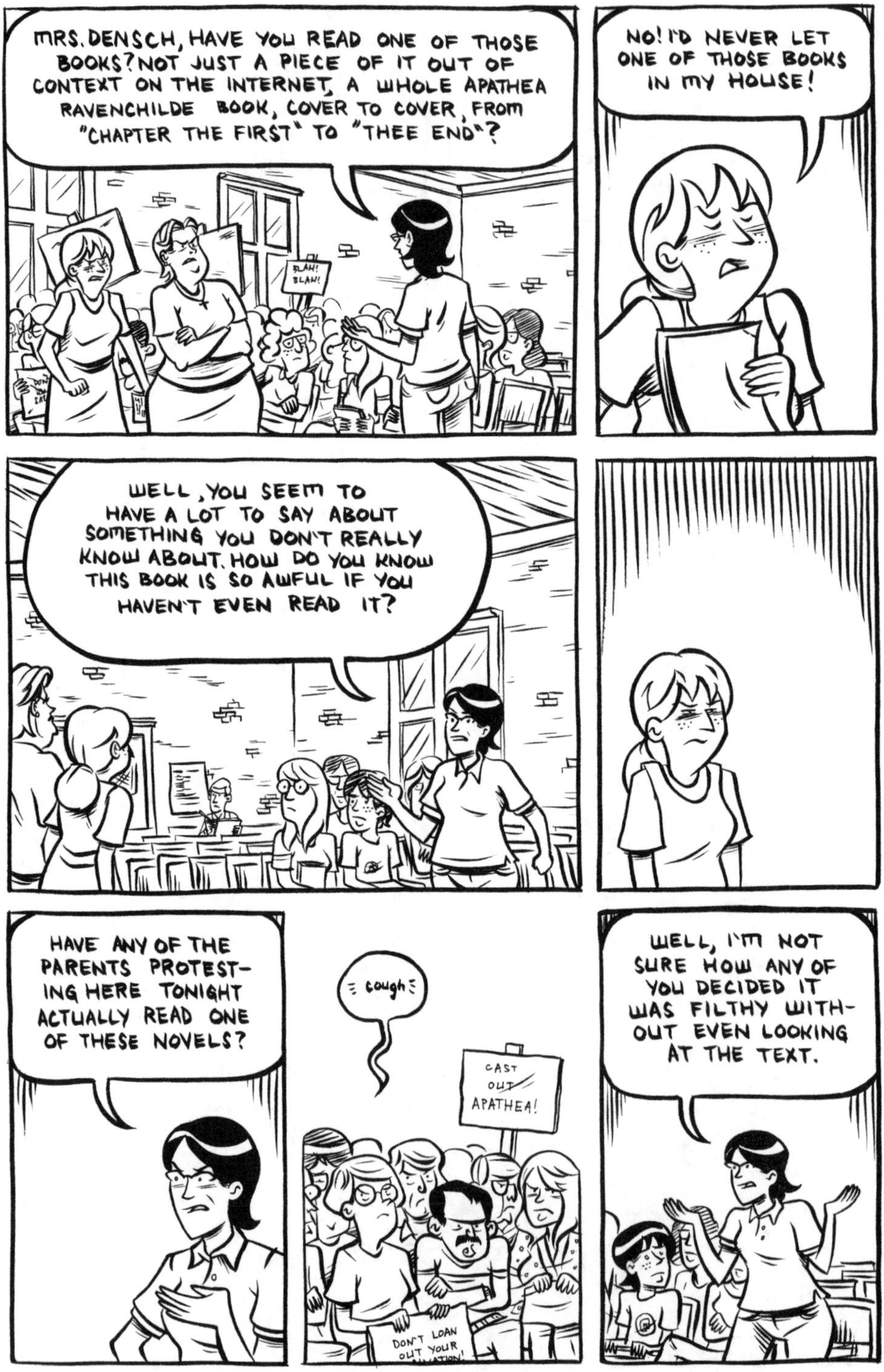
MRS. DENSCH, HAVE YOU READ ONE OF THOSE BOOKS? NOT JUST A PIECE OF IT OUT OF CONTEXT ON THE INTERNET, A WHOLE APATHEA RAVENCHILDE BOOK, COVER TO COVER, FROM "CHAPTER THE FIRST" TO "THEE END"?
BLAH! BLAH!
NO! I'D NEVER LET ONE OF THOSE BOOKS IN MY HOUSE!
WELL, YOU SEEM TO HAVE A LOT TO SAY ABOUT SOMETHING YOU DON'T REALLY KNOW ABOUT. HOW DO YOU KNOW THIS BOOK IS SO AWFUL IF YOU HAVEN'T EVEN READ IT?
HAVE ANY OF THE PARENTS PROTESTING HERE TONIGHT ACTUALLY READ ONE OF THESE NOVELS?
cough
CAST OUT APATHEA!
DON'T LOAN OUT YOUR
WELL, I'M NOT SURE HOW ANY OF YOU DECIDED IT WAS FILTHY WITHOUT EVEN LOOKING AT THE TEXT.

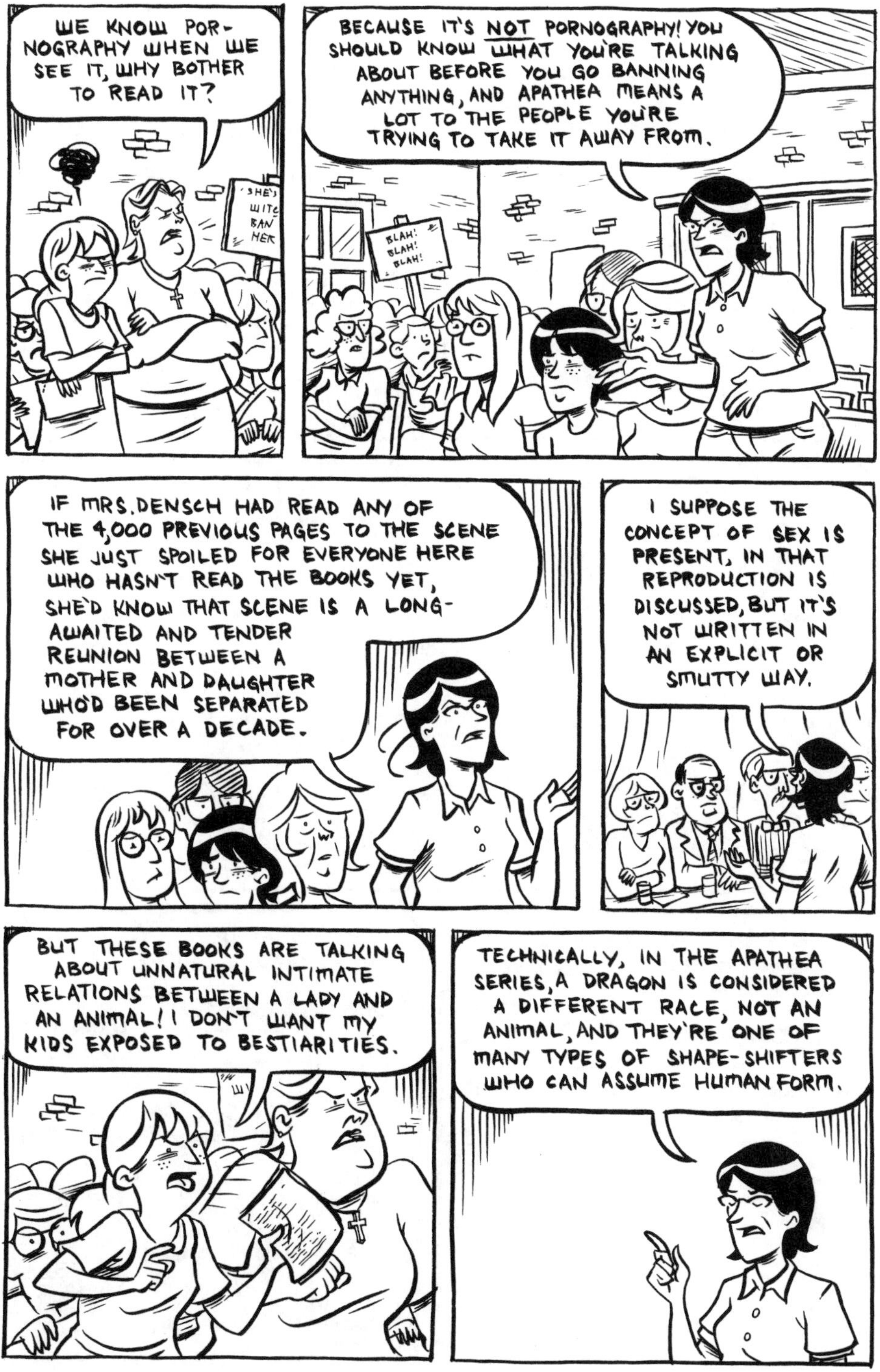
WE KNOW POR-NOGRAPHY WHEN WE SEE IT, WHY BOTHER TO READ IT?
BECAUSE IT'S NOT PORNOGRAPHY! YOU SHOULD KNOW WHAT YOU'RE TALKING ABOUT BEFORE YOU GO BANNING ANYTHING, AND APATHEA MEANS A LOT TO THE PEOPLE YOU'RE TRYING TO TAKE IT AWAY FROM.
BLAH! BLAH! BLAH!
IF MRS. DENSCH HAD READ ANY OF THE 4,000 PREVIOUS PAGES TO THE SCENE SHE JUST SPOILED FOR EVERYONE HERE WHO HASN'T READ THE BOOKS YET, SHE'D KNOW THAT SCENE IS A LONG-AWAITED AND TENDER REUNION BETWEEN A MOTHER AND DAUGHTER WHO'D BEEN SEPARATED FOR OVER A DECADE.
I SUPPOSE THE CONCEPT OF SEX IS PRESENT, IN THAT REPRODUCTION IS DISCUSSED, BUT IT'S NOT WRITTEN IN AN EXPLICIT OR SMUTTY WAY.
BUT THESE BOOKS ARE TALKING ABOUT UNNATURAL INTIMATE RELATIONS BETWEEN A LADY AND AN ANIMAL! I DON'T WANT MY KIDS EXPOSED TO BESTIARITIES.
TECHNICALLY, IN THE APATHEA SERIES, A DRAGON IS CONSIDERED A DIFFERENT RACE, NOT AN ANIMAL, AND THEY'RE ONE OF MANY TYPES OF SHAPE-SHIFTERS WHO CAN ASSUME HUMAN FORM.

TECHNICALLY, ANYTHING MATING WITH ANYTHING ELSE ISN'T APPROPRIATE READING MATERIAL FOR CHILDREN, EVEN IF THEY'RE THE SAME DARN SPECIES.

OKAY, IN THE INTEREST OF THIS NOT TAKING ALL NIGHT, I PROPOSE THAT THE BOARD POSTPONE VOTING ON REMOVAL OF THE BOOKS UNTIL AFTER A SUFFICIENT PERIOD TO ALLOW REVIEW.

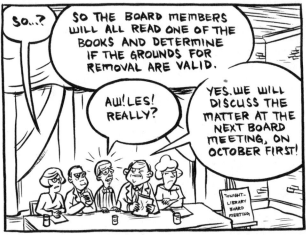

SO...?

SO THE BOARD MEMBERS WILL ALL READ ONE OF THE BOOKS AND DETERMINE IF THE GROUNDS FOR REMOVAL ARE VALID.

AW! LES! REALLY?

YES. WE WILL DISCUSS THE MATTER AT THE NEXT BOARD MEETING, ON OCTOBER FIRST!

TONIGHT— LIBRARY BOARD MEETING

NOW ANYONE INTERESTED IN DISCUSSING THE MERITS OF HAND DRIERS IS INVITED TO STAY.

I CAN'T GET OVER HER BEING HALF DRAGON. THE RAMIFACATIONS OF THIS ARE HUGE.

I KNOW!

IF THIS GETS TO THE COUNCIL OF ELF LORDS, THEY'RE GOING TO FREAK OUT!

BUT WHAT IF... THEY ALREADY KNOW?

GASP!

I HADN'T THOUGHT OF THAT!

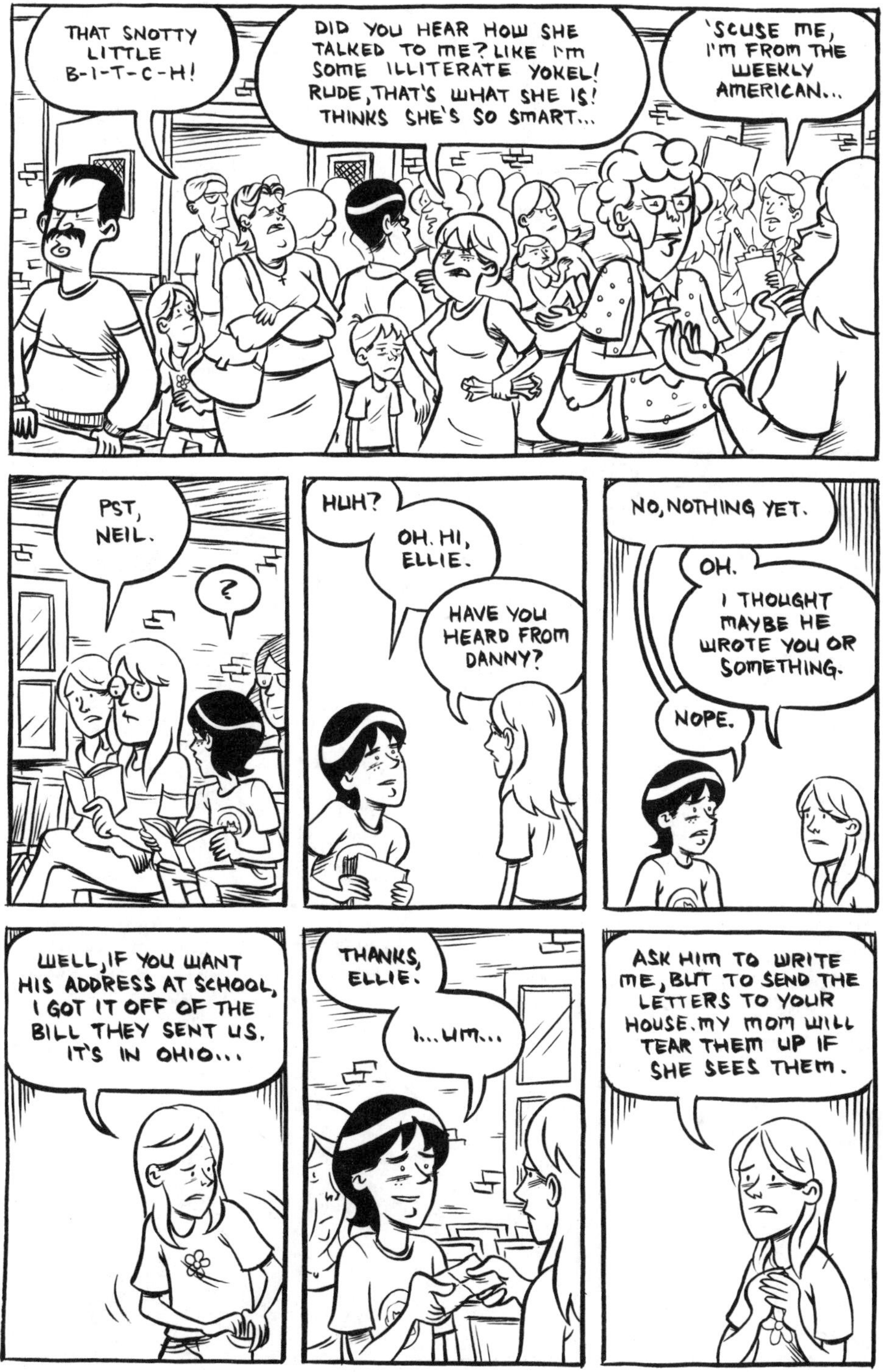
THAT SNOTTY LITTLE B-I-T-C-H!
DID YOU HEAR HOW SHE TALKED TO ME? LIKE I'M SOME ILLITERATE YOKEL! RUDE, THAT'S WHAT SHE IS! THINKS SHE'S SO SMART...
'SCUSE ME, I'M FROM THE WEEKLY AMERICAN...
PST, NEIL.
?
HUH?
OH. HI, ELLIE.
HAVE YOU HEARD FROM DANNY?
NO, NOTHING YET.
OH.
I THOUGHT MAYBE HE WROTE YOU OR SOMETHING.
NOPE.
WELL, IF YOU WANT HIS ADDRESS AT SCHOOL, I GOT IT OFF OF THE BILL THEY SENT US. IT'S IN OHIO...
THANKS, ELLIE.
I...UM...
ASK HIM TO WRITE ME, BUT TO SEND THE LETTERS TO YOUR HOUSE. MY MOM WILL TEAR THEM UP IF SHE SEES THEM.

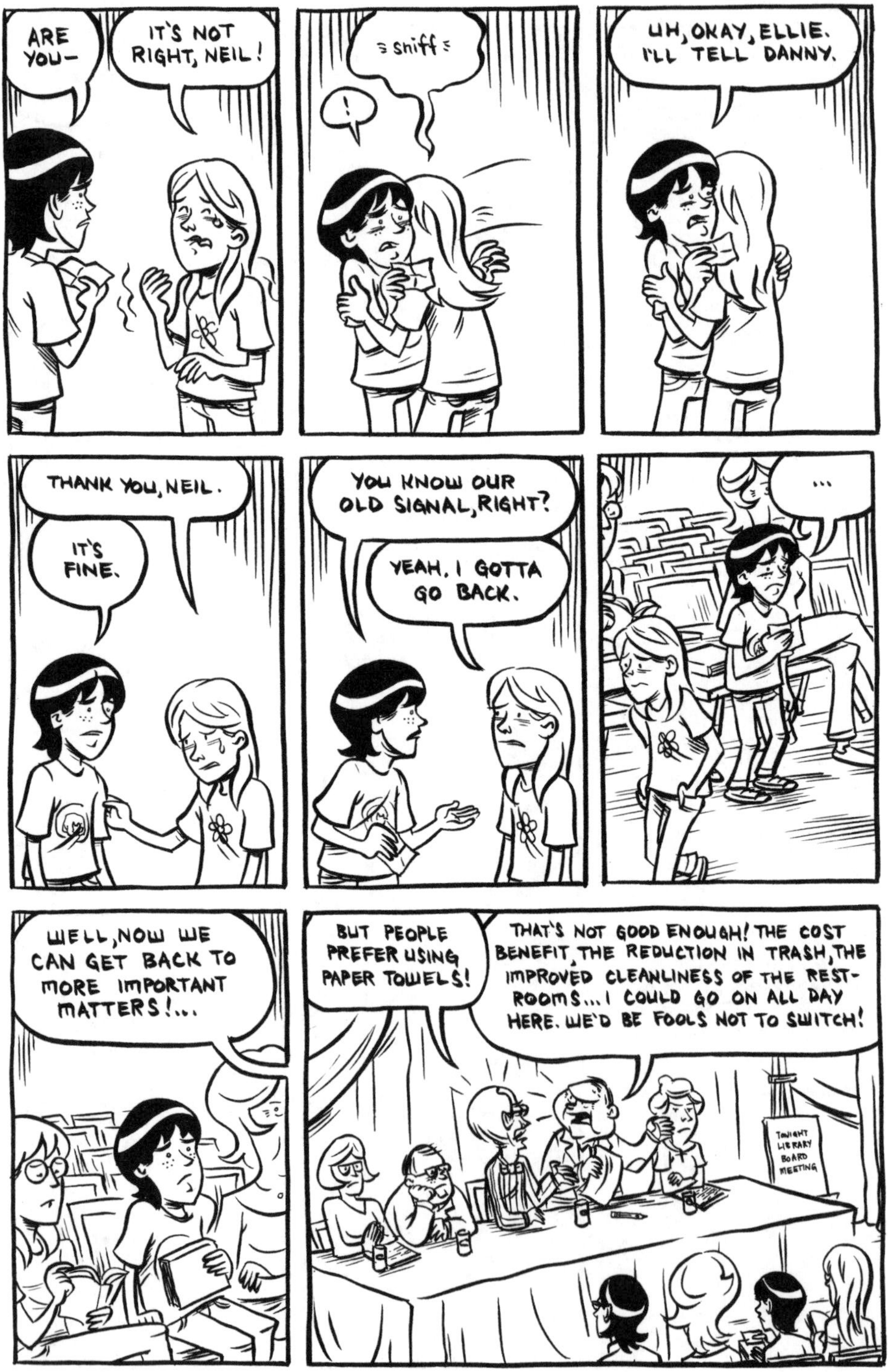
ARE YOU—
IT'S NOT RIGHT, NEIL!
!
sniff
UH, OKAY, ELLIE. I'LL TELL DANNY.
THANK YOU, NEIL.
IT'S FINE.
YOU KNOW OUR OLD SIGNAL, RIGHT?
YEAH, I GOTTA GO BACK.
...
WELL, NOW WE CAN GET BACK TO MORE IMPORTANT MATTERS!...
BUT PEOPLE PREFER USING PAPER TOWELS!
THAT'S NOT GOOD ENOUGH! THE COST BENEFIT, THE REDUCTION IN TRASH, THE IMPROVED CLEANLINESS OF THE REST-ROOMS... I COULD GO ON ALL DAY HERE. WE'D BE FOOLS NOT TO SWITCH!
TONIGHT LIBRARY BOARD MEETING

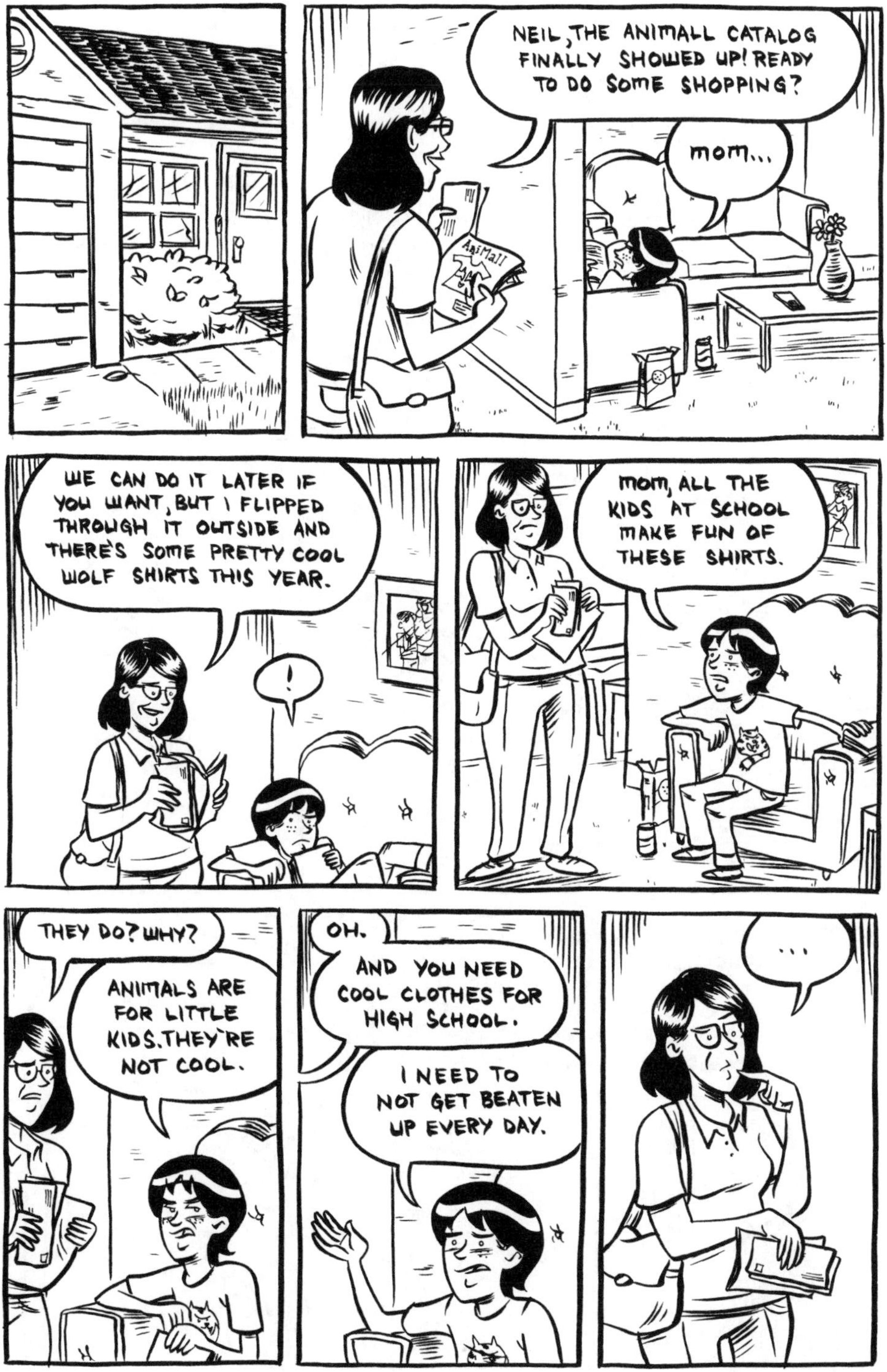
NEIL, THE ANIMALL CATALOG FINALLY SHOWED UP! READY TO DO SOME SHOPPING?
mom...
AniMall
WE CAN DO IT LATER IF YOU WANT, BUT I FLIPPED THROUGH IT OUTSIDE AND THERE'S SOME PRETTY COOL WOLF SHIRTS THIS YEAR.
!
mom, ALL THE KIDS AT SCHOOL MAKE FUN OF THESE SHIRTS.
THEY DO? WHY?
ANIMALS ARE FOR LITTLE KIDS. THEY'RE NOT COOL.
OH.
AND YOU NEED COOL CLOTHES FOR HIGH SCHOOL.
I NEED TO NOT GET BEATEN UP EVERY DAY.
...

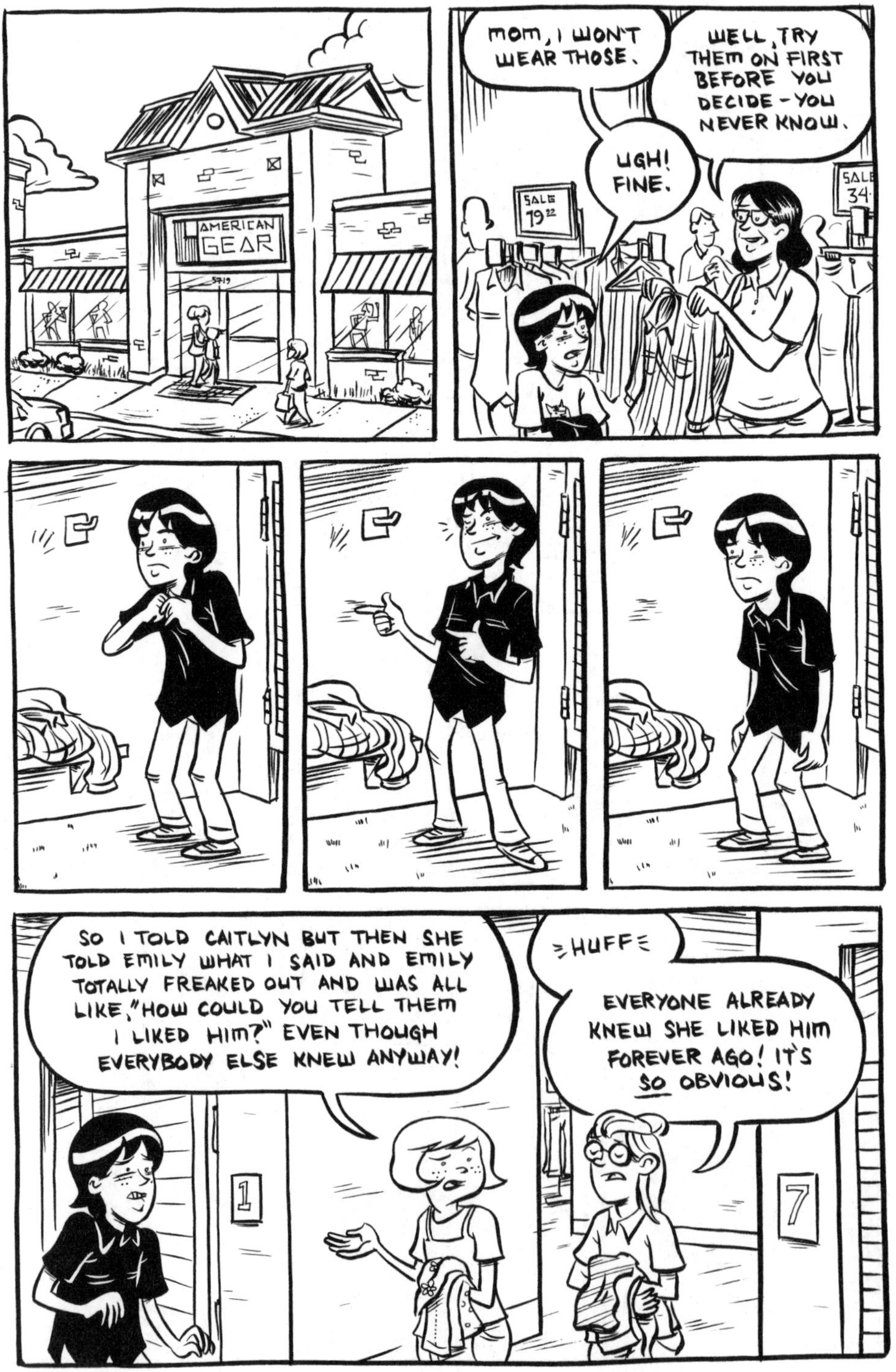
AMERICAN GEAR
5719
MOM, I WON'T WEAR THOSE.
WELL, TRY THEM ON FIRST BEFORE YOU DECIDE - YOU NEVER KNOW.
UGH! FINE.
SALE 19.22
SALE 34.
SO I TOLD CAITLYN BUT THEN SHE TOLD EMILY WHAT I SAID AND EMILY TOTALLY FREAKED OUT AND WAS ALL LIKE, "HOW COULD YOU TELL THEM I LIKED HIM?" EVEN THOUGH EVERYBODY ELSE KNEW ANYWAY!
HUFF
EVERYONE ALREADY KNEW SHE LIKED HIM FOREVER AGO! IT'S SO OBVIOUS!
1
7

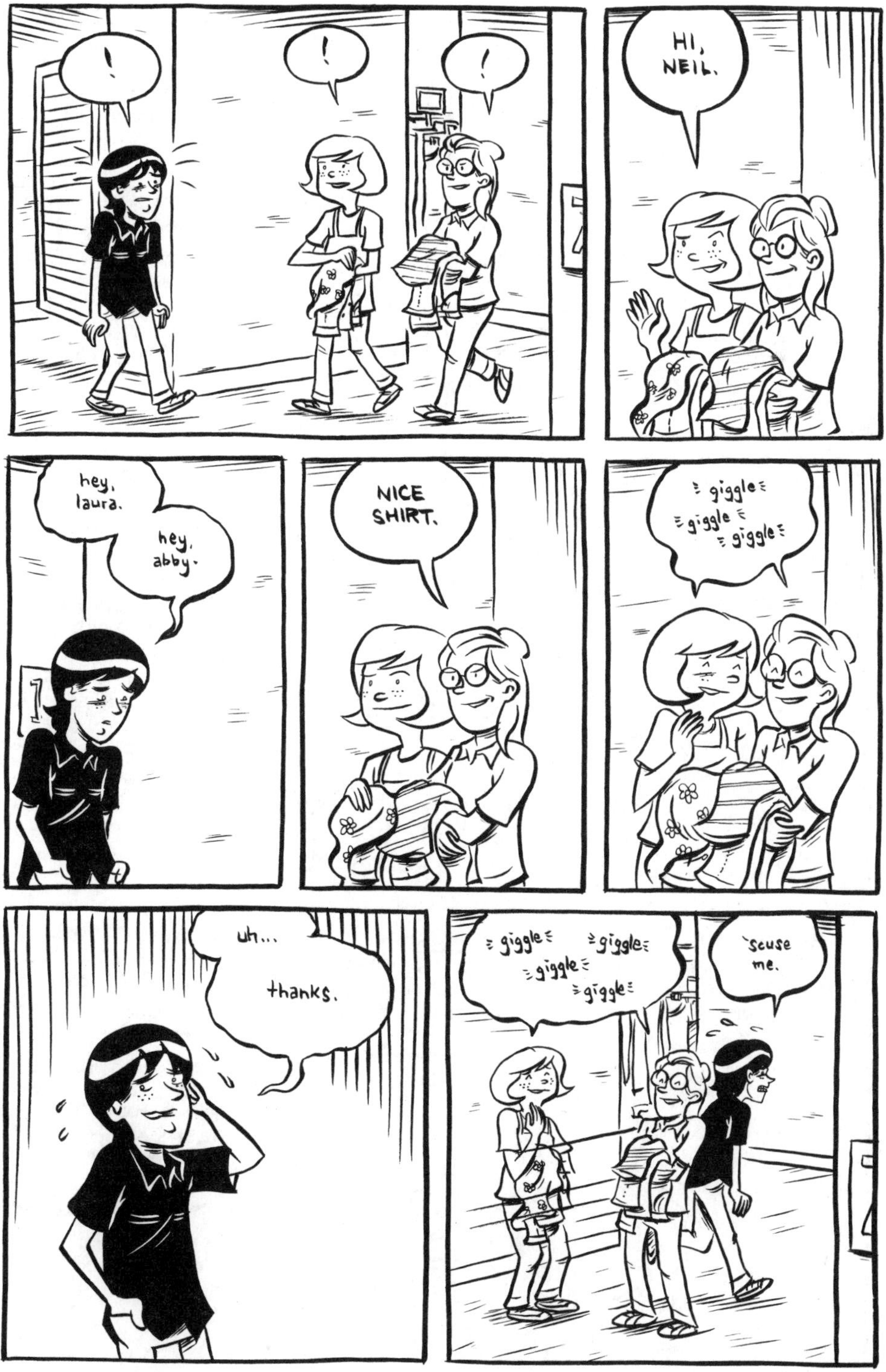
!
!
!
HI, NEIL.
hey, laura.
hey, abby.
NICE SHIRT.
giggle giggle giggle
uh...
thanks.
giggle giggle giggle giggle
'scuse me.

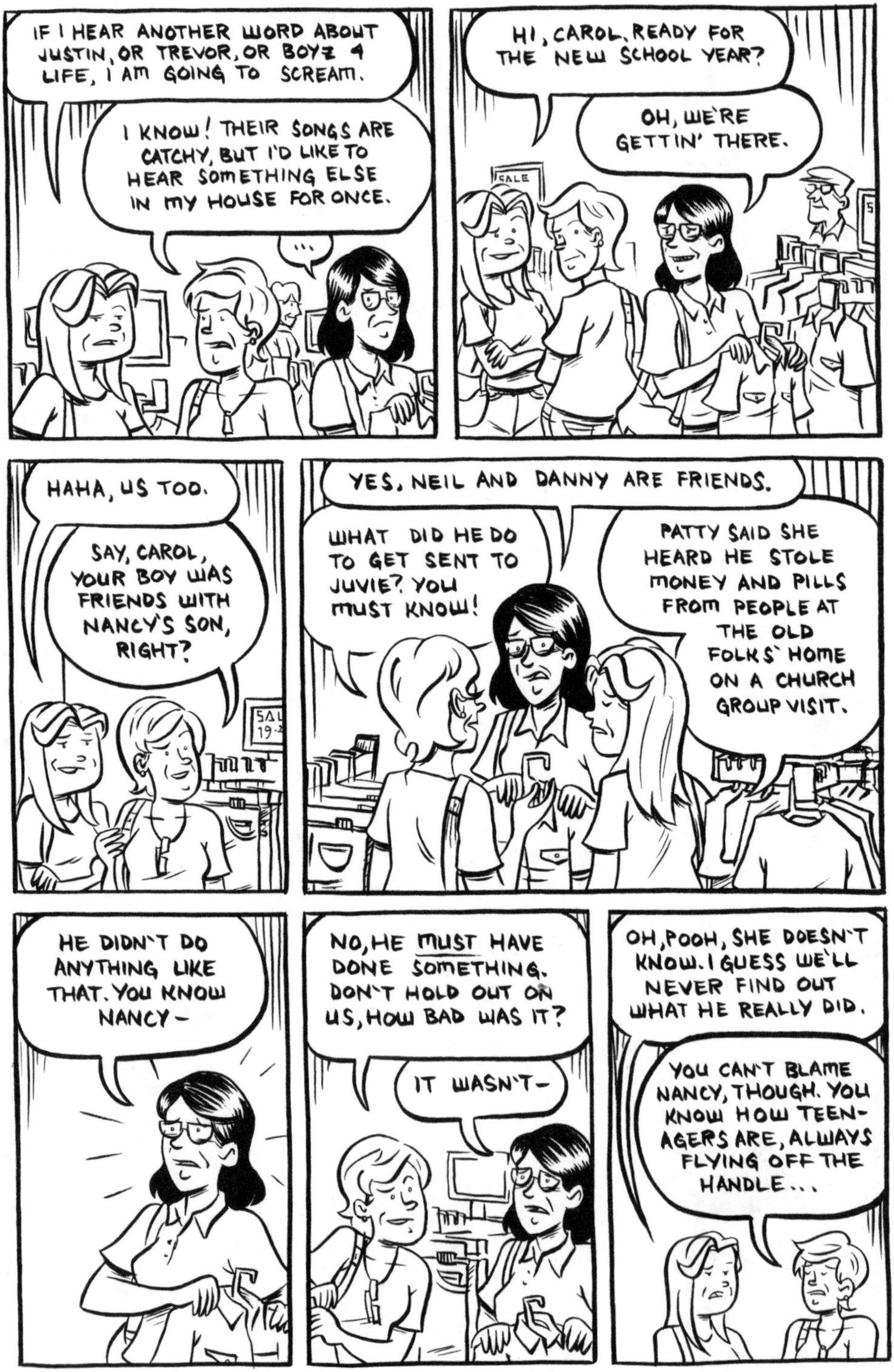
IF I HEAR ANOTHER WORD ABOUT JUSTIN, OR TREVOR, OR BOYZ 4 LIFE, I AM GOING TO SCREAM.
I KNOW! THEIR SONGS ARE CATCHY, BUT I'D LIKE TO HEAR SOMETHING ELSE IN MY HOUSE FOR ONCE.
...
HI, CAROL. READY FOR THE NEW SCHOOL YEAR?
OH, WE'RE GETTIN' THERE.
SALE
HAHA, US TOO.
SAY, CAROL, YOUR BOY WAS FRIENDS WITH NANCY'S SON, RIGHT?
YES. NEIL AND DANNY ARE FRIENDS.
WHAT DID HE DO TO GET SENT TO JUVIE? YOU MUST KNOW!
PATTY SAID SHE HEARD HE STOLE MONEY AND PILLS FROM PEOPLE AT THE OLD FOLKS' HOME ON A CHURCH GROUP VISIT.
HE DIDN'T DO ANYTHING LIKE THAT. YOU KNOW NANCY—
NO, HE MUST HAVE DONE SOMETHING. DON'T HOLD OUT ON US, HOW BAD WAS IT?
IT WASN'T—
OH, POOH, SHE DOESN'T KNOW. I GUESS WE'LL NEVER FIND OUT WHAT HE REALLY DID.
YOU CAN'T BLAME NANCY, THOUGH. YOU KNOW HOW TEEN-AGERS ARE, ALWAYS FLYING OFF THE HANDLE...

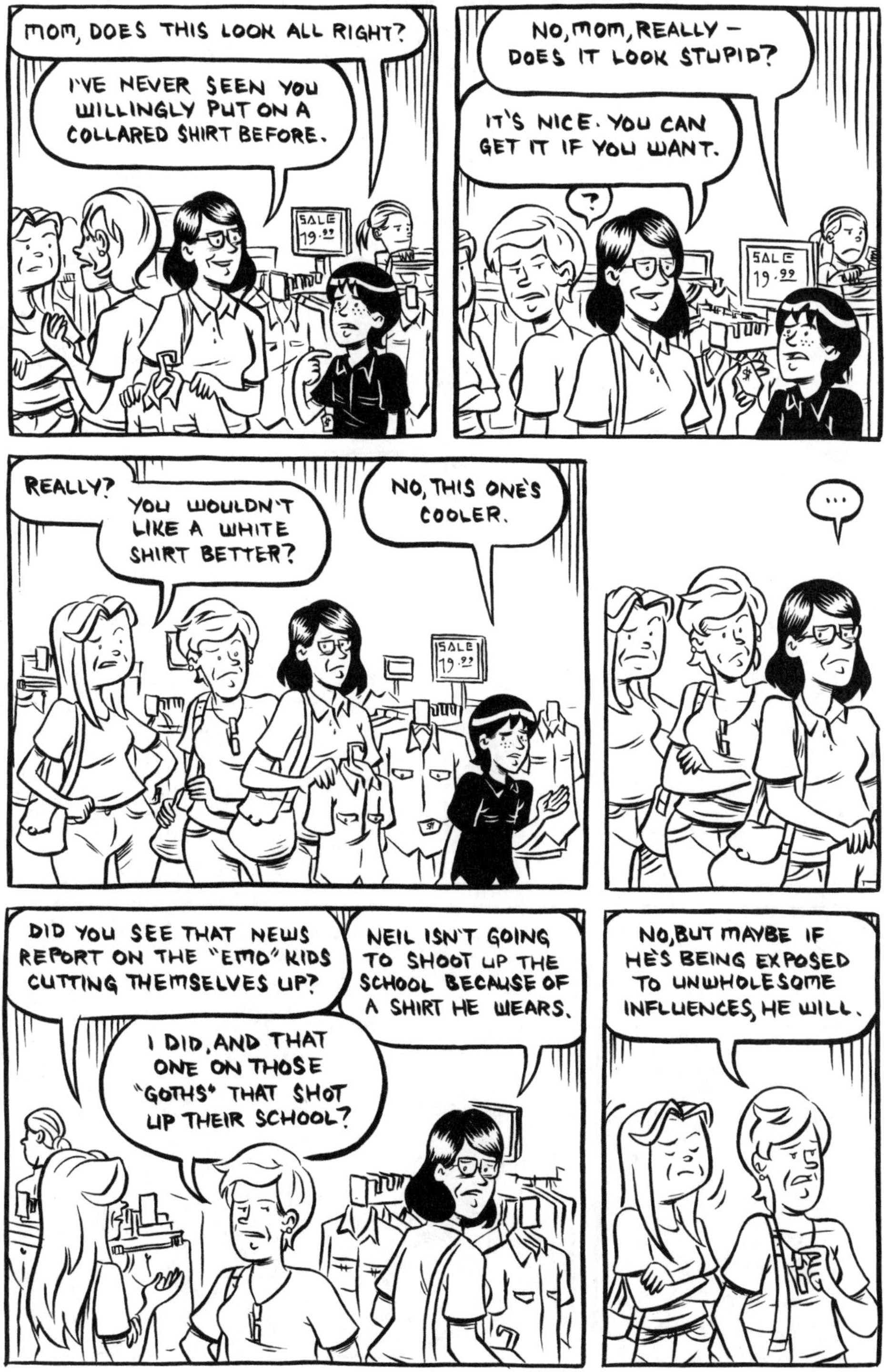
MOM, DOES THIS LOOK ALL RIGHT?
I'VE NEVER SEEN YOU WILLINGLY PUT ON A COLLARED SHIRT BEFORE.
SALE 19.99
NO, MOM, REALLY - DOES IT LOOK STUPID?
IT'S NICE. YOU CAN GET IT IF YOU WANT.
?
SALE 19.99
REALLY?
YOU WOULDN'T LIKE A WHITE SHIRT BETTER?
NO, THIS ONE'S COOLER.
SALE 19.99
...
DID YOU SEE THAT NEWS REPORT ON THE "EMO" KIDS CUTTING THEMSELVES UP?
I DID, AND THAT ONE ON THOSE "GOTHS" THAT SHOT UP THEIR SCHOOL?
NEIL ISN'T GOING TO SHOOT UP THE SCHOOL BECAUSE OF A SHIRT HE WEARS.
NO, BUT MAYBE IF HE'S BEING EXPOSED TO UNWHOLESOME INFLUENCES, HE WILL.

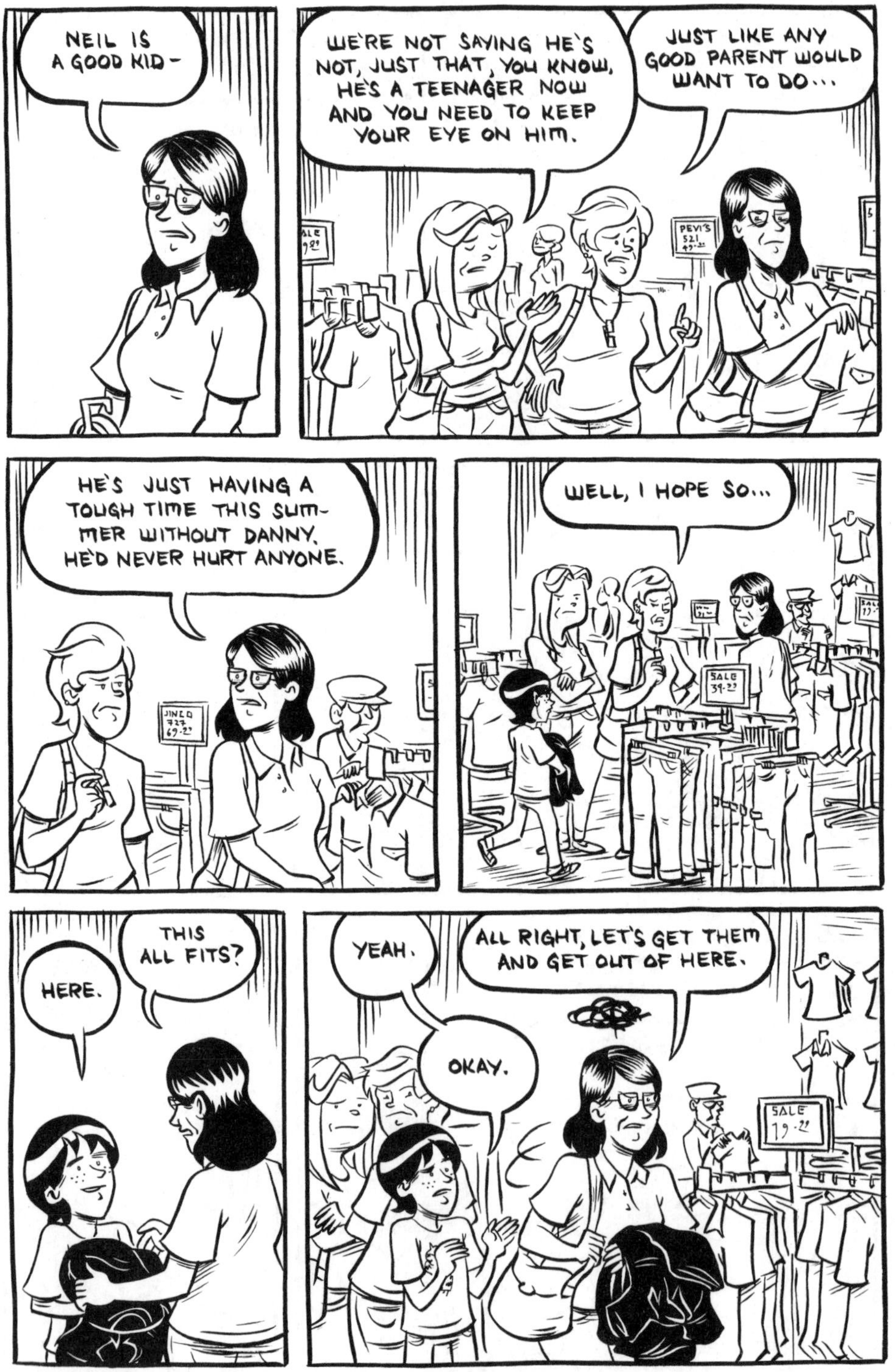
NEIL IS A GOOD KID –
WE'RE NOT SAYING HE'S NOT, JUST THAT, YOU KNOW, HE'S A TEENAGER NOW AND YOU NEED TO KEEP YOUR EYE ON HIM.
JUST LIKE ANY GOOD PARENT WOULD WANT TO DO...
HE'S JUST HAVING A TOUGH TIME THIS SUMMER WITHOUT DANNY. HE'D NEVER HURT ANYONE.
WELL, I HOPE SO...
SALE 39.99
HERE.
THIS ALL FITS?
YEAH.
ALL RIGHT, LET'S GET THEM AND GET OUT OF HERE.
OKAY.
SALE 19.99

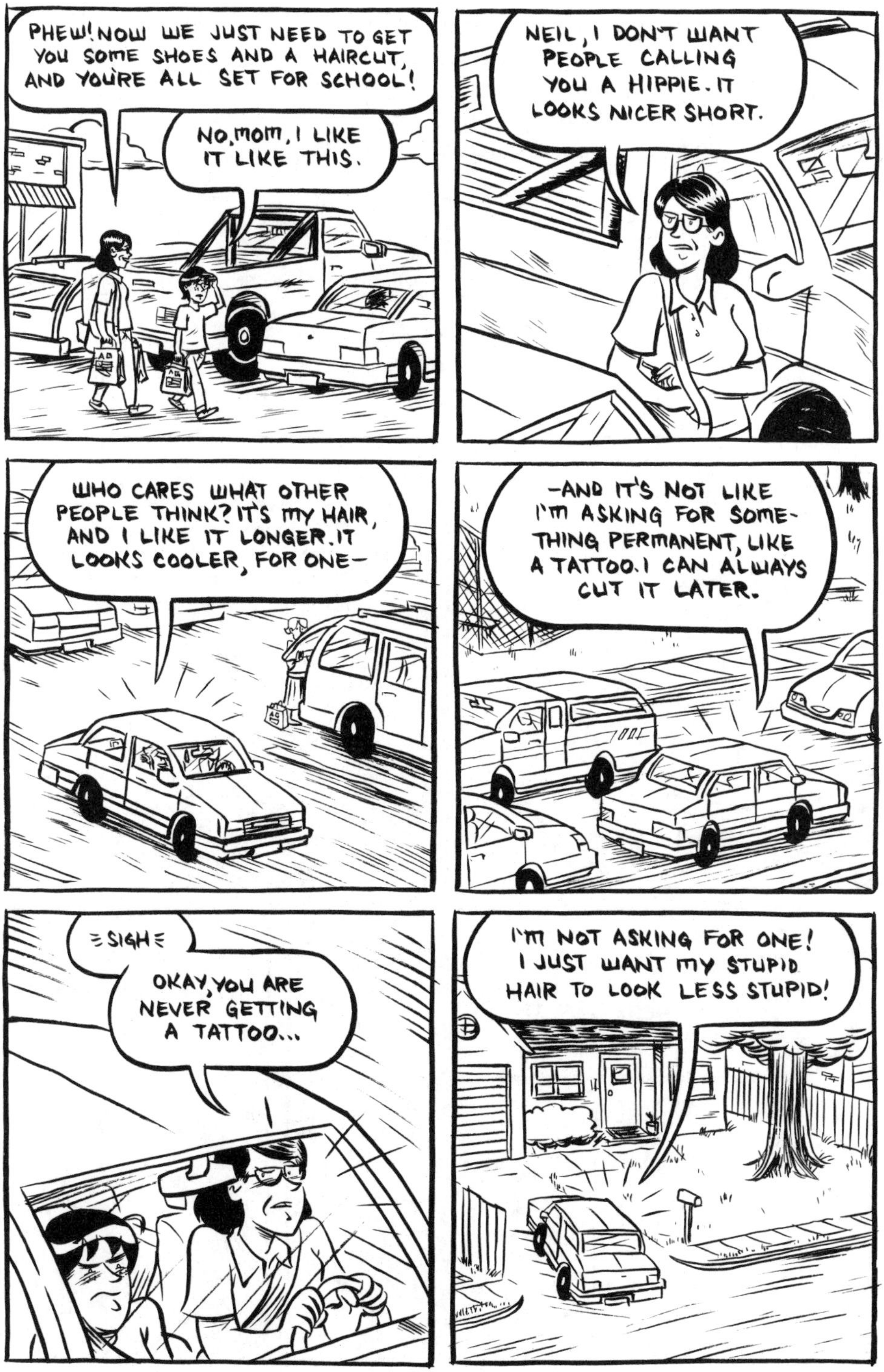
PHEW! NOW WE JUST NEED TO GET YOU SOME SHOES AND A HAIRCUT, AND YOU'RE ALL SET FOR SCHOOL!
NO, MOM, I LIKE IT LIKE THIS.
NEIL, I DON'T WANT PEOPLE CALLING YOU A HIPPIE. IT LOOKS NICER SHORT.
WHO CARES WHAT OTHER PEOPLE THINK? IT'S MY HAIR, AND I LIKE IT LONGER. IT LOOKS COOLER, FOR ONE–
–AND IT'S NOT LIKE I'M ASKING FOR SOMETHING PERMANENT, LIKE A TATTOO. I CAN ALWAYS CUT IT LATER.
≡SIGH≡
OKAY, YOU ARE NEVER GETTING A TATTOO...
I'M NOT ASKING FOR ONE! I JUST WANT MY STUPID HAIR TO LOOK LESS STUPID!

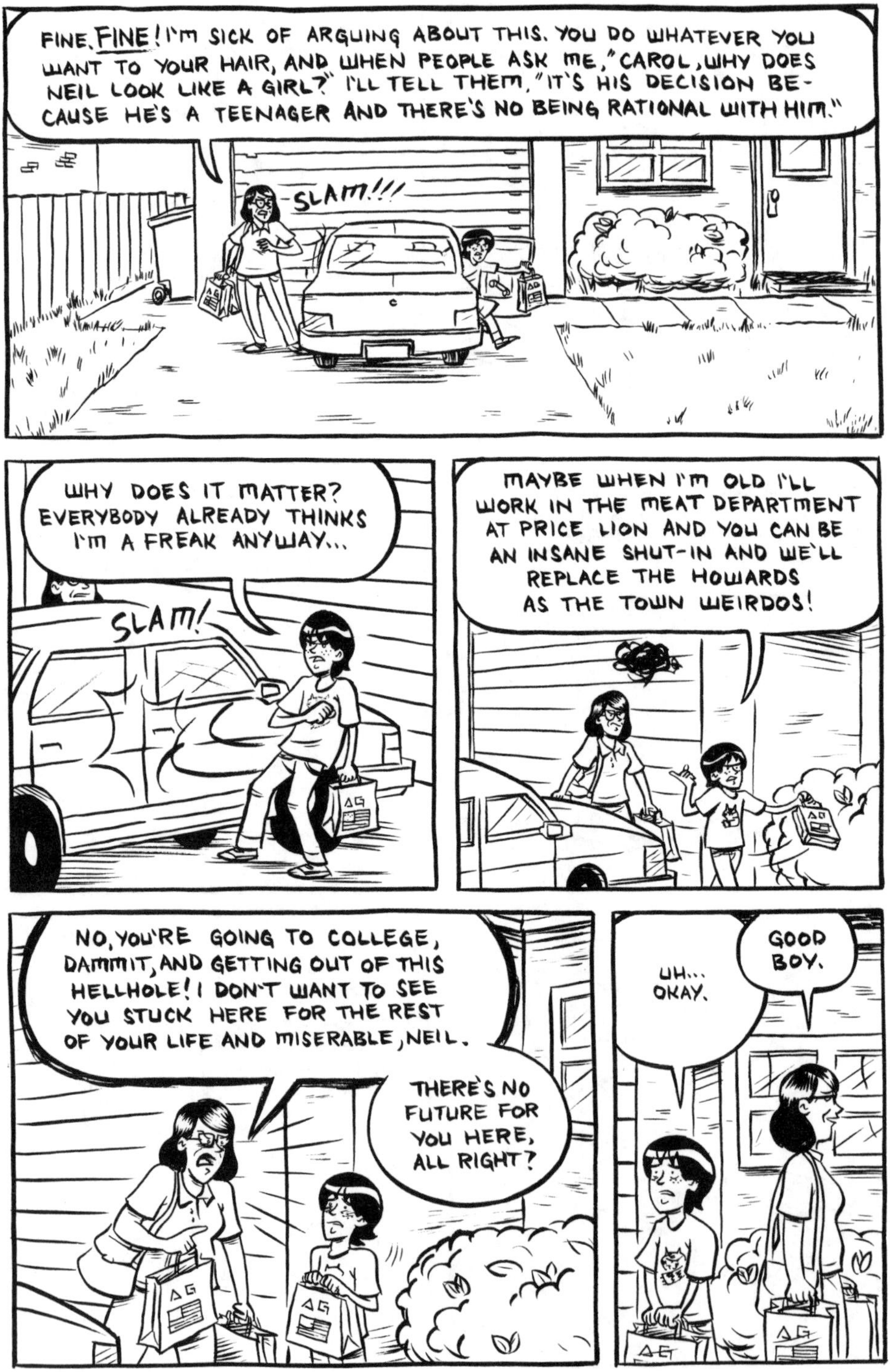

FINE. FINE! I'M SICK OF ARGUING ABOUT THIS. YOU DO WHATEVER YOU WANT TO YOUR HAIR, AND WHEN PEOPLE ASK ME, "CAROL, WHY DOES NEIL LOOK LIKE A GIRL?" I'LL TELL THEM, "IT'S HIS DECISION BECAUSE HE'S A TEENAGER AND THERE'S NO BEING RATIONAL WITH HIM."
SLAM!!!
WHY DOES IT MATTER? EVERYBODY ALREADY THINKS I'M A FREAK ANYWAY...
SLAM!
MAYBE WHEN I'M OLD I'LL WORK IN THE MEAT DEPARTMENT AT PRICE LION AND YOU CAN BE AN INSANE SHUT-IN AND WE'LL REPLACE THE HOWARDS AS THE TOWN WEIRDOS!
NO, YOU'RE GOING TO COLLEGE, DAMMIT, AND GETTING OUT OF THIS HELLHOLE! I DON'T WANT TO SEE YOU STUCK HERE FOR THE REST OF YOUR LIFE AND MISERABLE, NEIL.
THERE'S NO FUTURE FOR YOU HERE, ALL RIGHT?
UH... OKAY.
GOOD BOY.

CHAPTER 6

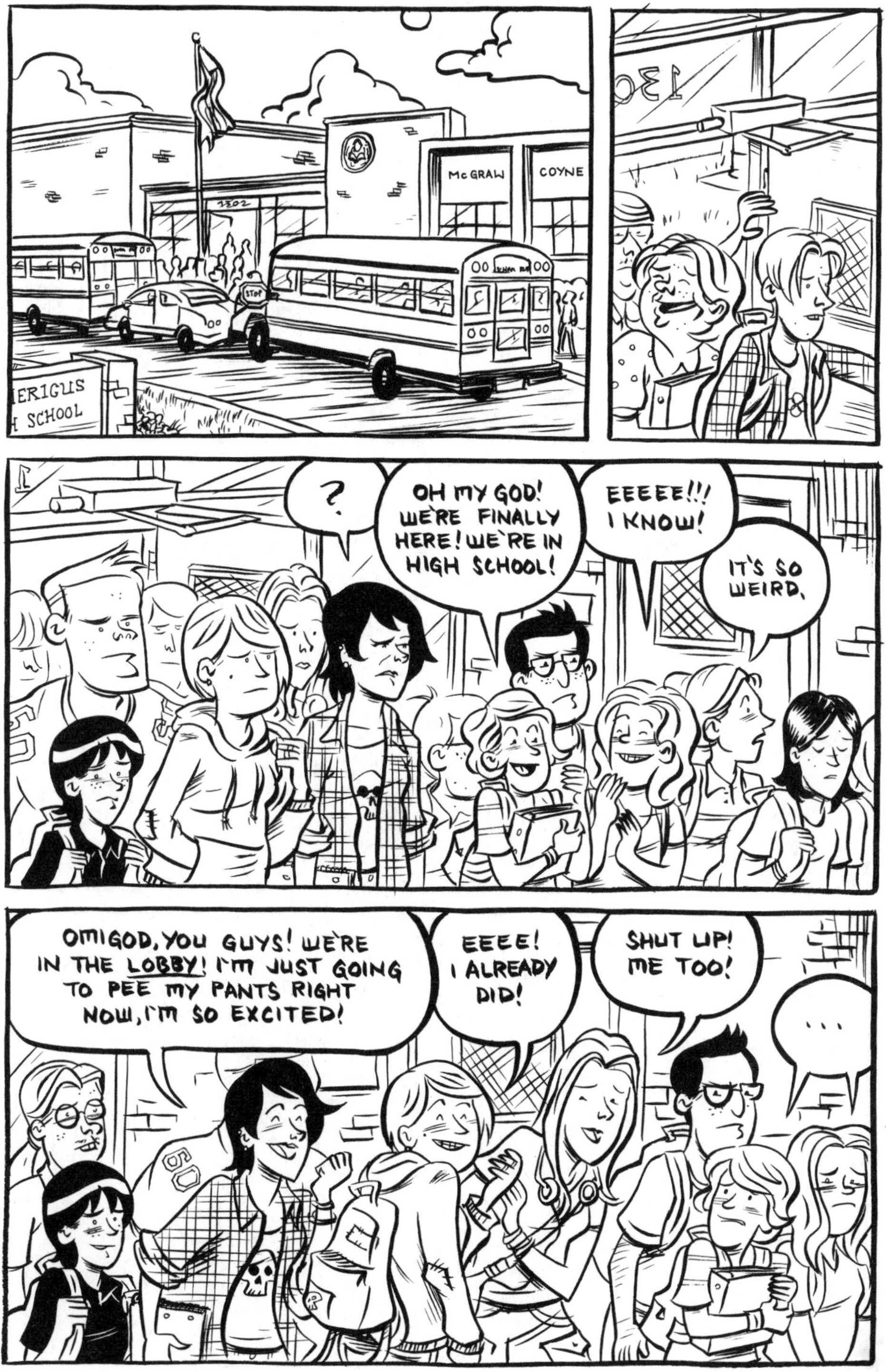
McGRAW
COYNE
1302
STOP
ERIGUS
H SCHOOL
?
OH MY GOD! WE'RE FINALLY HERE! WE'RE IN HIGH SCHOOL!
EEEEE!!! I KNOW!
IT'S SO WEIRD.
OMIGOD, YOU GUYS! WE'RE IN THE LOBBY! I'M JUST GOING TO PEE MY PANTS RIGHT NOW, I'M SO EXCITED!
EEEE! I ALREADY DID!
SHUT UP! ME TOO!
. . .

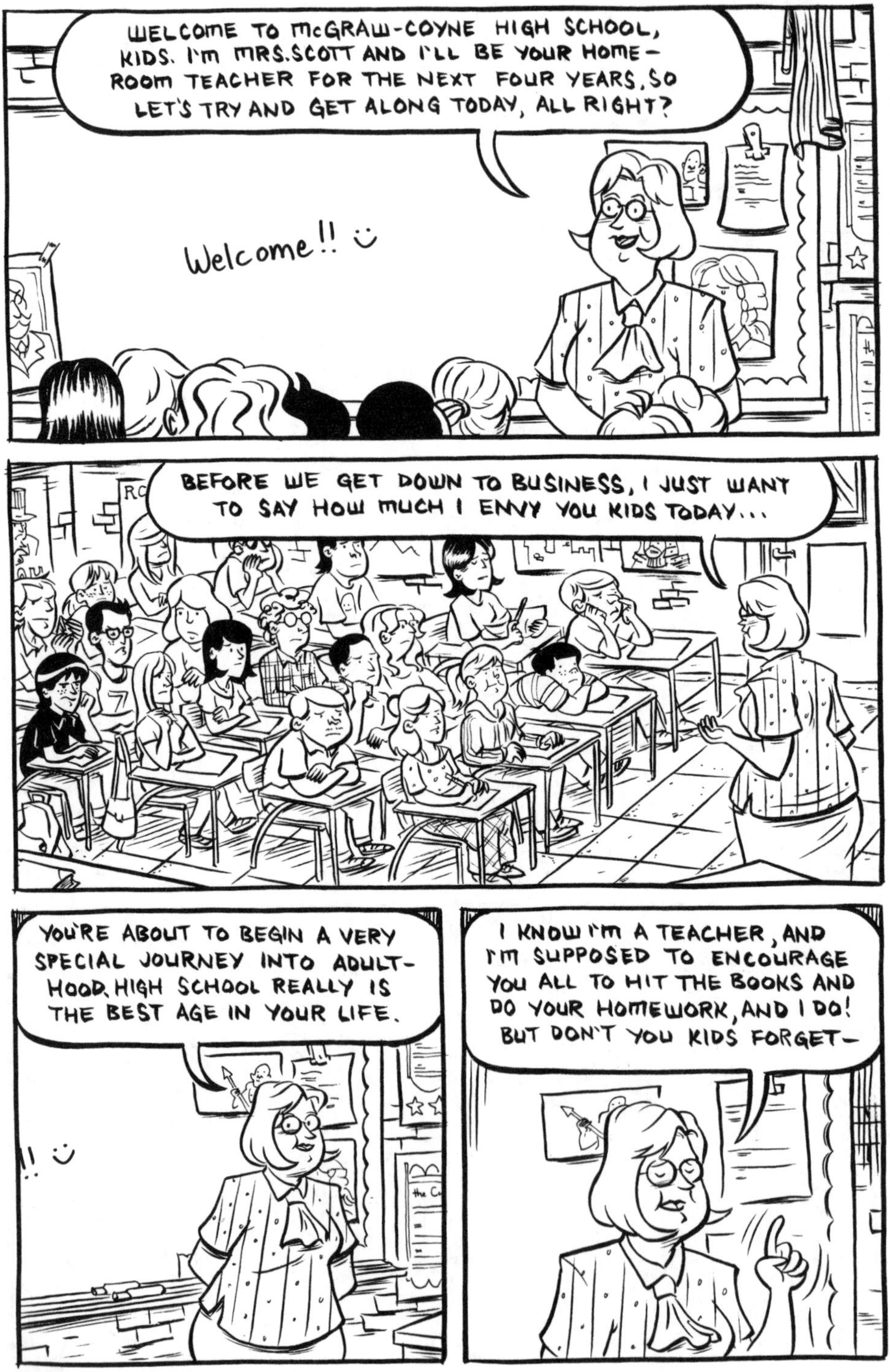
WELCOME TO McGRAW-COYNE HIGH SCHOOL, KIDS. I'M MRS. SCOTT AND I'LL BE YOUR HOME-ROOM TEACHER FOR THE NEXT FOUR YEARS, SO LET'S TRY AND GET ALONG TODAY, ALL RIGHT?
Welcome!! :)
BEFORE WE GET DOWN TO BUSINESS, I JUST WANT TO SAY HOW MUCH I ENVY YOU KIDS TODAY...
YOU'RE ABOUT TO BEGIN A VERY SPECIAL JOURNEY INTO ADULT-HOOD. HIGH SCHOOL REALLY IS THE BEST AGE IN YOUR LIFE.
I KNOW I'M A TEACHER, AND I'M SUPPOSED TO ENCOURAGE YOU ALL TO HIT THE BOOKS AND DO YOUR HOMEWORK, AND I DO! BUT DON'T YOU KIDS FORGET-

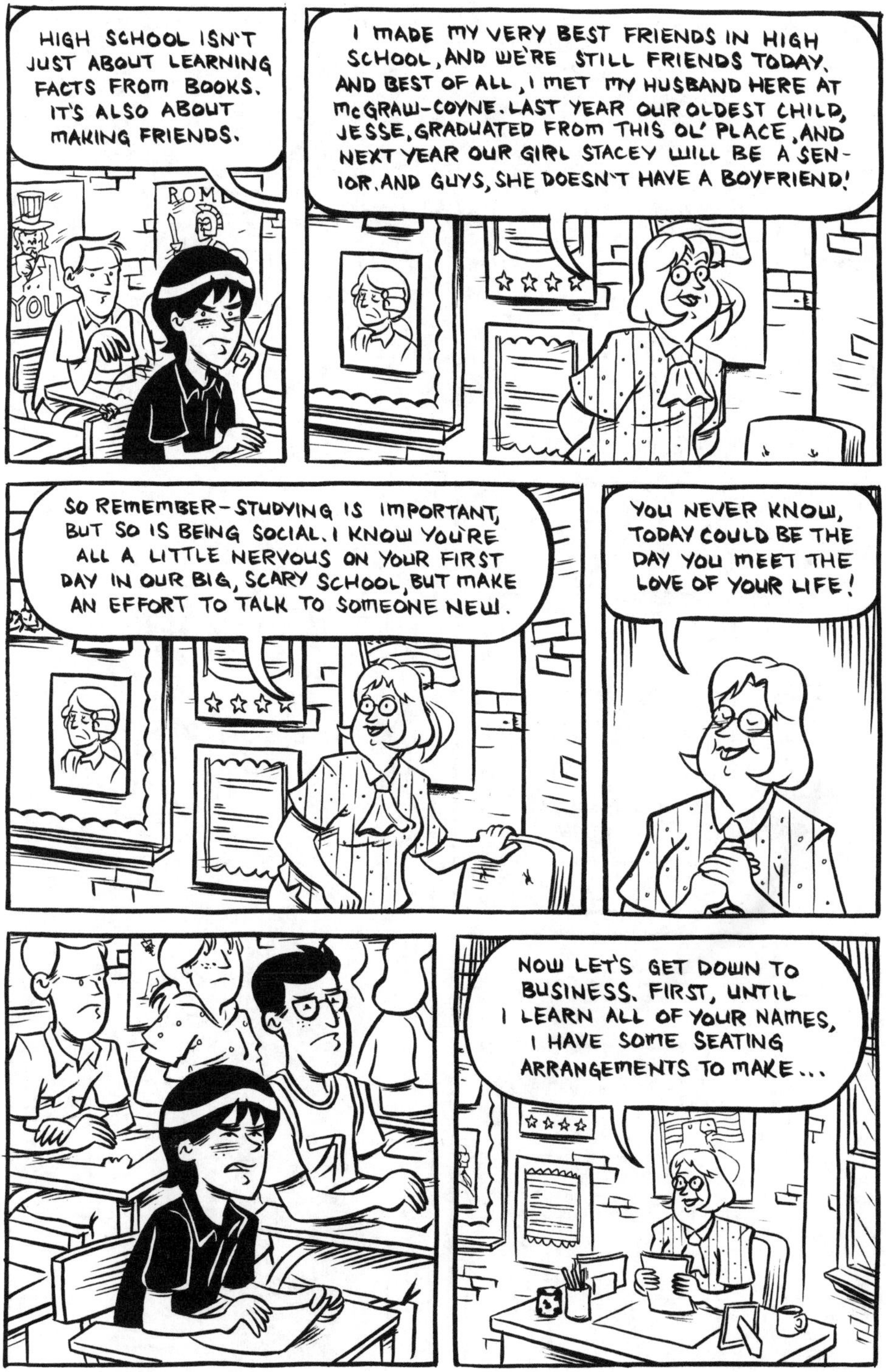
HIGH SCHOOL ISN'T JUST ABOUT LEARNING FACTS FROM BOOKS. IT'S ALSO ABOUT MAKING FRIENDS.
I MADE MY VERY BEST FRIENDS IN HIGH SCHOOL, AND WE'RE STILL FRIENDS TODAY. AND BEST OF ALL, I MET MY HUSBAND HERE AT McGRAW-COYNE. LAST YEAR OUR OLDEST CHILD, JESSE, GRADUATED FROM THIS OL' PLACE, AND NEXT YEAR OUR GIRL STACEY WILL BE A SENIOR. AND GUYS, SHE DOESN'T HAVE A BOYFRIEND!
SO REMEMBER—STUDYING IS IMPORTANT, BUT SO IS BEING SOCIAL. I KNOW YOU'RE ALL A LITTLE NERVOUS ON YOUR FIRST DAY IN OUR BIG, SCARY SCHOOL, BUT MAKE AN EFFORT TO TALK TO SOMEONE NEW.
YOU NEVER KNOW, TODAY COULD BE THE DAY YOU MEET THE LOVE OF YOUR LIFE!
NOW LET'S GET DOWN TO BUSINESS. FIRST, UNTIL I LEARN ALL OF YOUR NAMES, I HAVE SOME SEATING ARRANGEMENTS TO MAKE...

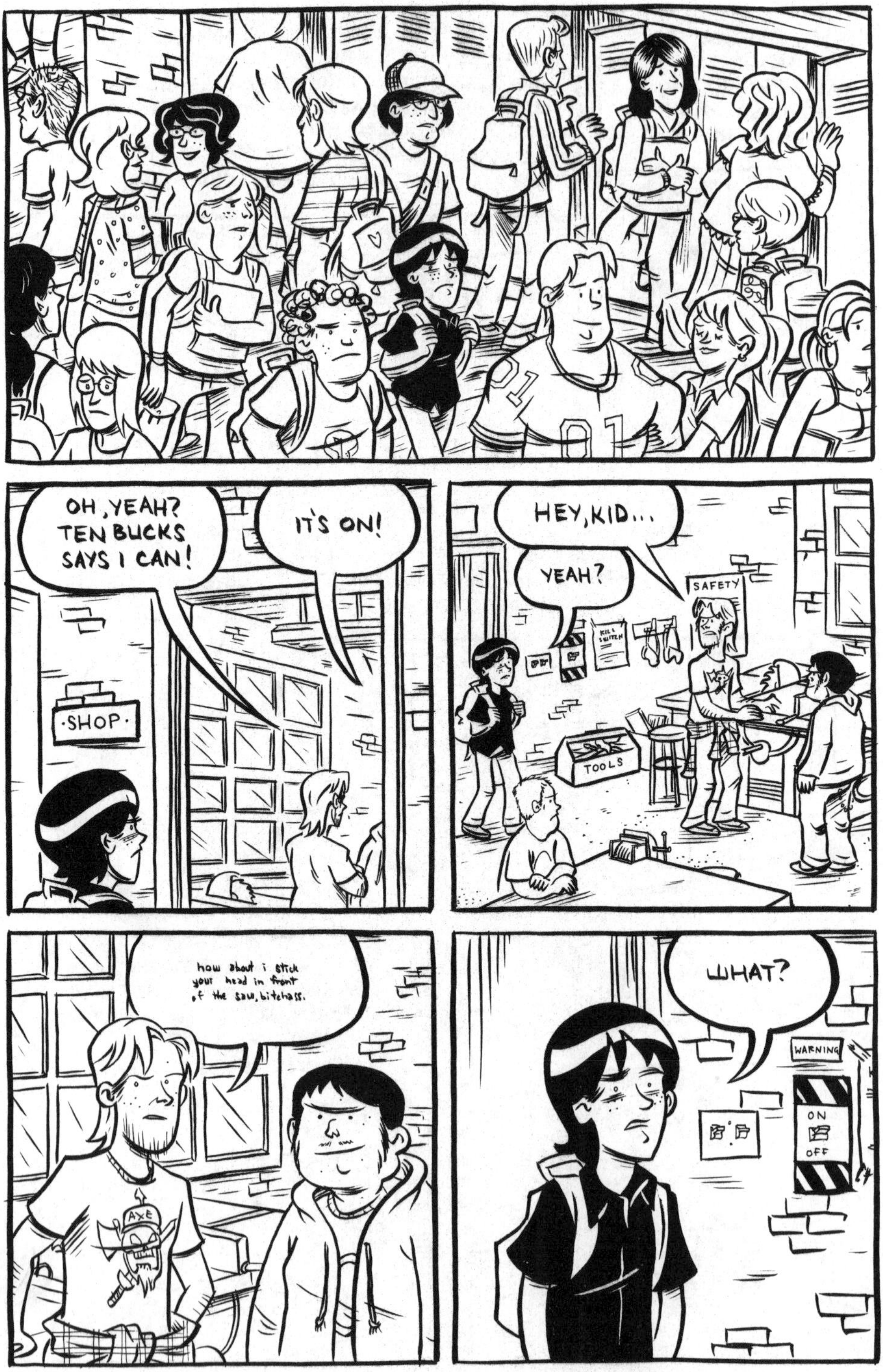
OH, YEAH? TEN BUCKS SAYS I CAN!
IT'S ON!
SHOP
HEY, KID...
YEAH?
SAFETY
TOOLS
how about i stick your head in front of the saw, bitchass.
WHAT?
WARNING
ON
OFF

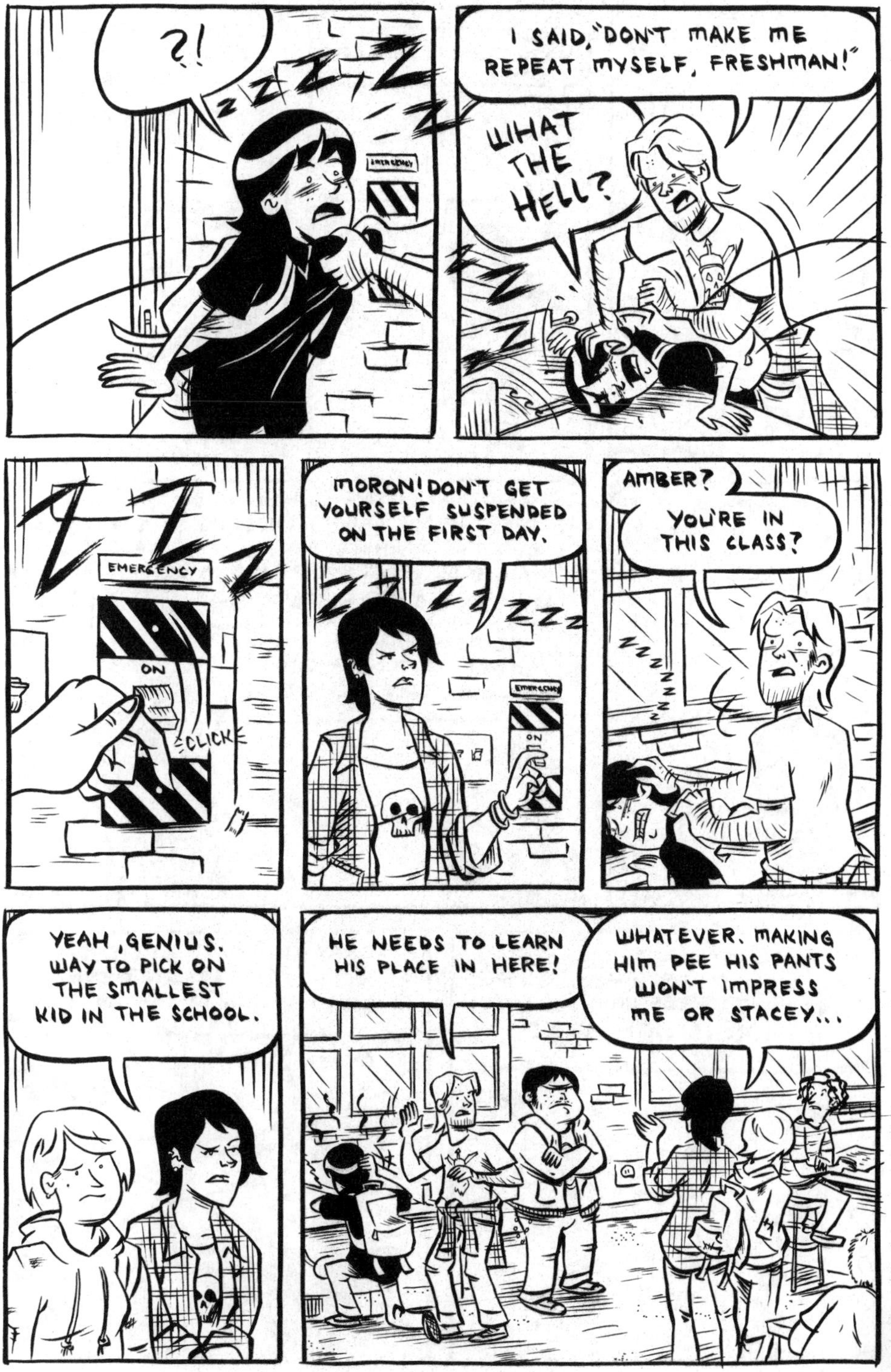
?!
I SAID, "DON'T MAKE ME REPEAT MYSELF, FRESHMAN!"
WHAT THE HELL?
EMERGENCY
ON
CLICK
MORON! DON'T GET YOURSELF SUSPENDED ON THE FIRST DAY.
AMBER?
YOU'RE IN THIS CLASS?
YEAH, GENIUS. WAY TO PICK ON THE SMALLEST KID IN THE SCHOOL.
HE NEEDS TO LEARN HIS PLACE IN HERE!
WHATEVER. MAKING HIM PEE HIS PANTS WON'T IMPRESS ME OR STACEY...

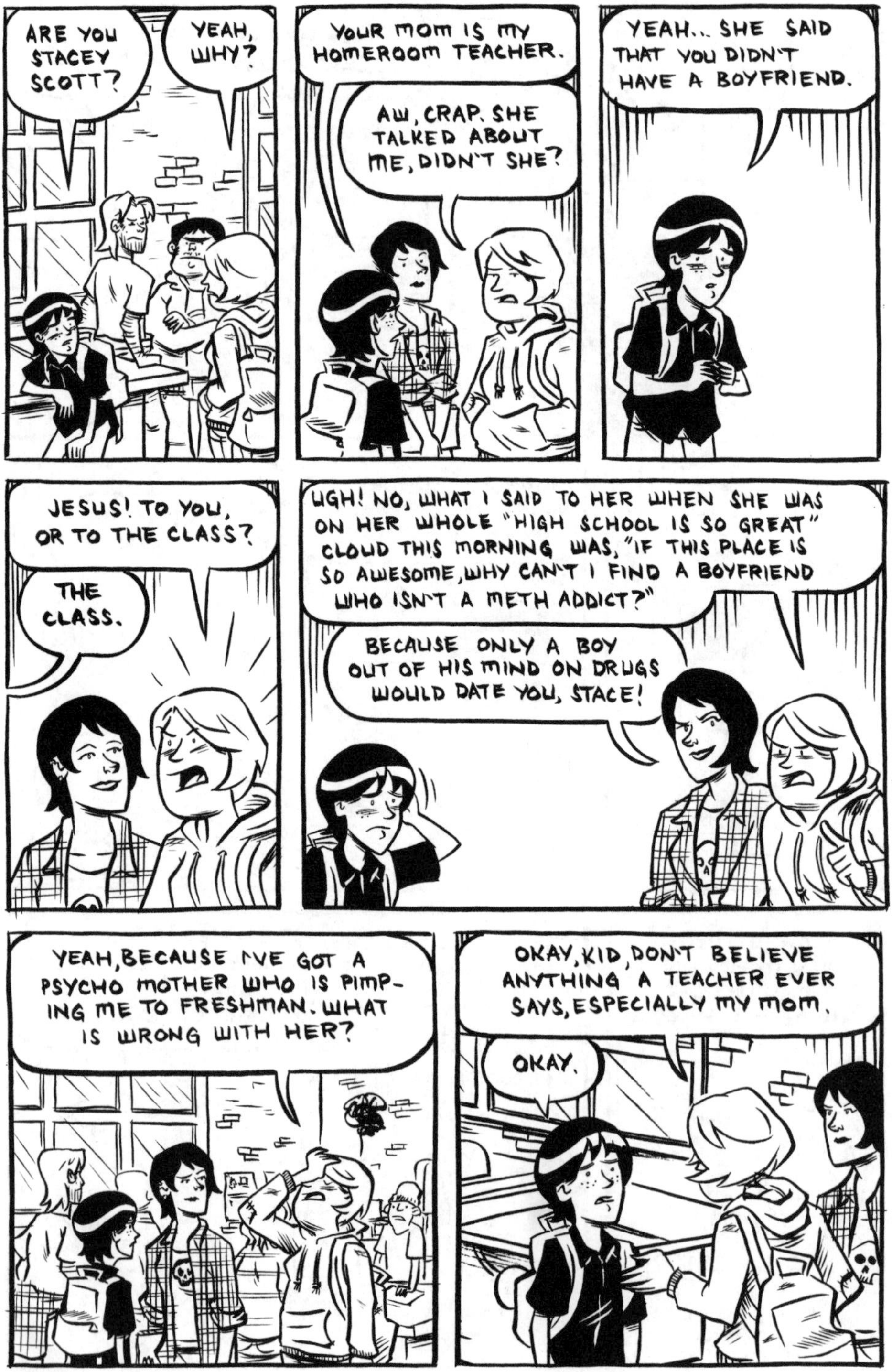
ARE YOU STACEY SCOTT?
YEAH, WHY?
YOUR MOM IS MY HOMEROOM TEACHER.
AW, CRAP. SHE TALKED ABOUT ME, DIDN'T SHE?
YEAH... SHE SAID THAT YOU DIDN'T HAVE A BOYFRIEND.
JESUS! TO YOU, OR TO THE CLASS?
THE CLASS.
UGH! NO, WHAT I SAID TO HER WHEN SHE WAS ON HER WHOLE "HIGH SCHOOL IS SO GREAT" CLOUD THIS MORNING WAS, "IF THIS PLACE IS SO AWESOME, WHY CAN'T I FIND A BOYFRIEND WHO ISN'T A METH ADDICT?"
BECAUSE ONLY A BOY OUT OF HIS MIND ON DRUGS WOULD DATE YOU, STACE!
YEAH, BECAUSE I'VE GOT A PSYCHO MOTHER WHO IS PIMP-ING ME TO FRESHMAN. WHAT IS WRONG WITH HER?
OKAY, KID, DON'T BELIEVE ANYTHING A TEACHER EVER SAYS, ESPECIALLY MY MOM.
OKAY.

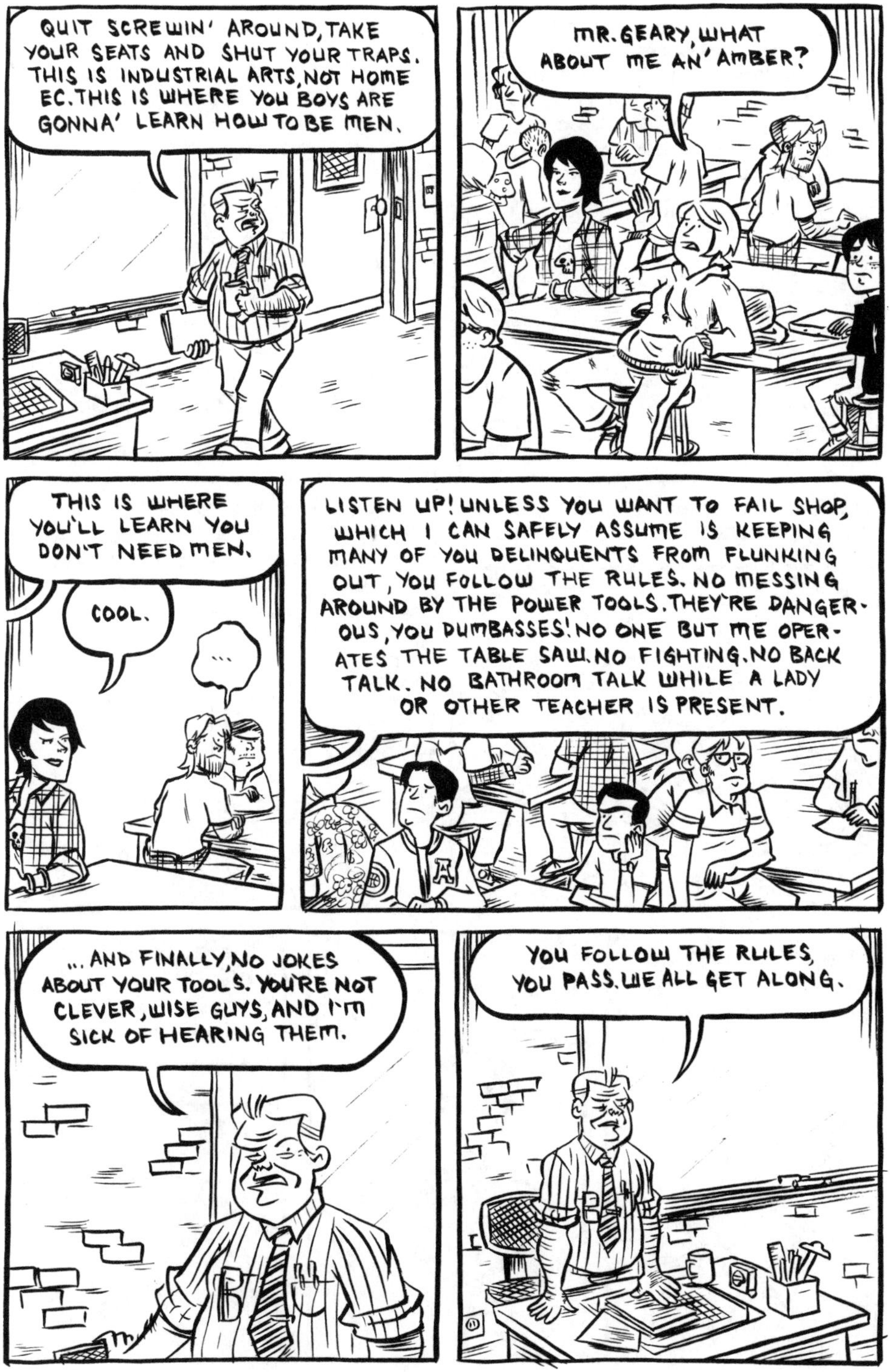
QUIT SCREWIN' AROUND, TAKE YOUR SEATS AND SHUT YOUR TRAPS. THIS IS INDUSTRIAL ARTS, NOT HOME EC. THIS IS WHERE YOU BOYS ARE GONNA' LEARN HOW TO BE MEN.
MR. GEARY, WHAT ABOUT ME AN' AMBER?
THIS IS WHERE YOU'LL LEARN YOU DON'T NEED MEN.
COOL.
...
LISTEN UP! UNLESS YOU WANT TO FAIL SHOP, WHICH I CAN SAFELY ASSUME IS KEEPING MANY OF YOU DELINQUENTS FROM FLUNKING OUT, YOU FOLLOW THE RULES. NO MESSING AROUND BY THE POWER TOOLS. THEY'RE DANGEROUS, YOU DUMBASSES! NO ONE BUT ME OPERATES THE TABLE SAW. NO FIGHTING. NO BACK TALK. NO BATHROOM TALK WHILE A LADY OR OTHER TEACHER IS PRESENT.
... AND FINALLY, NO JOKES ABOUT YOUR TOOLS. YOU'RE NOT CLEVER, WISE GUYS, AND I'M SICK OF HEARING THEM.
YOU FOLLOW THE RULES, YOU PASS. WE ALL GET ALONG.

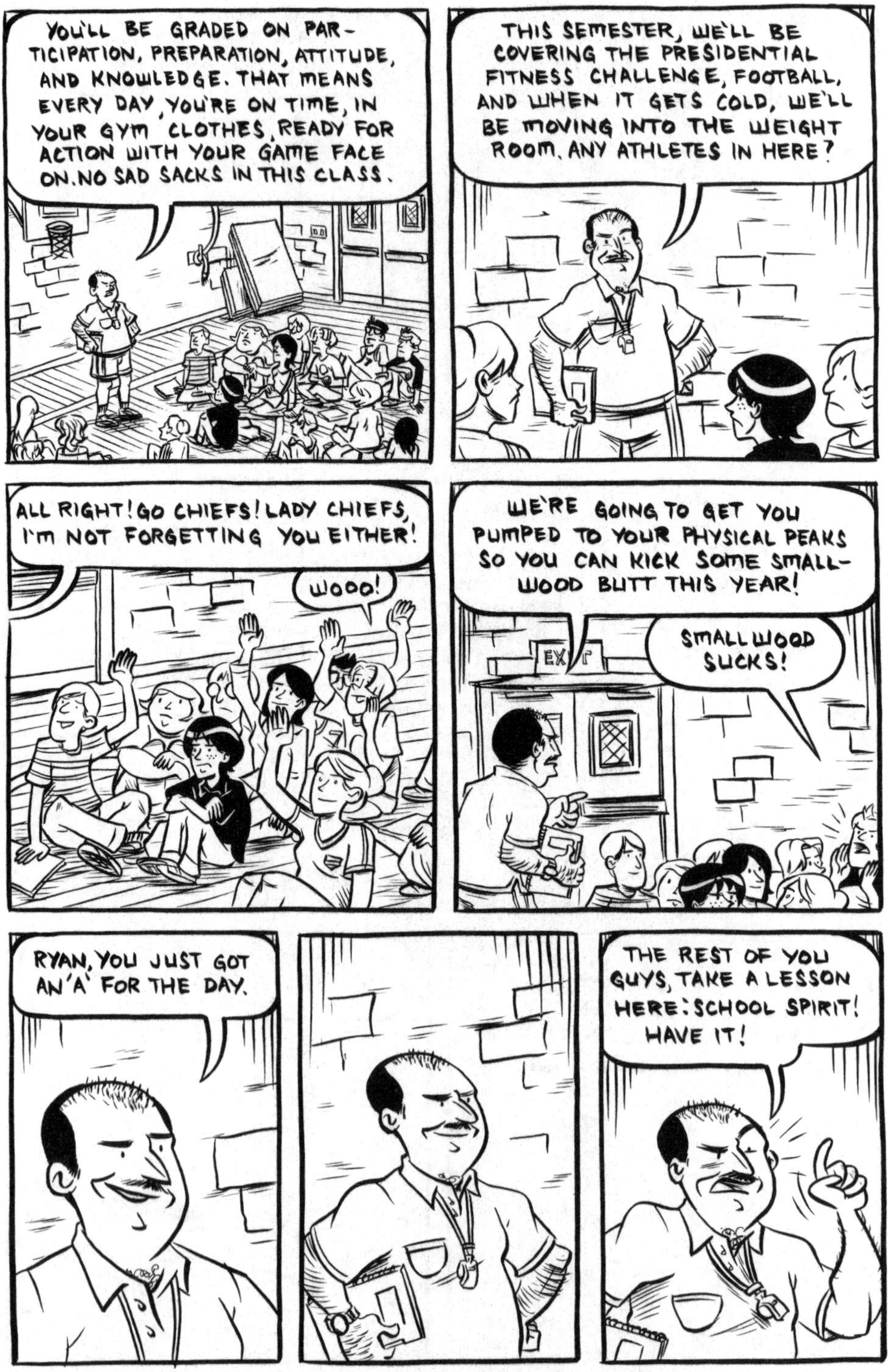
YOU'LL BE GRADED ON PARTICIPATION, PREPARATION, ATTITUDE, AND KNOWLEDGE. THAT MEANS EVERY DAY, YOU'RE ON TIME, IN YOUR GYM CLOTHES, READY FOR ACTION WITH YOUR GAME FACE ON. NO SAD SACKS IN THIS CLASS.
THIS SEMESTER, WE'LL BE COVERING THE PRESIDENTIAL FITNESS CHALLENGE, FOOTBALL, AND WHEN IT GETS COLD, WE'LL BE MOVING INTO THE WEIGHT ROOM. ANY ATHLETES IN HERE?
ALL RIGHT! GO CHIEFS! LADY CHIEFS, I'M NOT FORGETTING YOU EITHER!
WOOO!
WE'RE GOING TO GET YOU PUMPED TO YOUR PHYSICAL PEAKS SO YOU CAN KICK SOME SMALLWOOD BUTT THIS YEAR!
SMALLWOOD SUCKS!
RYAN, YOU JUST GOT AN 'A' FOR THE DAY.
THE REST OF YOU GUYS, TAKE A LESSON HERE: SCHOOL SPIRIT! HAVE IT!

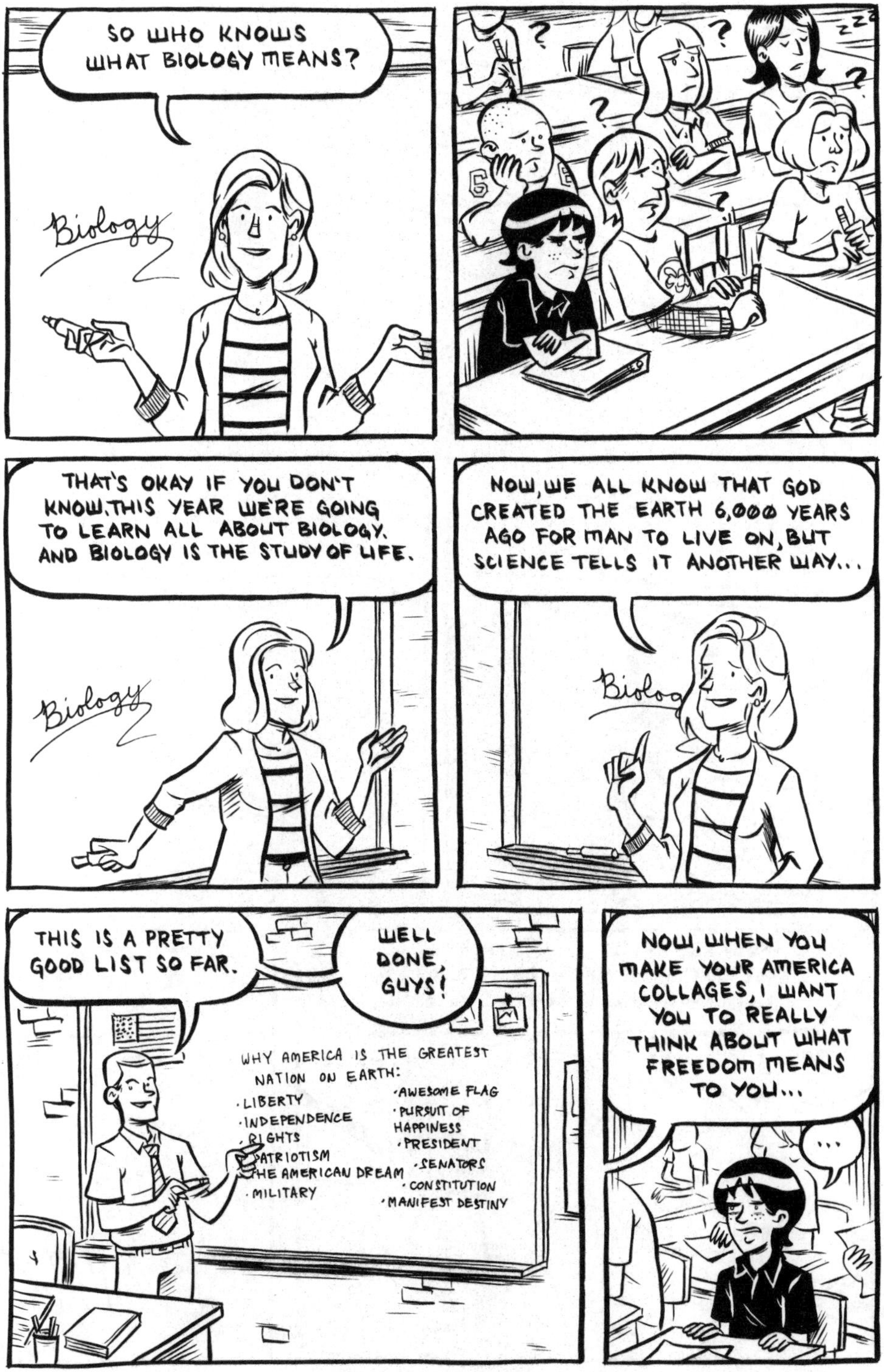
SO WHO KNOWS WHAT BIOLOGY MEANS?
Biology
THAT'S OKAY IF YOU DON'T KNOW. THIS YEAR WE'RE GOING TO LEARN ALL ABOUT BIOLOGY. AND BIOLOGY IS THE STUDY OF LIFE.
Biology
NOW, WE ALL KNOW THAT GOD CREATED THE EARTH 6,000 YEARS AGO FOR MAN TO LIVE ON, BUT SCIENCE TELLS IT ANOTHER WAY...
THIS IS A PRETTY GOOD LIST SO FAR.
WELL DONE, GUYS!
WHY AMERICA IS THE GREATEST NATION ON EARTH:
·LIBERTY
·INDEPENDENCE
·RIGHTS
·PATRIOTISM
·THE AMERICAN DREAM
·MILITARY
·AWESOME FLAG
·PURSUIT OF HAPPINESS
·PRESIDENT
·SENATORS
·CONSTITUTION
·MANIFEST DESTINY
NOW, WHEN YOU MAKE YOUR AMERICA COLLAGES, I WANT YOU TO REALLY THINK ABOUT WHAT FREEDOM MEANS TO YOU...
...

BONJOUR, CLASSE! JE M'APPELLE MADAME SAUNDERS. JE SUIS VOTRE PROFESSEUR DE FRANÇAIS.

PLEASE RAISE YOUR HANDS AS I CALL OUT YOUR NAME. DAVID ANDERSON. ...NEIL BARTON...HANNAH COULTER...

HERE.

HERE.

HERE.

PARIS

UH, I'M NOT SURE HOW YOU SAY THIS ONE... "JAIL"?

FRENCH I · PERIOD P
DAVID ANDERSON
NEIL BARTON
HANNAH COULTER
JAEL DeSELBY
LLY DRAKE
JENNIFER FAZIO
RDAN FYSH
ER GEENE
ILYN HOWARD
TIN KUROWSKI
NEWMAN
ROOKE PEETE
LEE PRESTON

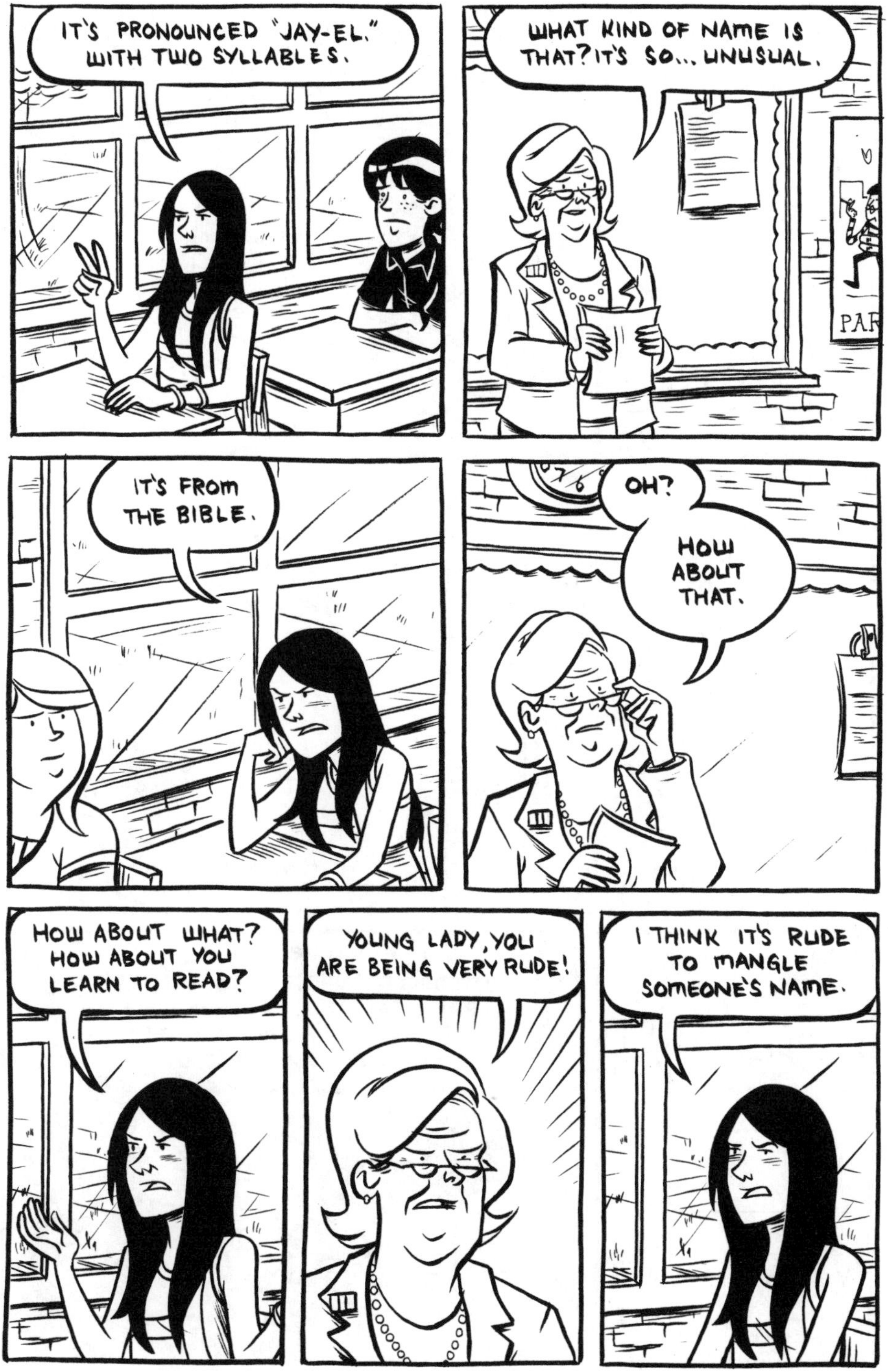
IT'S PRONOUNCED "JAY-EL," WITH TWO SYLLABLES.
WHAT KIND OF NAME IS THAT? IT'S SO... UNUSUAL.
PAR
IT'S FROM THE BIBLE.
OH?
HOW ABOUT THAT.
HOW ABOUT WHAT? HOW ABOUT YOU LEARN TO READ?
YOUNG LADY, YOU ARE BEING VERY RUDE!
I THINK IT'S RUDE TO MANGLE SOMEONE'S NAME.

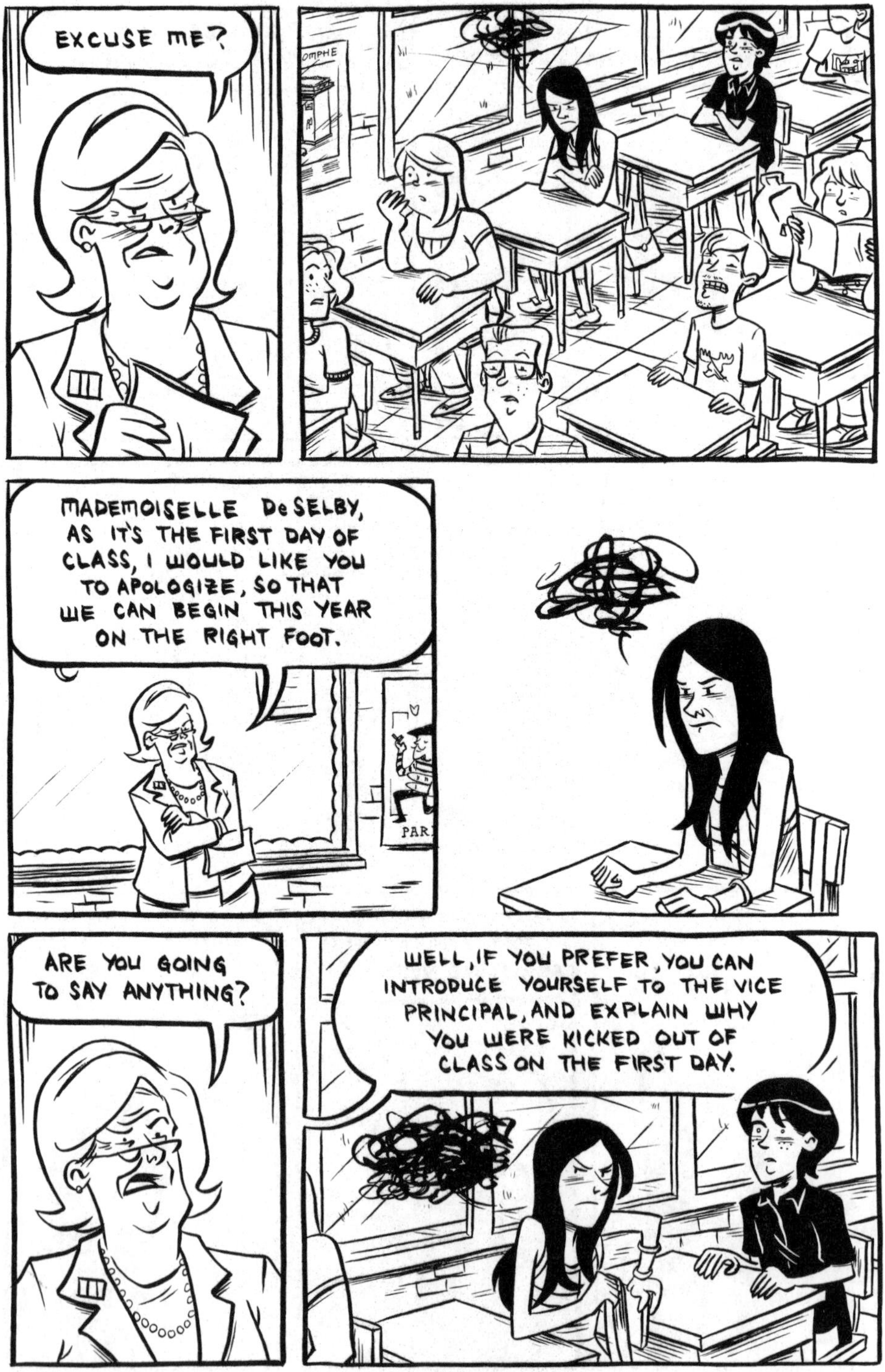
EXCUSE ME?
OMPHE
MADEMOISELLE De SELBY, AS IT'S THE FIRST DAY OF CLASS, I WOULD LIKE YOU TO APOLOGIZE, SO THAT WE CAN BEGIN THIS YEAR ON THE RIGHT FOOT.
PARI
ARE YOU GOING TO SAY ANYTHING?
WELL, IF YOU PREFER, YOU CAN INTRODUCE YOURSELF TO THE VICE PRINCIPAL, AND EXPLAIN WHY YOU WERE KICKED OUT OF CLASS ON THE FIRST DAY.

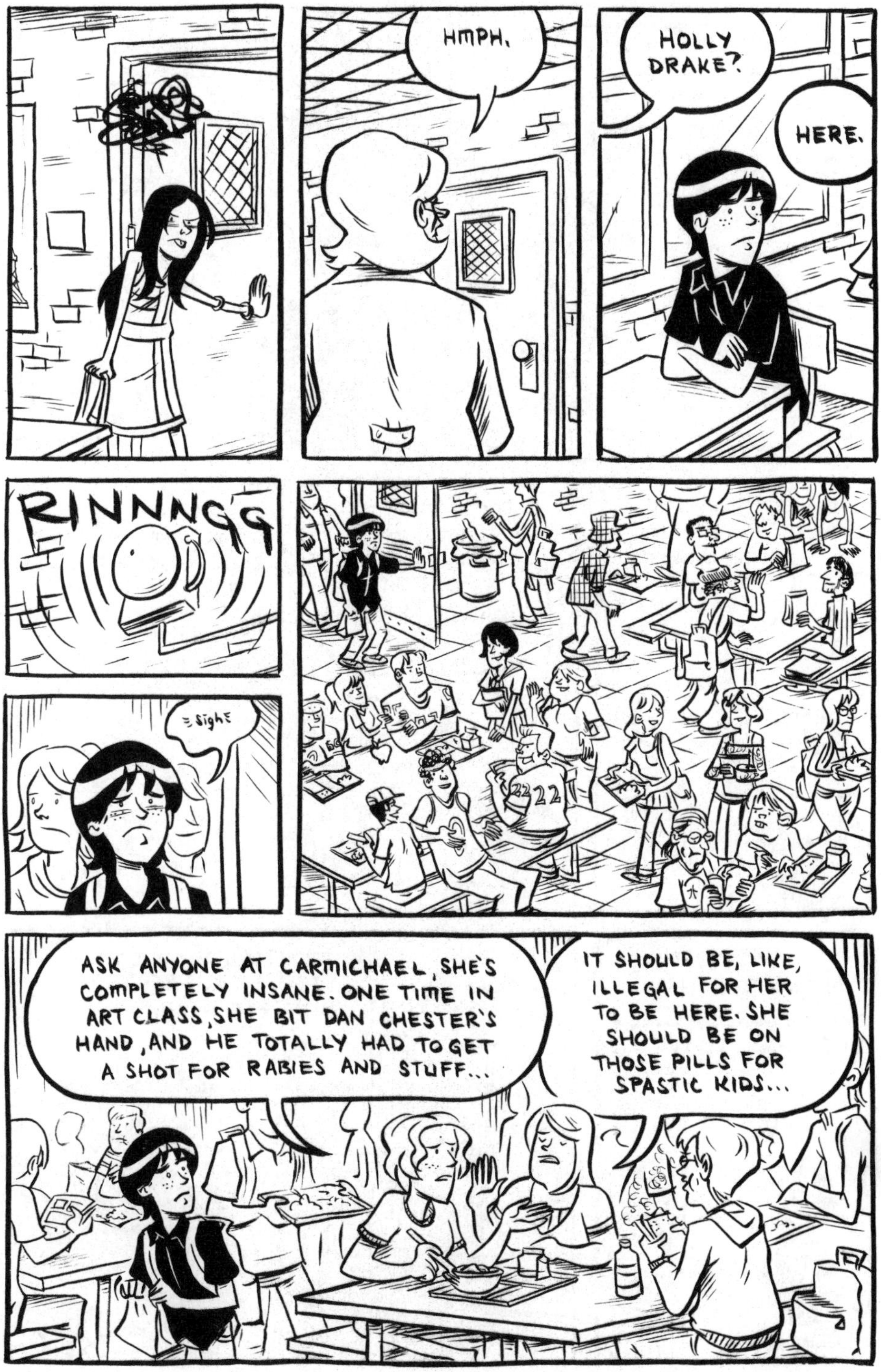
HMPH.
HOLLY DRAKE?
HERE.
RINNNGG
sigh
ASK ANYONE AT CARMICHAEL, SHE'S COMPLETELY INSANE. ONE TIME IN ART CLASS, SHE BIT DAN CHESTER'S HAND, AND HE TOTALLY HAD TO GET A SHOT FOR RABIES AND STUFF...
IT SHOULD BE, LIKE, ILLEGAL FOR HER TO BE HERE. SHE SHOULD BE ON THOSE PILLS FOR SPASTIC KIDS...

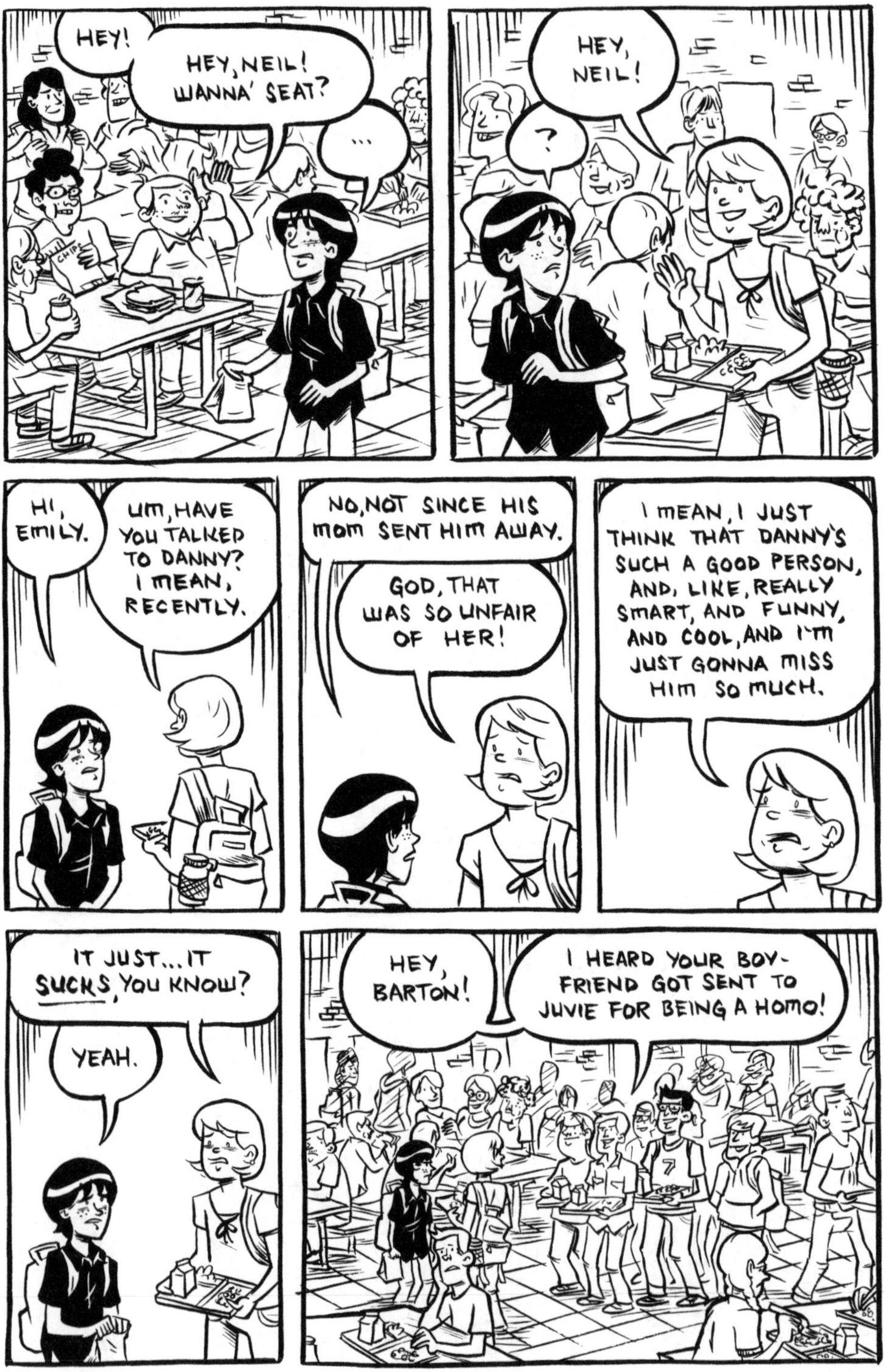
HEY!
HEY, NEIL! WANNA' SEAT?
...
HEY, NEIL!
?
HI, EMILY.
UM, HAVE YOU TALKED TO DANNY? I MEAN, RECENTLY.
NO, NOT SINCE HIS MOM SENT HIM AWAY.
GOD, THAT WAS SO UNFAIR OF HER!
I MEAN, I JUST THINK THAT DANNY'S SUCH A GOOD PERSON, AND, LIKE, REALLY SMART, AND FUNNY, AND COOL, AND I'M JUST GONNA MISS HIM SO MUCH.
IT JUST... IT SUCKS, YOU KNOW?
YEAH.
HEY, BARTON!
I HEARD YOUR BOY-FRIEND GOT SENT TO JUVIE FOR BEING A HOMO!

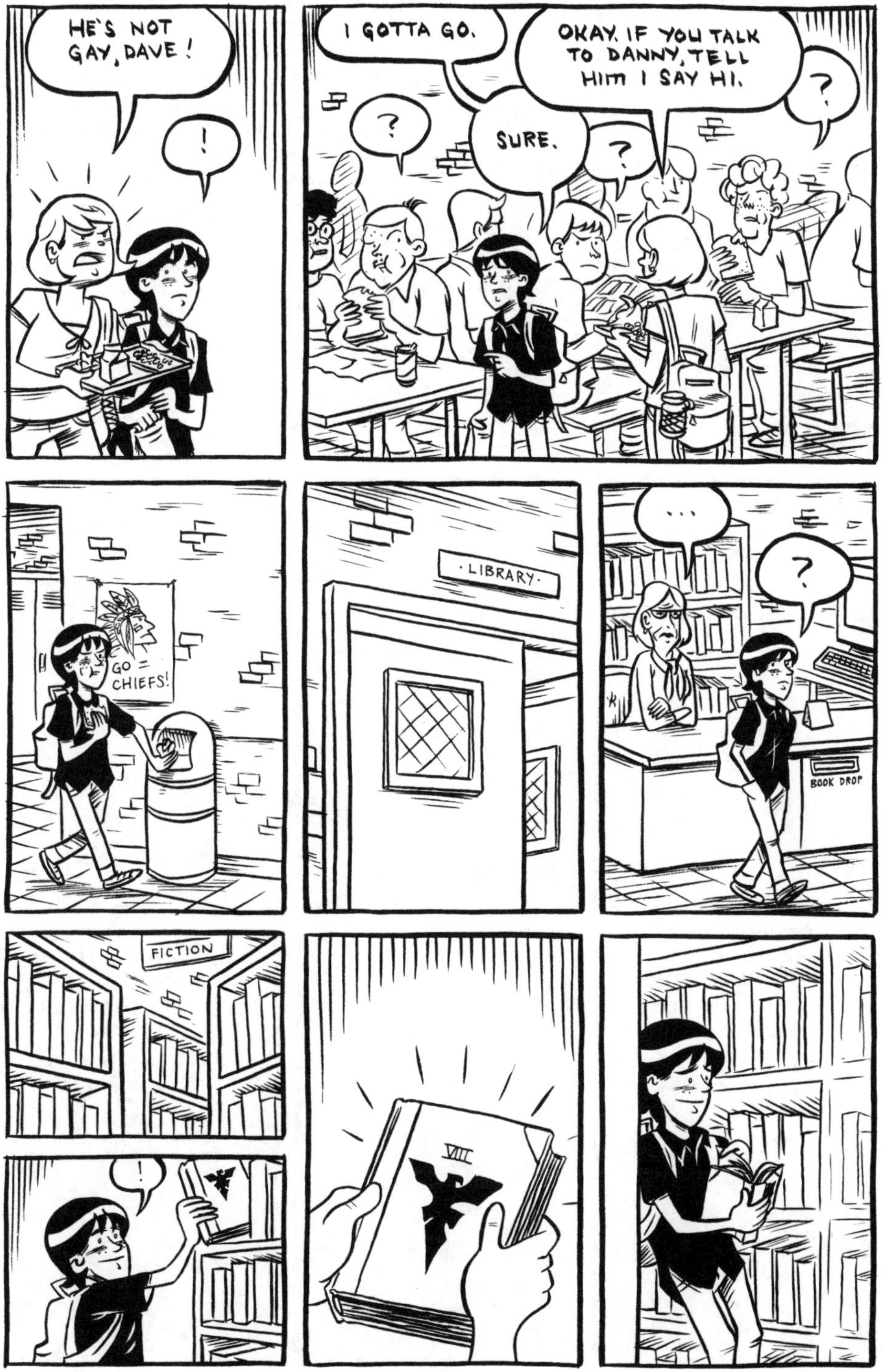

HE'S NOT GAY, DAVE!
!
I GOTTA GO.
OKAY. IF YOU TALK TO DANNY, TELL HIM I SAY HI.
?
SURE.
?
?
GO CHIEFS!
·LIBRARY·
...
?
BOOK DROP
FICTION
!
VIII

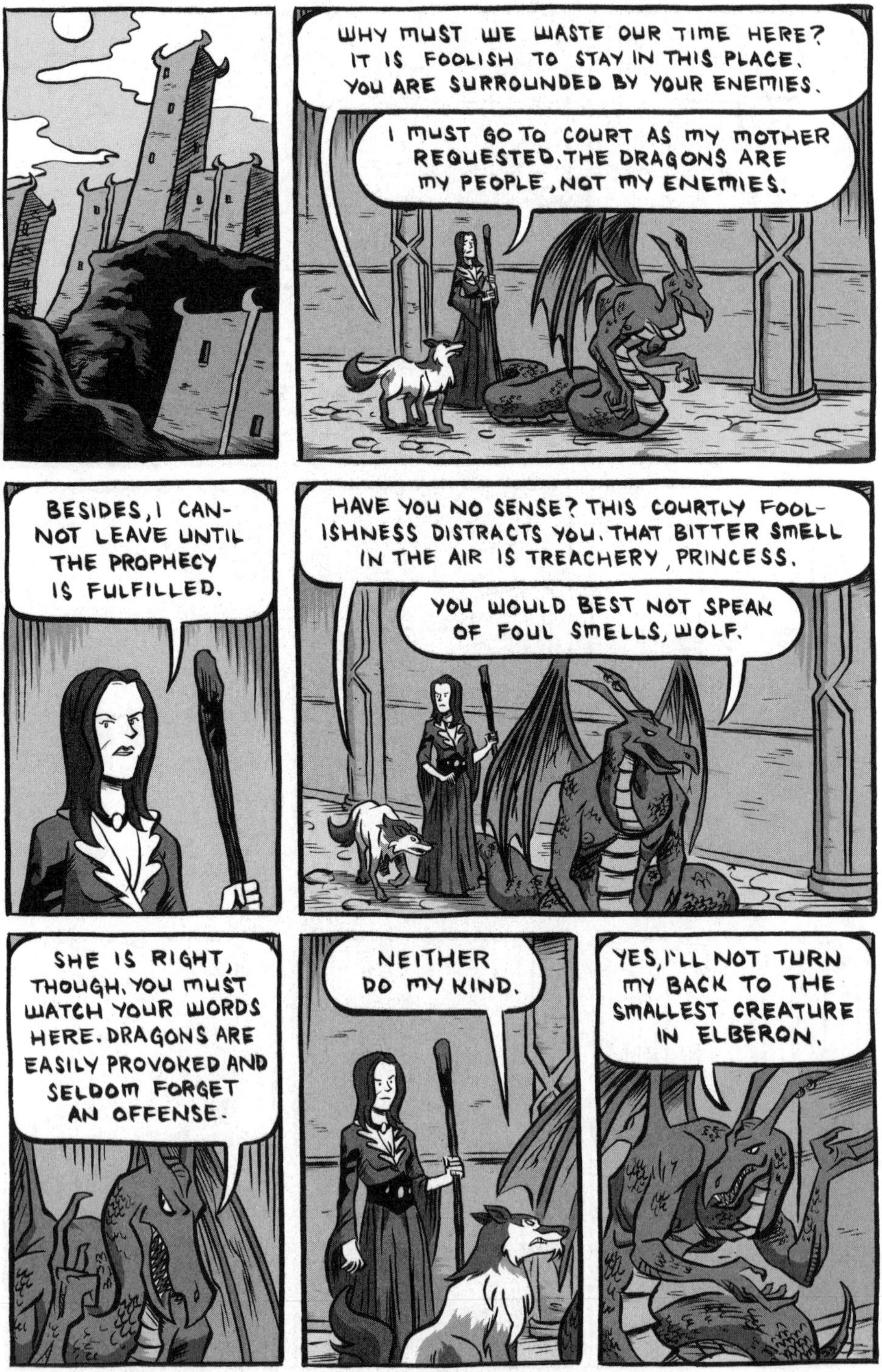
WHY MUST WE WASTE OUR TIME HERE? IT IS FOOLISH TO STAY IN THIS PLACE. YOU ARE SURROUNDED BY YOUR ENEMIES.
I MUST GO TO COURT AS MY MOTHER REQUESTED. THE DRAGONS ARE MY PEOPLE, NOT MY ENEMIES.
BESIDES, I CAN-NOT LEAVE UNTIL THE PROPHECY IS FULFILLED.
HAVE YOU NO SENSE? THIS COURTLY FOOL-ISHNESS DISTRACTS YOU. THAT BITTER SMELL IN THE AIR IS TREACHERY, PRINCESS.
YOU WOULD BEST NOT SPEAK OF FOUL SMELLS, WOLF.
SHE IS RIGHT, THOUGH. YOU MUST WATCH YOUR WORDS HERE. DRAGONS ARE EASILY PROVOKED AND SELDOM FORGET AN OFFENSE.
NEITHER DO MY KIND.
YES, I'LL NOT TURN MY BACK TO THE SMALLEST CREATURE IN ELBERON.

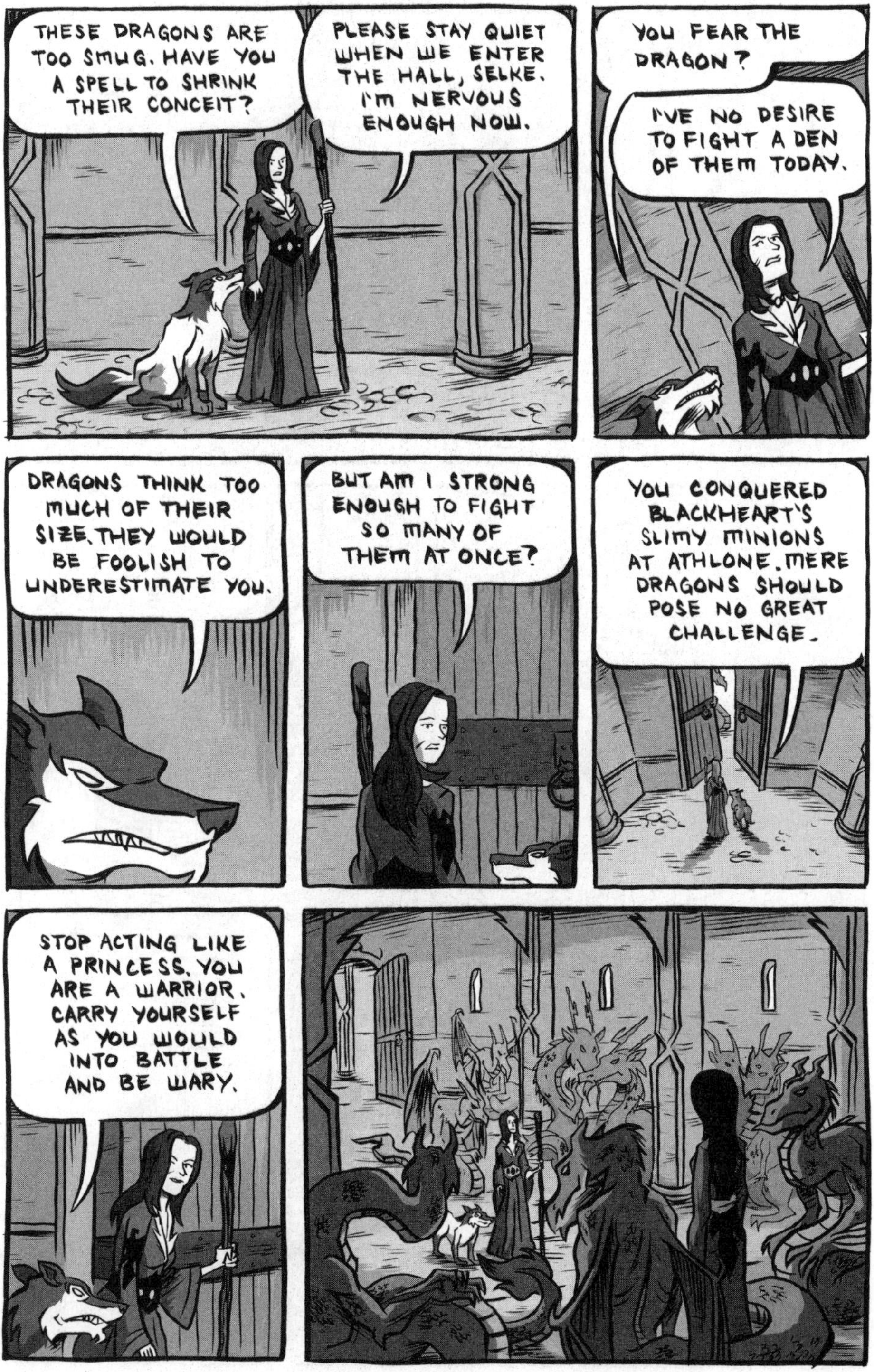
THESE DRAGONS ARE TOO SMUG. HAVE YOU A SPELL TO SHRINK THEIR CONCEIT?
PLEASE STAY QUIET WHEN WE ENTER THE HALL, SELKE. I'M NERVOUS ENOUGH NOW.
YOU FEAR THE DRAGON?
I'VE NO DESIRE TO FIGHT A DEN OF THEM TODAY.
DRAGONS THINK TOO MUCH OF THEIR SIZE. THEY WOULD BE FOOLISH TO UNDERESTIMATE YOU.
BUT AM I STRONG ENOUGH TO FIGHT SO MANY OF THEM AT ONCE?
YOU CONQUERED BLACKHEART'S SLIMY MINIONS AT ATHLONE. MERE DRAGONS SHOULD POSE NO GREAT CHALLENGE.
STOP ACTING LIKE A PRINCESS. YOU ARE A WARRIOR. CARRY YOURSELF AS YOU WOULD INTO BATTLE AND BE WARY.

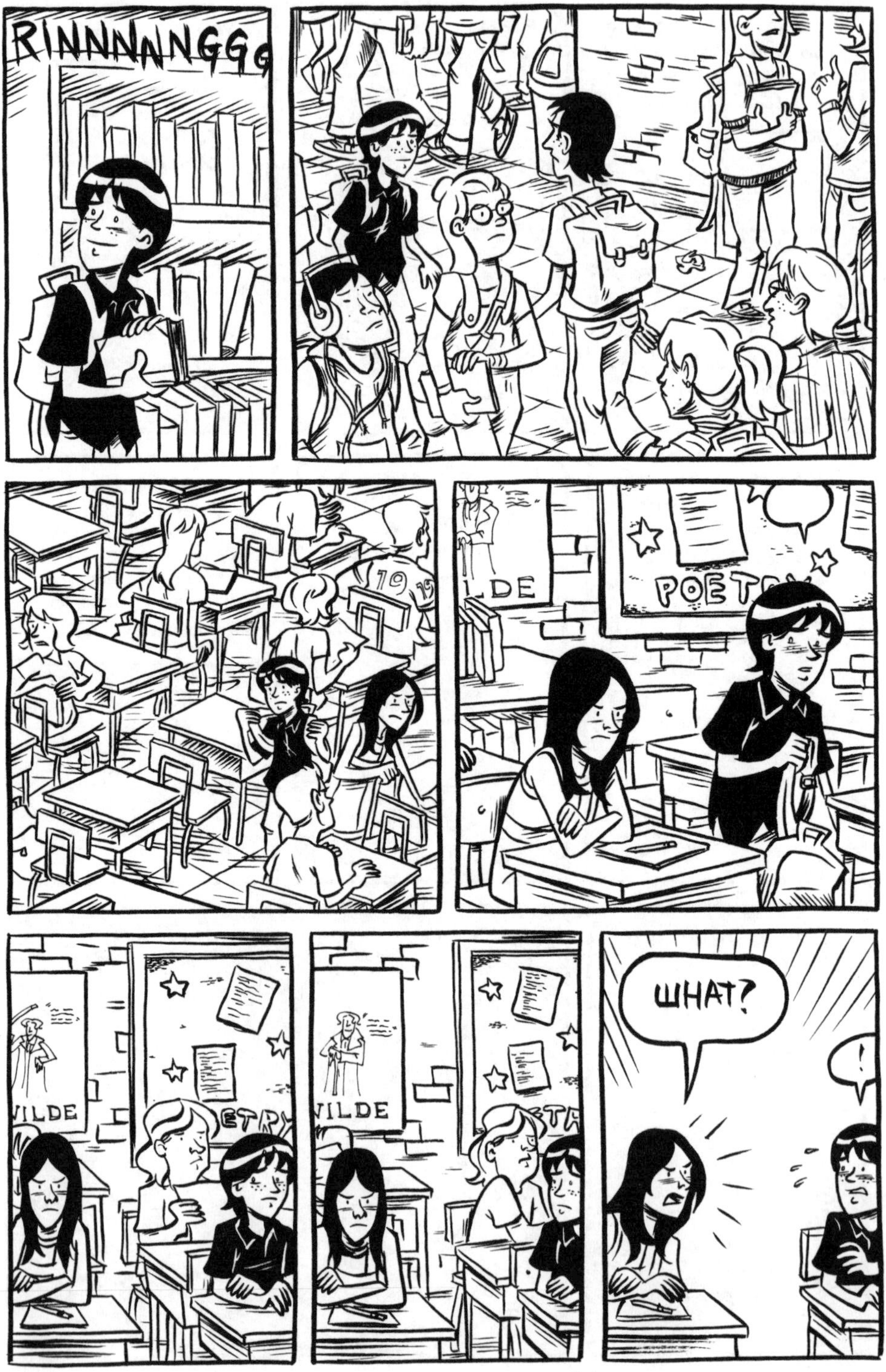
RINNNNNGGG
WILDE
POETRY
WILDE
WILDE
WHAT?
!

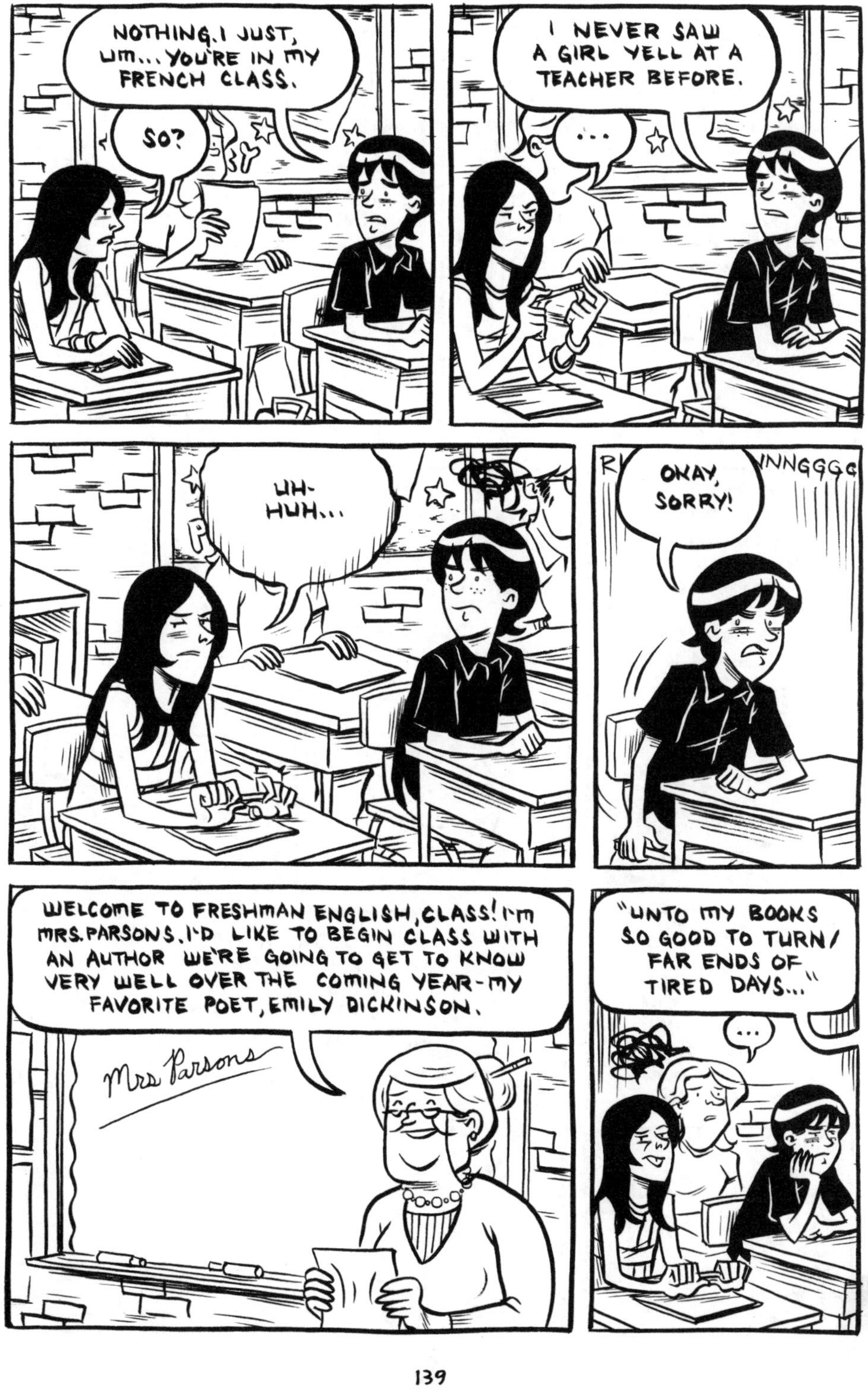
NOTHING. I JUST, UM... YOU'RE IN MY FRENCH CLASS.
SO?
I NEVER SAW A GIRL YELL AT A TEACHER BEFORE.
...
UH-HUH...
OKAY, SORRY!
WELCOME TO FRESHMAN ENGLISH, CLASS! I'M MRS. PARSONS. I'D LIKE TO BEGIN CLASS WITH AN AUTHOR WE'RE GOING TO GET TO KNOW VERY WELL OVER THE COMING YEAR- MY FAVORITE POET, EMILY DICKINSON.
Mrs Parsons
"UNTO MY BOOKS SO GOOD TO TURN/ FAR ENDS OF TIRED DAYS..."
...

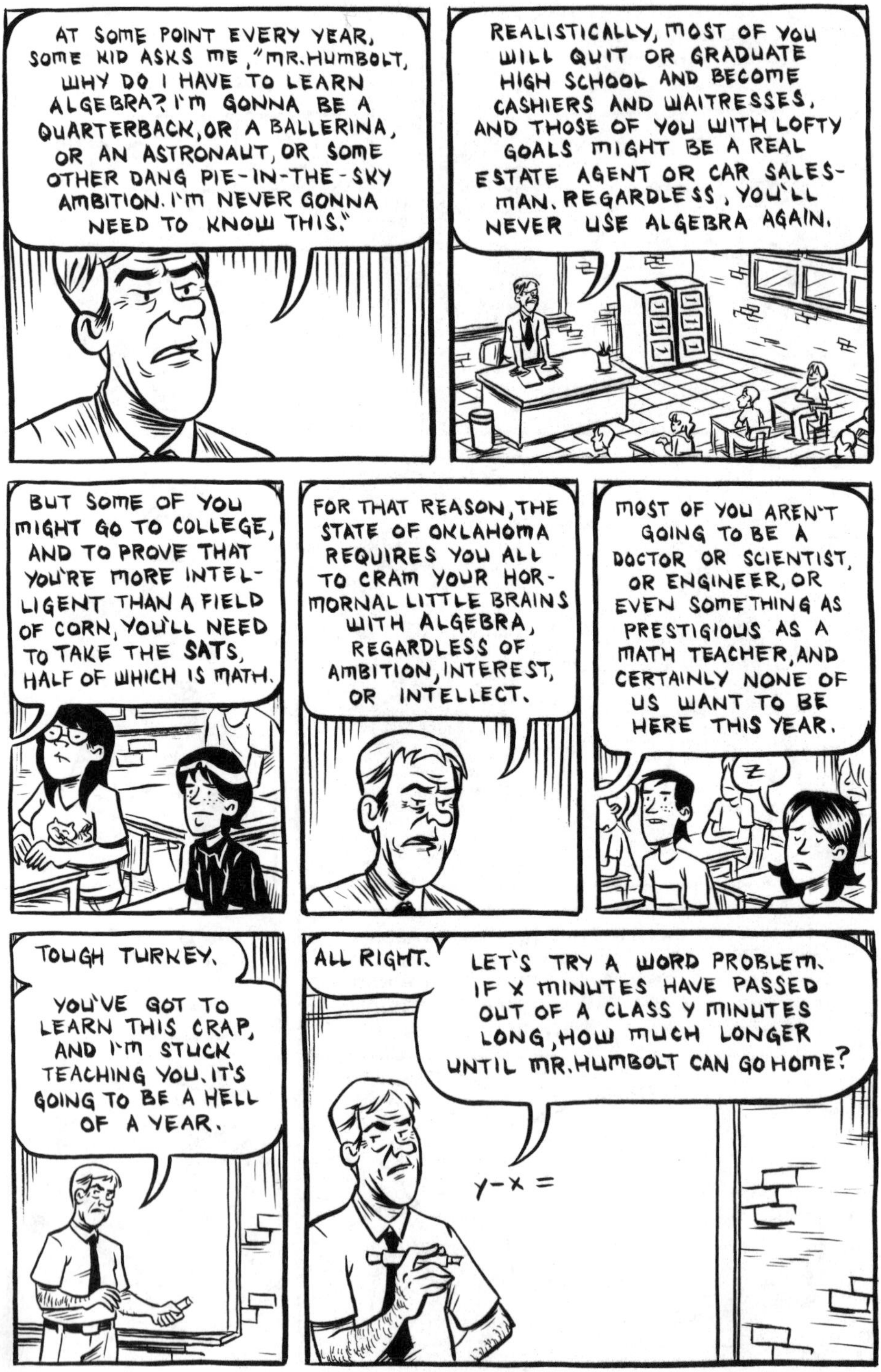
AT SOME POINT EVERY YEAR, SOME KID ASKS ME, "MR. HUMBOLT, WHY DO I HAVE TO LEARN ALGEBRA? I'M GONNA BE A QUARTERBACK, OR A BALLERINA, OR AN ASTRONAUT, OR SOME OTHER DANG PIE-IN-THE-SKY AMBITION. I'M NEVER GONNA NEED TO KNOW THIS."
REALISTICALLY, MOST OF YOU WILL QUIT OR GRADUATE HIGH SCHOOL AND BECOME CASHIERS AND WAITRESSES. AND THOSE OF YOU WITH LOFTY GOALS MIGHT BE A REAL ESTATE AGENT OR CAR SALESMAN. REGARDLESS, YOU'LL NEVER USE ALGEBRA AGAIN.
BUT SOME OF YOU MIGHT GO TO COLLEGE, AND TO PROVE THAT YOU'RE MORE INTELLIGENT THAN A FIELD OF CORN, YOU'LL NEED TO TAKE THE SATS, HALF OF WHICH IS MATH.
FOR THAT REASON, THE STATE OF OKLAHOMA REQUIRES YOU ALL TO CRAM YOUR HORMORNAL LITTLE BRAINS WITH ALGEBRA, REGARDLESS OF AMBITION, INTEREST, OR INTELLECT.
MOST OF YOU AREN'T GOING TO BE A DOCTOR OR SCIENTIST, OR ENGINEER, OR EVEN SOMETHING AS PRESTIGIOUS AS A MATH TEACHER, AND CERTAINLY NONE OF US WANT TO BE HERE THIS YEAR.
Z
TOUGH TURKEY.
YOU'VE GOT TO LEARN THIS CRAP, AND I'M STUCK TEACHING YOU. IT'S GOING TO BE A HELL OF A YEAR.
ALL RIGHT.
LET'S TRY A WORD PROBLEM. IF X MINUTES HAVE PASSED OUT OF A CLASS Y MINUTES LONG, HOW MUCH LONGER UNTIL MR. HUMBOLT CAN GO HOME?
Y-X =

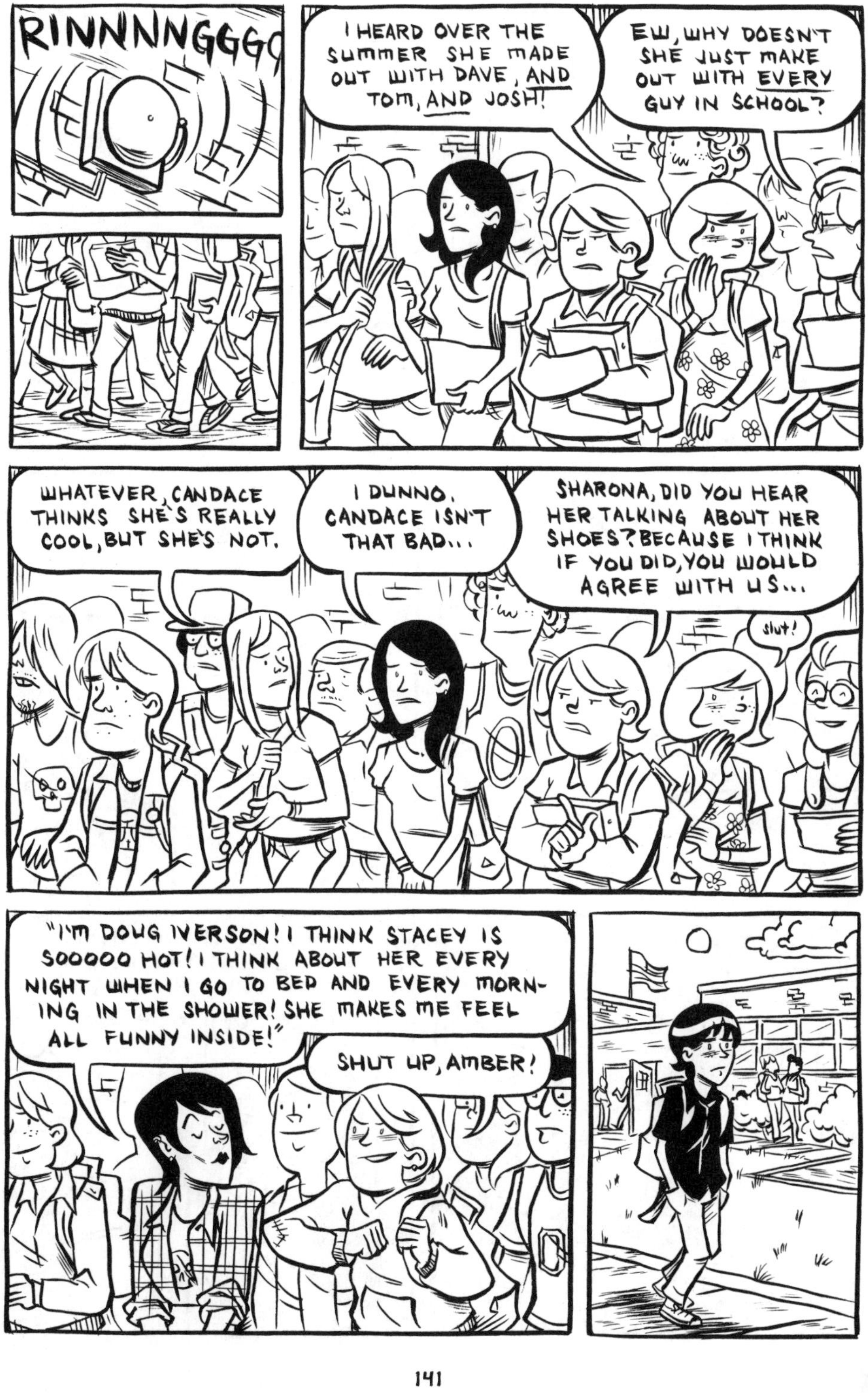
RINNNNGGG
I HEARD OVER THE SUMMER SHE MADE OUT WITH DAVE, AND TOM, AND JOSH!
EW, WHY DOESN'T SHE JUST MAKE OUT WITH EVERY GUY IN SCHOOL?
WHATEVER, CANDACE THINKS SHE'S REALLY COOL, BUT SHE'S NOT.
I DUNNO. CANDACE ISN'T THAT BAD...
SHARONA, DID YOU HEAR HER TALKING ABOUT HER SHOES? BECAUSE I THINK IF YOU DID, YOU WOULD AGREE WITH US...
slut!
"I'M DOUG IVERSON! I THINK STACEY IS SOOOOO HOT! I THINK ABOUT HER EVERY NIGHT WHEN I GO TO BED AND EVERY MORNING IN THE SHOWER! SHE MAKES ME FEEL ALL FUNNY INSIDE!"
SHUT UP, AMBER!

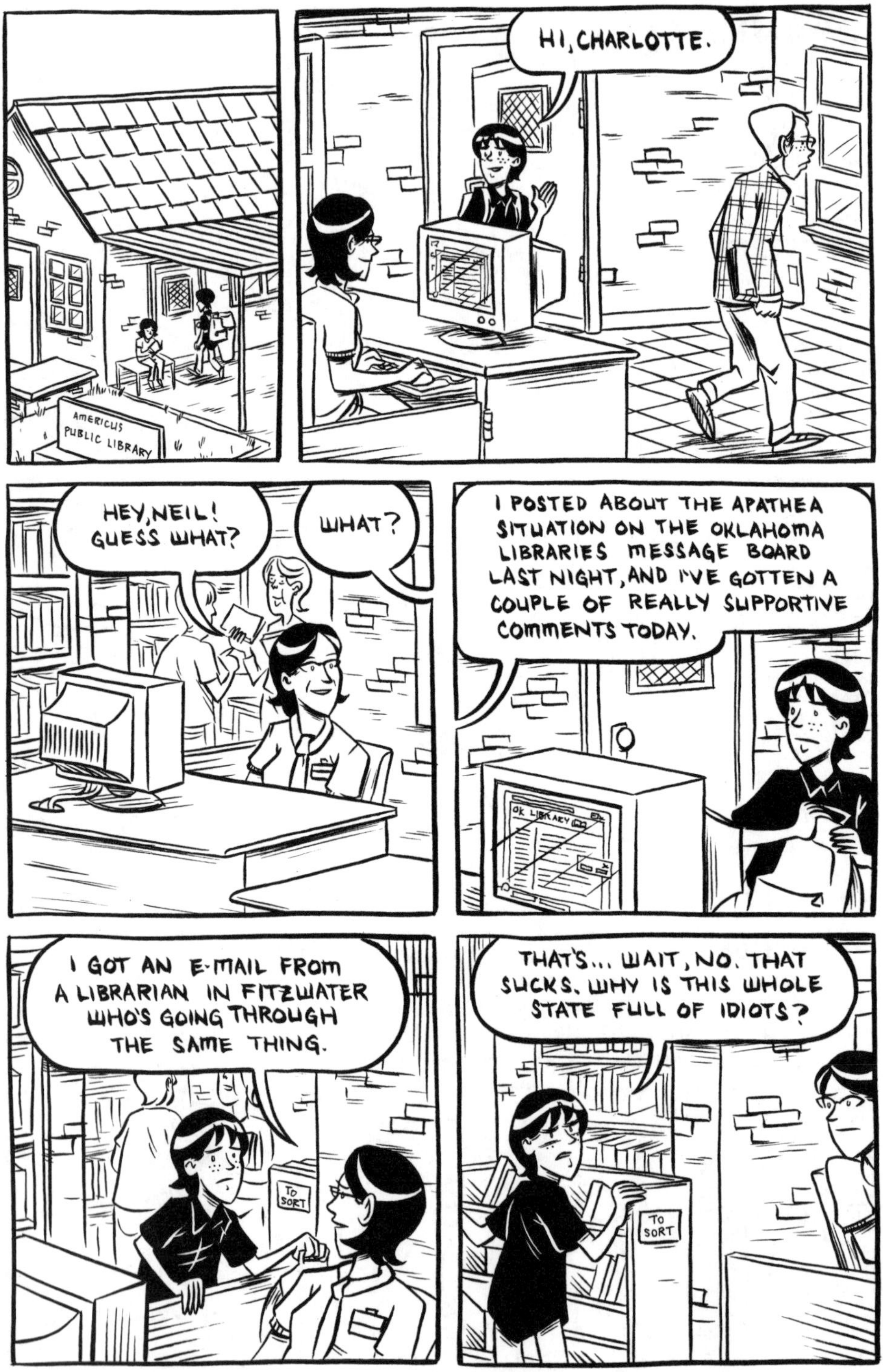
AMERICUS PUBLIC LIBRARY
HI, CHARLOTTE.
HEY, NEIL! GUESS WHAT?
WHAT?
I POSTED ABOUT THE APATHEA SITUATION ON THE OKLAHOMA LIBRARIES MESSAGE BOARD LAST NIGHT, AND I'VE GOTTEN A COUPLE OF REALLY SUPPORTIVE COMMENTS TODAY.
OK LIBRARY
I GOT AN E-MAIL FROM A LIBRARIAN IN FITZWATER WHO'S GOING THROUGH THE SAME THING.
TO SORT
THAT'S... WAIT, NO. THAT SUCKS. WHY IS THIS WHOLE STATE FULL OF IDIOTS?
TO SORT

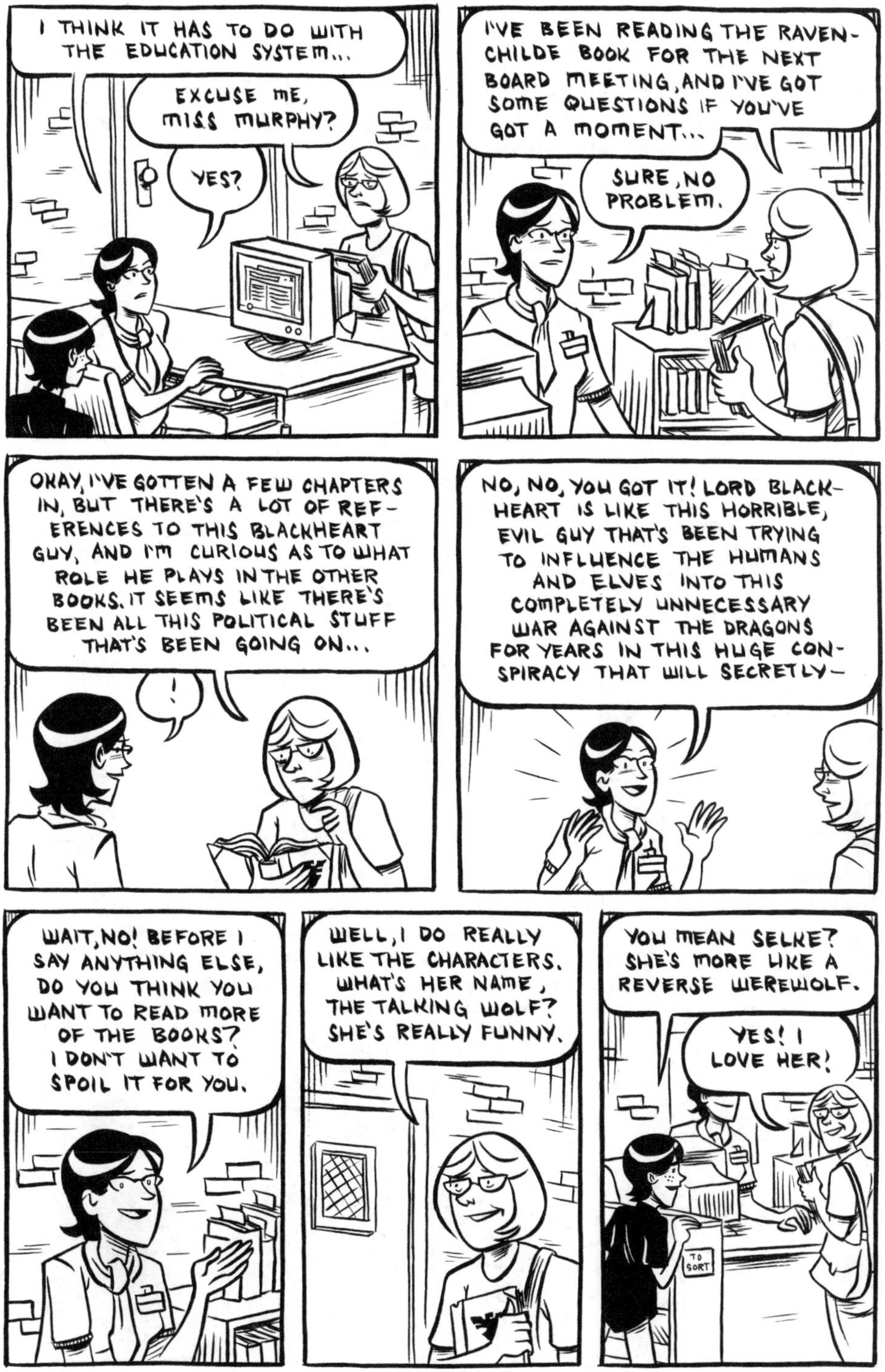
I THINK IT HAS TO DO WITH THE EDUCATION SYSTEM...
EXCUSE ME, MISS MURPHY?
YES?
I'VE BEEN READING THE RAVEN-CHILDE BOOK FOR THE NEXT BOARD MEETING, AND I'VE GOT SOME QUESTIONS IF YOU'VE GOT A MOMENT...
SURE, NO PROBLEM.
OKAY, I'VE GOTTEN A FEW CHAPTERS IN, BUT THERE'S A LOT OF REF-ERENCES TO THIS BLACKHEART GUY, AND I'M CURIOUS AS TO WHAT ROLE HE PLAYS IN THE OTHER BOOKS. IT SEEMS LIKE THERE'S BEEN ALL THIS POLITICAL STUFF THAT'S BEEN GOING ON...
!
NO, NO, YOU GOT IT! LORD BLACK-HEART IS LIKE THIS HORRIBLE, EVIL GUY THAT'S BEEN TRYING TO INFLUENCE THE HUMANS AND ELVES INTO THIS COMPLETELY UNNECESSARY WAR AGAINST THE DRAGONS FOR YEARS IN THIS HUGE CON-SPIRACY THAT WILL SECRETLY—
WAIT, NO! BEFORE I SAY ANYTHING ELSE, DO YOU THINK YOU WANT TO READ MORE OF THE BOOKS? I DON'T WANT TO SPOIL IT FOR YOU.
WELL, I DO REALLY LIKE THE CHARACTERS. WHAT'S HER NAME, THE TALKING WOLF? SHE'S REALLY FUNNY.
YOU MEAN SELKE? SHE'S MORE LIKE A REVERSE WEREWOLF.
YES! I LOVE HER!
TO SORT

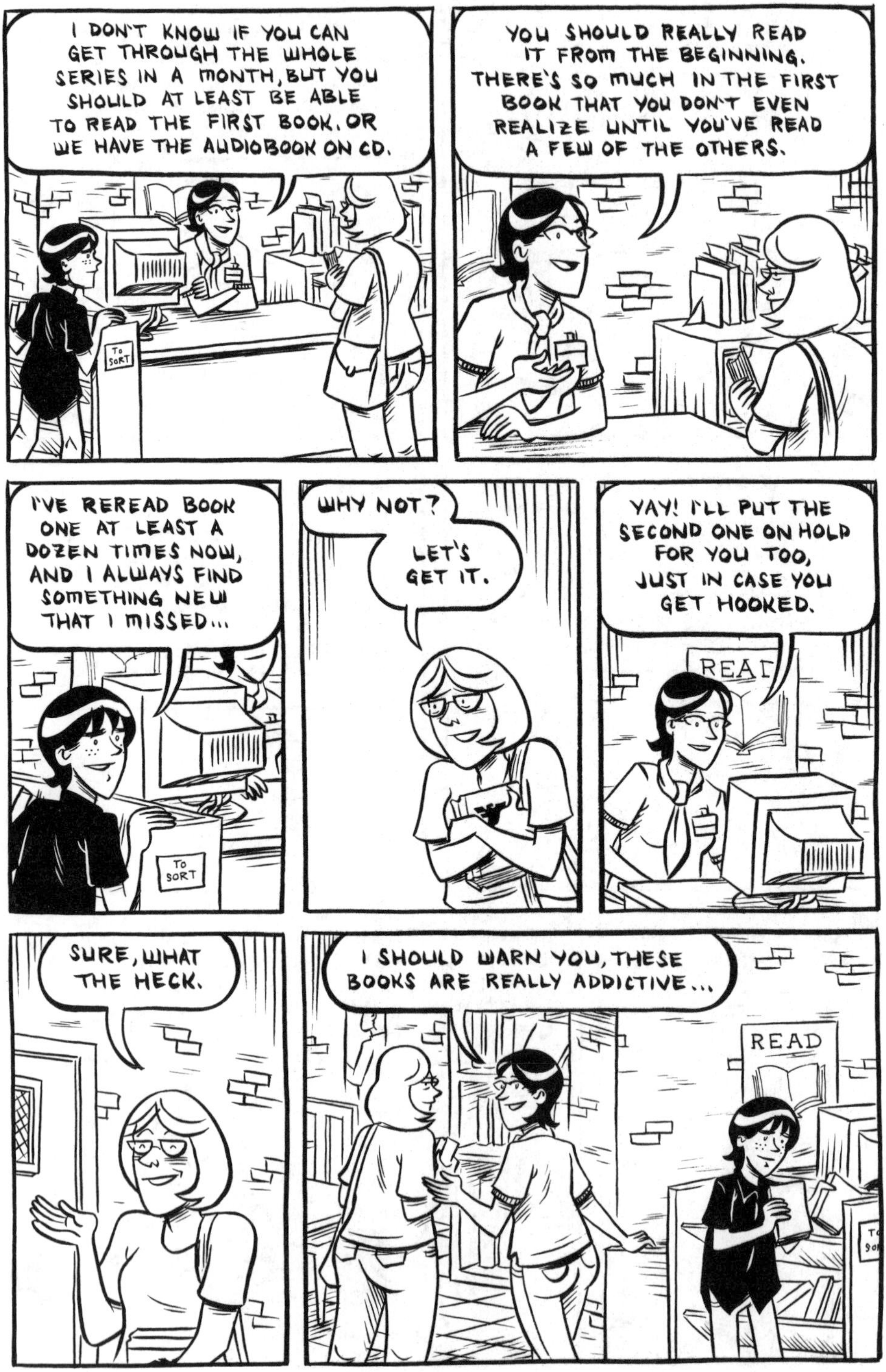
I DON'T KNOW IF YOU CAN GET THROUGH THE WHOLE SERIES IN A MONTH, BUT YOU SHOULD AT LEAST BE ABLE TO READ THE FIRST BOOK. OR WE HAVE THE AUDIOBOOK ON CD.
TO SORT
YOU SHOULD REALLY READ IT FROM THE BEGINNING. THERE'S SO MUCH IN THE FIRST BOOK THAT YOU DON'T EVEN REALIZE UNTIL YOU'VE READ A FEW OF THE OTHERS.
I'VE REREAD BOOK ONE AT LEAST A DOZEN TIMES NOW, AND I ALWAYS FIND SOMETHING NEW THAT I MISSED...
TO SORT
WHY NOT?
LET'S GET IT.
YAY! I'LL PUT THE SECOND ONE ON HOLD FOR YOU TOO, JUST IN CASE YOU GET HOOKED.
READ
SURE, WHAT THE HECK.
I SHOULD WARN YOU, THESE BOOKS ARE REALLY ADDICTIVE...
READ

CHAPTER 7

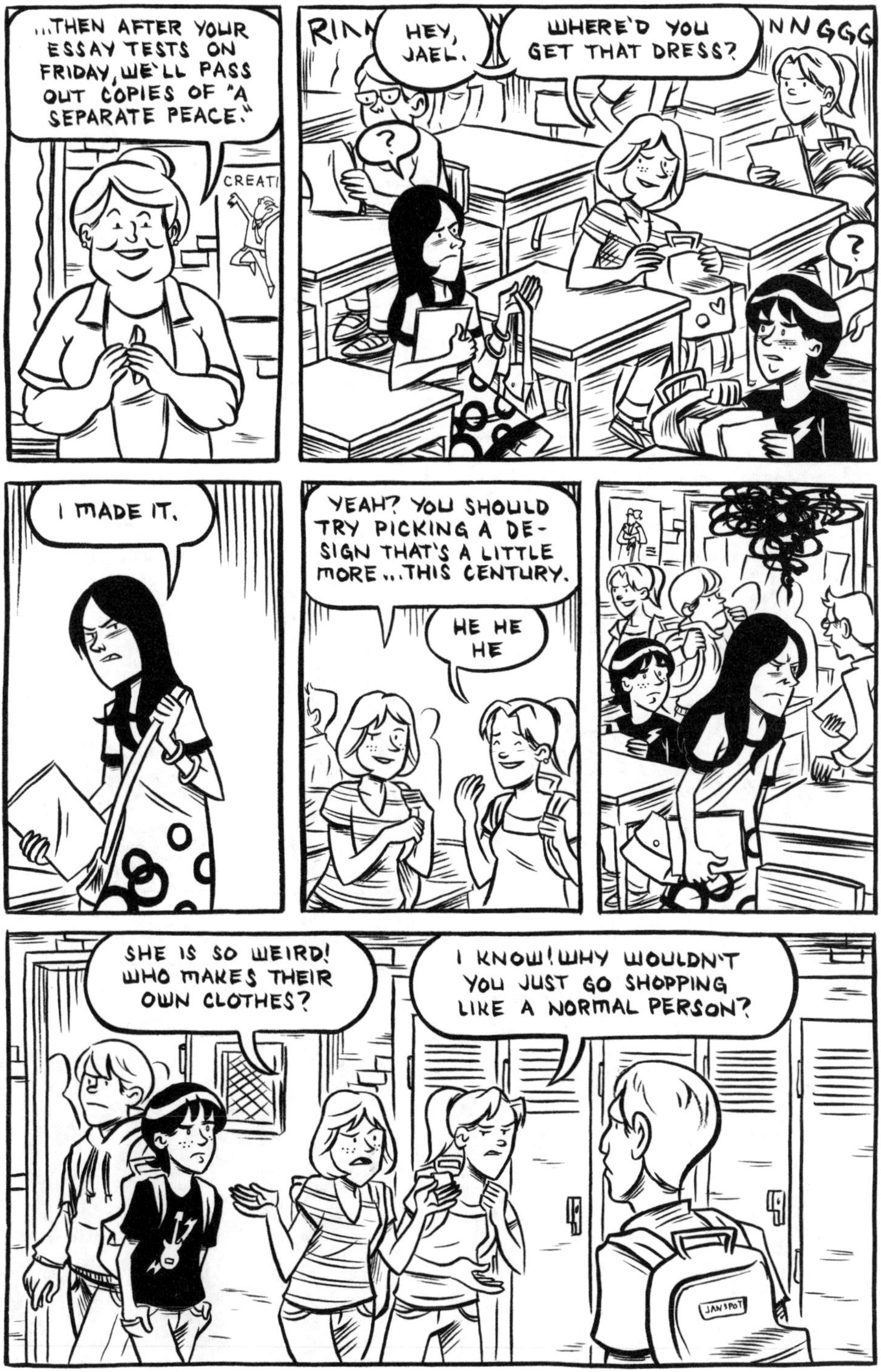
...THEN AFTER YOUR ESSAY TESTS ON FRIDAY, WE'LL PASS OUT COPIES OF "A SEPARATE PEACE."
CREATI
RIN
HEY, JAEL.
WHERE'D YOU GET THAT DRESS?
NNGGG
?
?
I MADE IT.
YEAH? YOU SHOULD TRY PICKING A DESIGN THAT'S A LITTLE MORE...THIS CENTURY.
HE HE HE
SHE IS SO WEIRD! WHO MAKES THEIR OWN CLOTHES?
I KNOW! WHY WOULDN'T YOU JUST GO SHOPPING LIKE A NORMAL PERSON?

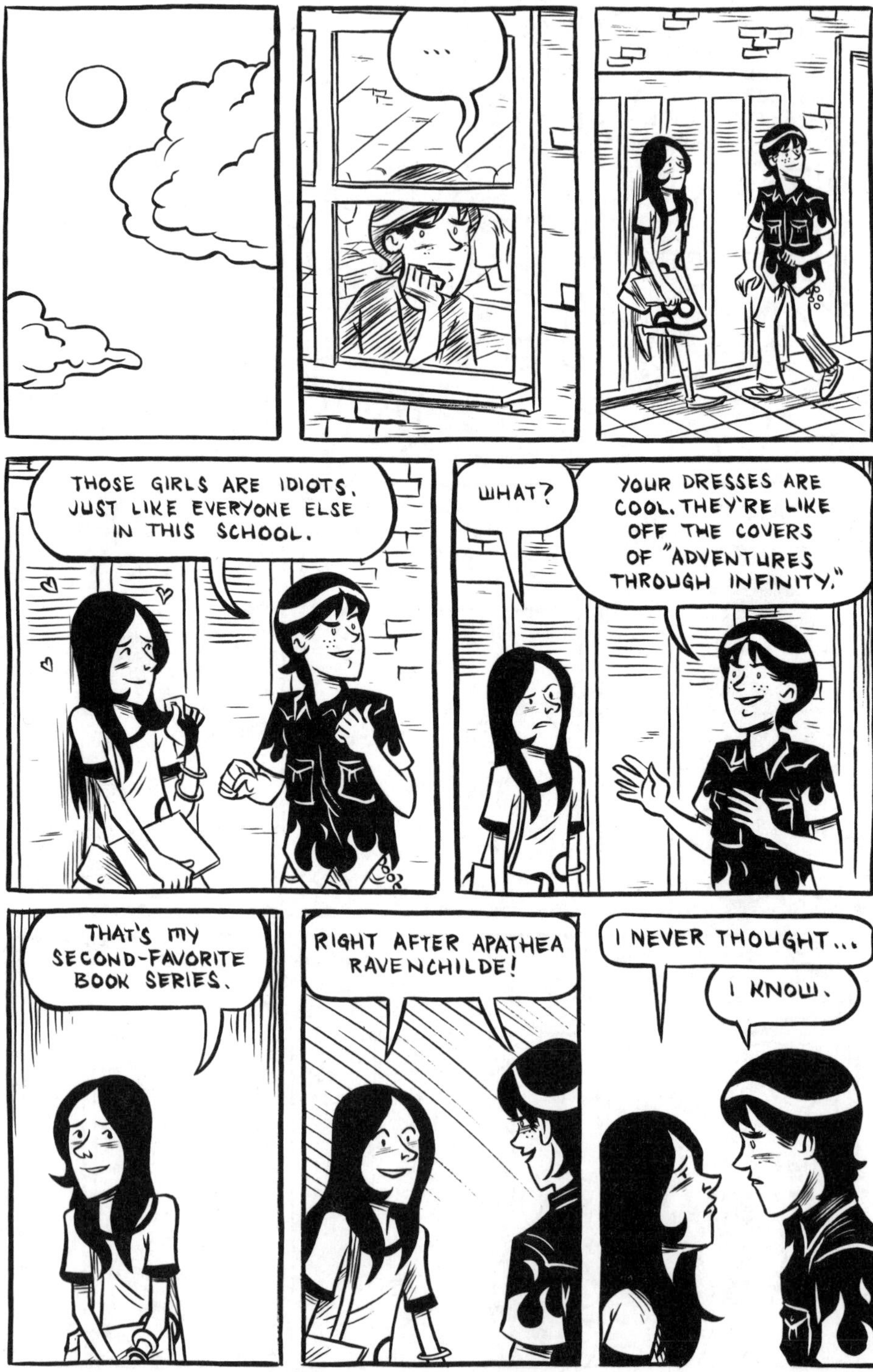
...
THOSE GIRLS ARE IDIOTS. JUST LIKE EVERYONE ELSE IN THIS SCHOOL.
WHAT?
YOUR DRESSES ARE COOL. THEY'RE LIKE OFF THE COVERS OF "ADVENTURES THROUGH INFINITY."
THAT'S MY SECOND-FAVORITE BOOK SERIES.
RIGHT AFTER APATHEA RAVENCHILDE!
I NEVER THOUGHT...
I KNOW.

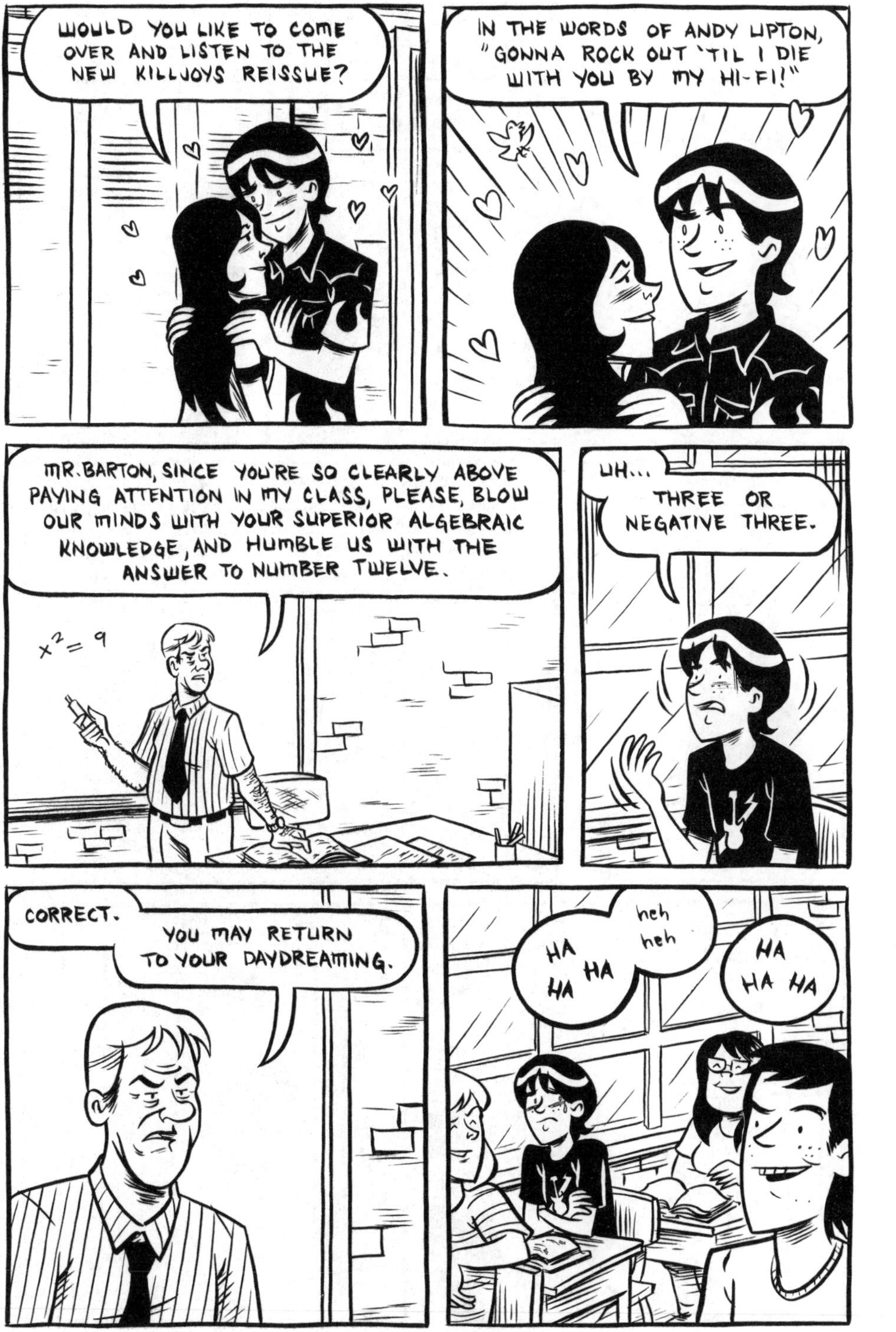
WOULD YOU LIKE TO COME OVER AND LISTEN TO THE NEW KILLJOYS REISSUE?
IN THE WORDS OF ANDY UPTON, "GONNA ROCK OUT 'TIL I DIE WITH YOU BY MY HI-FI!"
MR. BARTON, SINCE YOU'RE SO CLEARLY ABOVE PAYING ATTENTION IN MY CLASS, PLEASE, BLOW OUR MINDS WITH YOUR SUPERIOR ALGEBRAIC KNOWLEDGE, AND HUMBLE US WITH THE ANSWER TO NUMBER TWELVE.
$x^2 = 9$
UH...
THREE OR NEGATIVE THREE.
CORRECT.
YOU MAY RETURN TO YOUR DAYDREAMING.
HA HA HA
heh heh
HA HA HA

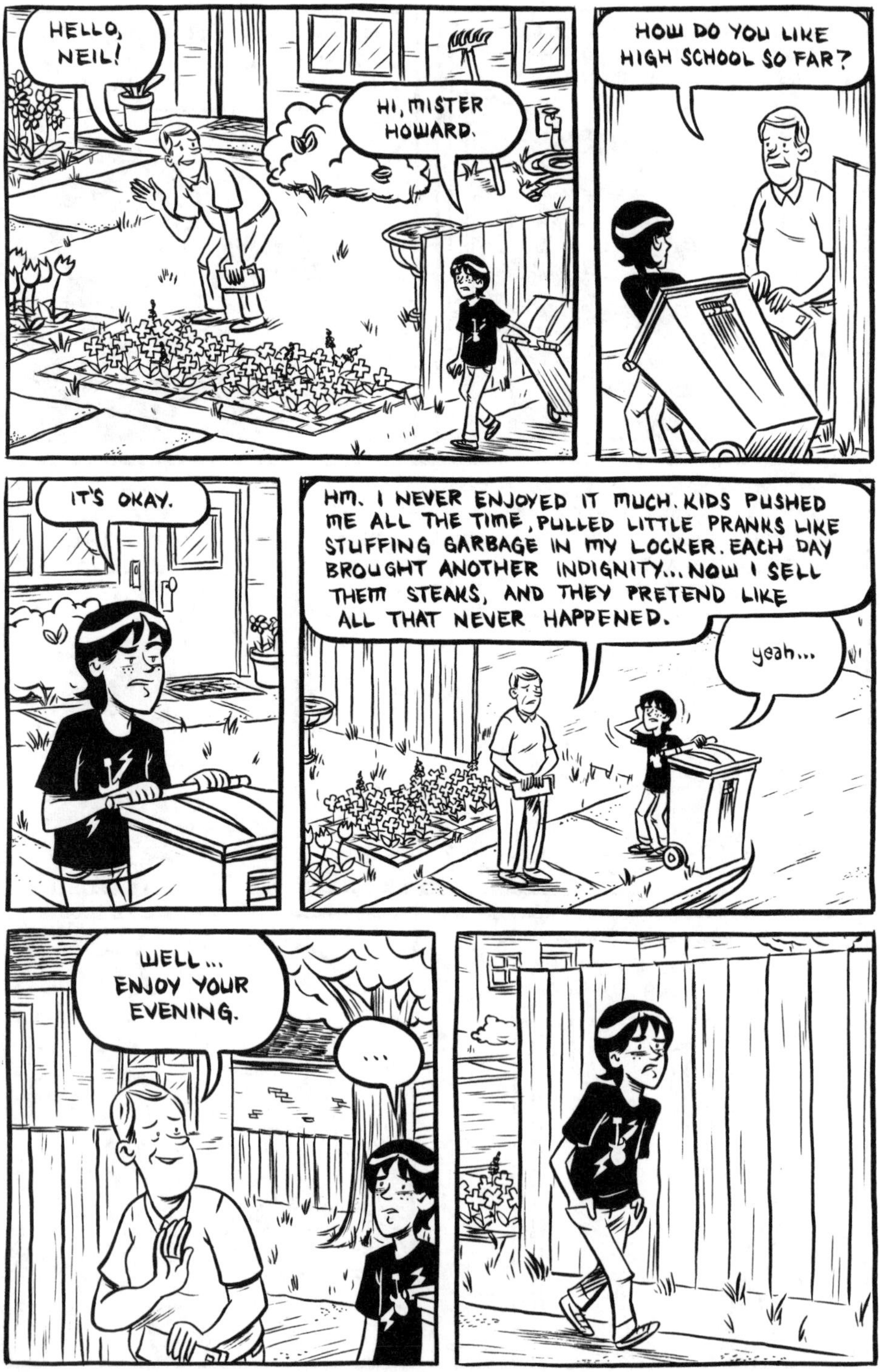
HELLO, NEIL!
HI, MISTER HOWARD.
HOW DO YOU LIKE HIGH SCHOOL SO FAR?
IT'S OKAY.
HM. I NEVER ENJOYED IT MUCH. KIDS PUSHED ME ALL THE TIME, PULLED LITTLE PRANKS LIKE STUFFING GARBAGE IN MY LOCKER. EACH DAY BROUGHT ANOTHER INDIGNITY... NOW I SELL THEM STEAKS, AND THEY PRETEND LIKE ALL THAT NEVER HAPPENED.
yeah...
WELL... ENJOY YOUR EVENING.
...

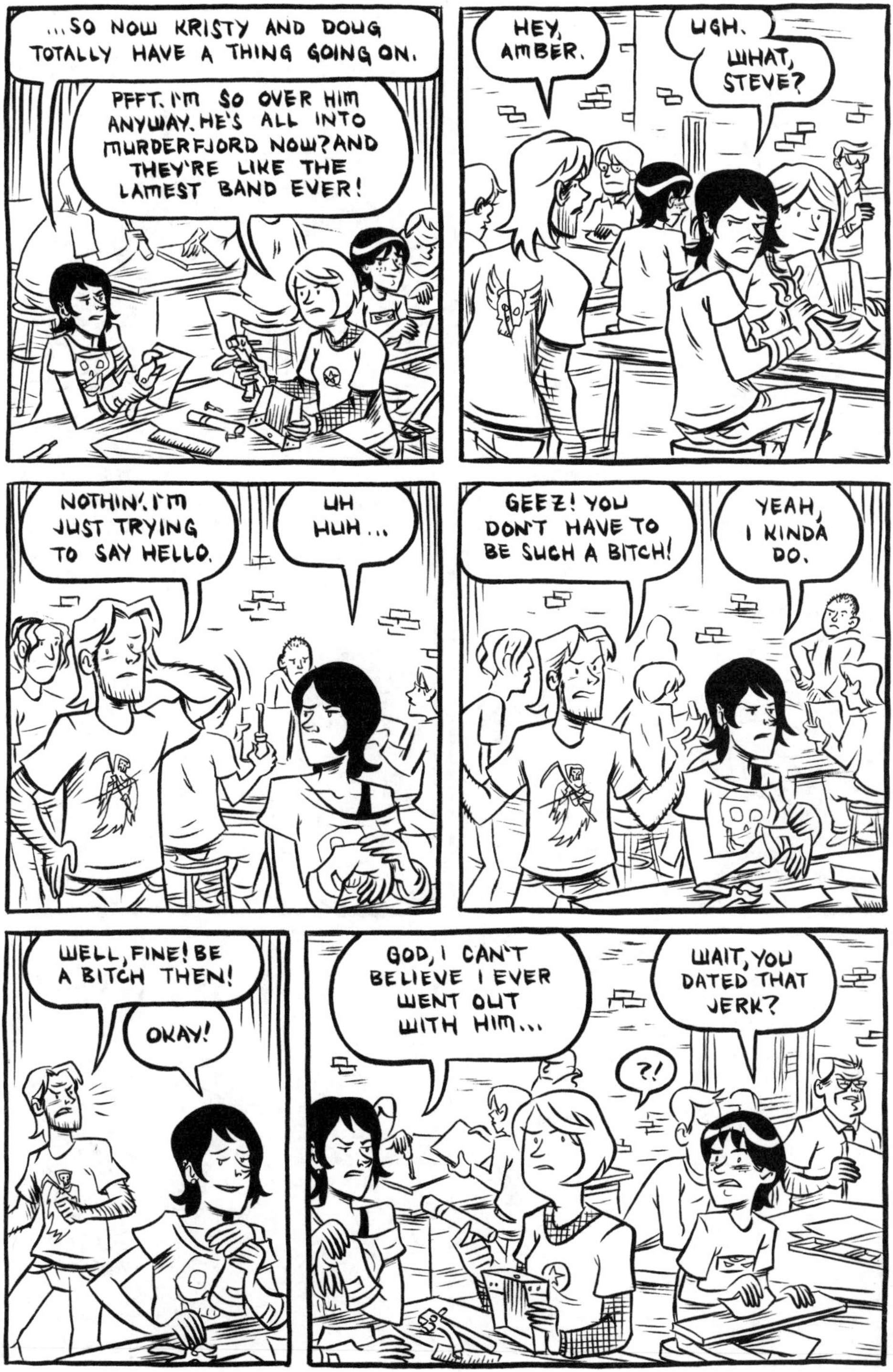
...SO NOW KRISTY AND DOUG TOTALLY HAVE A THING GOING ON.
PFFT. I'M SO OVER HIM ANYWAY. HE'S ALL INTO MURDERFJORD NOW? AND THEY'RE LIKE THE LAMEST BAND EVER!
HEY, AMBER.
UGH.
WHAT, STEVE?
NOTHIN'. I'M JUST TRYING TO SAY HELLO.
UH HUH...
GEEZ! YOU DON'T HAVE TO BE SUCH A BITCH!
YEAH, I KINDA DO.
WELL, FINE! BE A BITCH THEN!
OKAY!
GOD, I CAN'T BELIEVE I EVER WENT OUT WITH HIM...
WAIT, YOU DATED THAT JERK?
?!

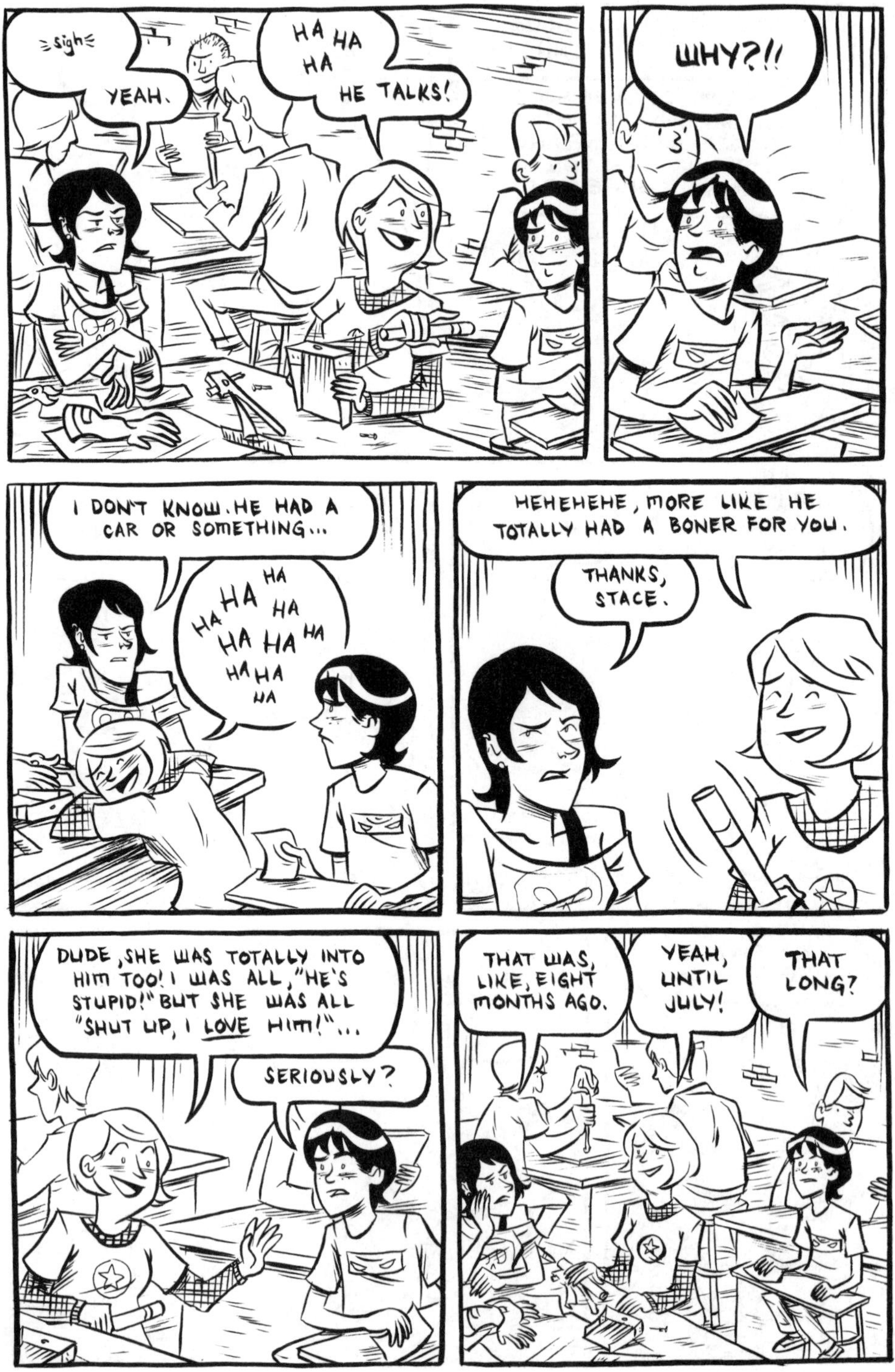

sigh
YEAH.
HA HA HA
HE TALKS!
WHY?!!
I DON'T KNOW. HE HAD A CAR OR SOMETHING...
HA HA HA HA HA HA HA HA HA HA HA
HEHEHEHE, MORE LIKE HE TOTALLY HAD A BONER FOR YOU.
THANKS, STACE.
DUDE, SHE WAS TOTALLY INTO HIM TOO! I WAS ALL, "HE'S STUPID!" BUT SHE WAS ALL "SHUT UP, I LOVE HIM!"...
SERIOUSLY?
THAT WAS, LIKE, EIGHT MONTHS AGO.
YEAH, UNTIL JULY!
THAT LONG?

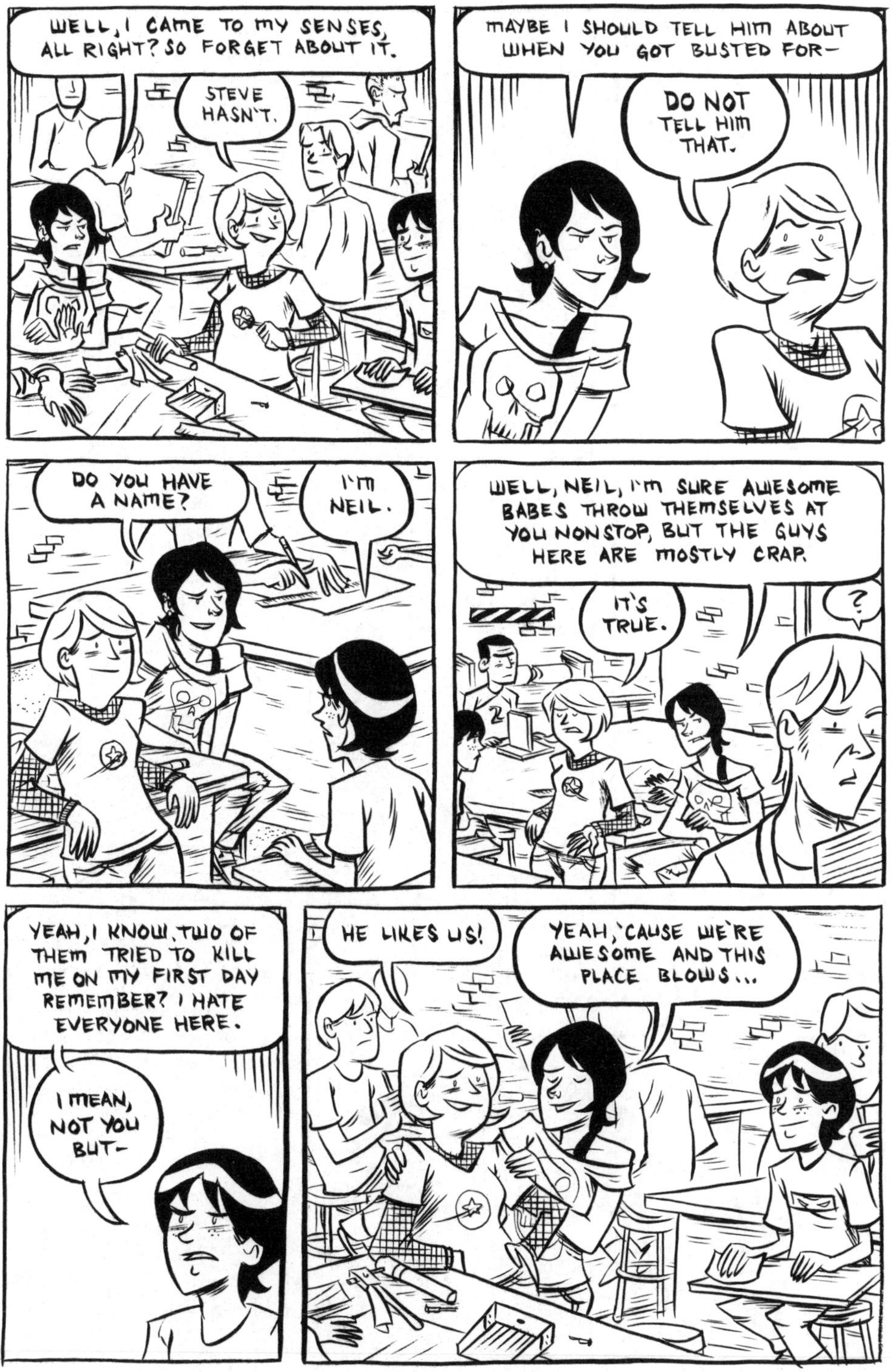
WELL, I CAME TO MY SENSES, ALL RIGHT? SO FORGET ABOUT IT.
STEVE HASN'T.
MAYBE I SHOULD TELL HIM ABOUT WHEN YOU GOT BUSTED FOR-
DO NOT TELL HIM THAT.
DO YOU HAVE A NAME?
I'M NEIL.
WELL, NEIL, I'M SURE AWESOME BABES THROW THEMSELVES AT YOU NONSTOP, BUT THE GUYS HERE ARE MOSTLY CRAP.
IT'S TRUE.
?
YEAH, I KNOW. TWO OF THEM TRIED TO KILL ME ON MY FIRST DAY REMEMBER? I HATE EVERYONE HERE.
I MEAN, NOT YOU BUT-
HE LIKES US!
YEAH, 'CAUSE WE'RE AWESOME AND THIS PLACE BLOWS...

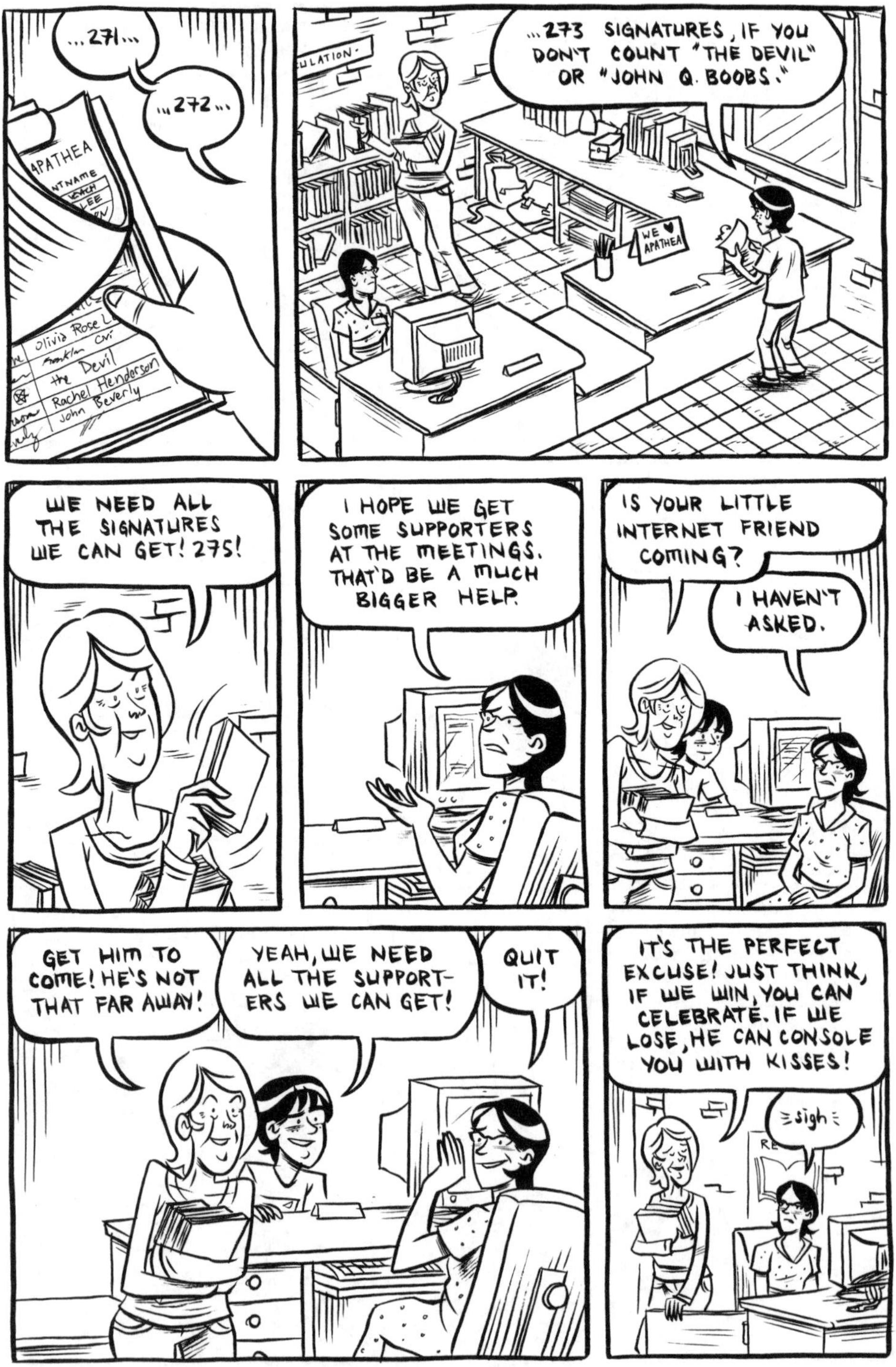
...271...
...272...
APATHEA
the Devil
Rachel Henderson
John Beverly
...273 SIGNATURES, IF YOU DON'T COUNT "THE DEVIL" OR "JOHN Q. BOOBS."
WE ♥ APATHEA
WE NEED ALL THE SIGNATURES WE CAN GET! 275!
I HOPE WE GET SOME SUPPORTERS AT THE MEETINGS. THAT'D BE A MUCH BIGGER HELP.
IS YOUR LITTLE INTERNET FRIEND COMING?
I HAVEN'T ASKED.
GET HIM TO COME! HE'S NOT THAT FAR AWAY!
YEAH, WE NEED ALL THE SUPPORTERS WE CAN GET!
QUIT IT!
IT'S THE PERFECT EXCUSE! JUST THINK, IF WE WIN, YOU CAN CELEBRATE. IF WE LOSE, HE CAN CONSOLE YOU WITH KISSES!
sigh

DON'T GET ANY IDEAS FROM AGNES.

HOW IS YOUR SPEECH COMING?

ALL RIGHT, I GUESS, I JUST WISH I COULD BE MORE CONFIDENT THAT LOGICAL REASONING WOULD WORK.

I'VE BEEN THINKING OF A COUPLE DIFFERENT STRATEGIES, THOUGH...

AND?

AND... I THINK YOU SHOULD SAY SOMETHING AT THE MEETING. IT WOULD HELP TO HAVE A YOUNG FAN TALKING ABOUT THE BOOKS IN A POSITIVE LIGHT.

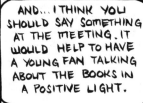

!

I KNOW IT'S INTIMIDATING, BUT I NEED YOU.

...

I MIGHT NOT BE THAT GOOD. WHAT IF I GET UP THERE AND I'M TOO NERVOUS TO EVEN SAY A WORD IN FRONT OF EVERYONE?

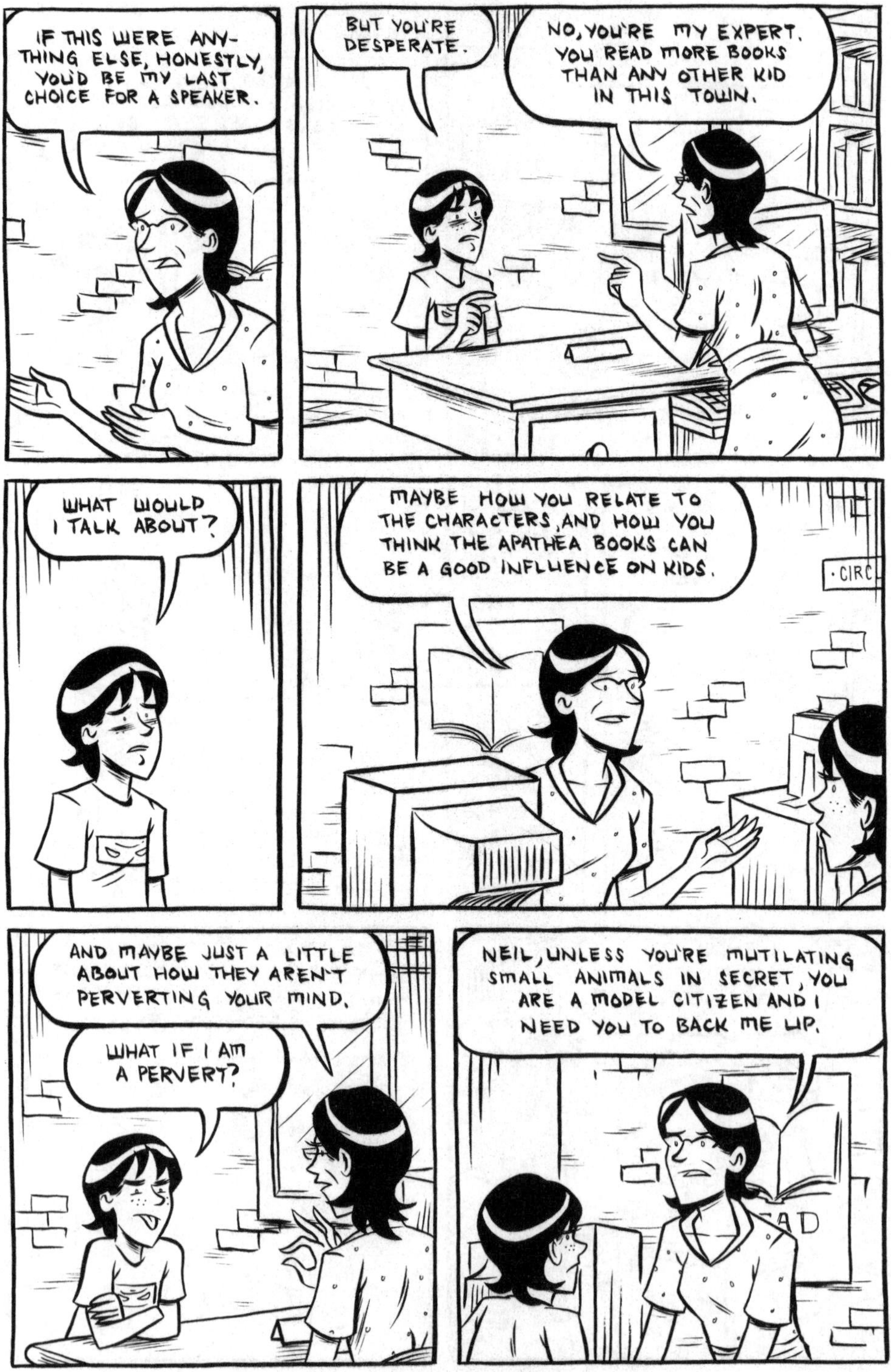
IF THIS WERE ANYTHING ELSE, HONESTLY, YOU'D BE MY LAST CHOICE FOR A SPEAKER.
BUT YOU'RE DESPERATE.
NO, YOU'RE MY EXPERT. YOU READ MORE BOOKS THAN ANY OTHER KID IN THIS TOWN.
WHAT WOULD I TALK ABOUT?
MAYBE HOW YOU RELATE TO THE CHARACTERS, AND HOW YOU THINK THE APATHEA BOOKS CAN BE A GOOD INFLUENCE ON KIDS.
·CIRC
AND MAYBE JUST A LITTLE ABOUT HOW THEY AREN'T PERVERTING YOUR MIND.
WHAT IF I AM A PERVERT?
NEIL, UNLESS YOU'RE MUTILATING SMALL ANIMALS IN SECRET, YOU ARE A MODEL CITIZEN AND I NEED YOU TO BACK ME UP.

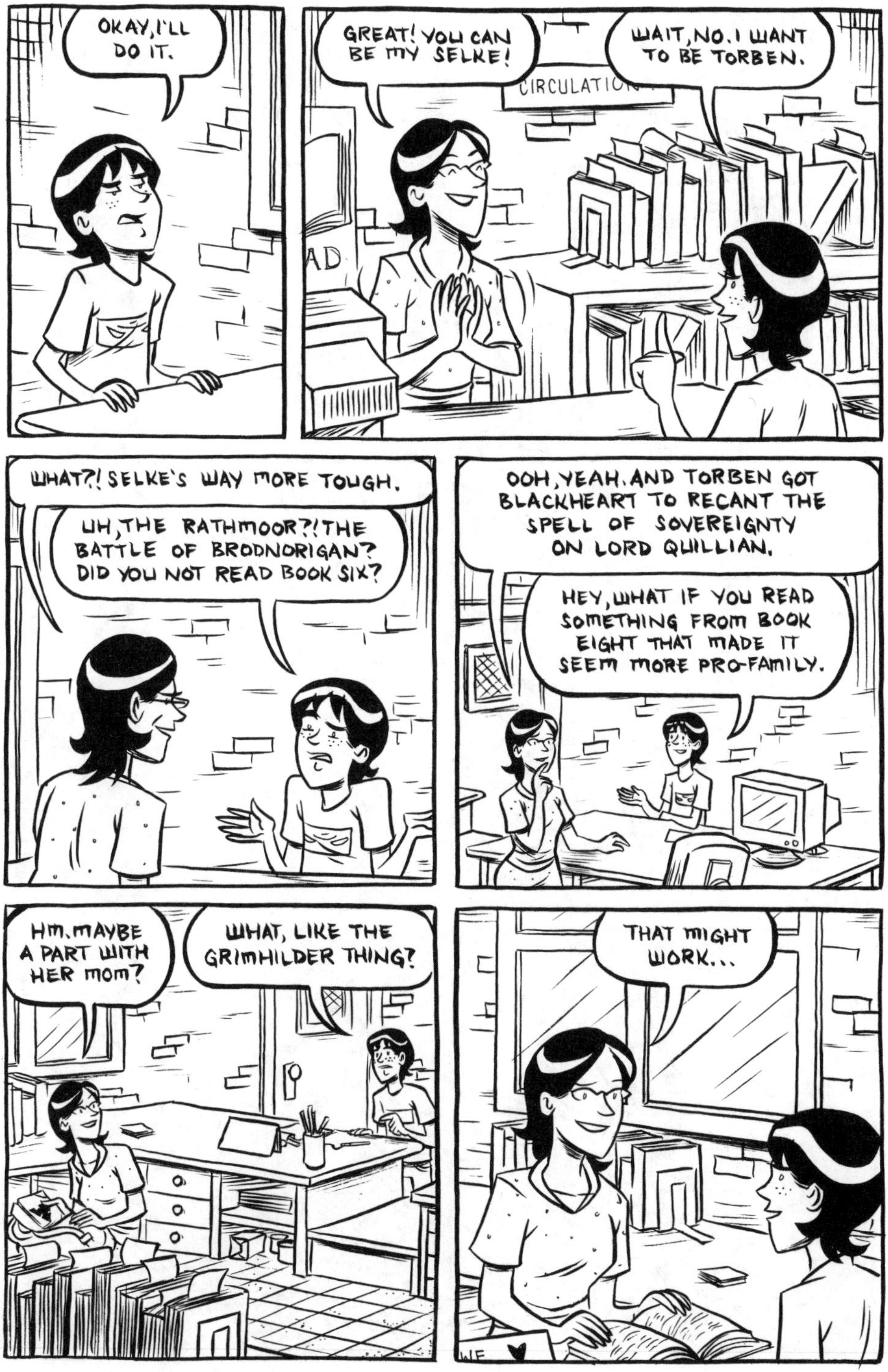
OKAY, I'LL DO IT.
GREAT! YOU CAN BE MY SELKE!
CIRCULATION
WAIT, NO. I WANT TO BE TORBEN.
AD
WHAT?! SELKE'S WAY MORE TOUGH.
UH, THE RATHMOOR?! THE BATTLE OF BRODNORIGAN? DID YOU NOT READ BOOK SIX?
OOH, YEAH. AND TORBEN GOT BLACKHEART TO RECANT THE SPELL OF SOVEREIGNTY ON LORD QUILLIAN.
HEY, WHAT IF YOU READ SOMETHING FROM BOOK EIGHT THAT MADE IT SEEM MORE PRO-FAMILY.
HM. MAYBE A PART WITH HER MOM?
WHAT, LIKE THE GRIMHILDER THING?
THAT MIGHT WORK...

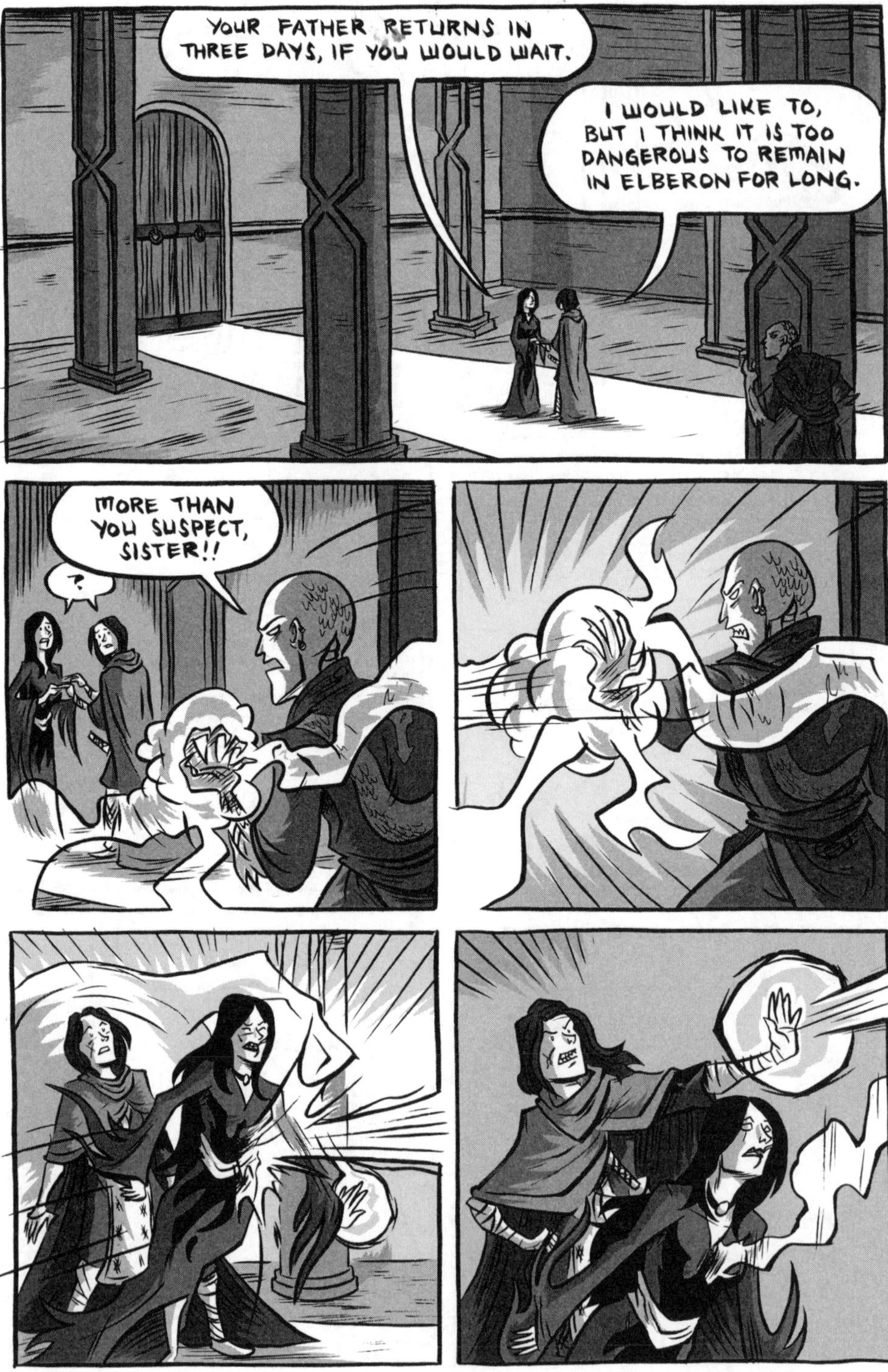
YOUR FATHER RETURNS IN THREE DAYS, IF YOU WOULD WAIT.
I WOULD LIKE TO, BUT I THINK IT IS TOO DANGEROUS TO REMAIN IN ELBERON FOR LONG.
?
MORE THAN YOU SUSPECT, SISTER!!

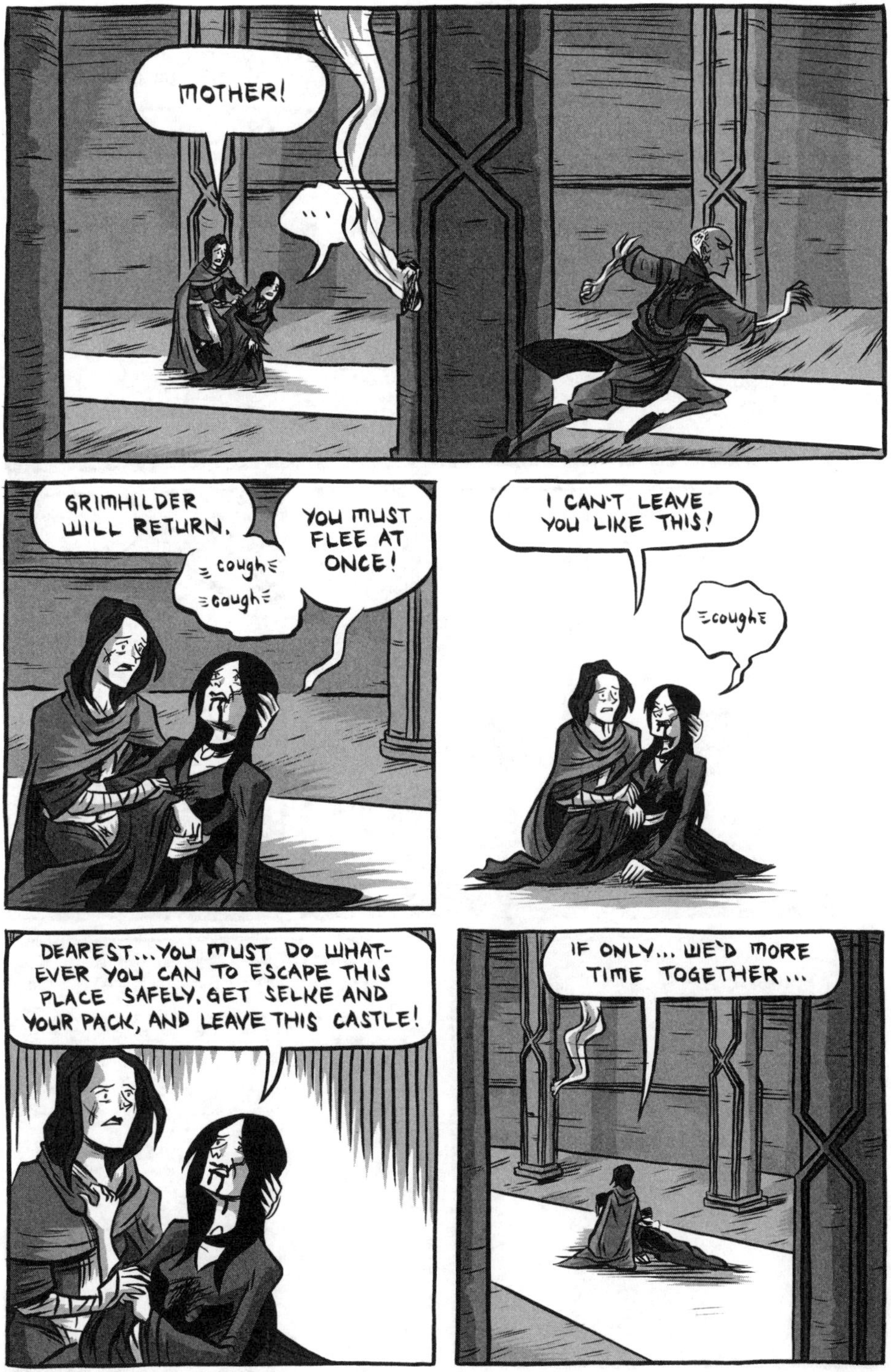
MOTHER!
...
GRIMHILDER WILL RETURN.
cough
cough
YOU MUST FLEE AT ONCE!
I CAN'T LEAVE YOU LIKE THIS!
cough
DEAREST... YOU MUST DO WHAT-EVER YOU CAN TO ESCAPE THIS PLACE SAFELY. GET SELKE AND YOUR PACK, AND LEAVE THIS CASTLE!
IF ONLY... WE'D MORE TIME TOGETHER...

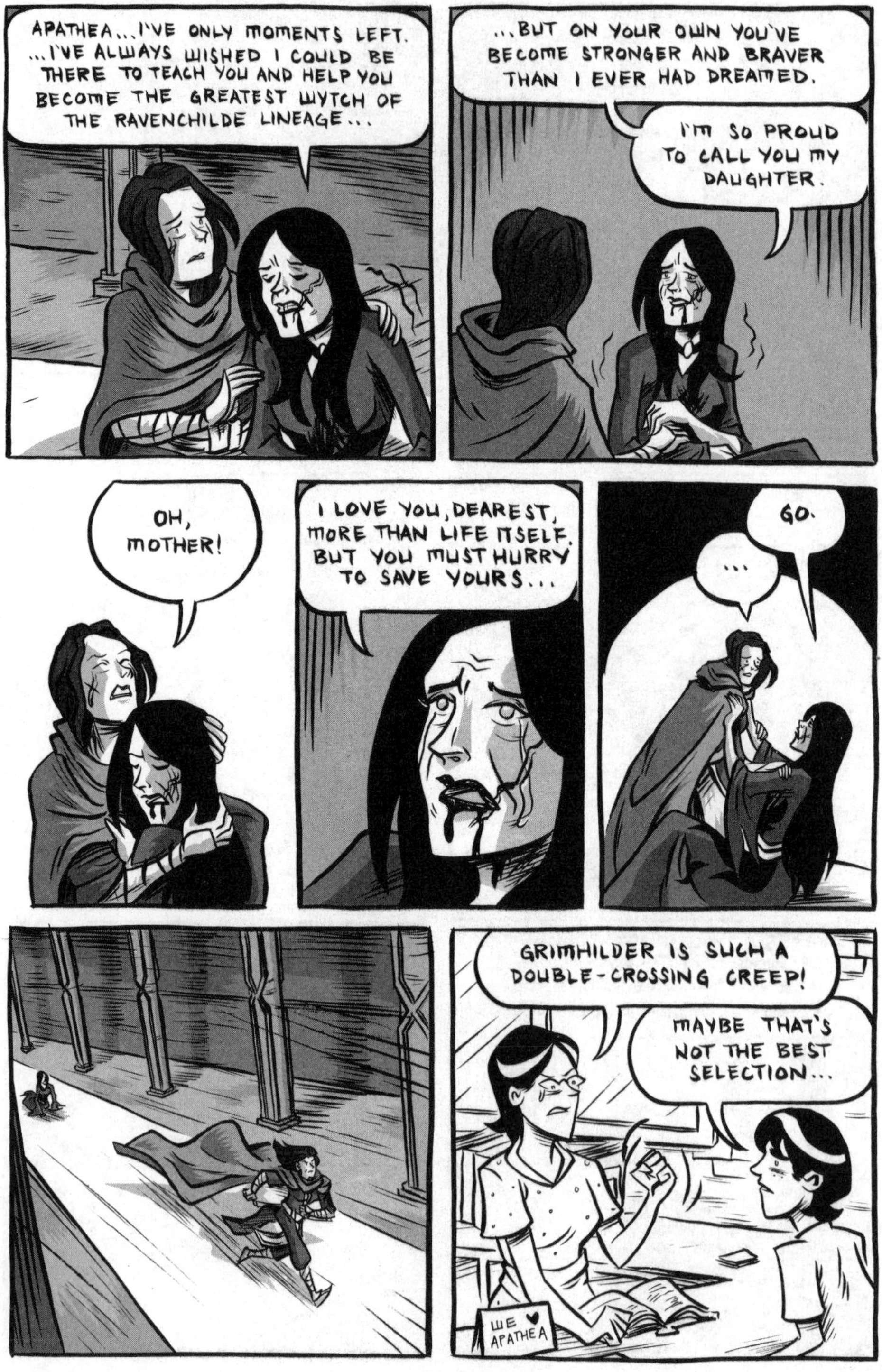
APATHEA...I'VE ONLY MOMENTS LEFT. ...I'VE ALWAYS WISHED I COULD BE THERE TO TEACH YOU AND HELP YOU BECOME THE GREATEST WYTCH OF THE RAVENCHILDE LINEAGE...
...BUT ON YOUR OWN YOU'VE BECOME STRONGER AND BRAVER THAN I EVER HAD DREAMED.
I'M SO PROUD TO CALL YOU MY DAUGHTER.
OH, MOTHER!
I LOVE YOU, DEAREST, MORE THAN LIFE ITSELF. BUT YOU MUST HURRY TO SAVE YOURS...
...
GO.
GRIMHILDER IS SUCH A DOUBLE-CROSSING CREEP!
MAYBE THAT'S NOT THE BEST SELECTION...
WE ♥ APATHEA

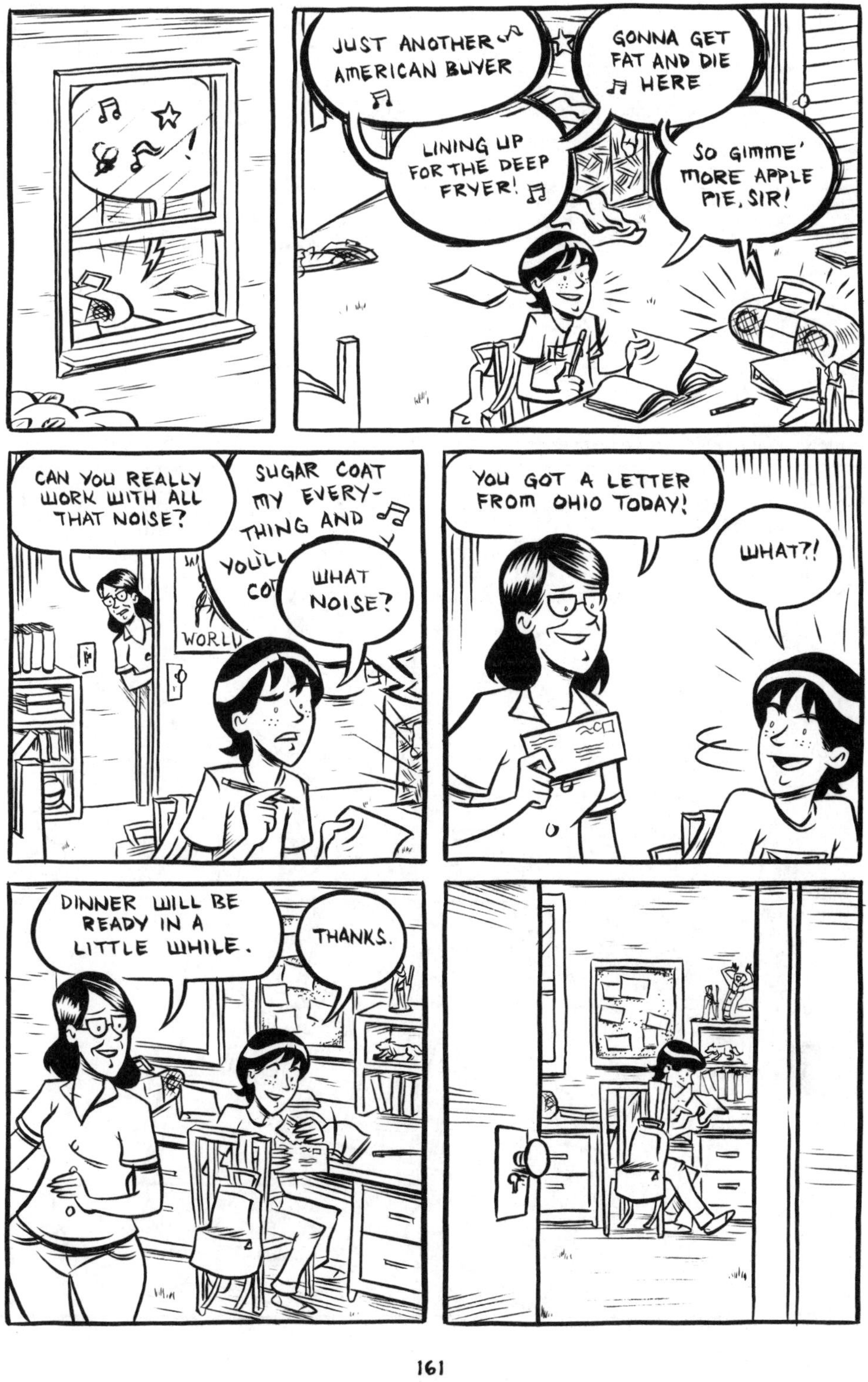
JUST ANOTHER AMERICAN BUYER
GONNA GET FAT AND DIE HERE
LINING UP FOR THE DEEP FRYER!
SO GIMME' MORE APPLE PIE, SIR!
CAN YOU REALLY WORK WITH ALL THAT NOISE?
SUGAR COAT MY EVERY-THING AND
WHAT NOISE?
YOU GOT A LETTER FROM OHIO TODAY!
WHAT?!
DINNER WILL BE READY IN A LITTLE WHILE.
THANKS.

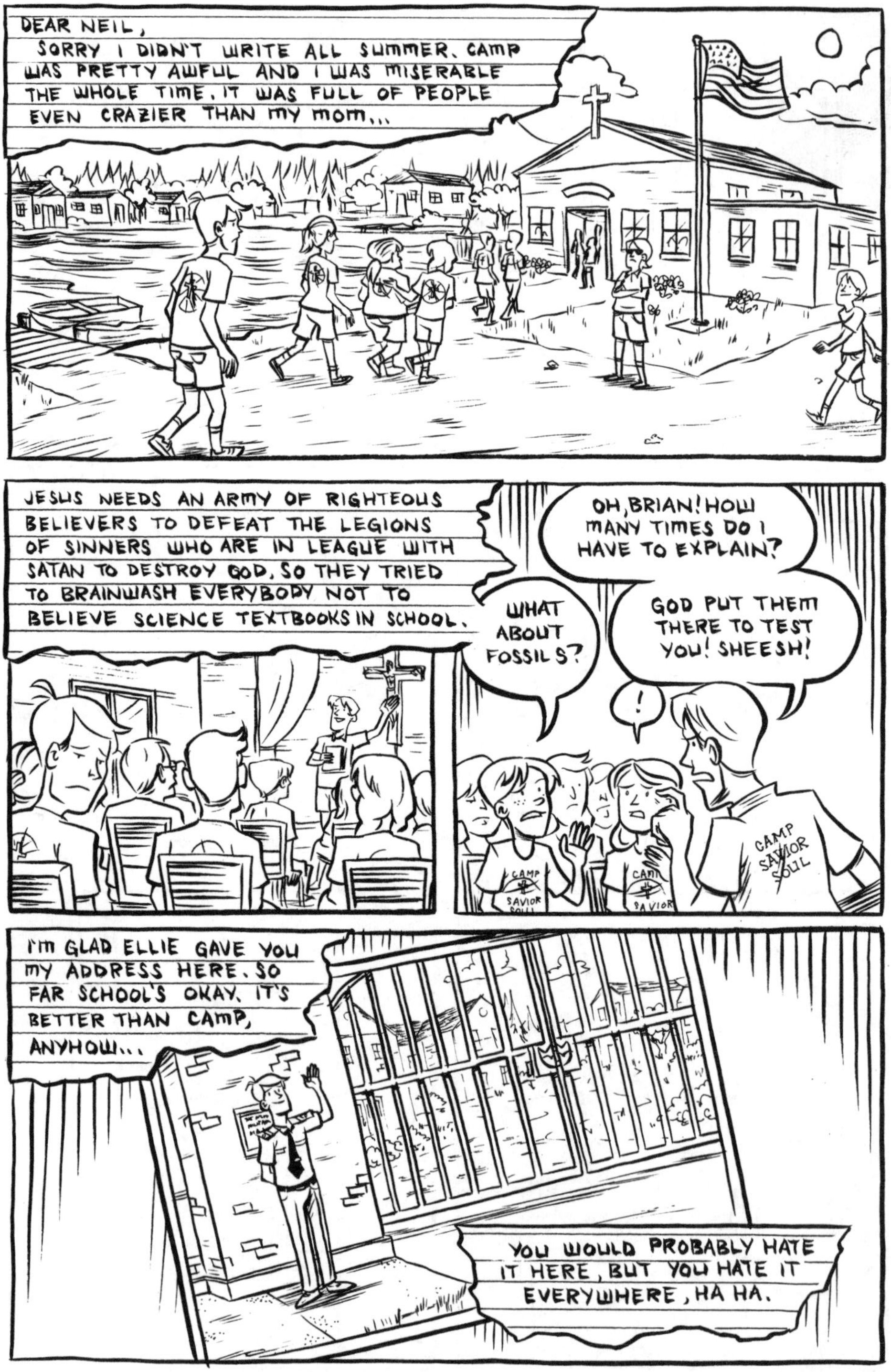
DEAR NEIL,
SORRY I DIDN'T WRITE ALL SUMMER. CAMP WAS PRETTY AWFUL AND I WAS MISERABLE THE WHOLE TIME. IT WAS FULL OF PEOPLE EVEN CRAZIER THAN MY MOM...
JESUS NEEDS AN ARMY OF RIGHTEOUS BELIEVERS TO DEFEAT THE LEGIONS OF SINNERS WHO ARE IN LEAGUE WITH SATAN TO DESTROY GOD. SO THEY TRIED TO BRAINWASH EVERYBODY NOT TO BELIEVE SCIENCE TEXTBOOKS IN SCHOOL.
WHAT ABOUT FOSSILS?
OH, BRIAN! HOW MANY TIMES DO I HAVE TO EXPLAIN?
GOD PUT THEM THERE TO TEST YOU! SHEESH!
!
CAMP SAVIOR SOUL
I'M GLAD ELLIE GAVE YOU MY ADDRESS HERE. SO FAR SCHOOL'S OKAY. IT'S BETTER THAN CAMP, ANYHOW...
YOU WOULD PROBABLY HATE IT HERE, BUT YOU HATE IT EVERYWHERE, HA HA.

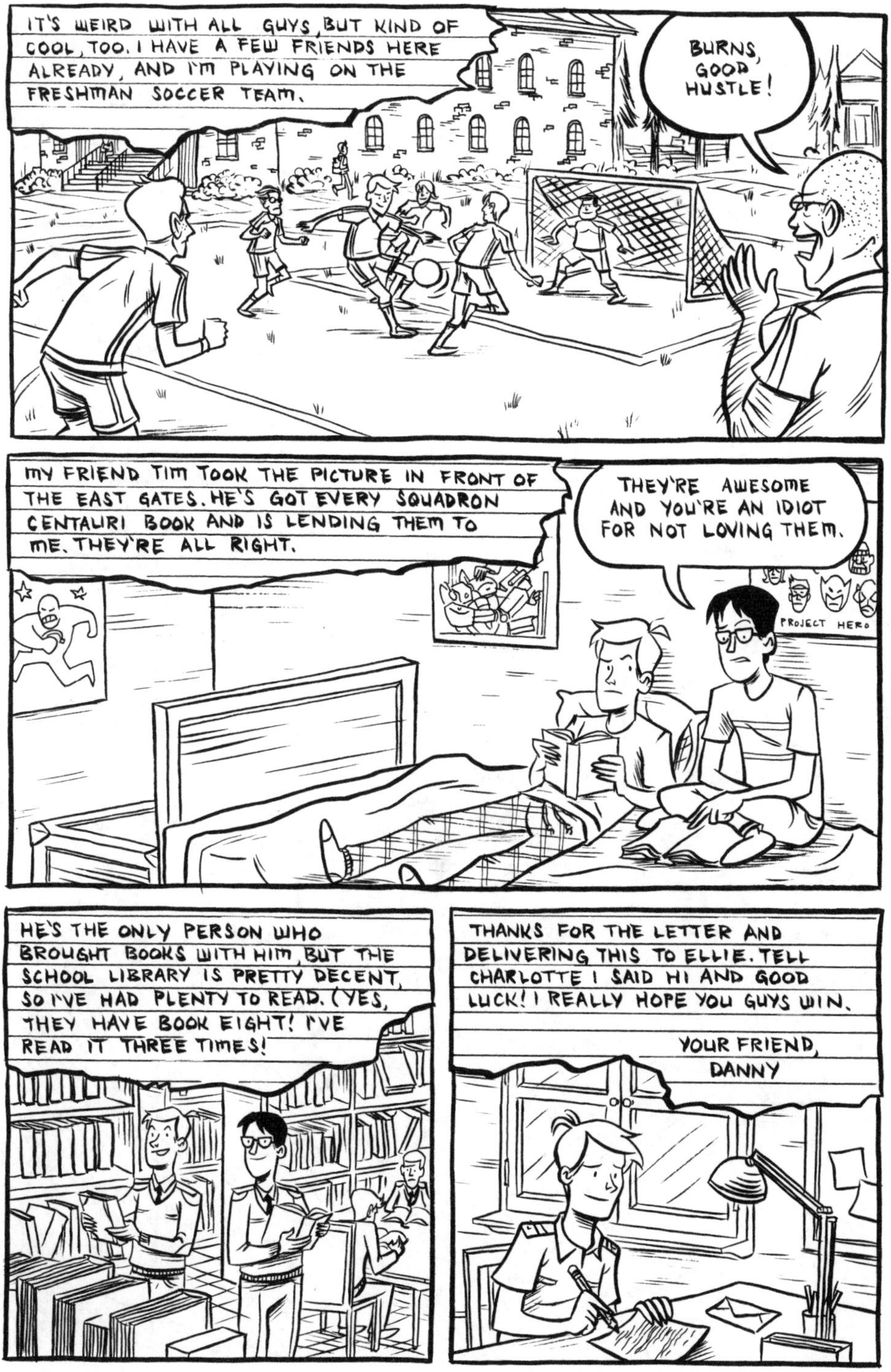
IT'S WEIRD WITH ALL GUYS, BUT KIND OF COOL, TOO. I HAVE A FEW FRIENDS HERE ALREADY, AND I'M PLAYING ON THE FRESHMAN SOCCER TEAM.
BURNS, GOOD HUSTLE!
MY FRIEND TIM TOOK THE PICTURE IN FRONT OF THE EAST GATES. HE'S GOT EVERY SQUADRON CENTAURI BOOK AND IS LENDING THEM TO ME. THEY'RE ALL RIGHT.
THEY'RE AWESOME AND YOU'RE AN IDIOT FOR NOT LOVING THEM.
PROJECT HERO
HE'S THE ONLY PERSON WHO BROUGHT BOOKS WITH HIM, BUT THE SCHOOL LIBRARY IS PRETTY DECENT, SO I'VE HAD PLENTY TO READ. (YES, THEY HAVE BOOK EIGHT! I'VE READ IT THREE TIMES!
THANKS FOR THE LETTER AND DELIVERING THIS TO ELLIE. TELL CHARLOTTE I SAID HI AND GOOD LUCK! I REALLY HOPE YOU GUYS WIN.
YOUR FRIEND,
DANNY

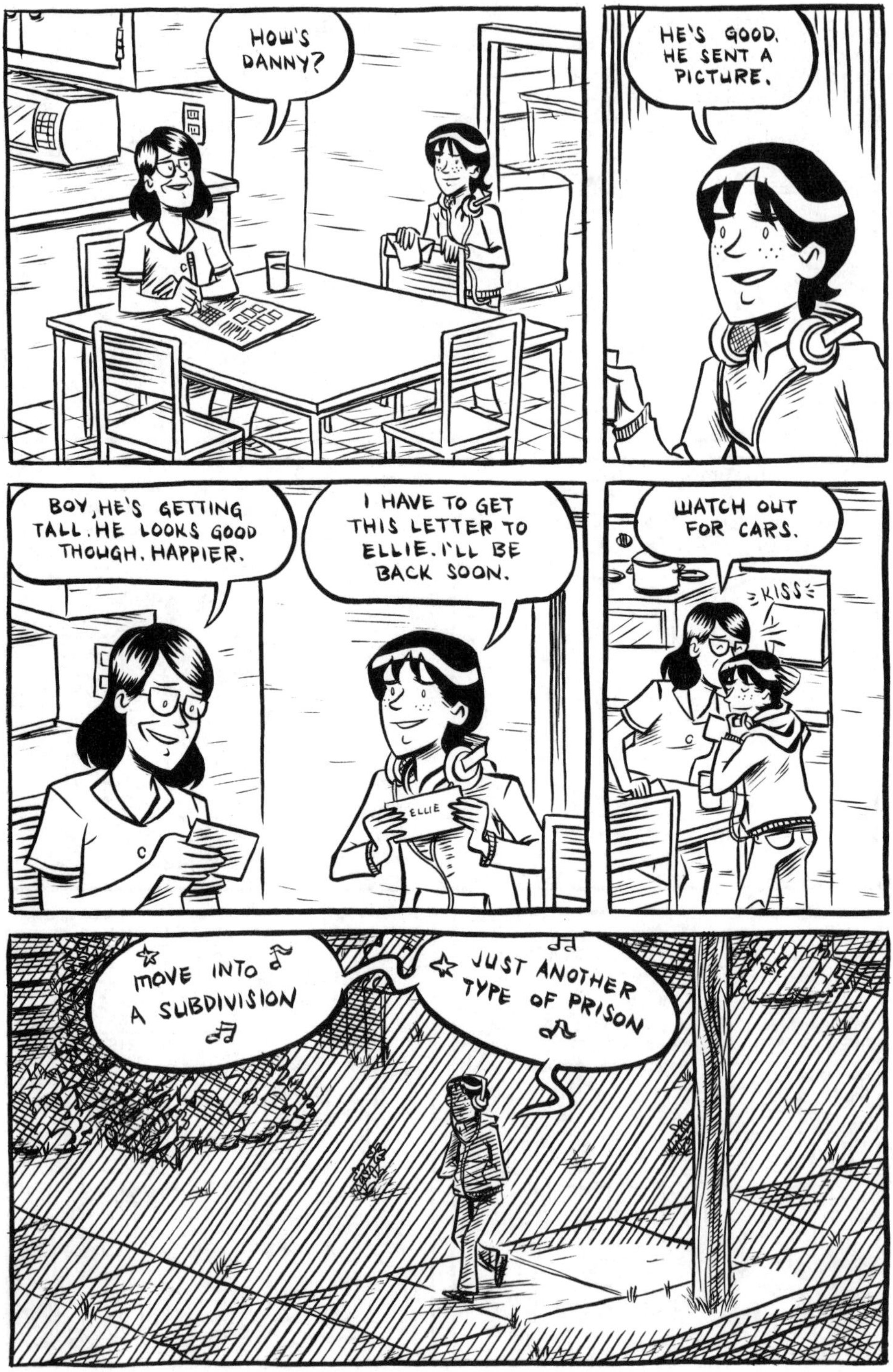
HOW'S DANNY?
HE'S GOOD. HE SENT A PICTURE.
BOY, HE'S GETTING TALL. HE LOOKS GOOD THOUGH. HAPPIER.
I HAVE TO GET THIS LETTER TO ELLIE. I'LL BE BACK SOON.
ELLIE
WATCH OUT FOR CARS.
KISS
MOVE INTO A SUBDIVISION
JUST ANOTHER TYPE OF PRISON

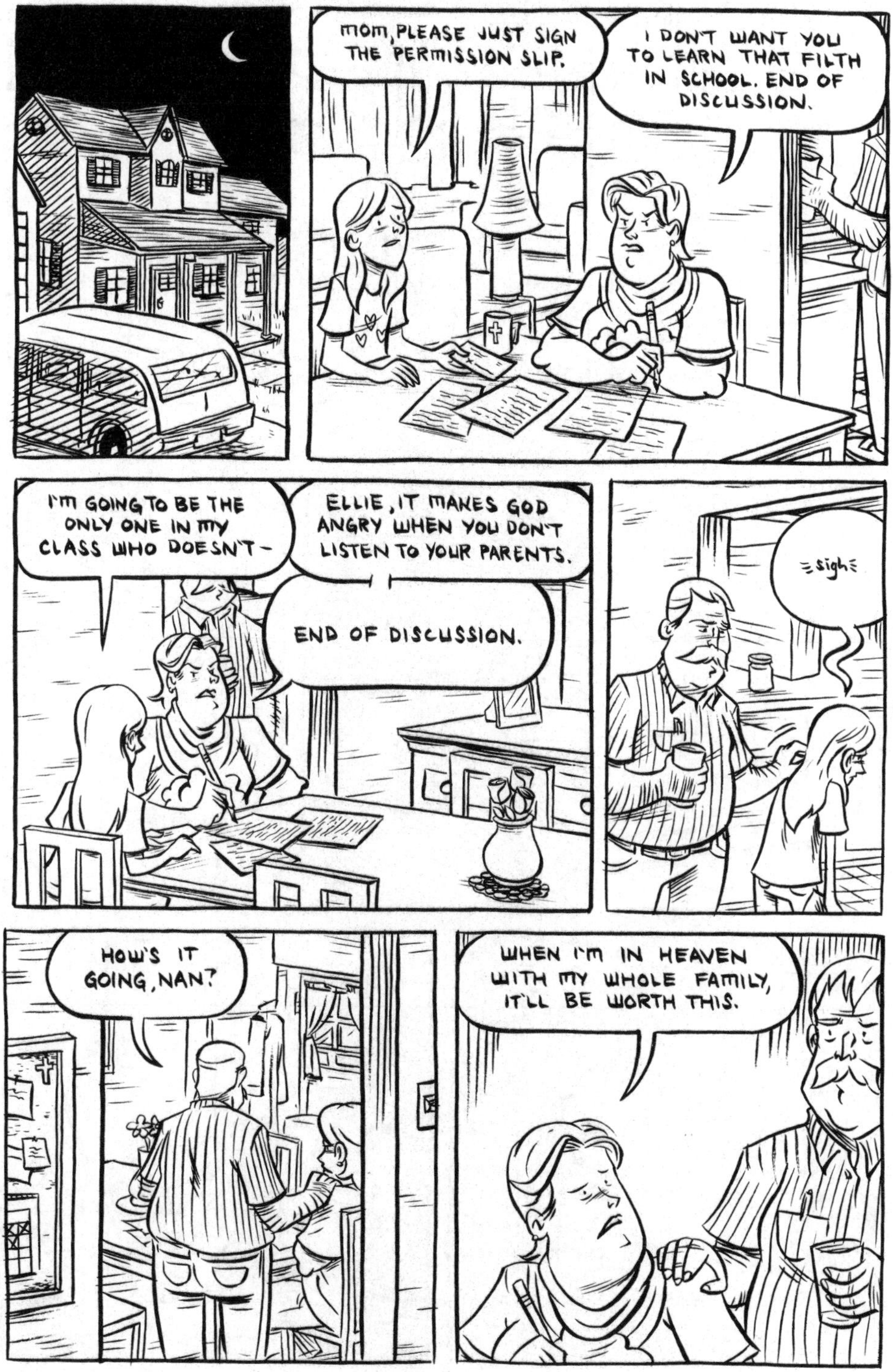
MOM, PLEASE JUST SIGN THE PERMISSION SLIP.
I DON'T WANT YOU TO LEARN THAT FILTH IN SCHOOL. END OF DISCUSSION.
I'M GOING TO BE THE ONLY ONE IN MY CLASS WHO DOESN'T-
ELLIE, IT MAKES GOD ANGRY WHEN YOU DON'T LISTEN TO YOUR PARENTS.
END OF DISCUSSION.
sigh
HOW'S IT GOING, NAN?
WHEN I'M IN HEAVEN WITH MY WHOLE FAMILY, IT'LL BE WORTH THIS.

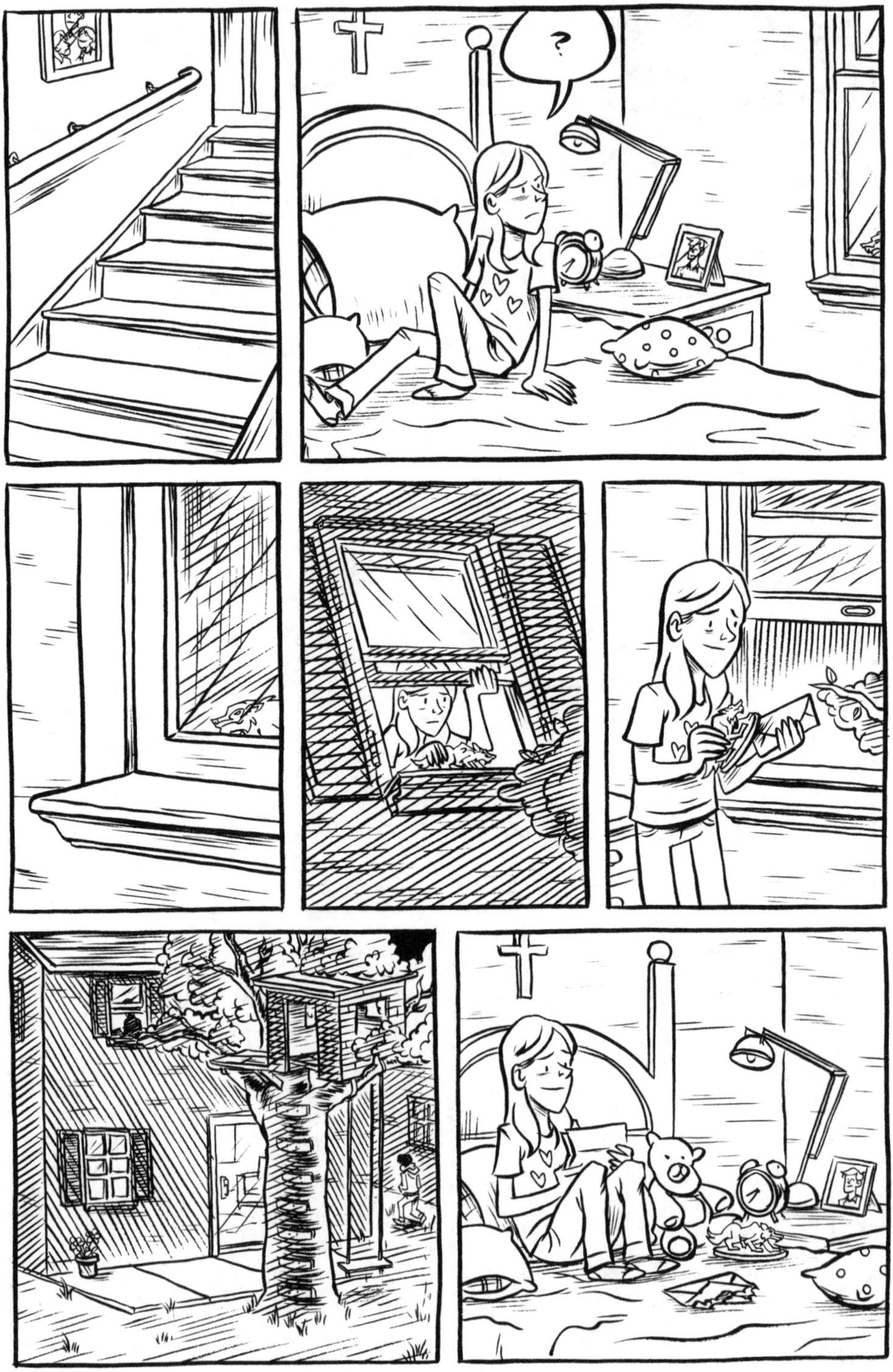
?

CHAPTER 8

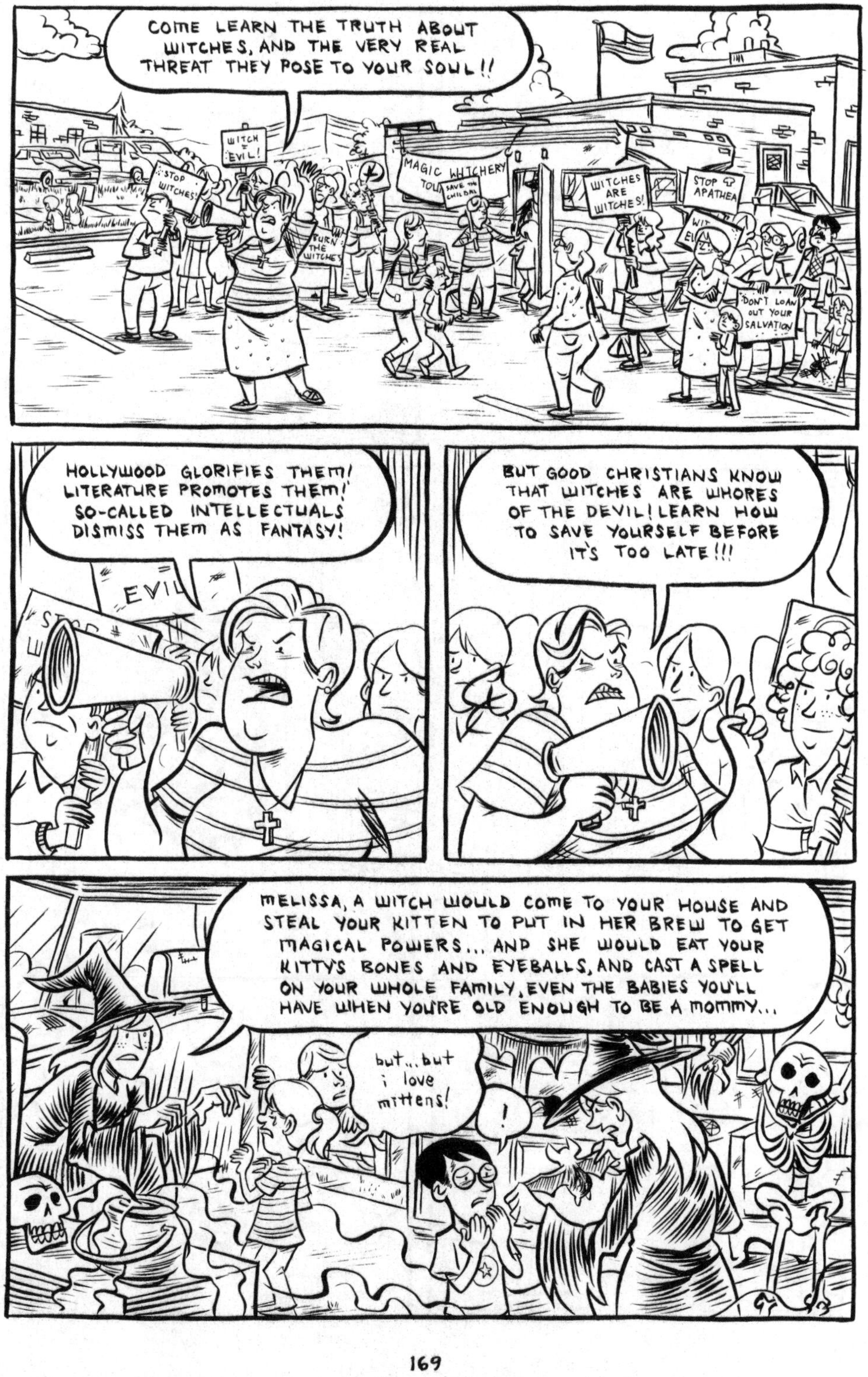
COME LEARN THE TRUTH ABOUT WITCHES, AND THE VERY REAL THREAT THEY POSE TO YOUR SOUL!!
WITCH = EVIL!
STOP WITCHES!
BURN THE WITCHES
MAGIC WITCHERY TOU
WITCHES ARE WITCHES!
STOP APATHEA
DON'T LOAN OUT YOUR SALVATION
HOLLYWOOD GLORIFIES THEM! LITERATURE PROMOTES THEM! SO-CALLED INTELLECTUALS DISMISS THEM AS FANTASY!
EVIL
BUT GOOD CHRISTIANS KNOW THAT WITCHES ARE WHORES OF THE DEVIL! LEARN HOW TO SAVE YOURSELF BEFORE IT'S TOO LATE!!!
MELISSA, A WITCH WOULD COME TO YOUR HOUSE AND STEAL YOUR KITTEN TO PUT IN HER BREW TO GET MAGICAL POWERS... AND SHE WOULD EAT YOUR KITTY'S BONES AND EYEBALLS, AND CAST A SPELL ON YOUR WHOLE FAMILY, EVEN THE BABIES YOU'LL HAVE WHEN YOU'RE OLD ENOUGH TO BE A MOMMY...
but... but i love mittens!
!

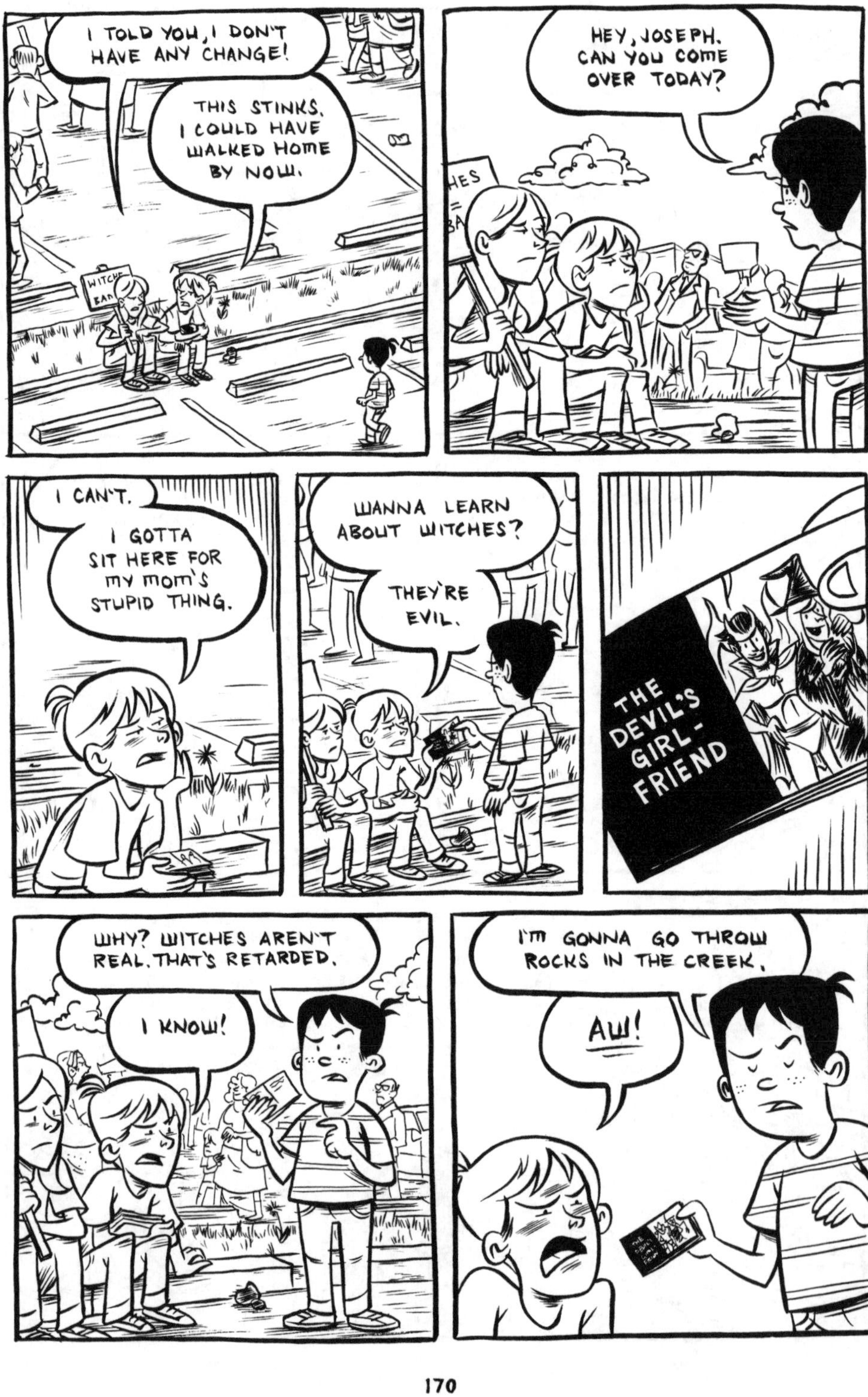

I TOLD YOU, I DON'T HAVE ANY CHANGE!
THIS STINKS. I COULD HAVE WALKED HOME BY NOW.
HEY, JOSEPH. CAN YOU COME OVER TODAY?
I CAN'T.
I GOTTA SIT HERE FOR MY MOM'S STUPID THING.
WANNA LEARN ABOUT WITCHES?
THEY'RE EVIL.
THE DEVIL'S GIRL-FRIEND
WHY? WITCHES AREN'T REAL. THAT'S RETARDED.
I KNOW!
I'M GONNA GO THROW ROCKS IN THE CREEK.
AW!

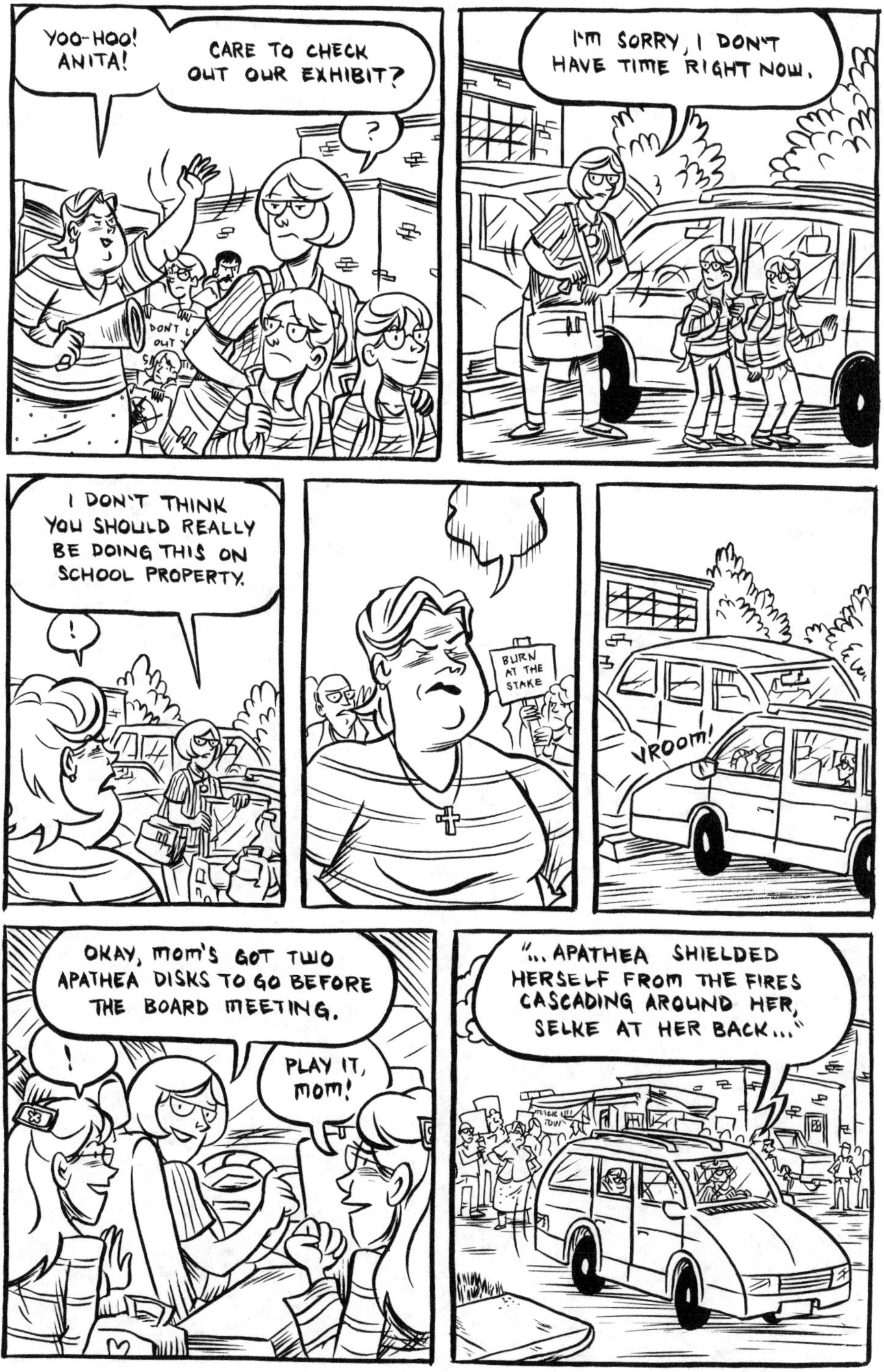
YOO-HOO! ANITA!
CARE TO CHECK OUT OUR EXHIBIT?
?
I'M SORRY, I DON'T HAVE TIME RIGHT NOW.
I DON'T THINK YOU SHOULD REALLY BE DOING THIS ON SCHOOL PROPERTY.
!
BURN AT THE STAKE
VROOM!
OKAY, MOM'S GOT TWO APATHEA DISKS TO GO BEFORE THE BOARD MEETING.
!
PLAY IT, MOM!
"...APATHEA SHIELDED HERSELF FROM THE FIRES CASCADING AROUND HER, SELKE AT HER BACK..."

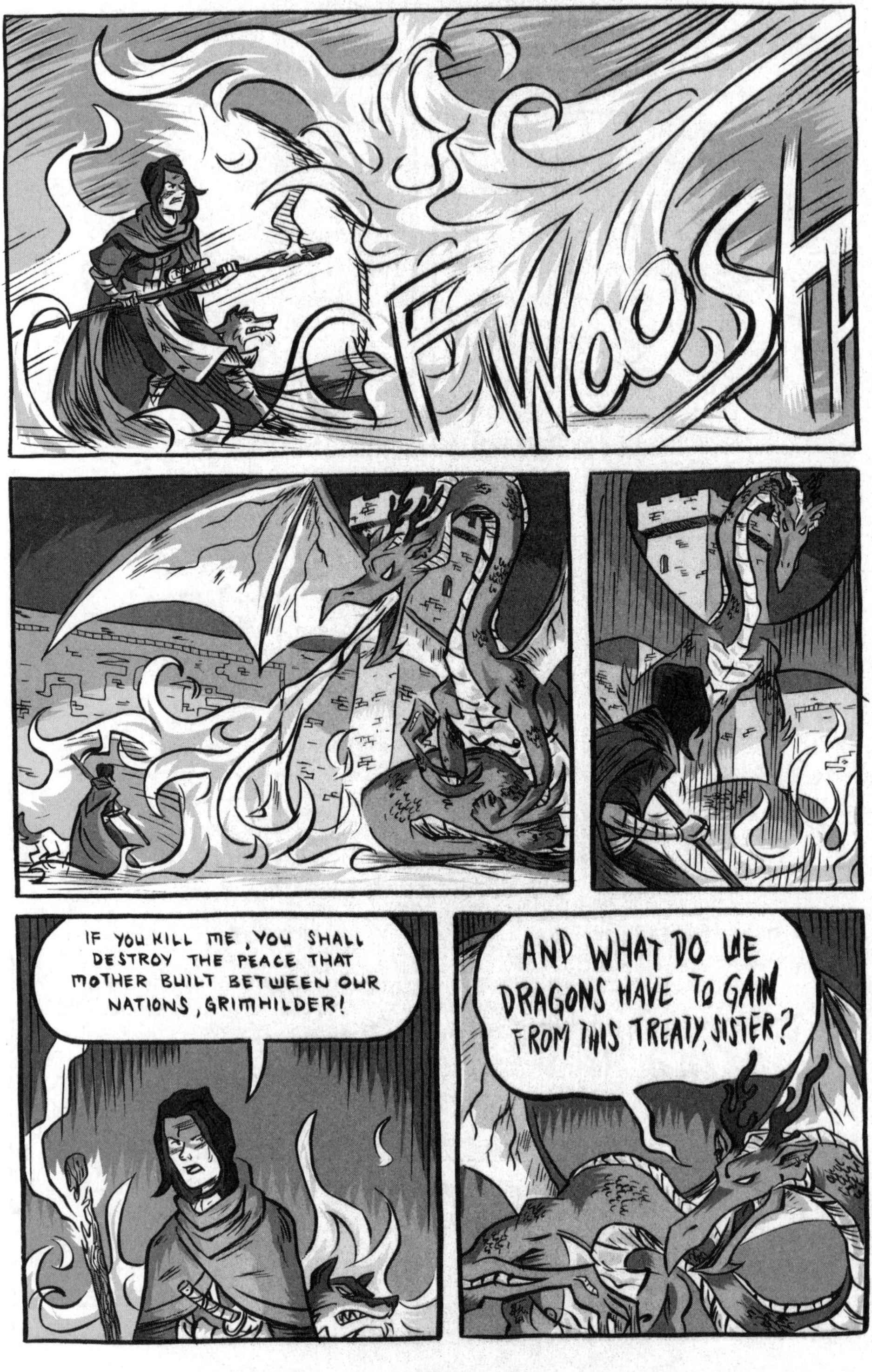
FWOOSH
IF YOU KILL ME, YOU SHALL DESTROY THE PEACE THAT MOTHER BUILT BETWEEN OUR NATIONS, GRIMHILDER!
AND WHAT DO WE DRAGONS HAVE TO GAIN FROM THIS TREATY, SISTER?

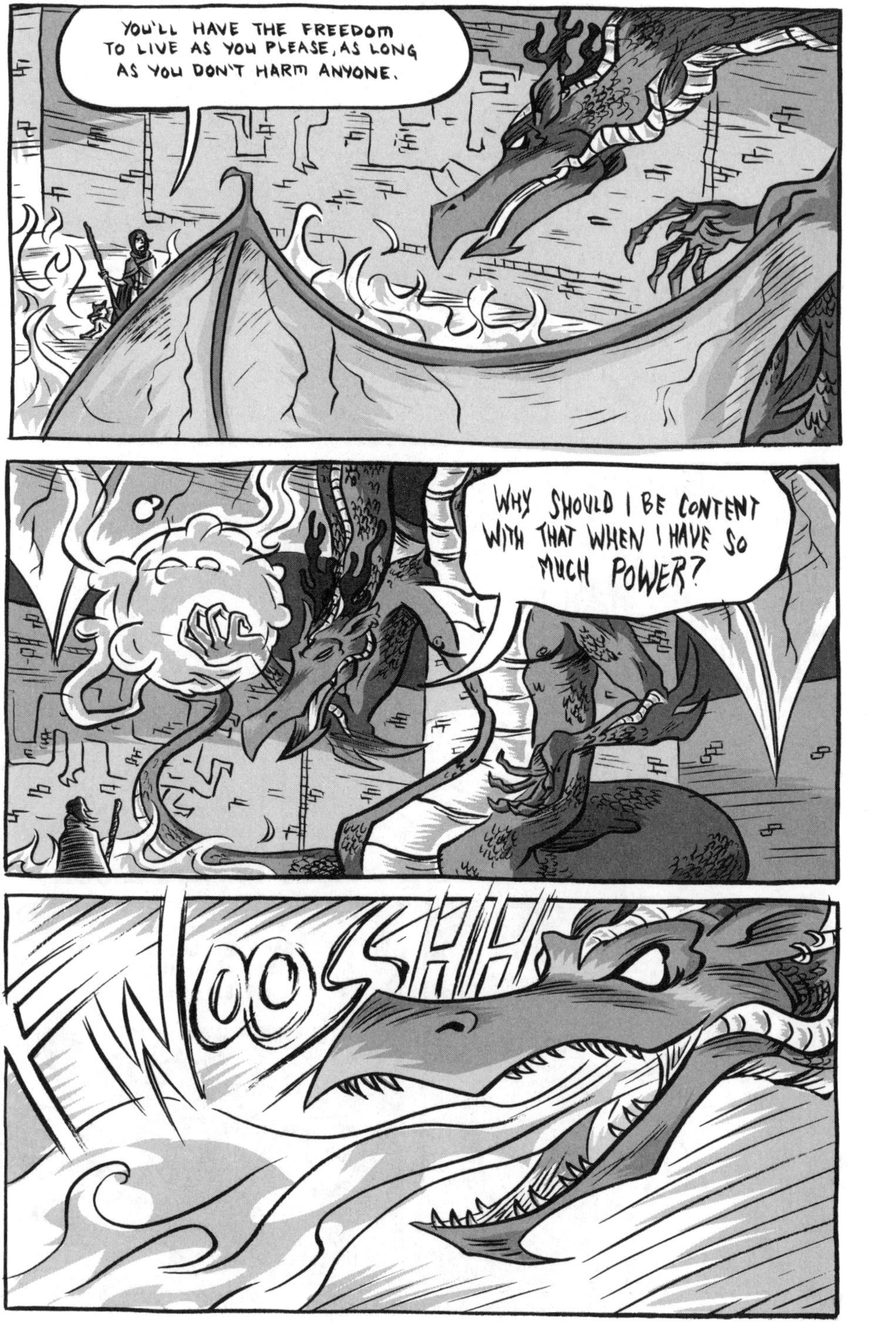
YOU'LL HAVE THE FREEDOM TO LIVE AS YOU PLEASE, AS LONG AS YOU DON'T HARM ANYONE.
WHY SHOULD I BE CONTENT WITH THAT WHEN I HAVE SO MUCH POWER?
WOOSHHH

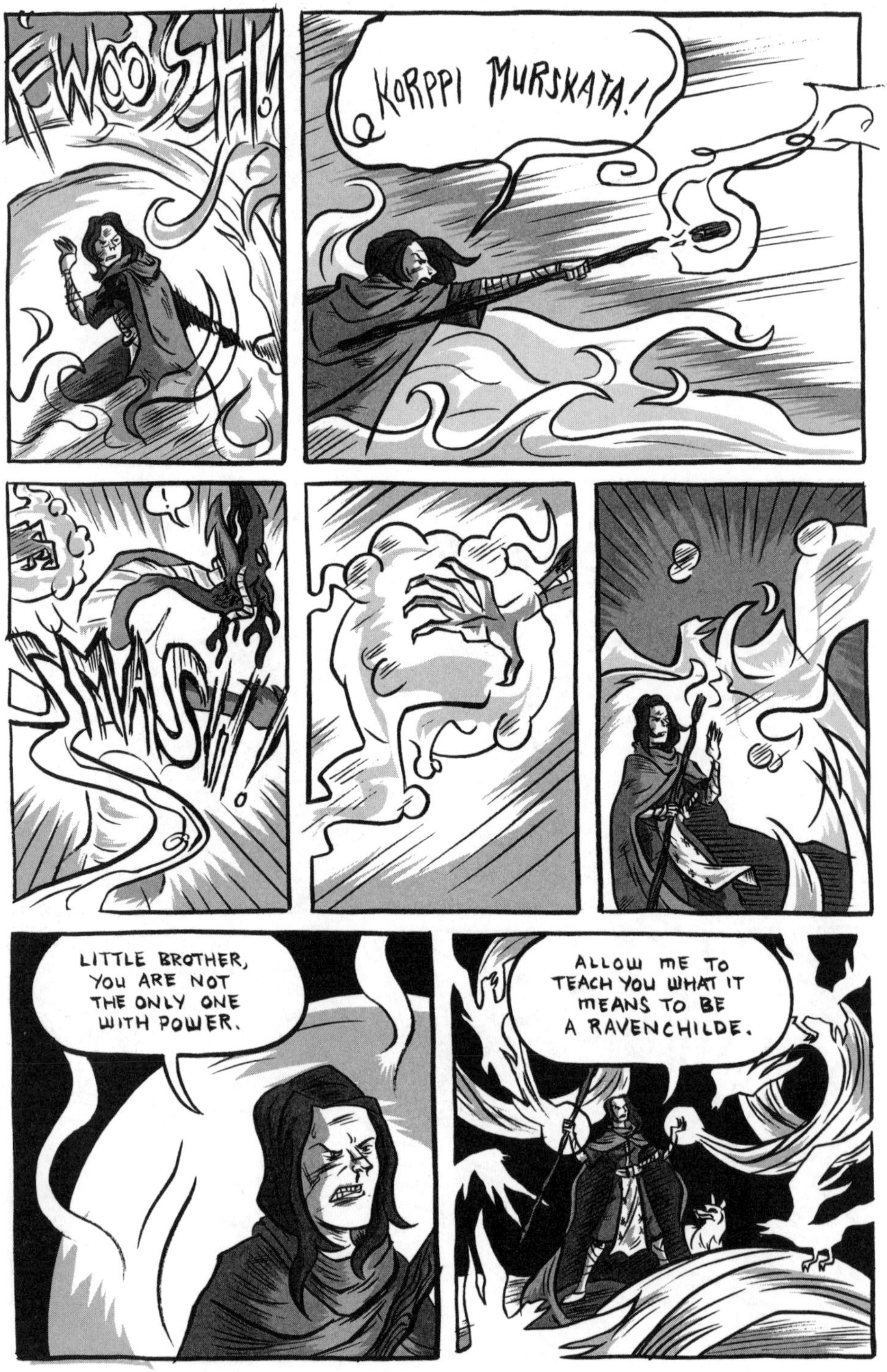
FWOOSH!
KORPPI MURSKATA!
!
SMASH!!
LITTLE BROTHER, YOU ARE NOT THE ONLY ONE WITH POWER.
ALLOW ME TO TEACH YOU WHAT IT MEANS TO BE A RAVENCHILDE.

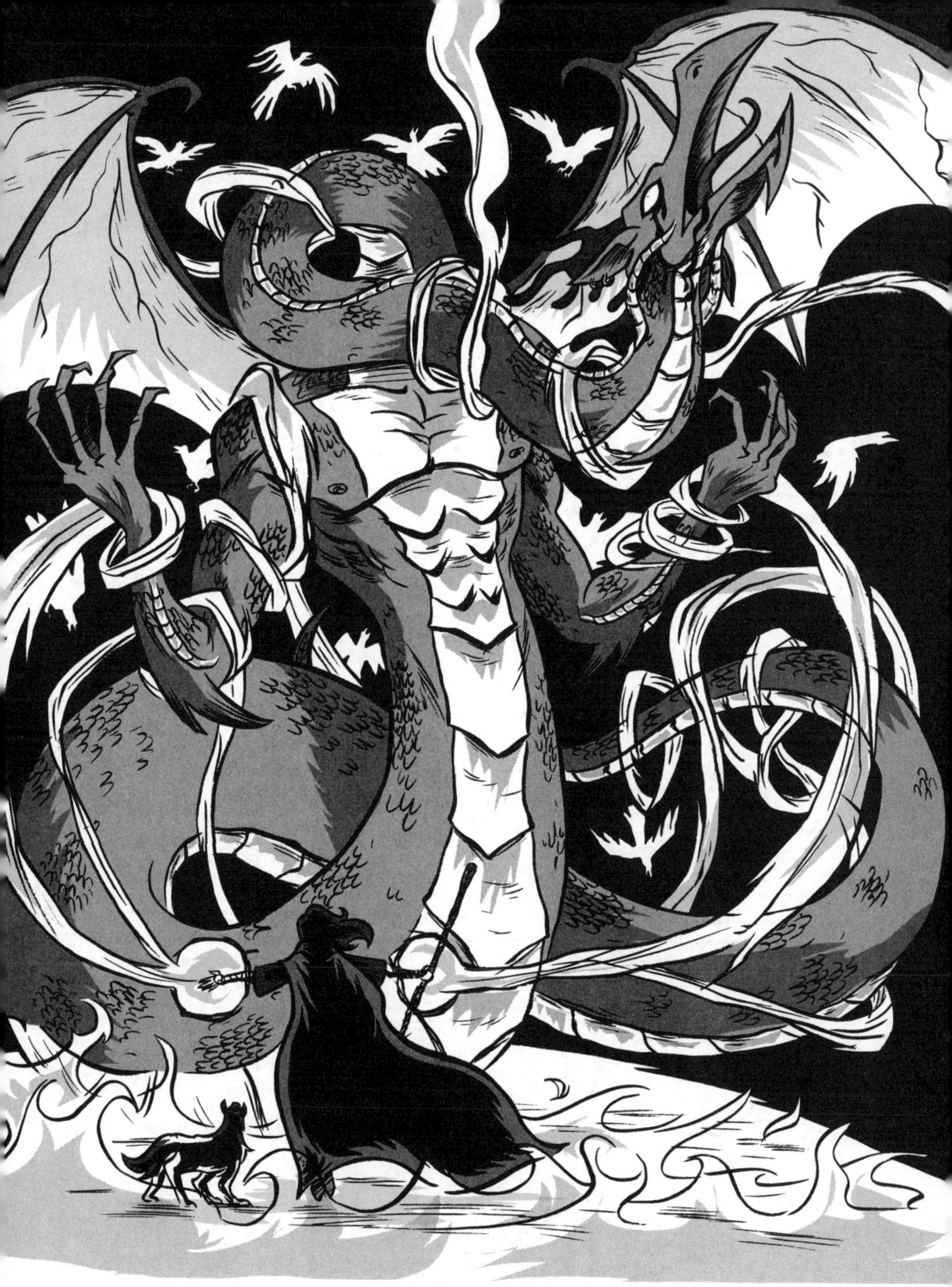

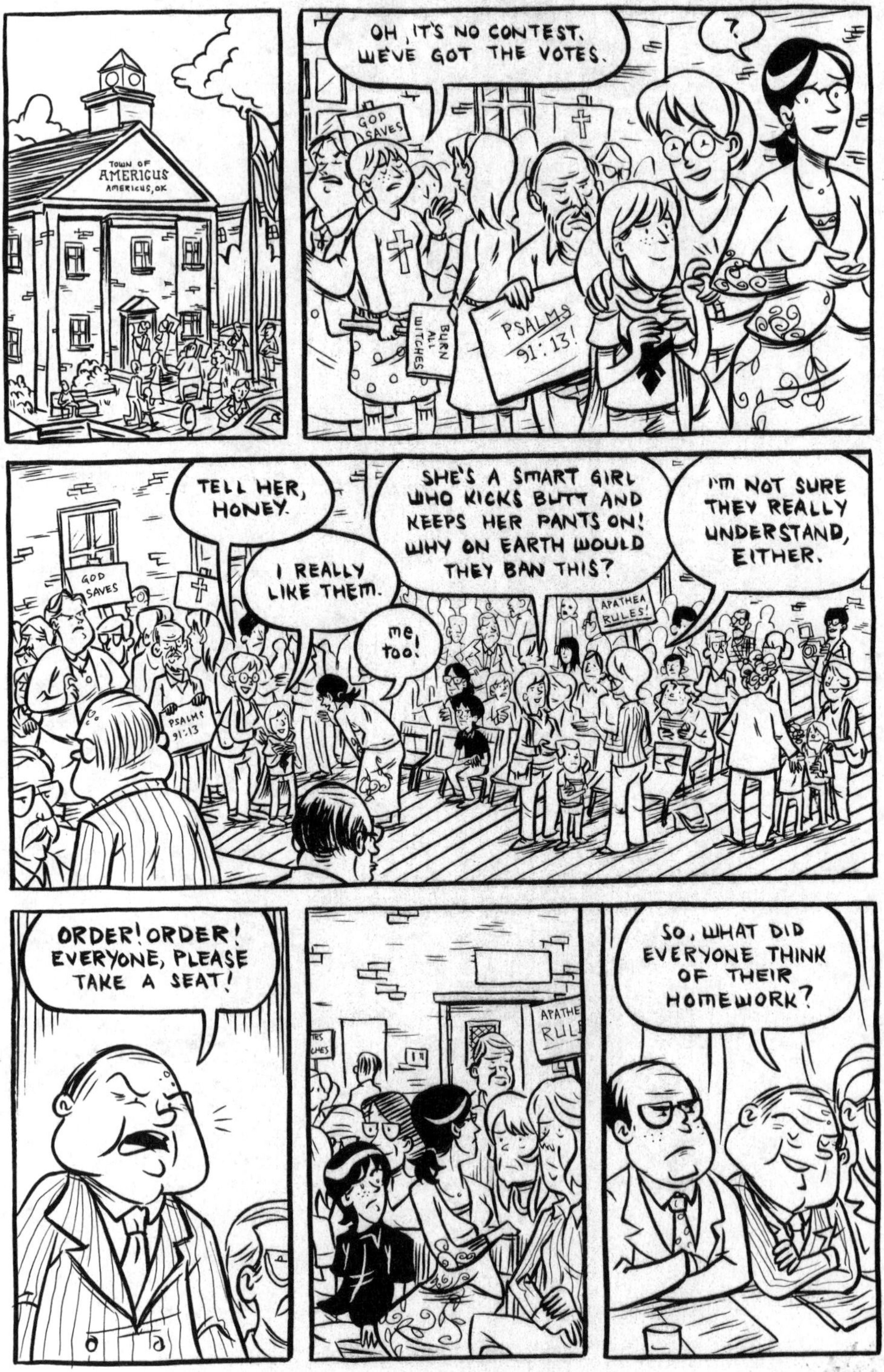
TOWN OF
AMERICUS
AMERICUS, OK
OH, IT'S NO CONTEST. WE'VE GOT THE VOTES.
?
GOD SAVES
BURN ALL WITCHES
PSALMS 91:13!
TELL HER, HONEY.
I REALLY LIKE THEM.
me, too!
SHE'S A SMART GIRL WHO KICKS BUTT AND KEEPS HER PANTS ON! WHY ON EARTH WOULD THEY BAN THIS?
I'M NOT SURE THEY REALLY UNDERSTAND, EITHER.
GOD SAVES
PSALMS 91:13
APATHEA RULES!
ORDER! ORDER! EVERYONE, PLEASE TAKE A SEAT!
SO, WHAT DID EVERYONE THINK OF THEIR HOMEWORK?

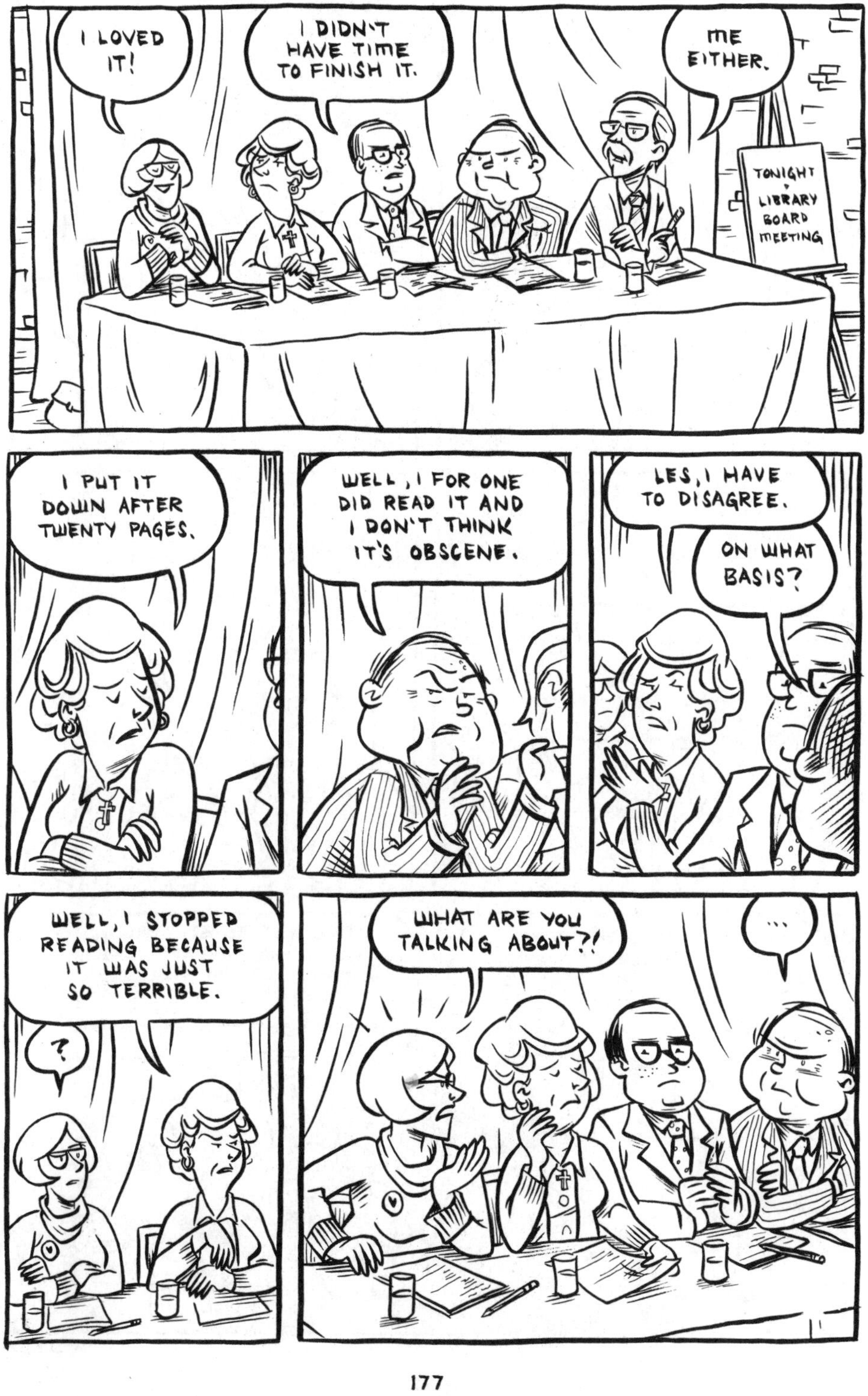
I LOVED IT!
I DIDN'T HAVE TIME TO FINISH IT.
ME EITHER.
TONIGHT LIBRARY BOARD MEETING
I PUT IT DOWN AFTER TWENTY PAGES.
WELL, I FOR ONE DID READ IT AND I DON'T THINK IT'S OBSCENE.
LES, I HAVE TO DISAGREE.
ON WHAT BASIS?
WELL, I STOPPED READING BECAUSE IT WAS JUST SO TERRIBLE.
?
WHAT ARE YOU TALKING ABOUT?!
...

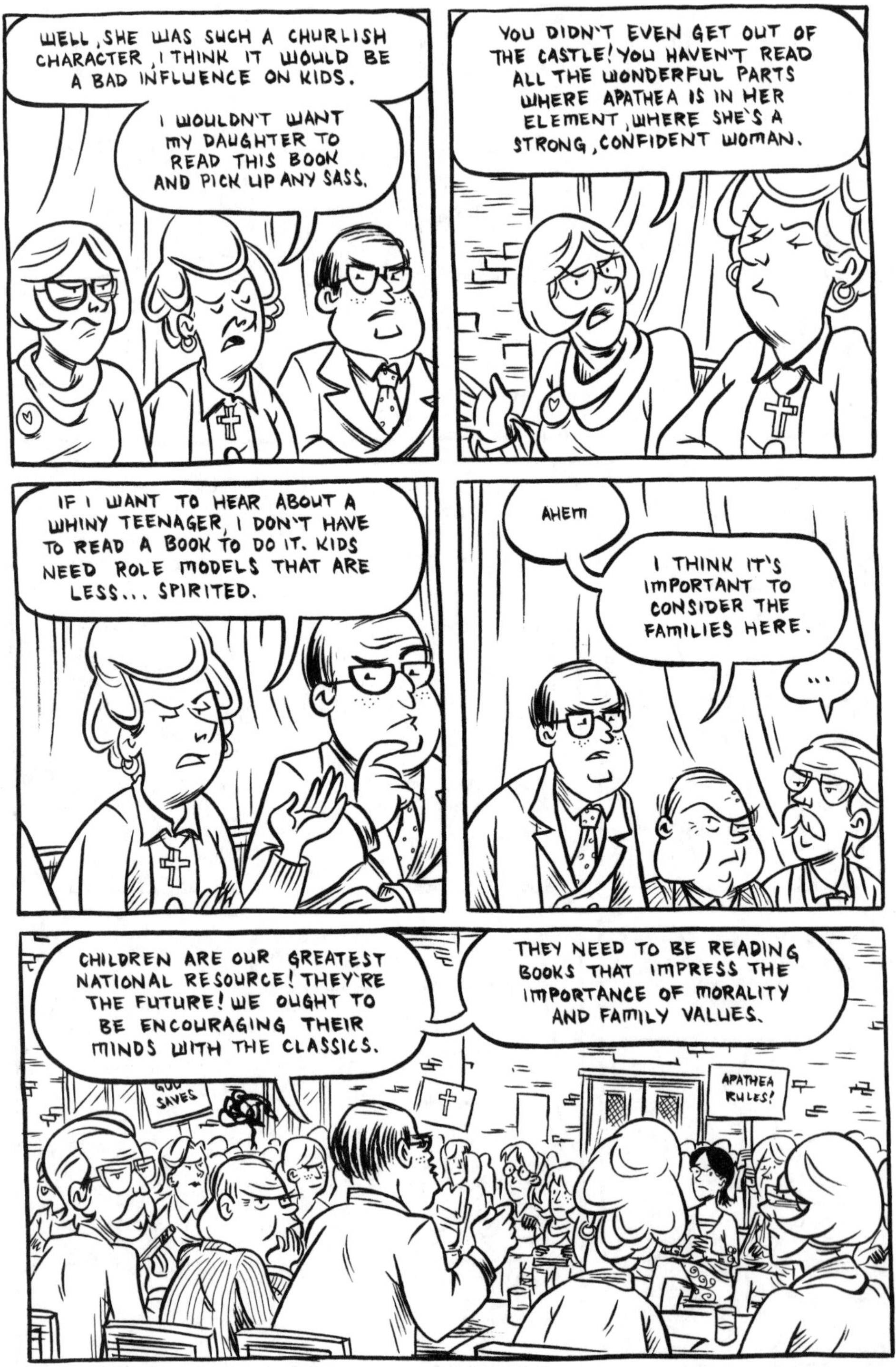
WELL, SHE WAS SUCH A CHURLISH CHARACTER, I THINK IT WOULD BE A BAD INFLUENCE ON KIDS.
I WOULDN'T WANT MY DAUGHTER TO READ THIS BOOK AND PICK UP ANY SASS.
YOU DIDN'T EVEN GET OUT OF THE CASTLE! YOU HAVEN'T READ ALL THE WONDERFUL PARTS WHERE APATHEA IS IN HER ELEMENT, WHERE SHE'S A STRONG, CONFIDENT WOMAN.
IF I WANT TO HEAR ABOUT A WHINY TEENAGER, I DON'T HAVE TO READ A BOOK TO DO IT. KIDS NEED ROLE MODELS THAT ARE LESS... SPIRITED.
AHEM
I THINK IT'S IMPORTANT TO CONSIDER THE FAMILIES HERE.
...
CHILDREN ARE OUR GREATEST NATIONAL RESOURCE! THEY'RE THE FUTURE! WE OUGHT TO BE ENCOURAGING THEIR MINDS WITH THE CLASSICS.
THEY NEED TO BE READING BOOKS THAT IMPRESS THE IMPORTANCE OF MORALITY AND FAMILY VALUES.
SAVES
APATHEA RULES!

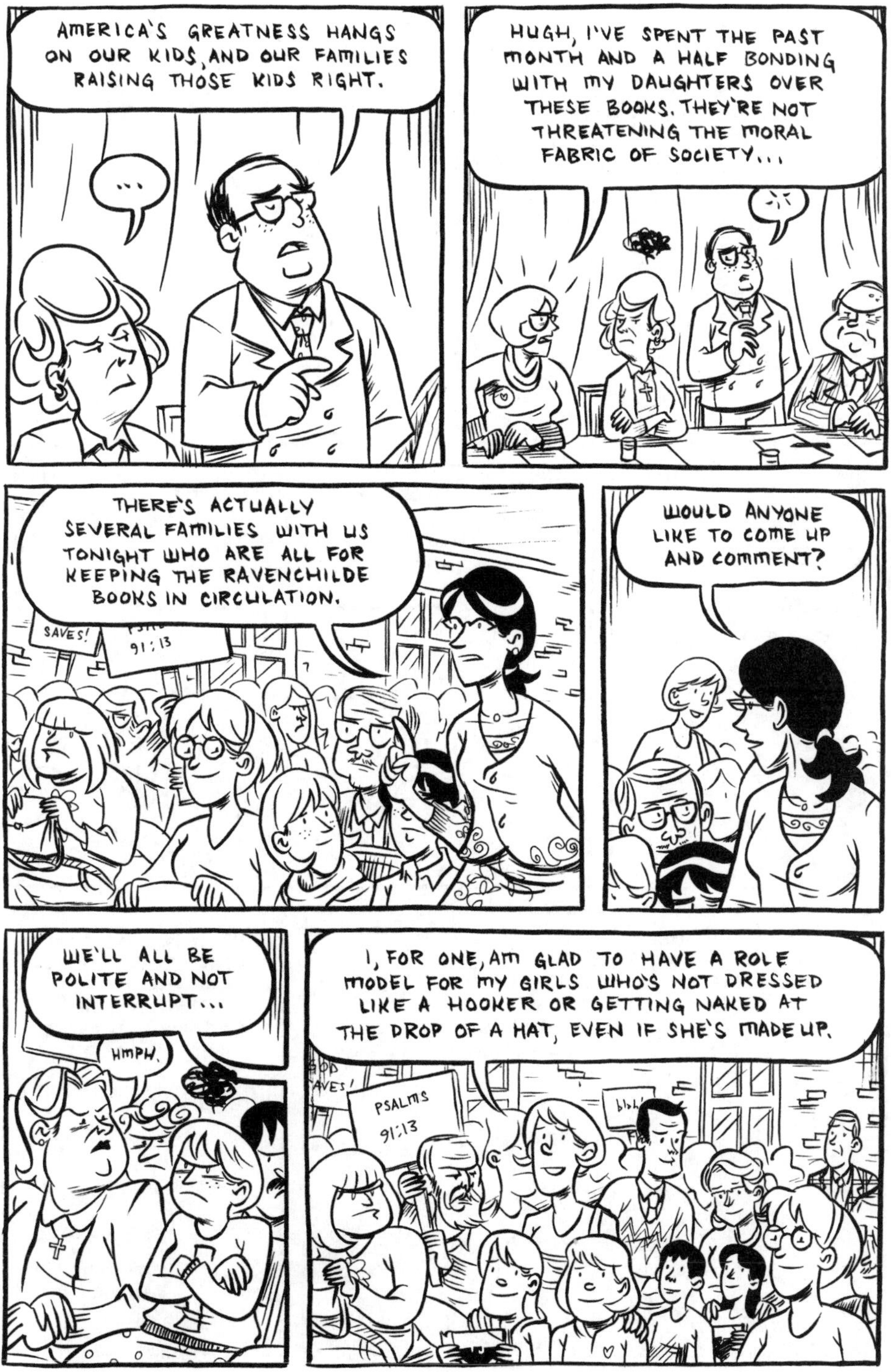
AMERICA'S GREATNESS HANGS ON OUR KIDS, AND OUR FAMILIES RAISING THOSE KIDS RIGHT.
...
HUGH, I'VE SPENT THE PAST MONTH AND A HALF BONDING WITH MY DAUGHTERS OVER THESE BOOKS. THEY'RE NOT THREATENING THE MORAL FABRIC OF SOCIETY...
THERE'S ACTUALLY SEVERAL FAMILIES WITH US TONIGHT WHO ARE ALL FOR KEEPING THE RAVENCHILDE BOOKS IN CIRCULATION.
SAVES!
91:13
WOULD ANYONE LIKE TO COME UP AND COMMENT?
WE'LL ALL BE POLITE AND NOT INTERRUPT...
HMPH.
I, FOR ONE, AM GLAD TO HAVE A ROLE MODEL FOR MY GIRLS WHO'S NOT DRESSED LIKE A HOOKER OR GETTING NAKED AT THE DROP OF A HAT, EVEN IF SHE'S MADE UP.
PSALMS 91:13
blah

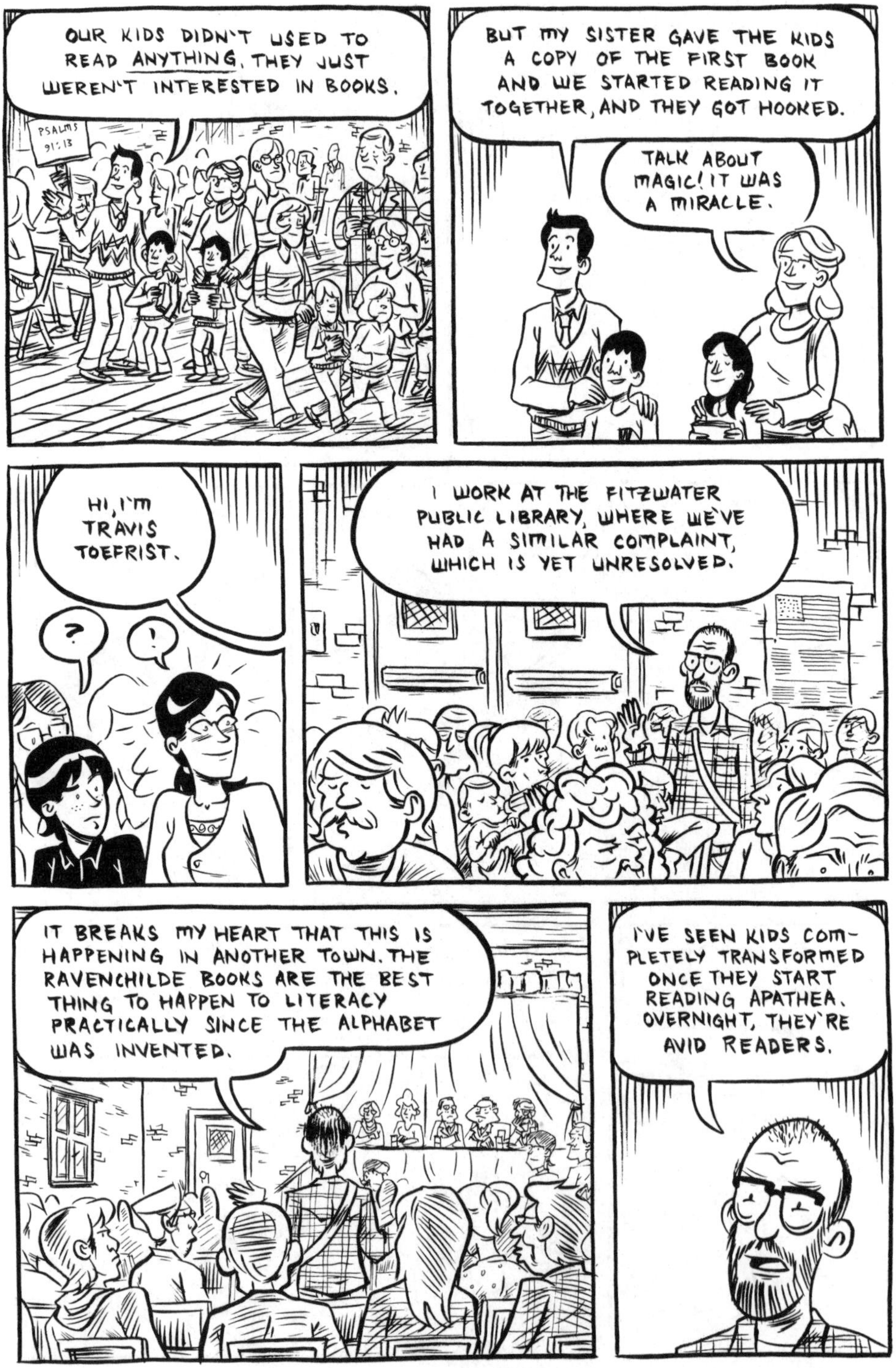
OUR KIDS DIDN'T USED TO READ ANYTHING. THEY JUST WEREN'T INTERESTED IN BOOKS.
PSALMS 91:13
BUT MY SISTER GAVE THE KIDS A COPY OF THE FIRST BOOK AND WE STARTED READING IT TOGETHER, AND THEY GOT HOOKED.
TALK ABOUT MAGIC! IT WAS A MIRACLE.
HI, I'M TRAVIS TOEFRIST.
?
!
I WORK AT THE FITZWATER PUBLIC LIBRARY, WHERE WE'VE HAD A SIMILAR COMPLAINT, WHICH IS YET UNRESOLVED.
IT BREAKS MY HEART THAT THIS IS HAPPENING IN ANOTHER TOWN. THE RAVENCHILDE BOOKS ARE THE BEST THING TO HAPPEN TO LITERACY PRACTICALLY SINCE THE ALPHABET WAS INVENTED.
I'VE SEEN KIDS COMPLETELY TRANSFORMED ONCE THEY START READING APATHEA. OVERNIGHT, THEY'RE AVID READERS.

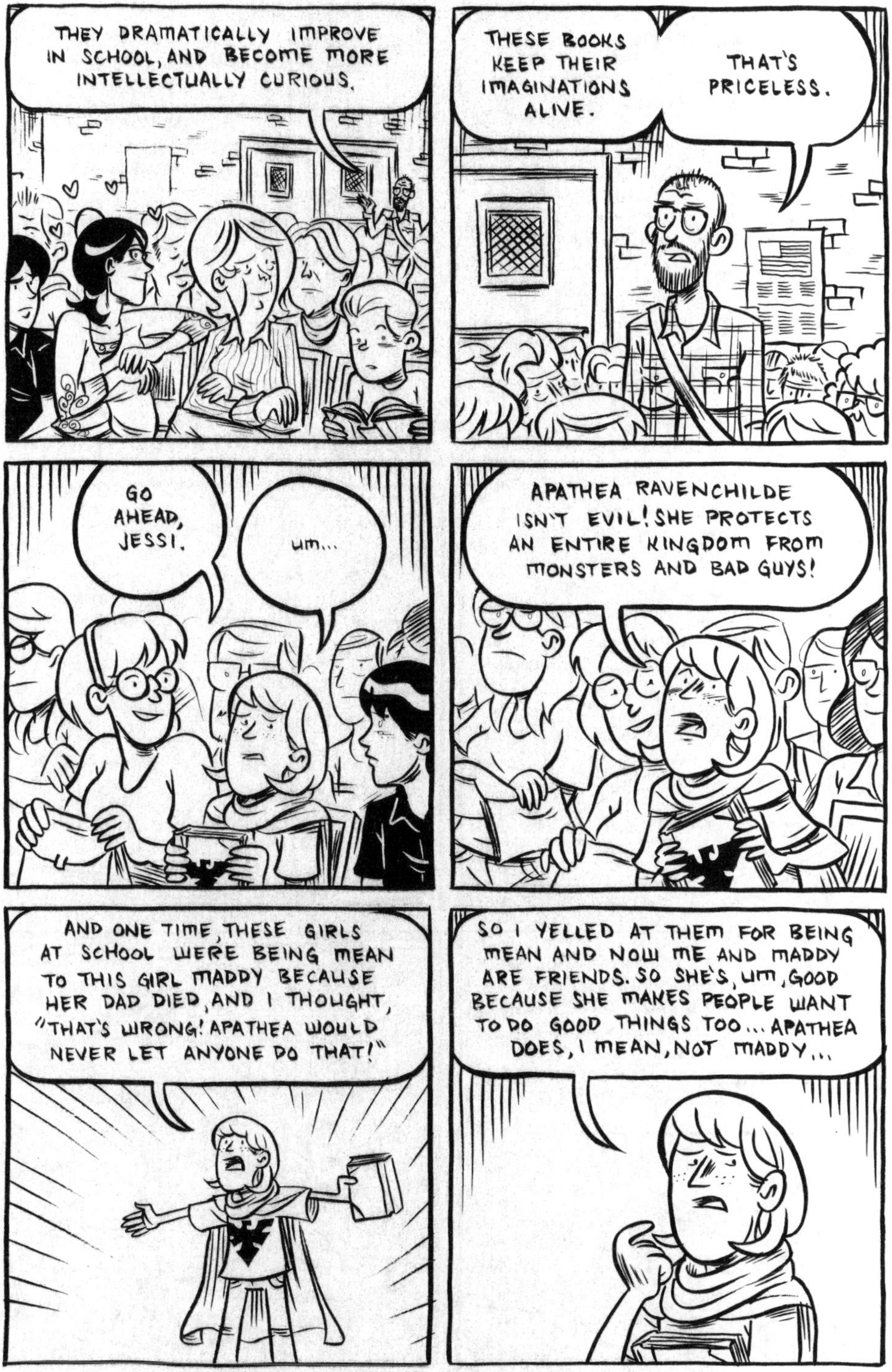
THEY DRAMATICALLY IMPROVE IN SCHOOL, AND BECOME MORE INTELLECTUALLY CURIOUS.
THESE BOOKS KEEP THEIR IMAGINATIONS ALIVE.
THAT'S PRICELESS.
GO AHEAD, JESSI.
um...
APATHEA RAVENCHILDE ISN'T EVIL! SHE PROTECTS AN ENTIRE KINGDOM FROM MONSTERS AND BAD GUYS!
AND ONE TIME, THESE GIRLS AT SCHOOL WERE BEING MEAN TO THIS GIRL MADDY BECAUSE HER DAD DIED, AND I THOUGHT, "THAT'S WRONG! APATHEA WOULD NEVER LET ANYONE DO THAT!"
SO I YELLED AT THEM FOR BEING MEAN AND NOW ME AND MADDY ARE FRIENDS. SO SHE'S, UM, GOOD BECAUSE SHE MAKES PEOPLE WANT TO DO GOOD THINGS TOO... APATHEA DOES, I MEAN, NOT MADDY...

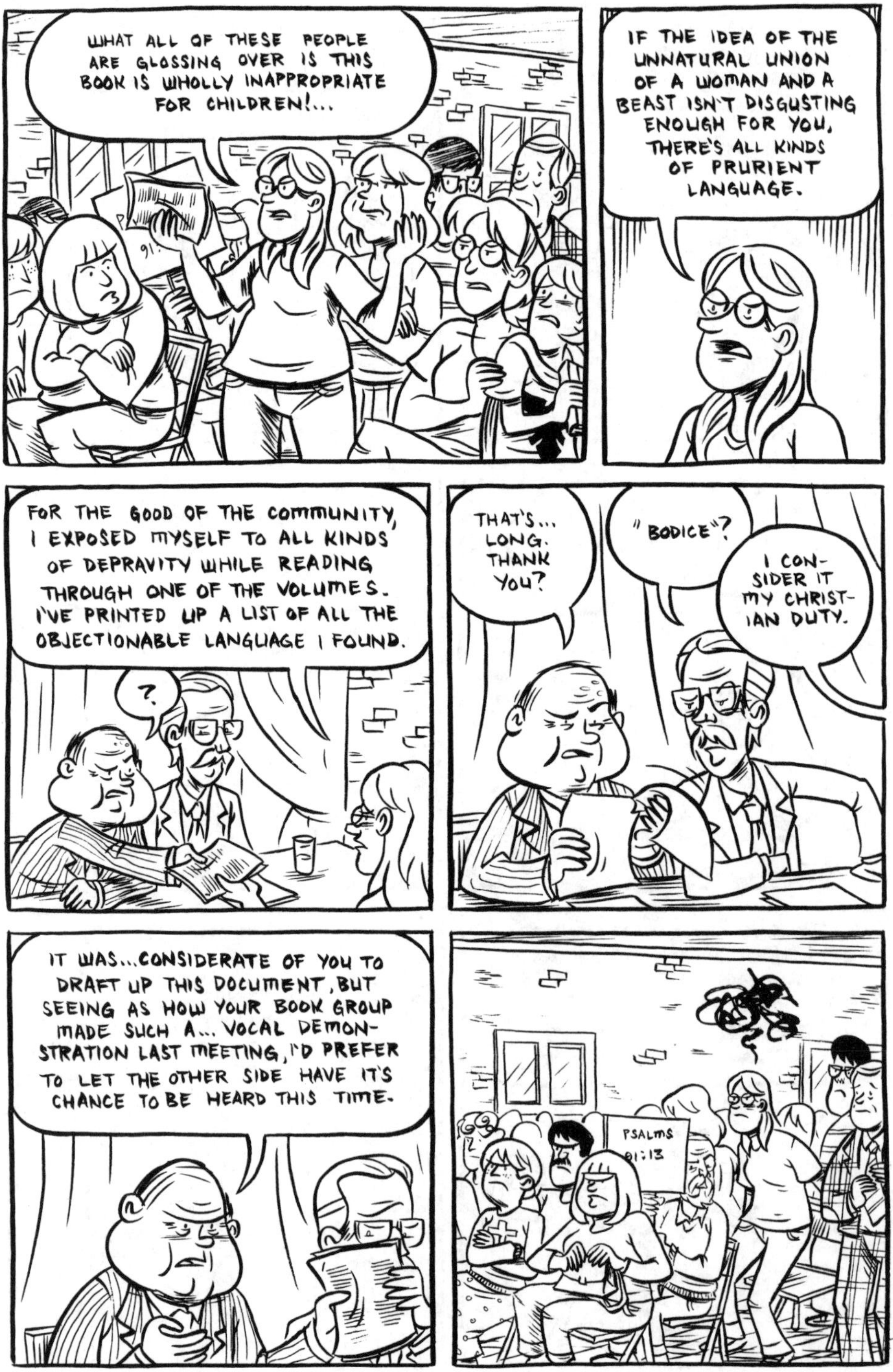
WHAT ALL OF THESE PEOPLE ARE GLOSSING OVER IS THIS BOOK IS WHOLLY INAPPROPRIATE FOR CHILDREN!...
IF THE IDEA OF THE UNNATURAL UNION OF A WOMAN AND A BEAST ISN'T DISGUSTING ENOUGH FOR YOU, THERE'S ALL KINDS OF PRURIENT LANGUAGE.
FOR THE GOOD OF THE COMMUNITY, I EXPOSED MYSELF TO ALL KINDS OF DEPRAVITY WHILE READING THROUGH ONE OF THE VOLUMES. I'VE PRINTED UP A LIST OF ALL THE OBJECTIONABLE LANGUAGE I FOUND.
?
THAT'S... LONG. THANK YOU?
"BODICE"?
I CONSIDER IT MY CHRISTIAN DUTY.
IT WAS...CONSIDERATE OF YOU TO DRAFT UP THIS DOCUMENT, BUT SEEING AS HOW YOUR BOOK GROUP MADE SUCH A... VOCAL DEMONSTRATION LAST MEETING, I'D PREFER TO LET THE OTHER SIDE HAVE IT'S CHANCE TO BE HEARD THIS TIME.
PSALMS 91:13

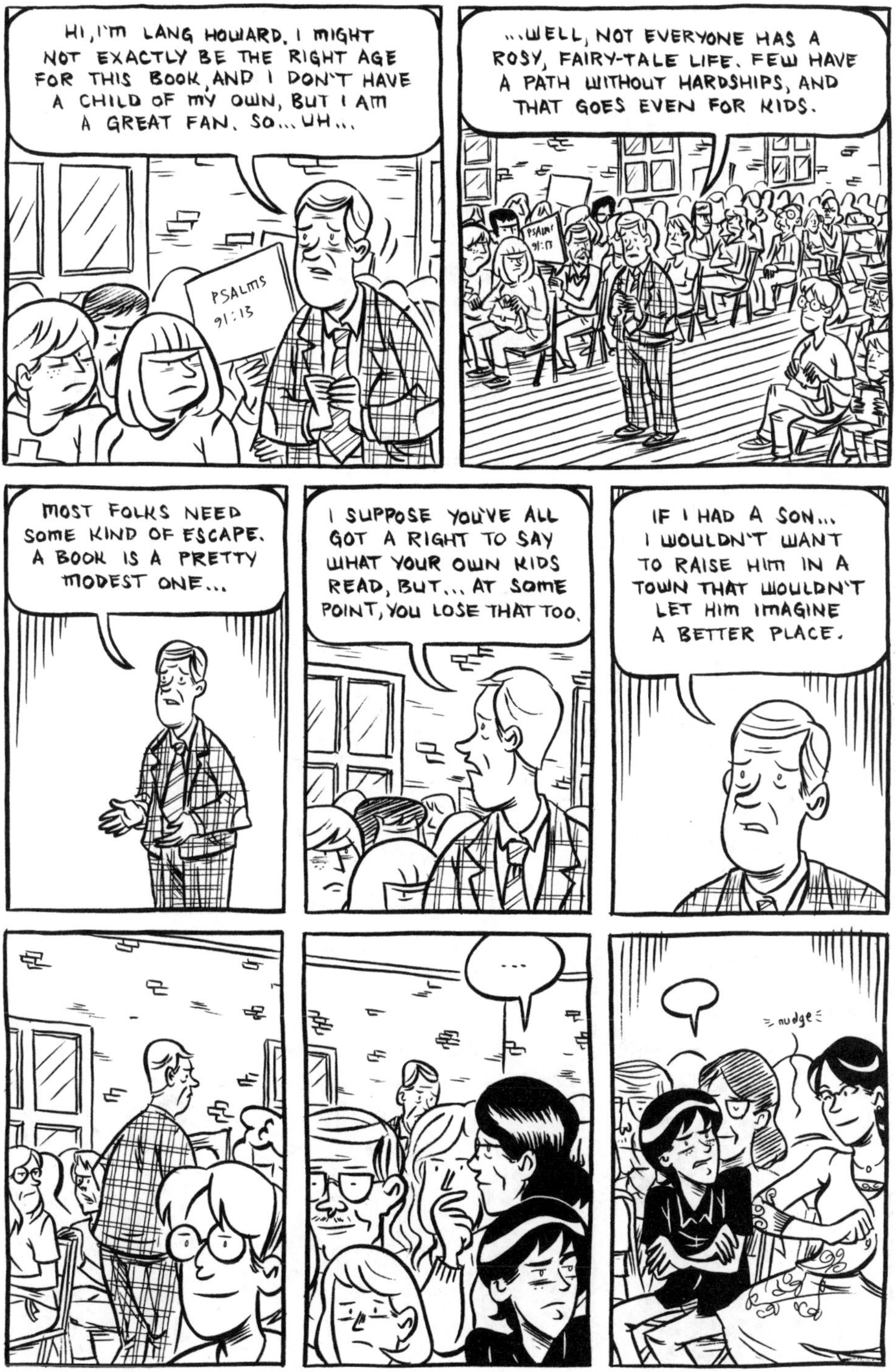
HI, I'M LANG HOWARD. I MIGHT NOT EXACTLY BE THE RIGHT AGE FOR THIS BOOK, AND I DON'T HAVE A CHILD OF MY OWN, BUT I AM A GREAT FAN. SO... UH...
PSALMS 91:13
...WELL, NOT EVERYONE HAS A ROSY, FAIRY-TALE LIFE. FEW HAVE A PATH WITHOUT HARDSHIPS, AND THAT GOES EVEN FOR KIDS.
MOST FOLKS NEED SOME KIND OF ESCAPE. A BOOK IS A PRETTY MODEST ONE...
I SUPPOSE YOU'VE ALL GOT A RIGHT TO SAY WHAT YOUR OWN KIDS READ, BUT... AT SOME POINT, YOU LOSE THAT TOO.
IF I HAD A SON... I WOULDN'T WANT TO RAISE HIM IN A TOWN THAT WOULDN'T LET HIM IMAGINE A BETTER PLACE.
...
nudge

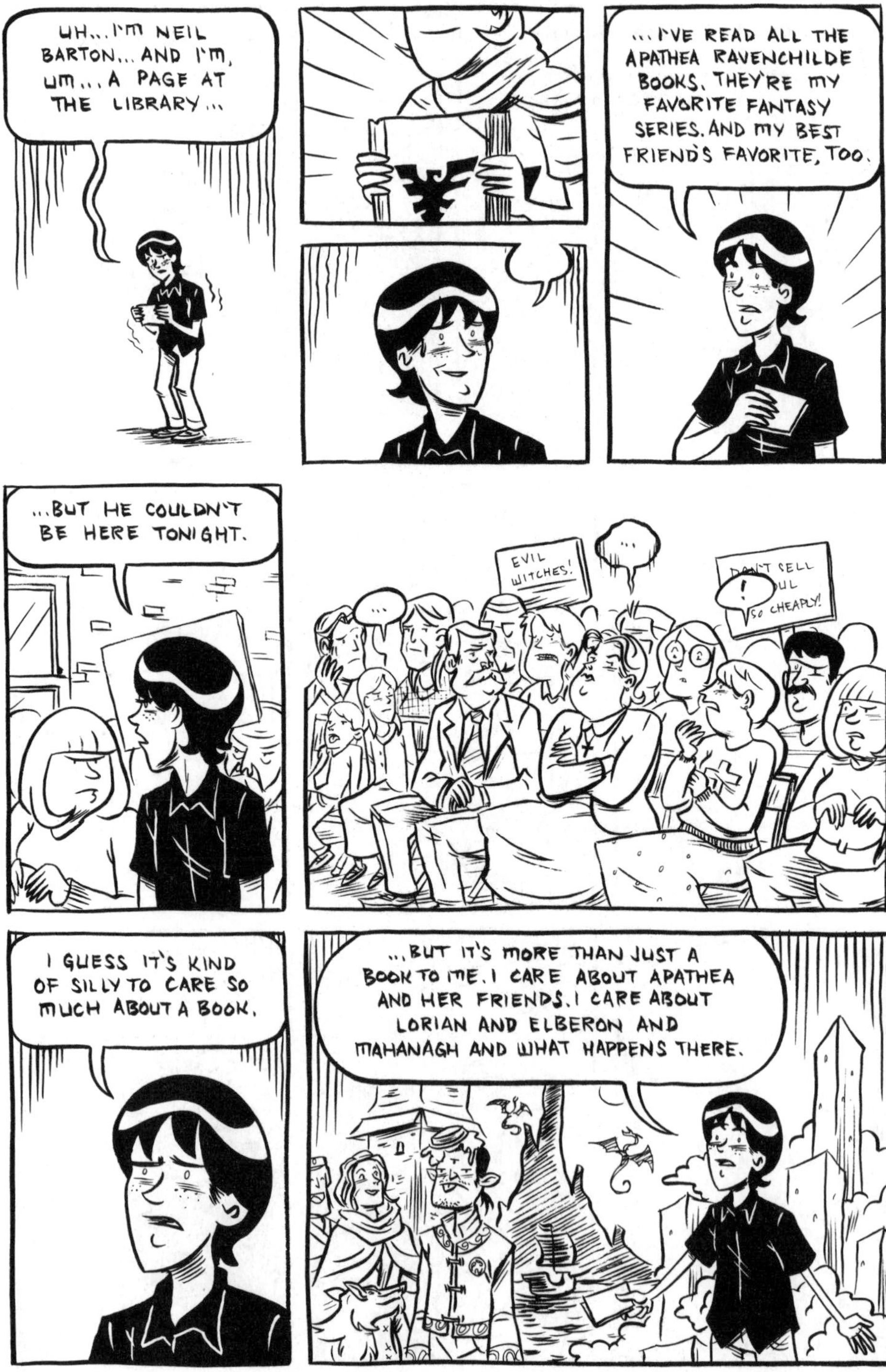
UH...I'M NEIL BARTON...AND I'M, UM...A PAGE AT THE LIBRARY...
...I'VE READ ALL THE APATHEA RAVENCHILDE BOOKS. THEY'RE MY FAVORITE FANTASY SERIES. AND MY BEST FRIEND'S FAVORITE, TOO.
...BUT HE COULDN'T BE HERE TONIGHT.
EVIL WITCHES!
SO CHEAPLY!
I GUESS IT'S KIND OF SILLY TO CARE SO MUCH ABOUT A BOOK.
...BUT IT'S MORE THAN JUST A BOOK TO ME. I CARE ABOUT APATHEA AND HER FRIENDS. I CARE ABOUT LORIAN AND ELBERON AND MAHANAGH AND WHAT HAPPENS THERE.

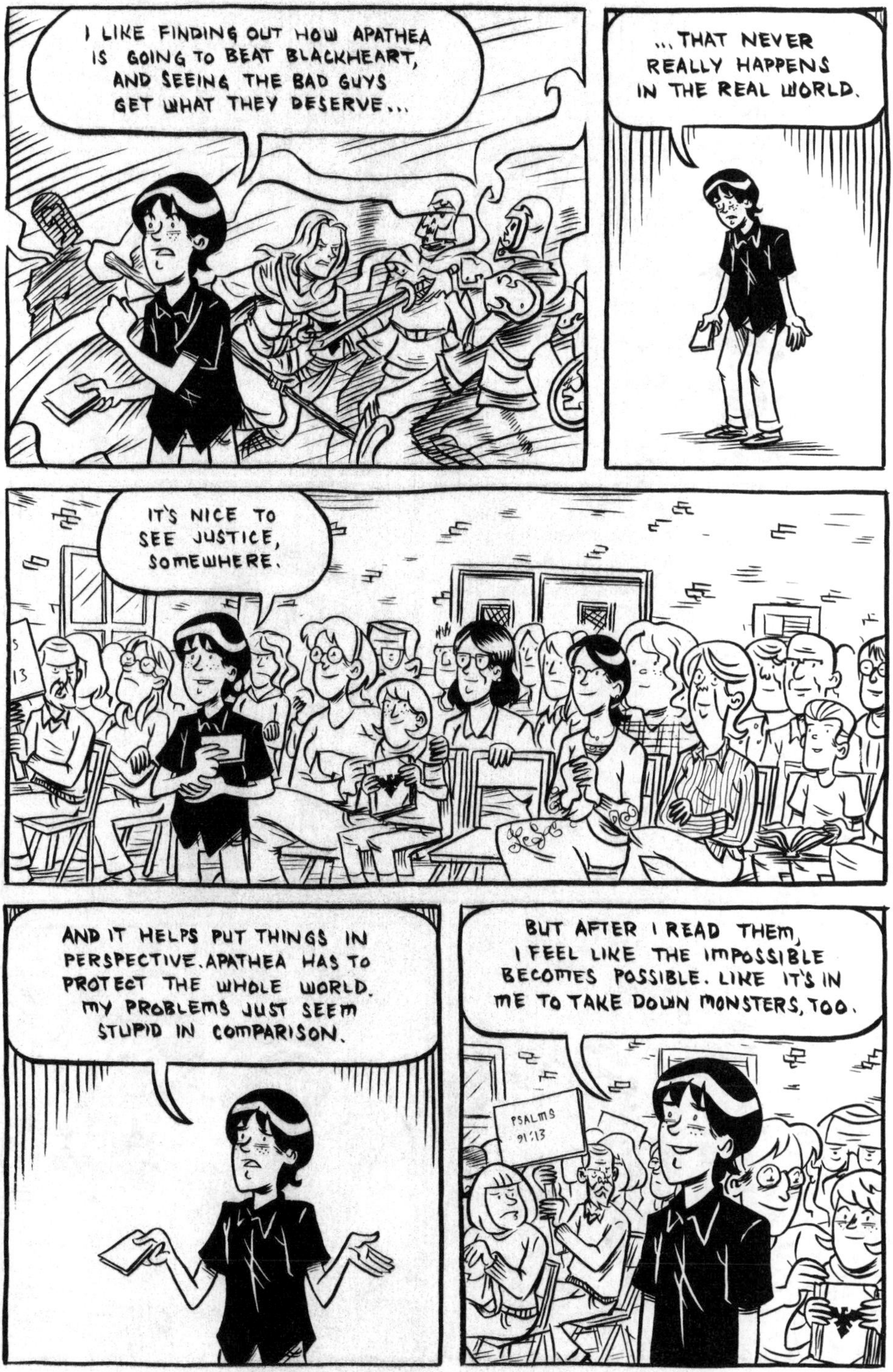
I LIKE FINDING OUT HOW APATHEA IS GOING TO BEAT BLACKHEART, AND SEEING THE BAD GUYS GET WHAT THEY DESERVE...
...THAT NEVER REALLY HAPPENS IN THE REAL WORLD.
IT'S NICE TO SEE JUSTICE, SOMEWHERE.
AND IT HELPS PUT THINGS IN PERSPECTIVE. APATHEA HAS TO PROTECT THE WHOLE WORLD. MY PROBLEMS JUST SEEM STUPID IN COMPARISON.
BUT AFTER I READ THEM, I FEEL LIKE THE IMPOSSIBLE BECOMES POSSIBLE. LIKE IT'S IN ME TO TAKE DOWN MONSTERS, TOO.
PSALMS 91:13

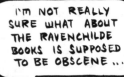

I'M NOT REALLY SURE WHAT ABOUT THE RAVENCHILDE BOOKS IS SUPPOSED TO BE OBSCENE ...

... BUT BANNING THEM WOULD JUST BE A SIN.

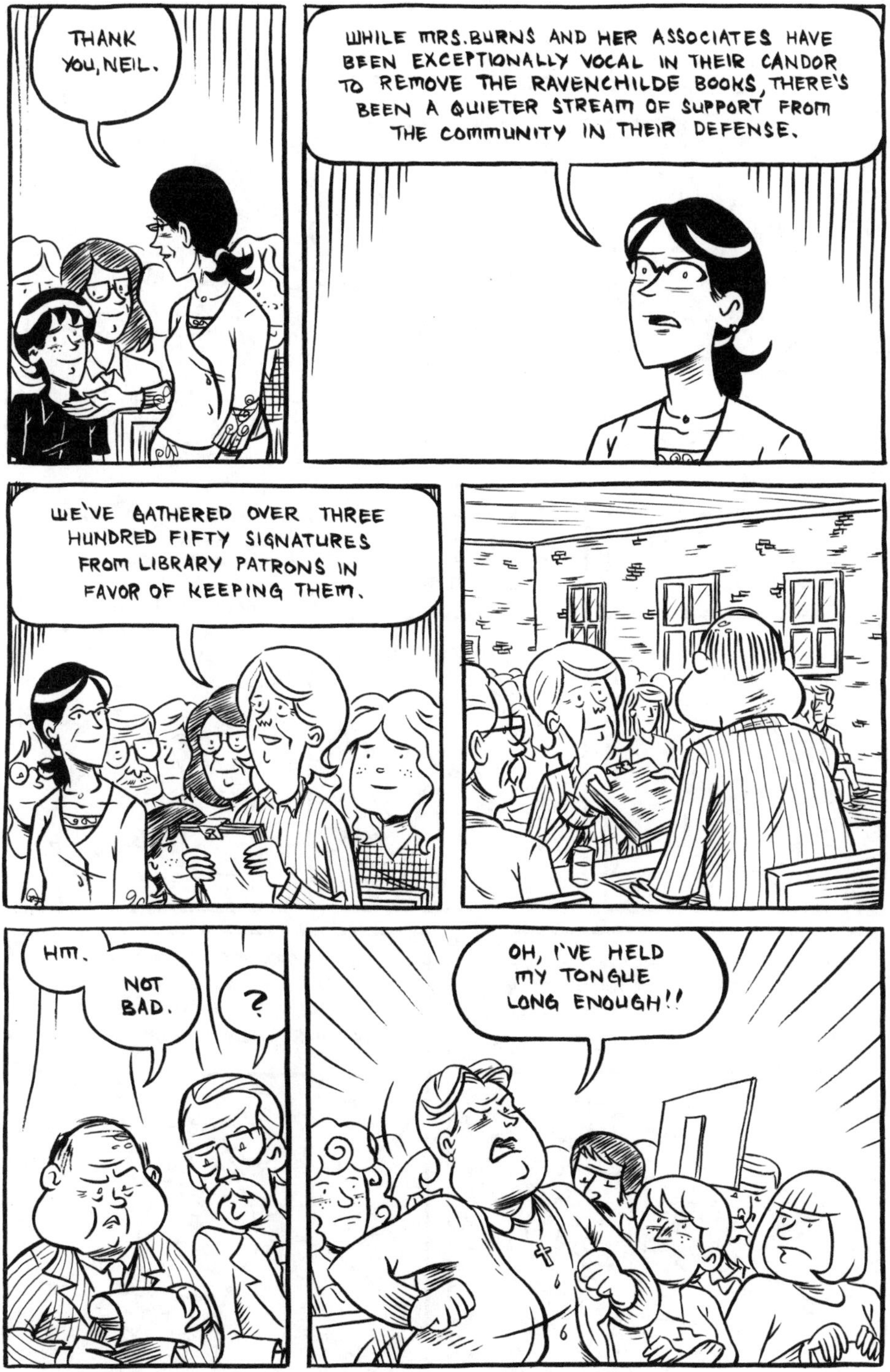
THANK YOU, NEIL.
WHILE MRS. BURNS AND HER ASSOCIATES HAVE BEEN EXCEPTIONALLY VOCAL IN THEIR CANDOR TO REMOVE THE RAVENCHILDE BOOKS, THERE'S BEEN A QUIETER STREAM OF SUPPORT FROM THE COMMUNITY IN THEIR DEFENSE.
WE'VE GATHERED OVER THREE HUNDRED FIFTY SIGNATURES FROM LIBRARY PATRONS IN FAVOR OF KEEPING THEM.
HM.
NOT BAD.
?
OH, I'VE HELD MY TONGUE LONG ENOUGH!!

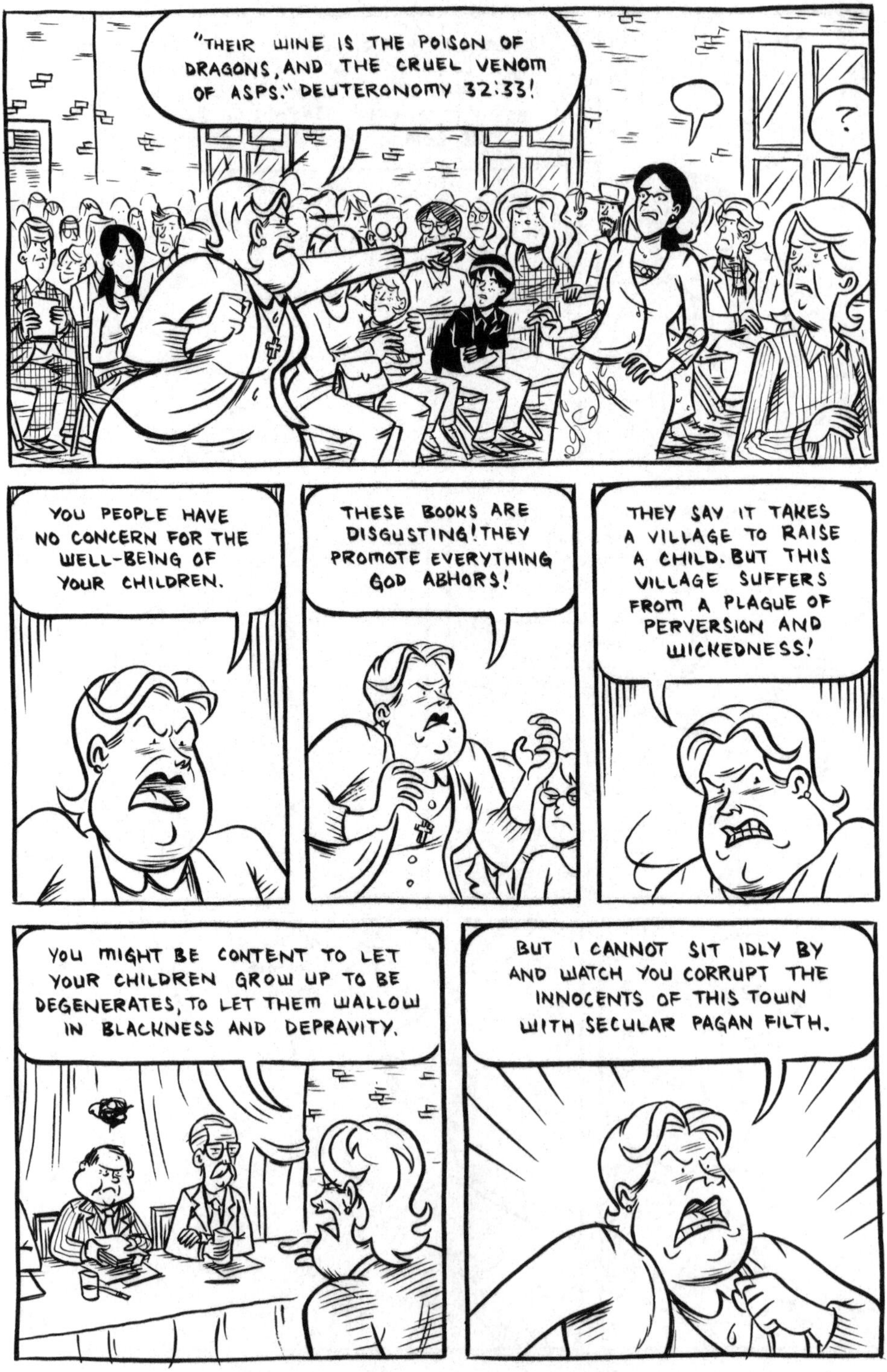
"THEIR WINE IS THE POISON OF DRAGONS, AND THE CRUEL VENOM OF ASPS." DEUTERONOMY 32:33!
?
YOU PEOPLE HAVE NO CONCERN FOR THE WELL-BEING OF YOUR CHILDREN.
THESE BOOKS ARE DISGUSTING! THEY PROMOTE EVERYTHING GOD ABHORS!
THEY SAY IT TAKES A VILLAGE TO RAISE A CHILD. BUT THIS VILLAGE SUFFERS FROM A PLAGUE OF PERVERSION AND WICKEDNESS!
YOU MIGHT BE CONTENT TO LET YOUR CHILDREN GROW UP TO BE DEGENERATES, TO LET THEM WALLOW IN BLACKNESS AND DEPRAVITY.
BUT I CANNOT SIT IDLY BY AND WATCH YOU CORRUPT THE INNOCENTS OF THIS TOWN WITH SECULAR PAGAN FILTH.

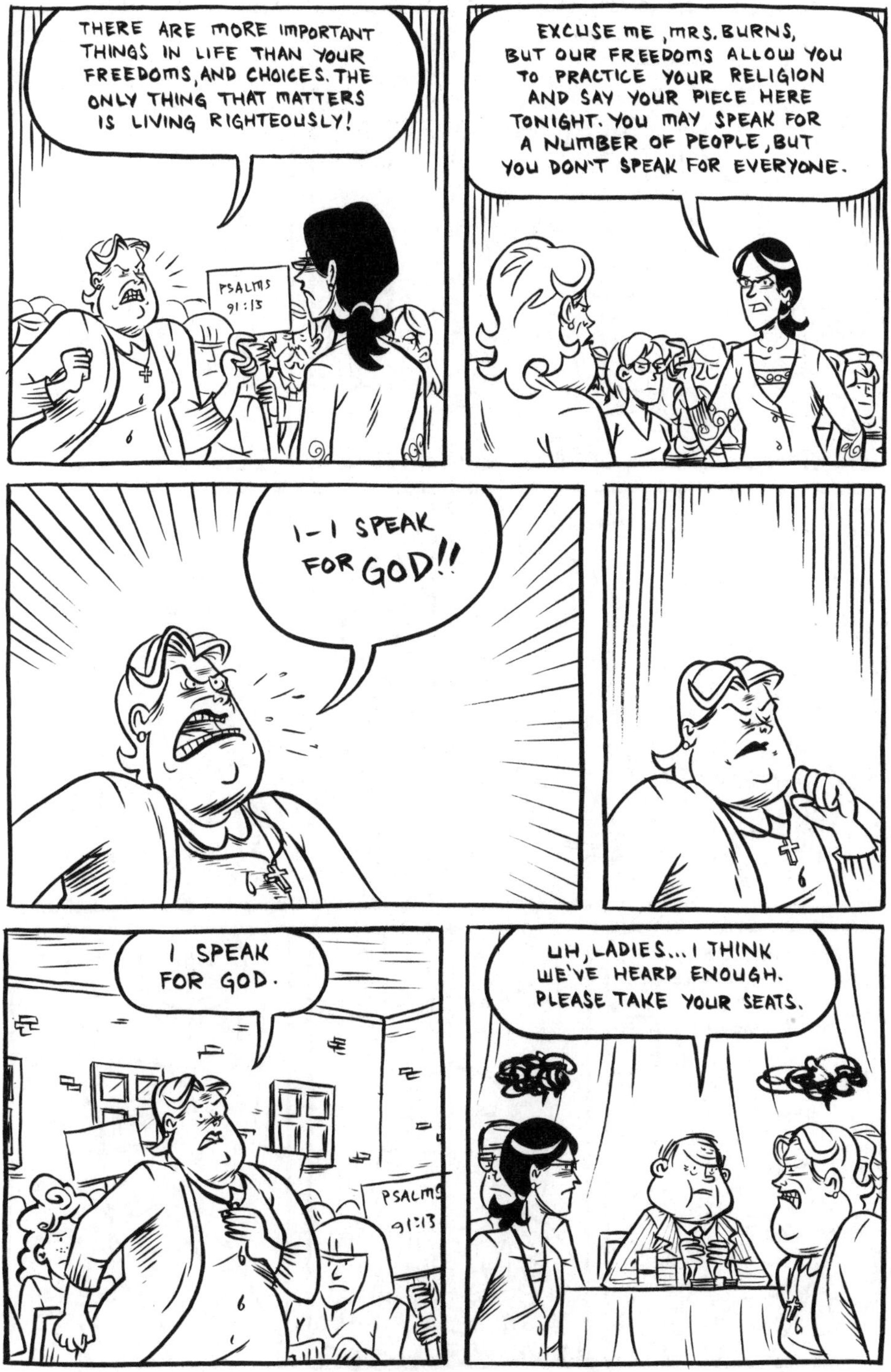

THERE ARE MORE IMPORTANT THINGS IN LIFE THAN YOUR FREEDOMS, AND CHOICES. THE ONLY THING THAT MATTERS IS LIVING RIGHTEOUSLY!
PSALMS 91:13
EXCUSE ME, MRS. BURNS, BUT OUR FREEDOMS ALLOW YOU TO PRACTICE YOUR RELIGION AND SAY YOUR PIECE HERE TONIGHT. YOU MAY SPEAK FOR A NUMBER OF PEOPLE, BUT YOU DON'T SPEAK FOR EVERYONE.
I-I SPEAK FOR GOD!!
I SPEAK FOR GOD.
PSALMS 91:13
UH, LADIES... I THINK WE'VE HEARD ENOUGH. PLEASE TAKE YOUR SEATS.

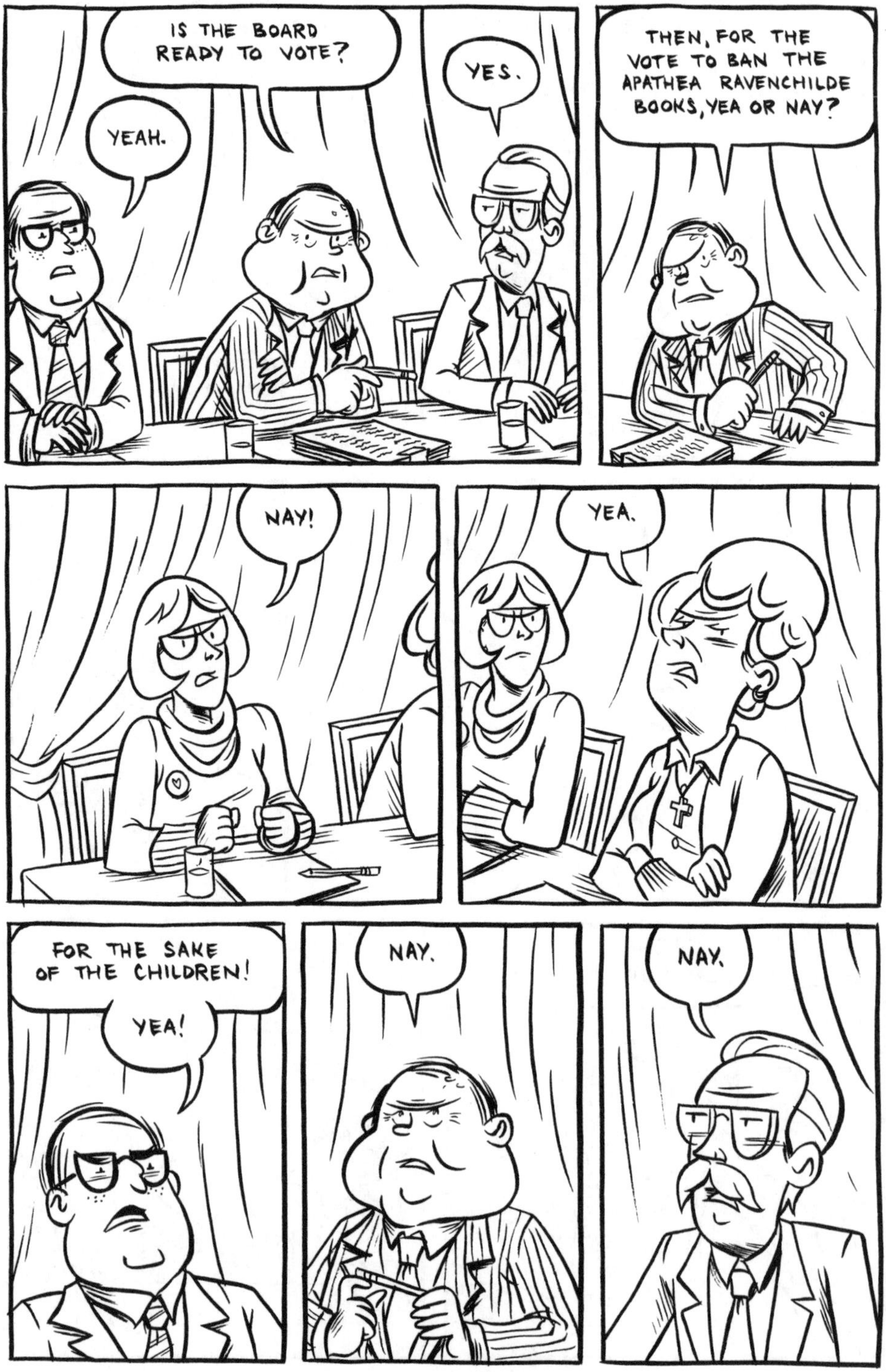
IS THE BOARD READY TO VOTE?
YEAH.
YES.
THEN, FOR THE VOTE TO BAN THE APATHEA RAVENCHILDE BOOKS, YEA OR NAY?
NAY!
YEA.
FOR THE SAKE OF THE CHILDREN!
YEA!
NAY.
NAY.

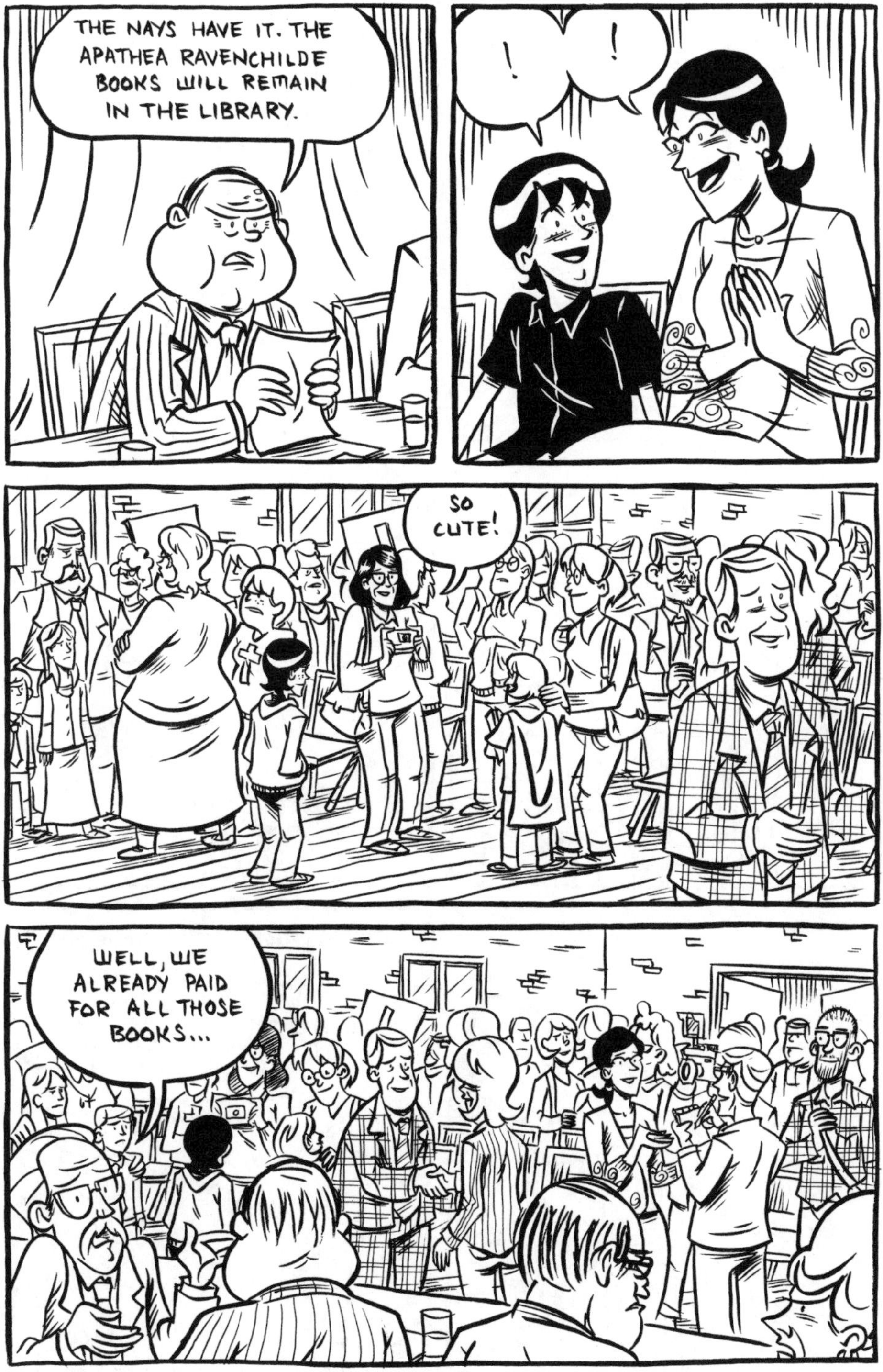
THE NAYS HAVE IT. THE APATHEA RAVENCHILDE BOOKS WILL REMAIN IN THE LIBRARY.
!
!
SO CUTE!
WELL, WE ALREADY PAID FOR ALL THOSE BOOKS...

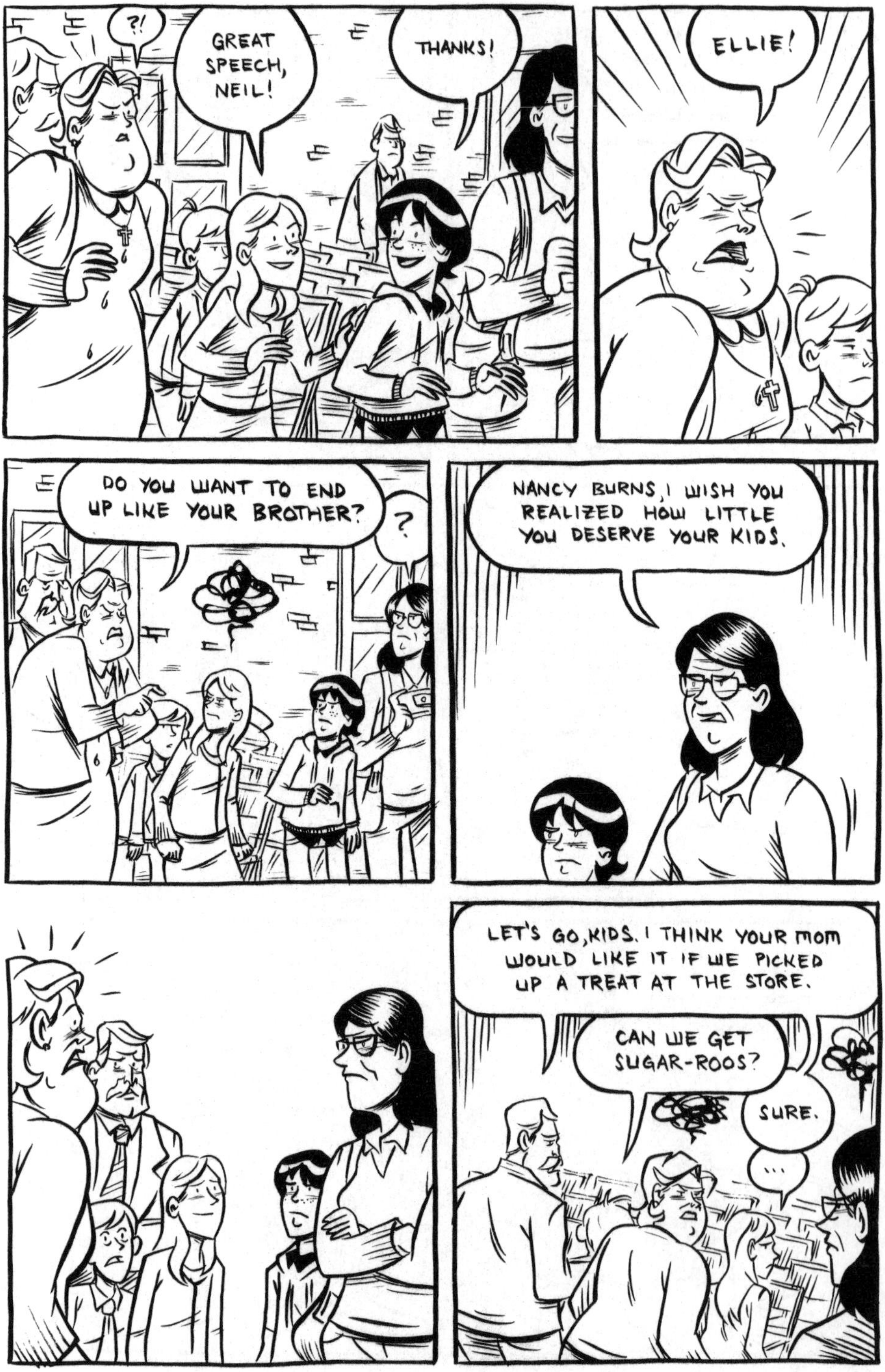
?!
GREAT SPEECH, NEIL!
THANKS!
ELLIE!
DO YOU WANT TO END UP LIKE YOUR BROTHER?
?
NANCY BURNS, I WISH YOU REALIZED HOW LITTLE YOU DESERVE YOUR KIDS.
LET'S GO, KIDS. I THINK YOUR MOM WOULD LIKE IT IF WE PICKED UP A TREAT AT THE STORE.
CAN WE GET SUGAR-ROOS?
SURE.
...

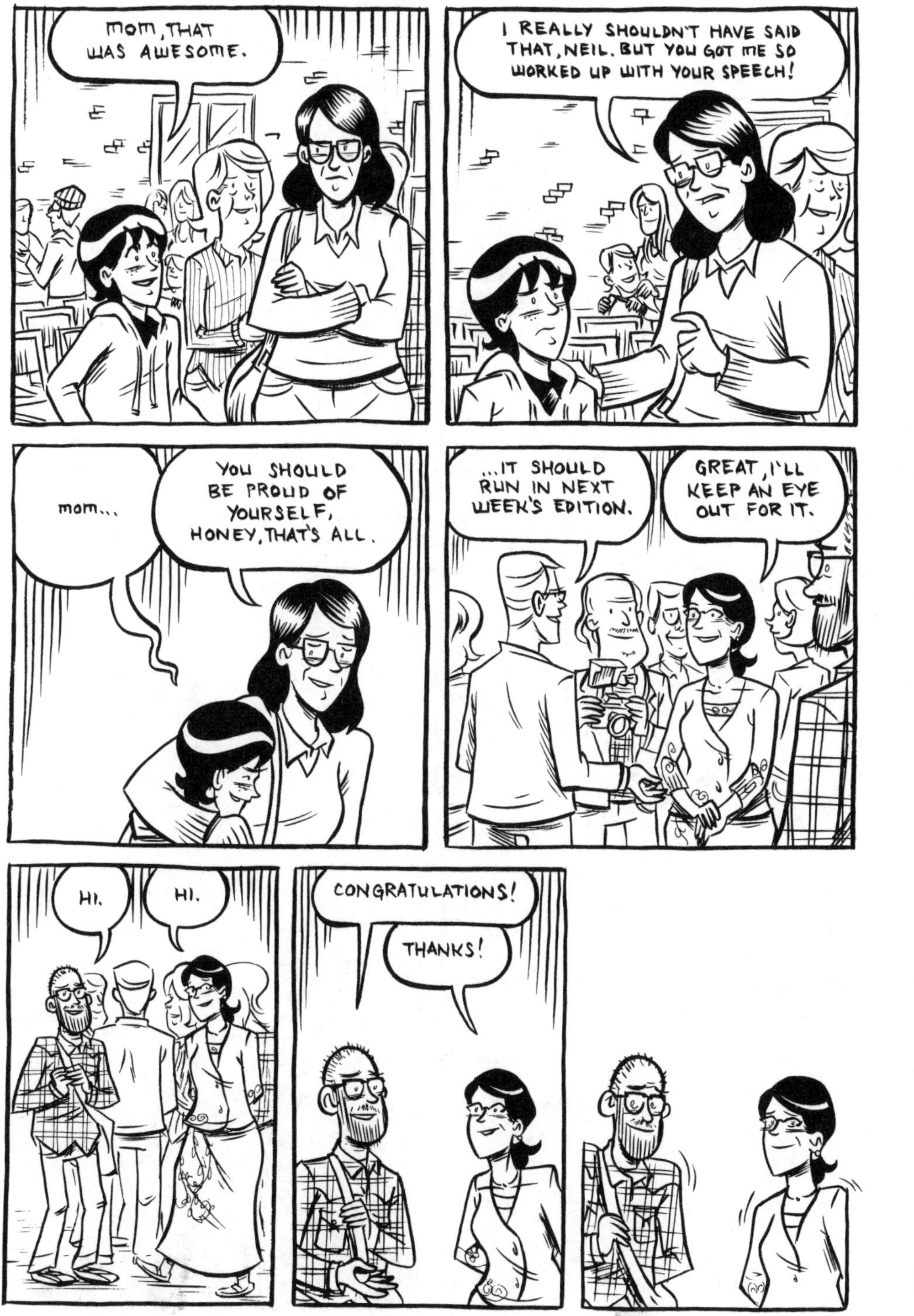
MOM, THAT WAS AWESOME.
I REALLY SHOULDN'T HAVE SAID THAT, NEIL. BUT YOU GOT ME SO WORKED UP WITH YOUR SPEECH!
MOM...
YOU SHOULD BE PROUD OF YOURSELF, HONEY, THAT'S ALL.
...IT SHOULD RUN IN NEXT WEEK'S EDITION.
GREAT, I'LL KEEP AN EYE OUT FOR IT.
HI.
HI.
CONGRATULATIONS!
THANKS!

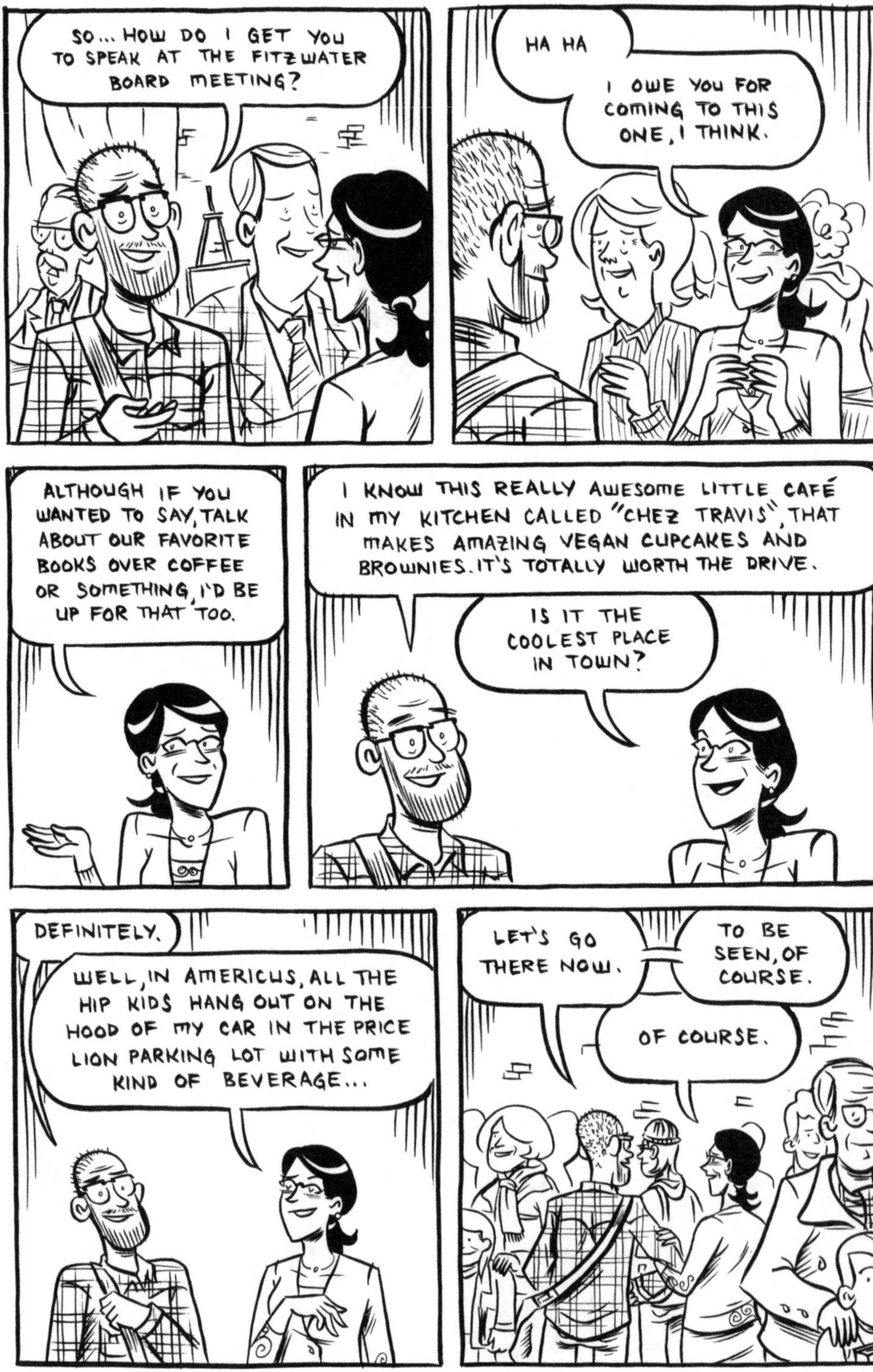
SO... HOW DO I GET YOU TO SPEAK AT THE FITZWATER BOARD MEETING?
HA HA
I OWE YOU FOR COMING TO THIS ONE, I THINK.
ALTHOUGH IF YOU WANTED TO SAY, TALK ABOUT OUR FAVORITE BOOKS OVER COFFEE OR SOMETHING, I'D BE UP FOR THAT TOO.
I KNOW THIS REALLY AWESOME LITTLE CAFÉ IN MY KITCHEN CALLED "CHEZ TRAVIS", THAT MAKES AMAZING VEGAN CUPCAKES AND BROWNIES. IT'S TOTALLY WORTH THE DRIVE.
IS IT THE COOLEST PLACE IN TOWN?
DEFINITELY.
WELL, IN AMERICUS, ALL THE HIP KIDS HANG OUT ON THE HOOD OF MY CAR IN THE PRICE LION PARKING LOT WITH SOME KIND OF BEVERAGE...
LET'S GO THERE NOW.
TO BE SEEN, OF COURSE.
OF COURSE.

CHAPTER 9

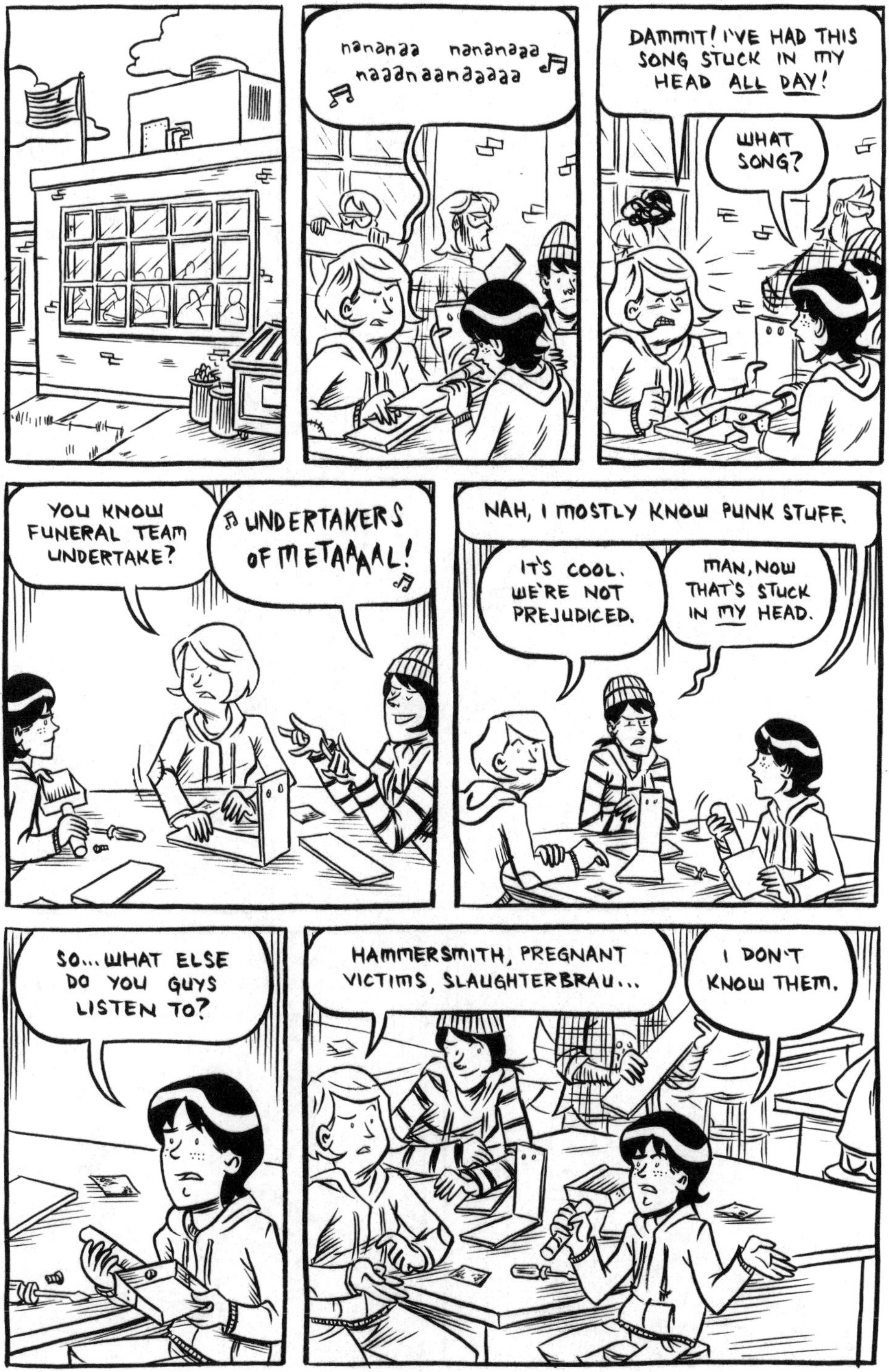
nananaa nananaaa naaanaanaaaaa
DAMMIT! I'VE HAD THIS SONG STUCK IN MY HEAD ALL DAY!
WHAT SONG?
YOU KNOW FUNERAL TEAM UNDERTAKE?
UNDERTAKERS OF METAAAAL!
NAH, I MOSTLY KNOW PUNK STUFF.
IT'S COOL. WE'RE NOT PREJUDICED.
MAN, NOW THAT'S STUCK IN MY HEAD.
SO... WHAT ELSE DO YOU GUYS LISTEN TO?
HAMMERSMITH, PREGNANT VICTIMS, SLAUGHTERBRAU...
I DON'T KNOW THEM.

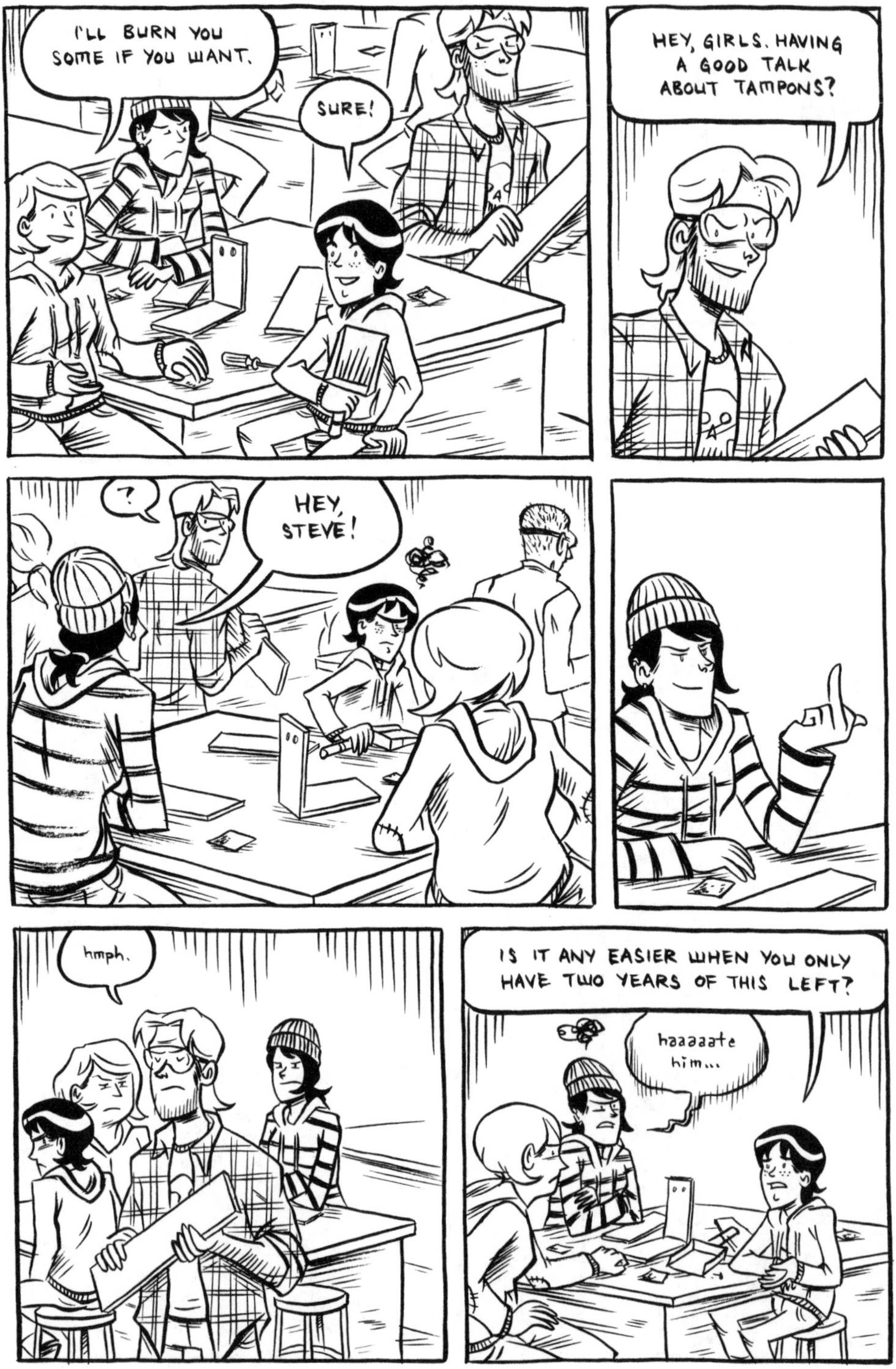
I'LL BURN YOU SOME IF YOU WANT.
SURE!
HEY, GIRLS. HAVING A GOOD TALK ABOUT TAMPONS?
?
HEY, STEVE!
hmph.
IS IT ANY EASIER WHEN YOU ONLY HAVE TWO YEARS OF THIS LEFT?
haaaaate him...

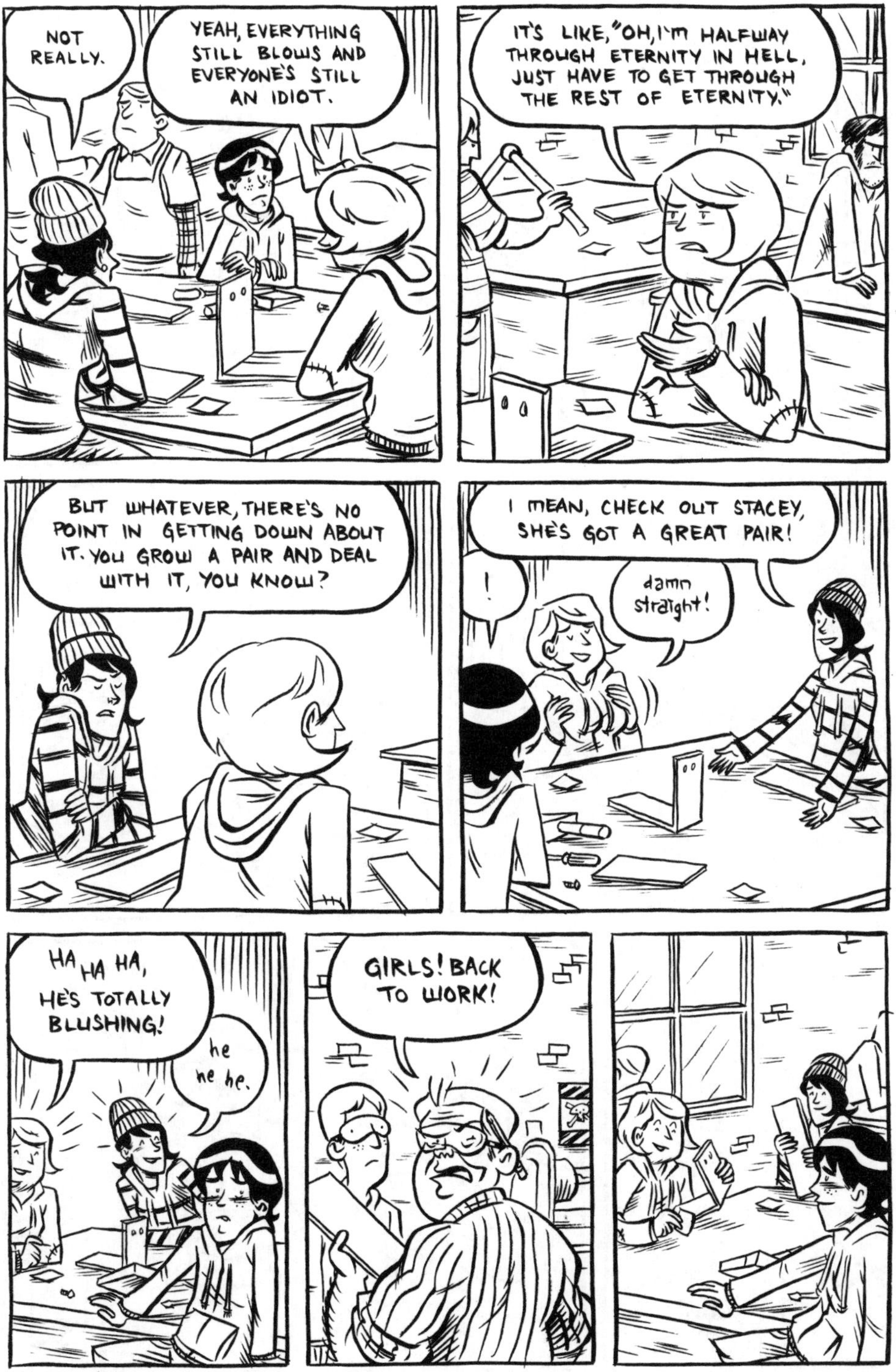
NOT REALLY.
YEAH, EVERYTHING STILL BLOWS AND EVERYONE'S STILL AN IDIOT.
IT'S LIKE, "OH, I'M HALFWAY THROUGH ETERNITY IN HELL, JUST HAVE TO GET THROUGH THE REST OF ETERNITY."
BUT WHATEVER, THERE'S NO POINT IN GETTING DOWN ABOUT IT. YOU GROW A PAIR AND DEAL WITH IT, YOU KNOW?
I MEAN, CHECK OUT STACEY, SHE'S GOT A GREAT PAIR!
!
damn straight!
HA HA HA, HE'S TOTALLY BLUSHING!
he he he.
GIRLS! BACK TO WORK!

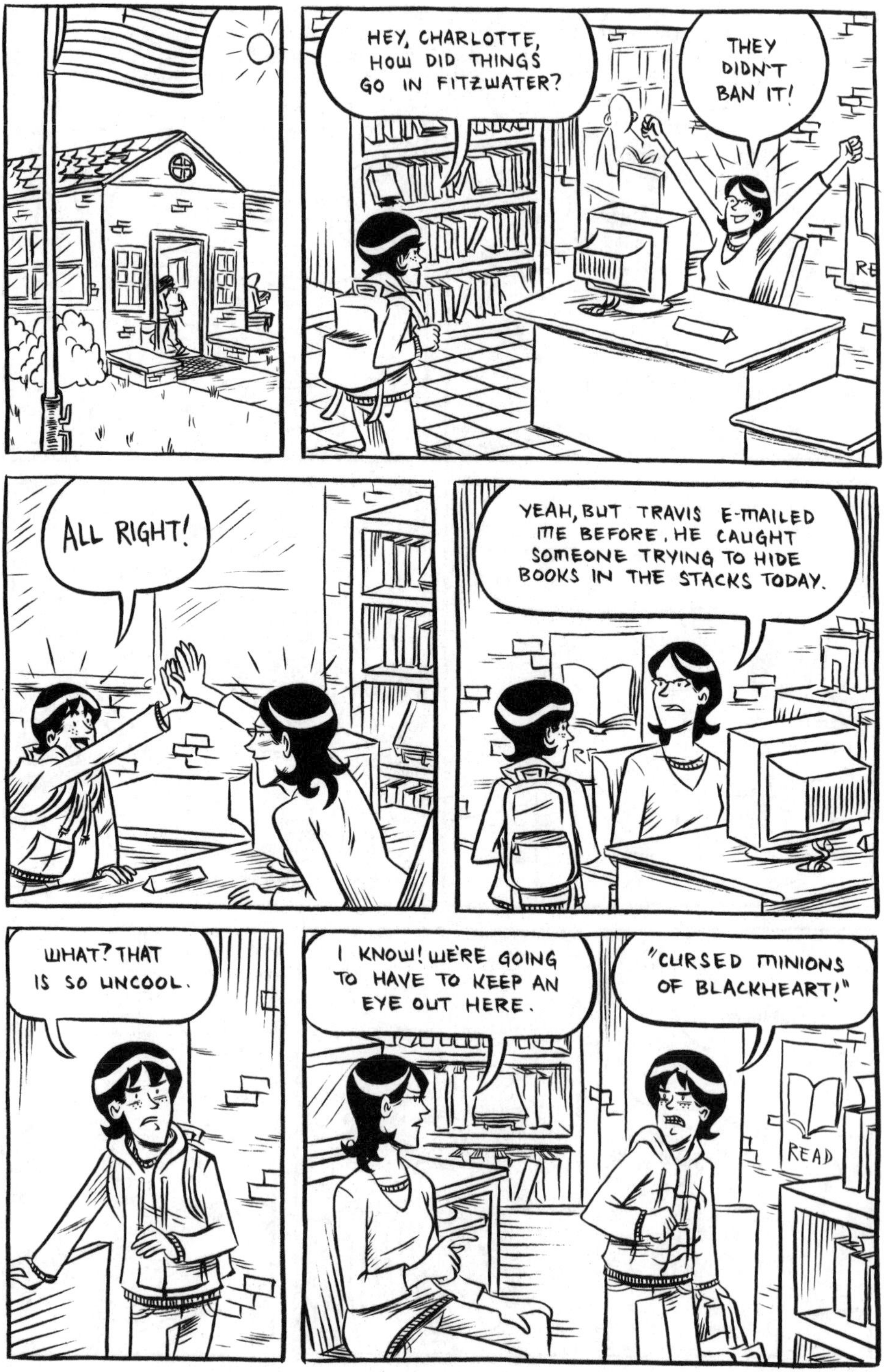
HEY, CHARLOTTE, HOW DID THINGS GO IN FITZWATER?
THEY DIDN'T BAN IT!
ALL RIGHT!
YEAH, BUT TRAVIS E-MAILED ME BEFORE. HE CAUGHT SOMEONE TRYING TO HIDE BOOKS IN THE STACKS TODAY.
WHAT? THAT IS SO UNCOOL.
I KNOW! WE'RE GOING TO HAVE TO KEEP AN EYE OUT HERE.
"CURSED MINIONS OF BLACKHEART!"
READ

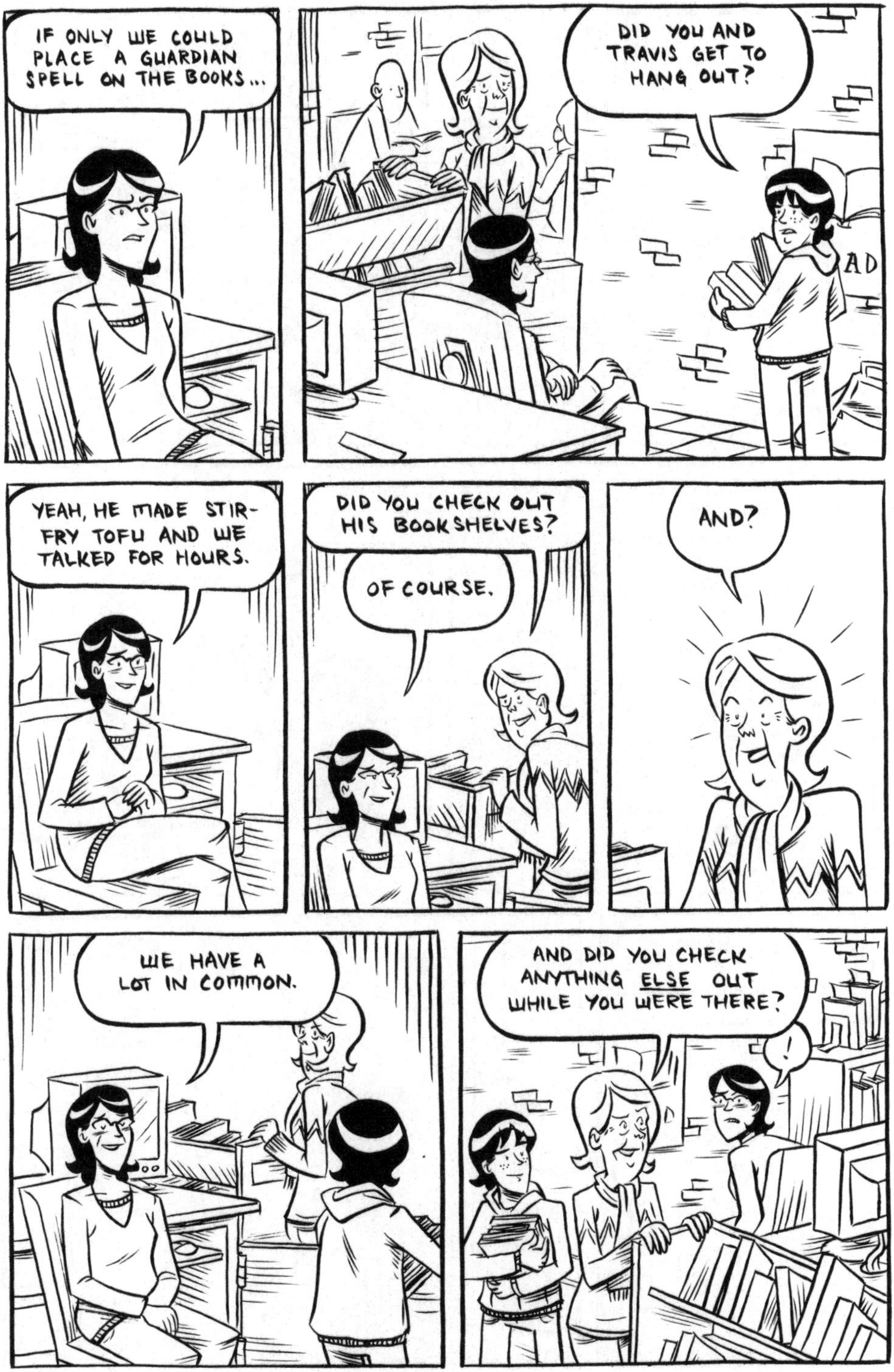
IF ONLY WE COULD PLACE A GUARDIAN SPELL ON THE BOOKS...
DID YOU AND TRAVIS GET TO HANG OUT?
AD
YEAH, HE MADE STIR-FRY TOFU AND WE TALKED FOR HOURS.
DID YOU CHECK OUT HIS BOOKSHELVES?
OF COURSE.
AND?
WE HAVE A LOT IN COMMON.
AND DID YOU CHECK ANYTHING ELSE OUT WHILE YOU WERE THERE?
!

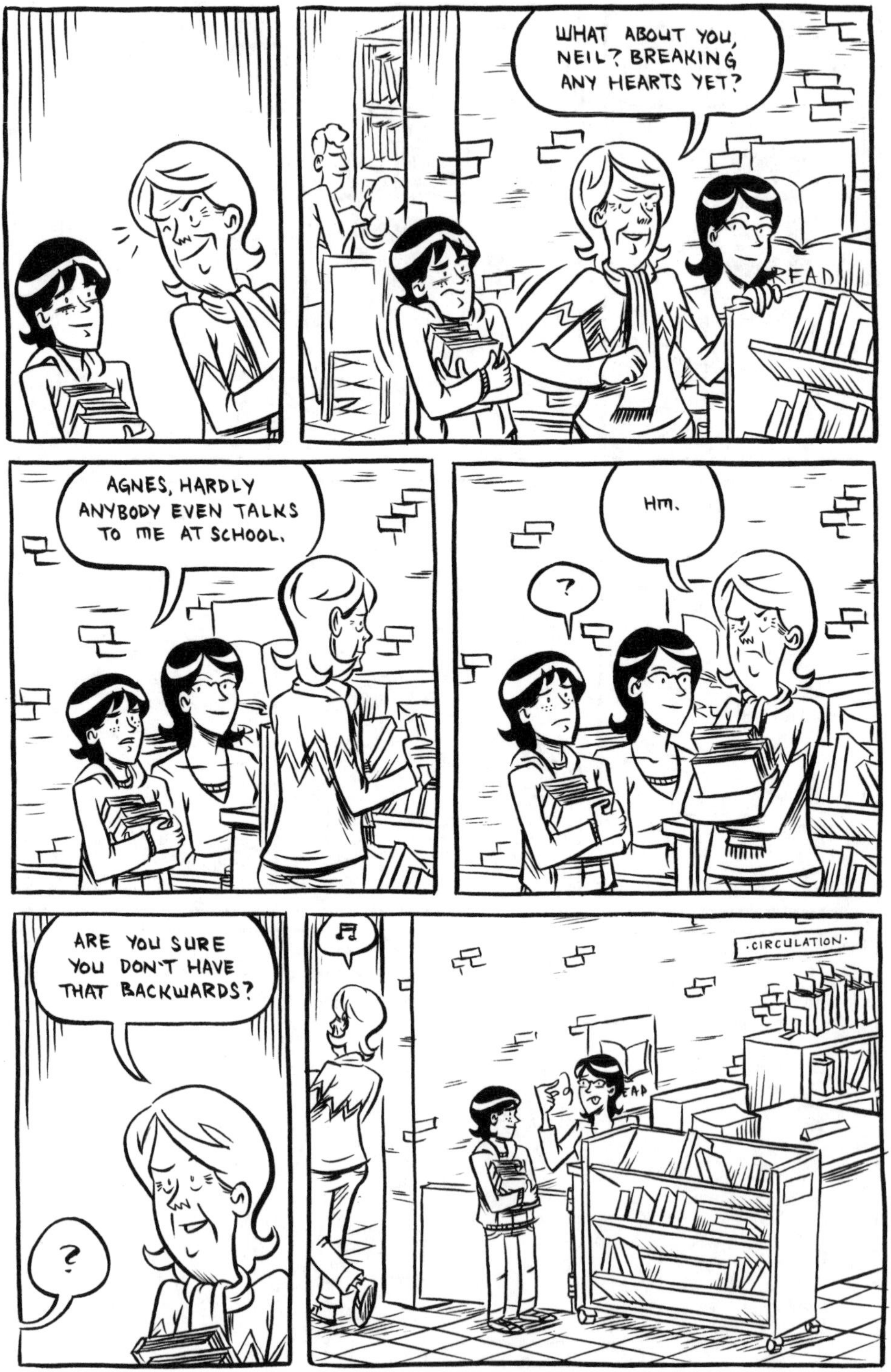
WHAT ABOUT YOU, NEIL? BREAKING ANY HEARTS YET?
READ
AGNES, HARDLY ANYBODY EVEN TALKS TO ME AT SCHOOL.
Hm.
?
ARE YOU SURE YOU DON'T HAVE THAT BACKWARDS?
?
♫
·CIRCULATION·

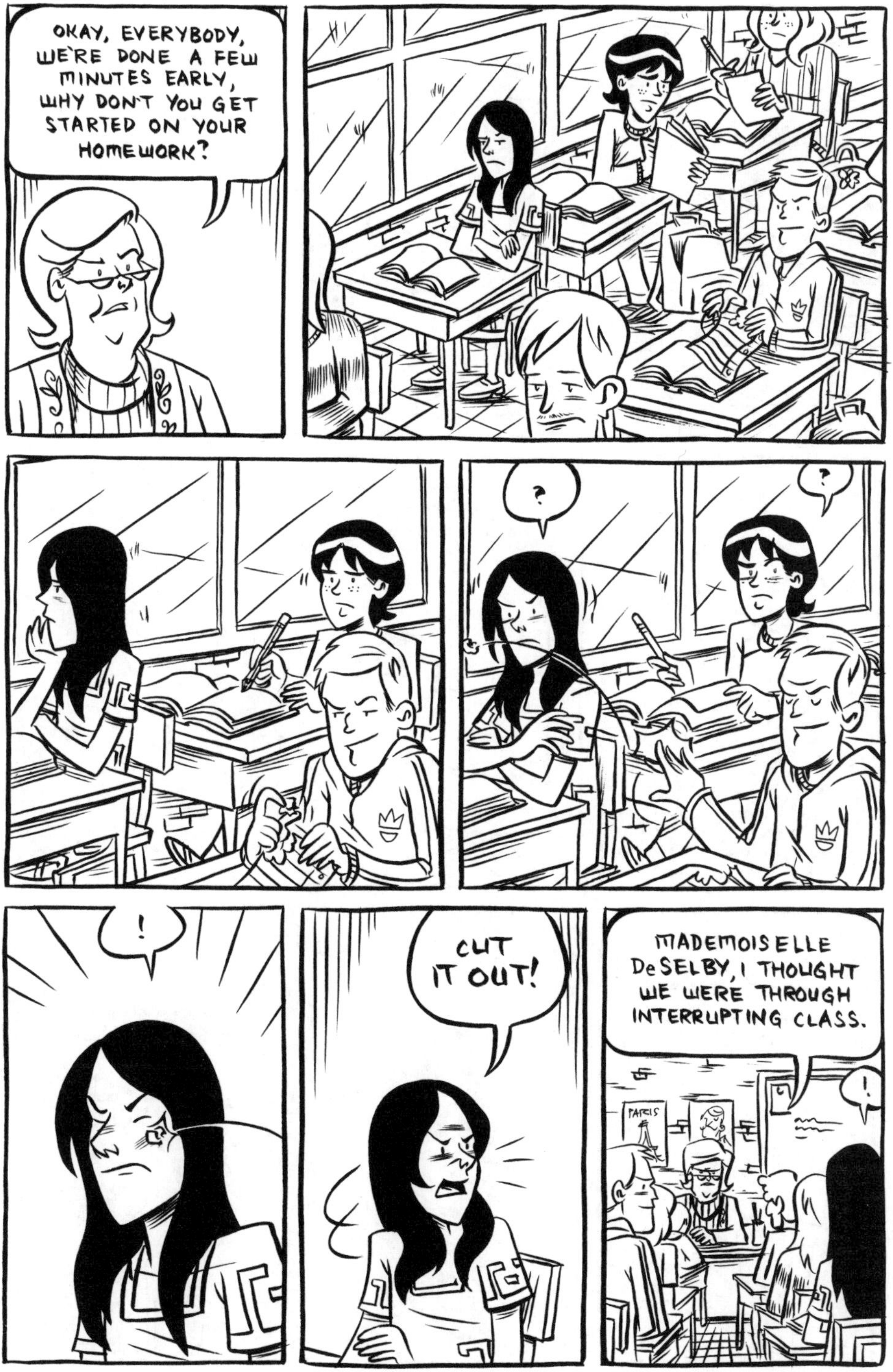
OKAY, EVERYBODY, WE'RE DONE A FEW MINUTES EARLY, WHY DON'T YOU GET STARTED ON YOUR HOMEWORK?
?
?
!
CUT IT OUT!
MADEMOISELLE DeSELBY, I THOUGHT WE WERE THROUGH INTERRUPTING CLASS.
!
PARIS

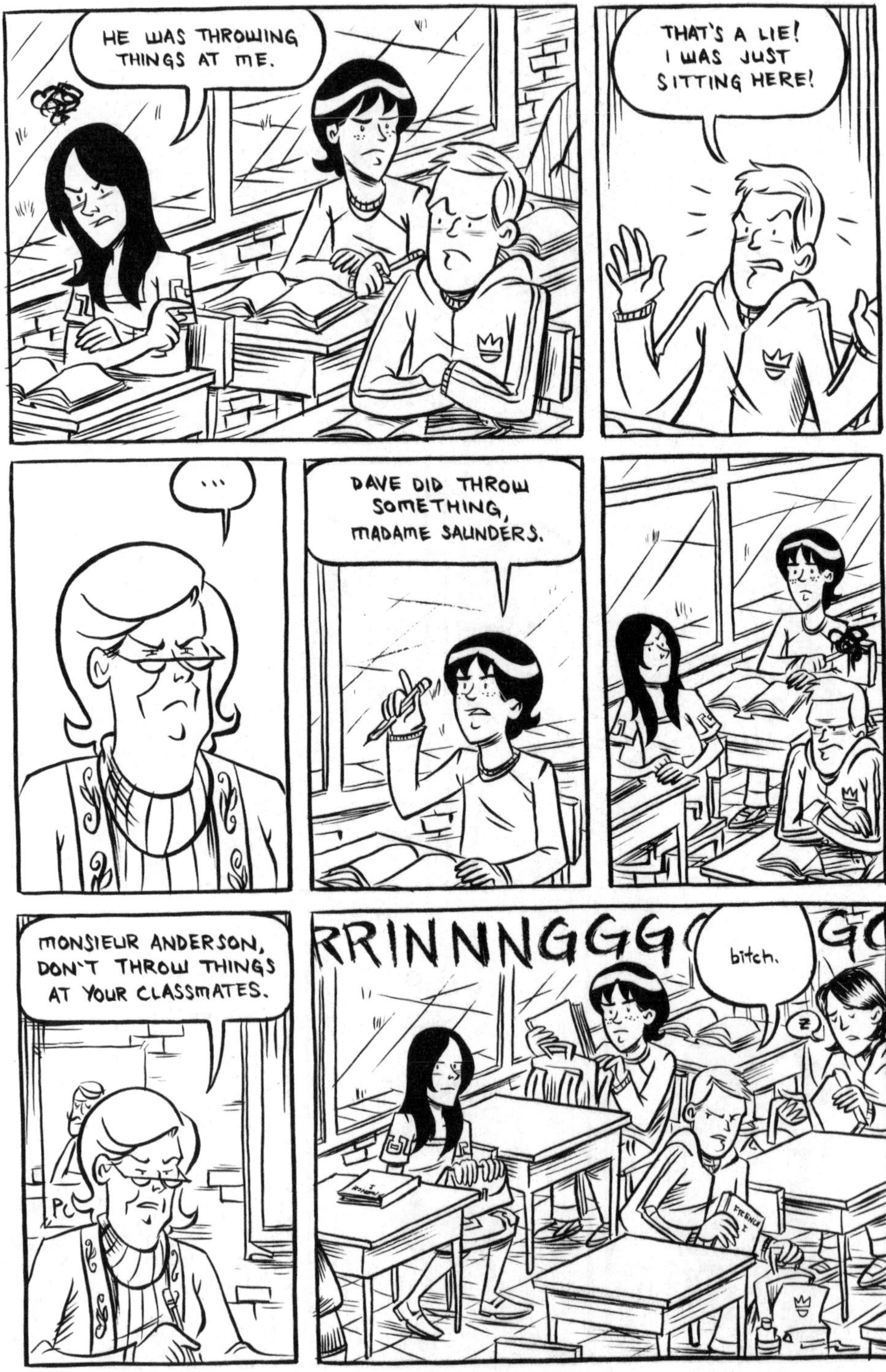
HE WAS THROWING THINGS AT ME.
THAT'S A LIE! I WAS JUST SITTING HERE!
...
DAVE DID THROW SOMETHING, MADAME SAUNDERS.
MONSIEUR ANDERSON, DON'T THROW THINGS AT YOUR CLASSMATES.
RRINNNGGG
GG
bitch.
Z
FRENCH I

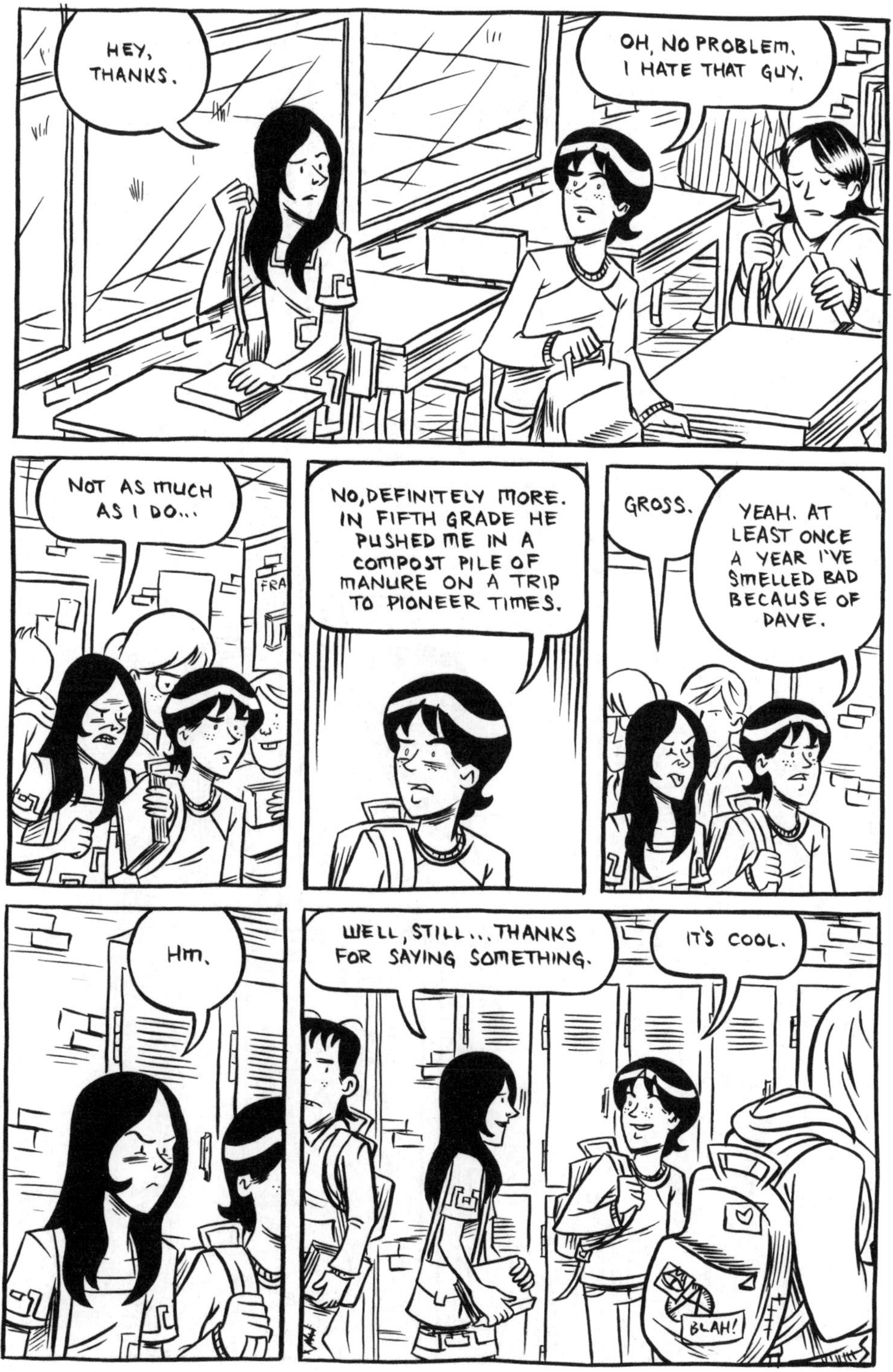
HEY, THANKS.
OH, NO PROBLEM. I HATE THAT GUY.
NOT AS MUCH AS I DO...
FRA
NO, DEFINITELY MORE. IN FIFTH GRADE HE PUSHED ME IN A COMPOST PILE OF MANURE ON A TRIP TO PIONEER TIMES.
GROSS.
YEAH. AT LEAST ONCE A YEAR I'VE SMELLED BAD BECAUSE OF DAVE.
Hm.
WELL, STILL... THANKS FOR SAYING SOMETHING.
IT'S COOL.
BLAH!

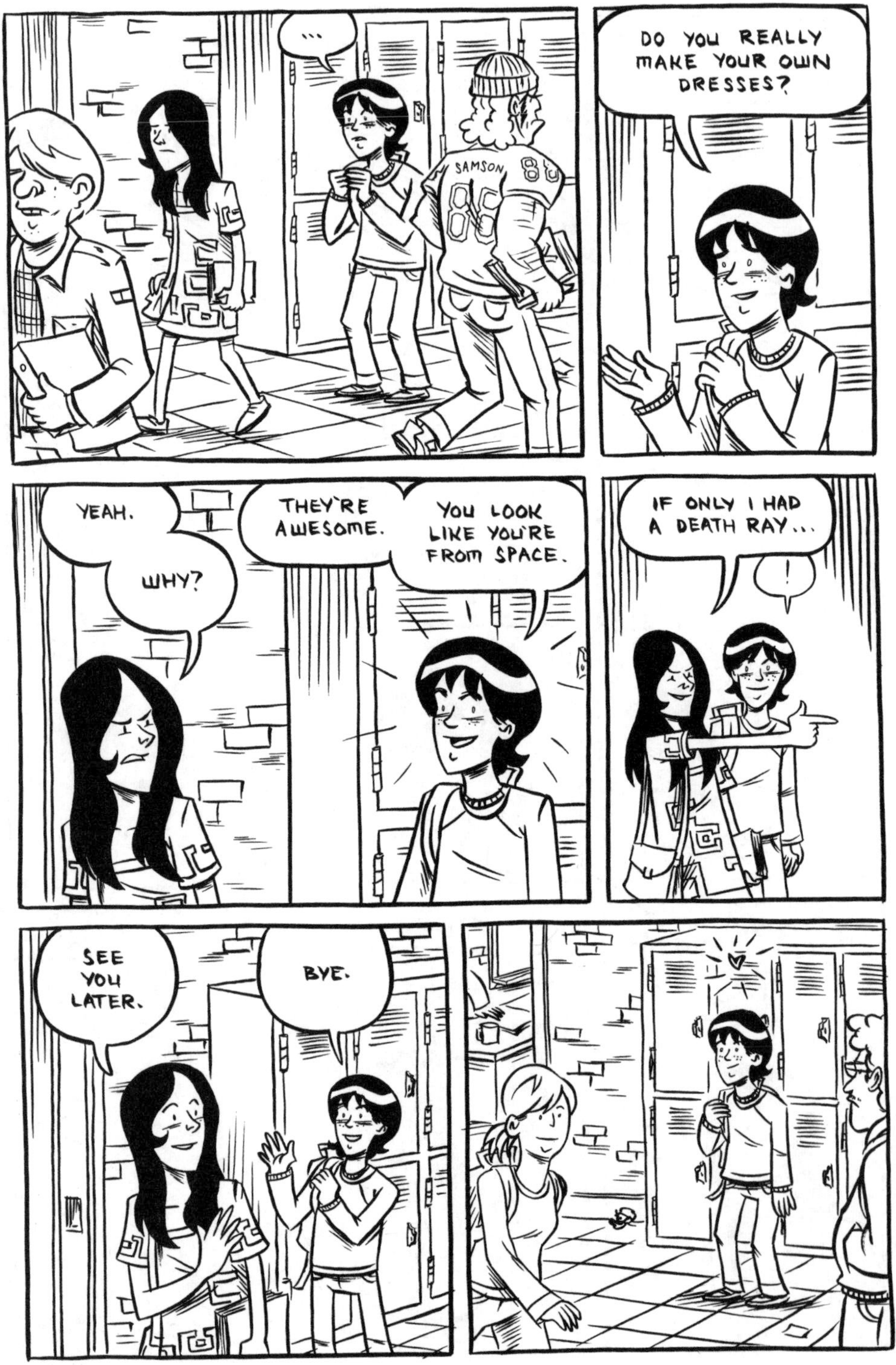
...
SAMSON 88
DO YOU REALLY MAKE YOUR OWN DRESSES?
YEAH.
WHY?
THEY'RE AWESOME.
YOU LOOK LIKE YOU'RE FROM SPACE.
IF ONLY I HAD A DEATH RAY...
!
SEE YOU LATER.
BYE.

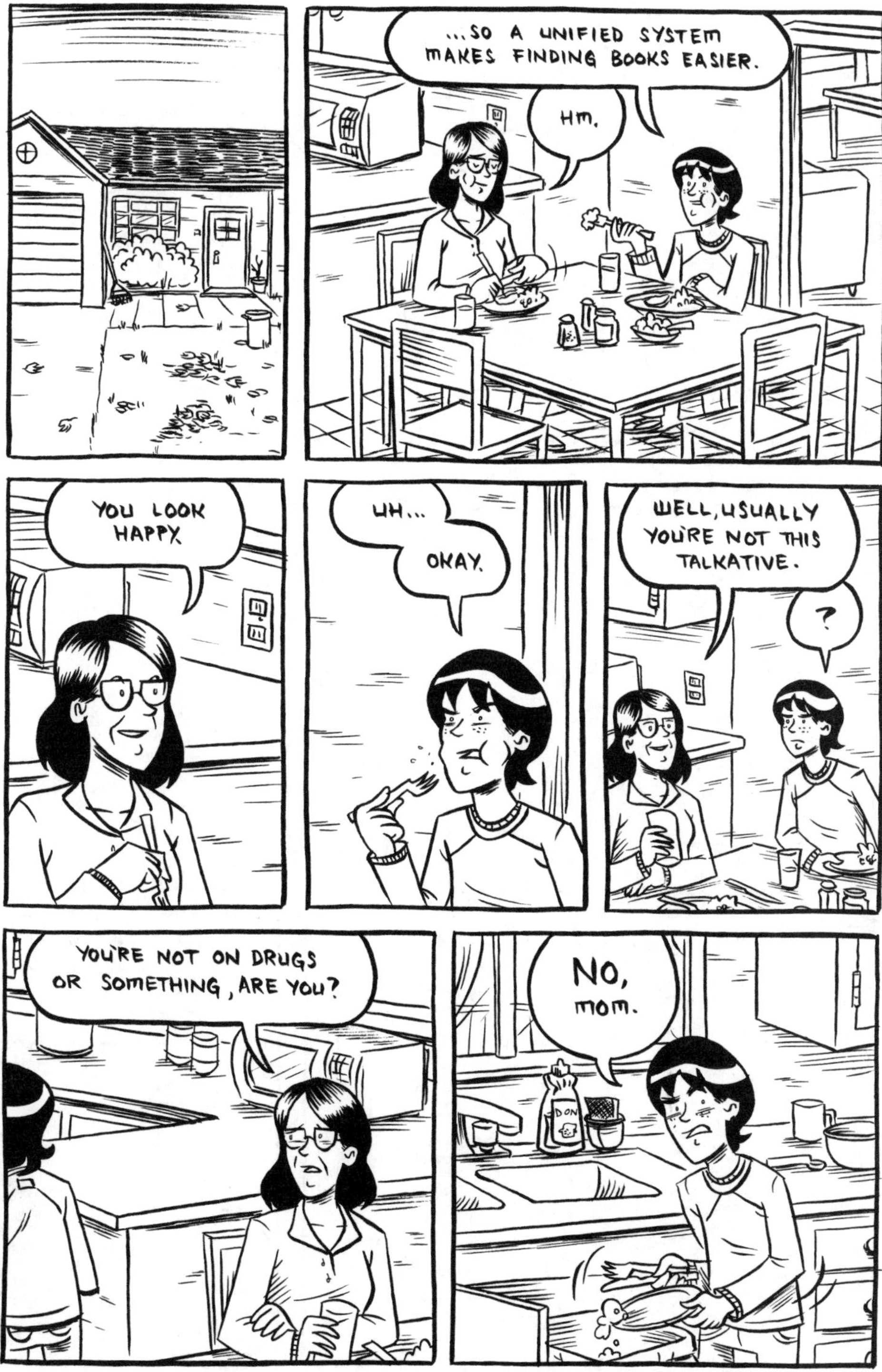
...SO A UNIFIED SYSTEM MAKES FINDING BOOKS EASIER.
HM.
YOU LOOK HAPPY.
UH...
OKAY.
WELL, USUALLY YOU'RE NOT THIS TALKATIVE.
?
YOU'RE NOT ON DRUGS OR SOMETHING, ARE YOU?
NO, MOM.

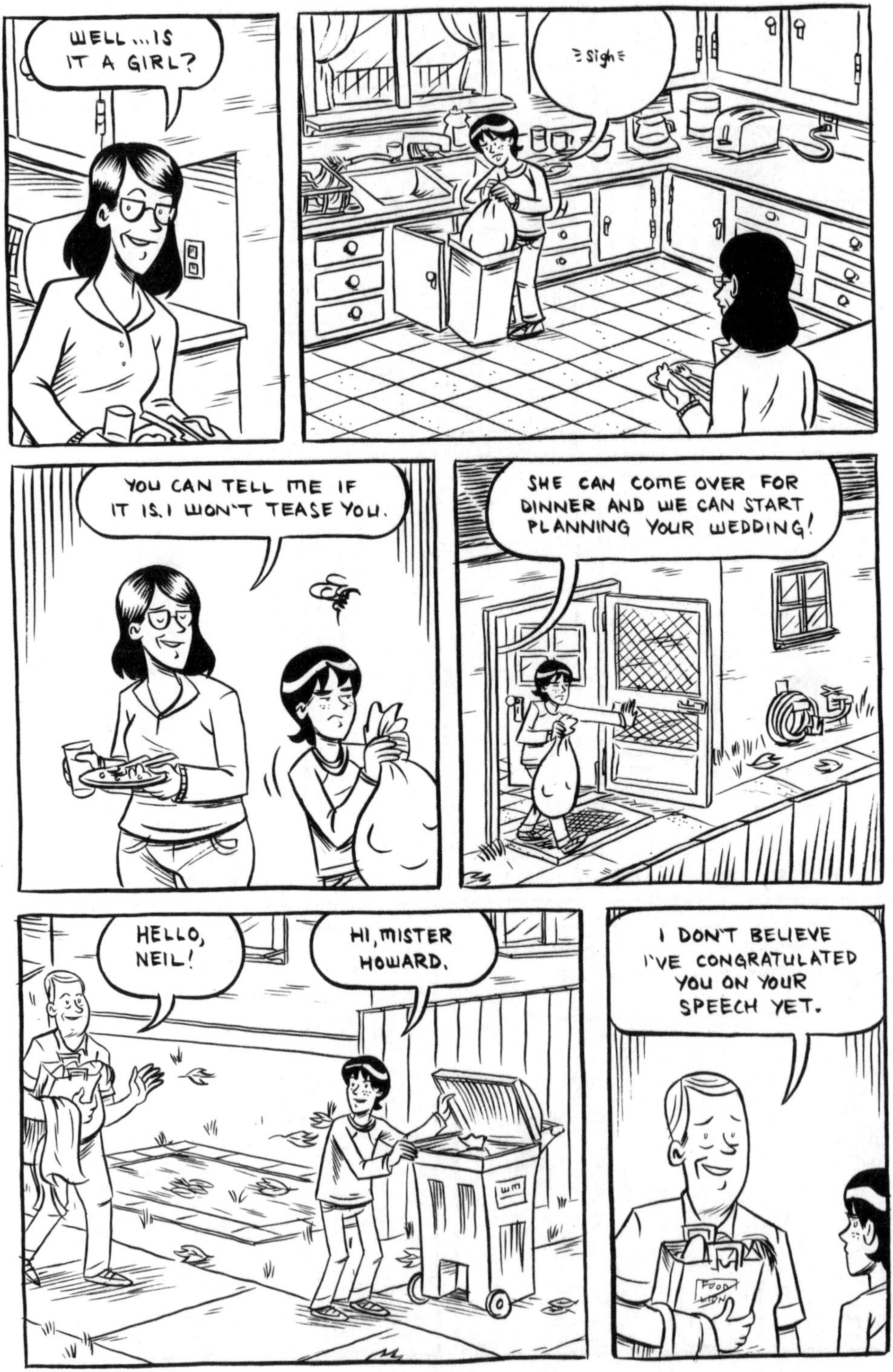
WELL... IS IT A GIRL?
sigh
YOU CAN TELL ME IF IT IS. I WON'T TEASE YOU.
SHE CAN COME OVER FOR DINNER AND WE CAN START PLANNING YOUR WEDDING!
HELLO, NEIL!
HI, MISTER HOWARD.
I DON'T BELIEVE I'VE CONGRATULATED YOU ON YOUR SPEECH YET.

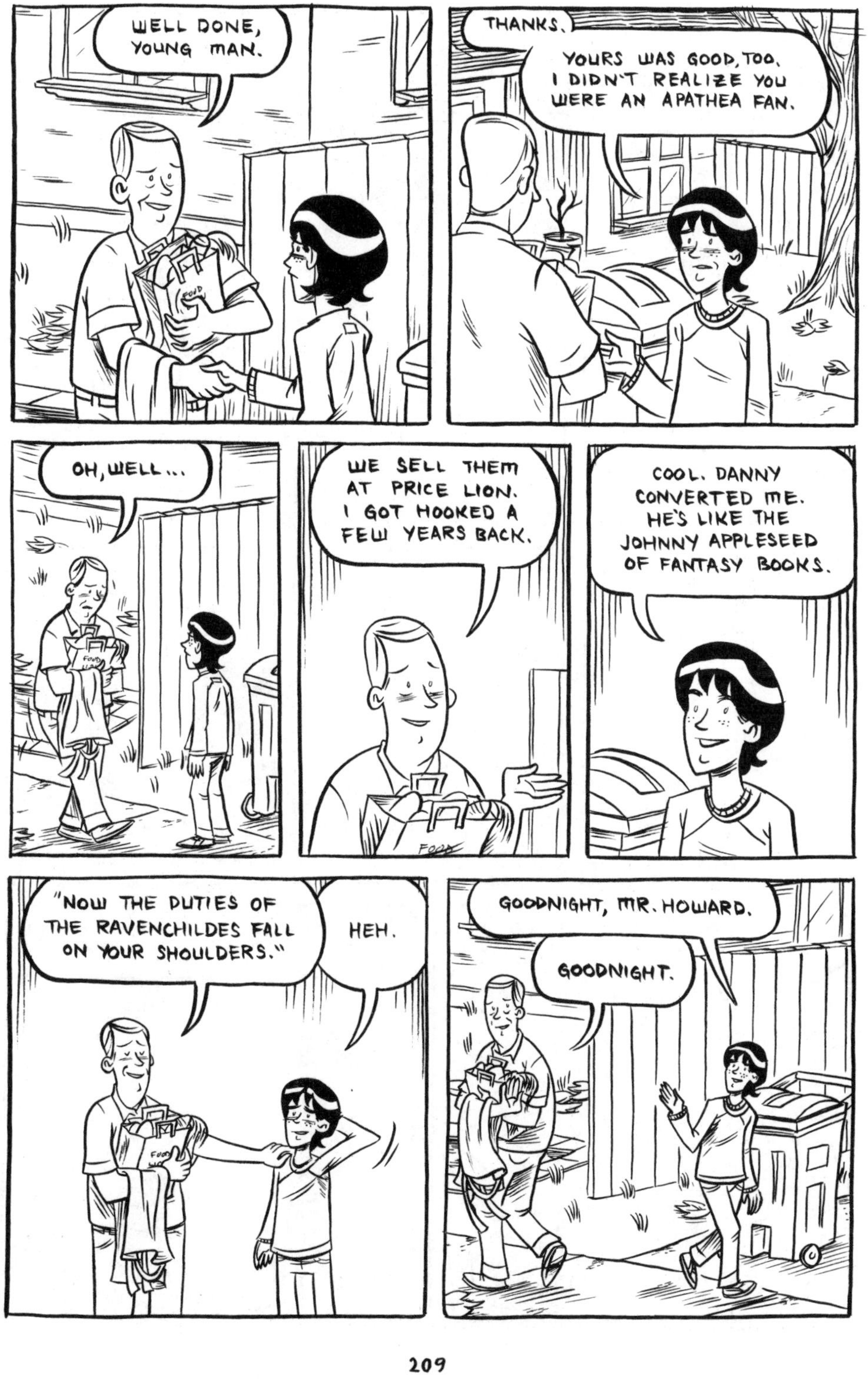
WELL DONE, YOUNG MAN.
THANKS.
YOURS WAS GOOD, TOO. I DIDN'T REALIZE YOU WERE AN APATHEA FAN.
OH, WELL...
WE SELL THEM AT PRICE LION. I GOT HOOKED A FEW YEARS BACK.
COOL. DANNY CONVERTED ME. HE'S LIKE THE JOHNNY APPLESEED OF FANTASY BOOKS.
"NOW THE DUTIES OF THE RAVENCHILDES FALL ON YOUR SHOULDERS."
HEH.
GOODNIGHT, MR. HOWARD.
GOODNIGHT.

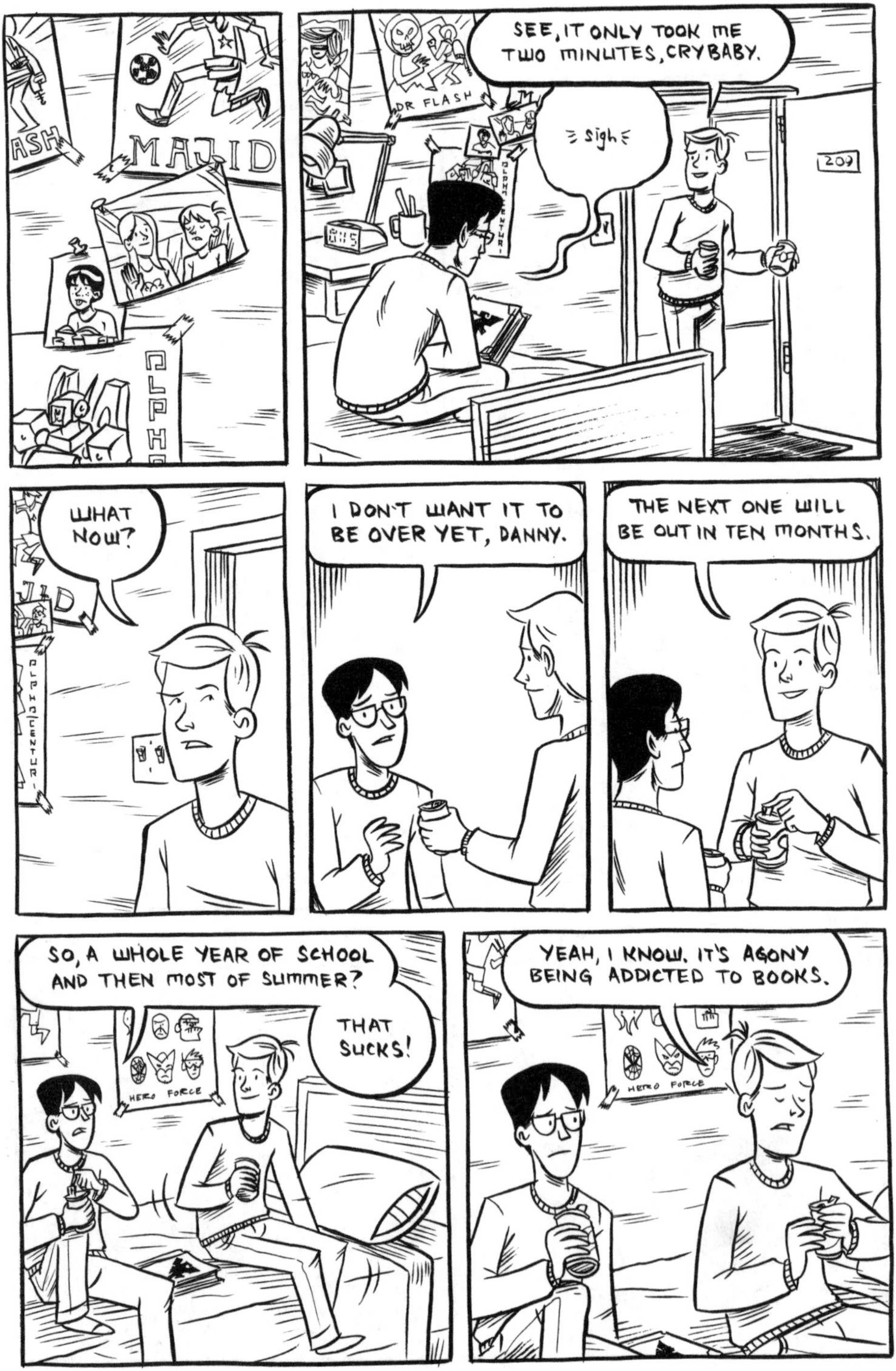
MAJID
ALPHA
DR FLASH
SEE, IT ONLY TOOK ME TWO MINUTES, CRYBABY.
sigh
209
WHAT NOW?
I DON'T WANT IT TO BE OVER YET, DANNY.
THE NEXT ONE WILL BE OUT IN TEN MONTHS.
SO, A WHOLE YEAR OF SCHOOL AND THEN MOST OF SUMMER?
THAT SUCKS!
HERO FORCE
YEAH, I KNOW. IT'S AGONY BEING ADDICTED TO BOOKS.

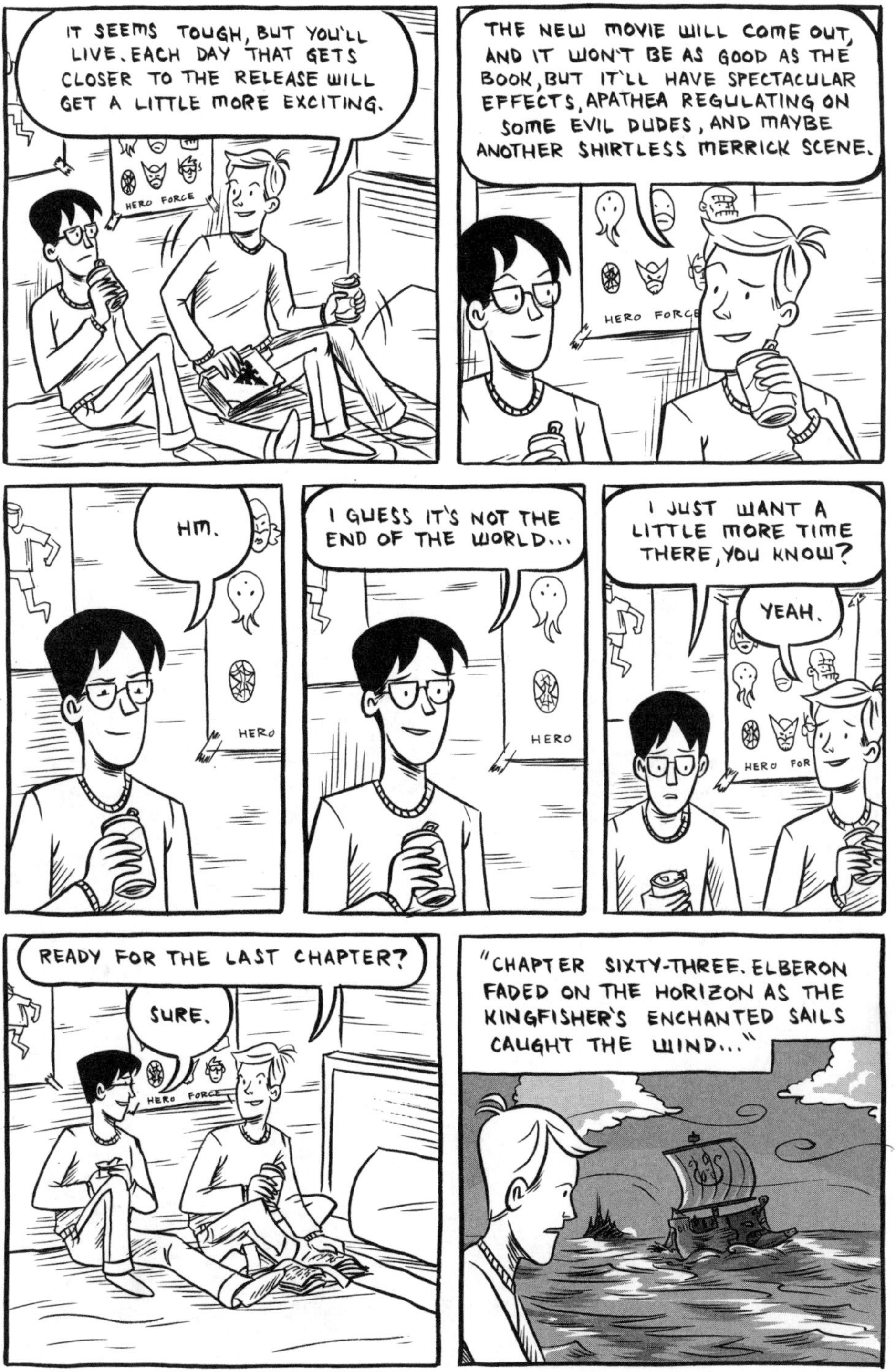
IT SEEMS TOUGH, BUT YOU'LL LIVE. EACH DAY THAT GETS CLOSER TO THE RELEASE WILL GET A LITTLE MORE EXCITING.
HERO FORCE
THE NEW MOVIE WILL COME OUT, AND IT WON'T BE AS GOOD AS THE BOOK, BUT IT'LL HAVE SPECTACULAR EFFECTS, APATHEA REGULATING ON SOME EVIL DUDES, AND MAYBE ANOTHER SHIRTLESS MERRICK SCENE.
HERO FORCE
HM.
HERO
I GUESS IT'S NOT THE END OF THE WORLD...
HERO
I JUST WANT A LITTLE MORE TIME THERE, YOU KNOW?
YEAH.
HERO FOR
READY FOR THE LAST CHAPTER?
SURE.
HERO FORCE
"CHAPTER SIXTY-THREE. ELBERON FADED ON THE HORIZON AS THE KINGFISHER'S ENCHANTED SAILS CAUGHT THE WIND..."

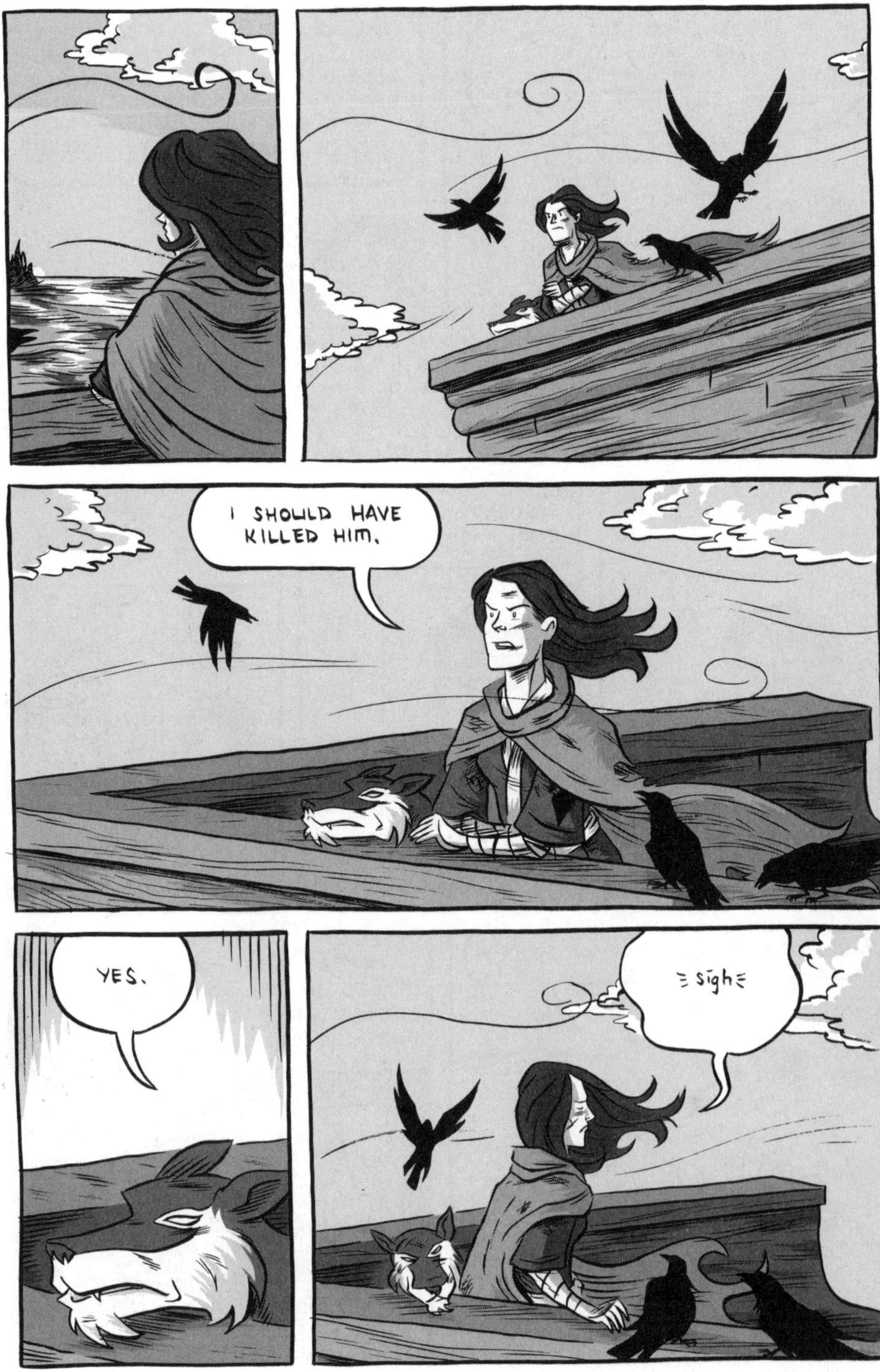
I SHOULD HAVE KILLED HIM.
YES.
sigh

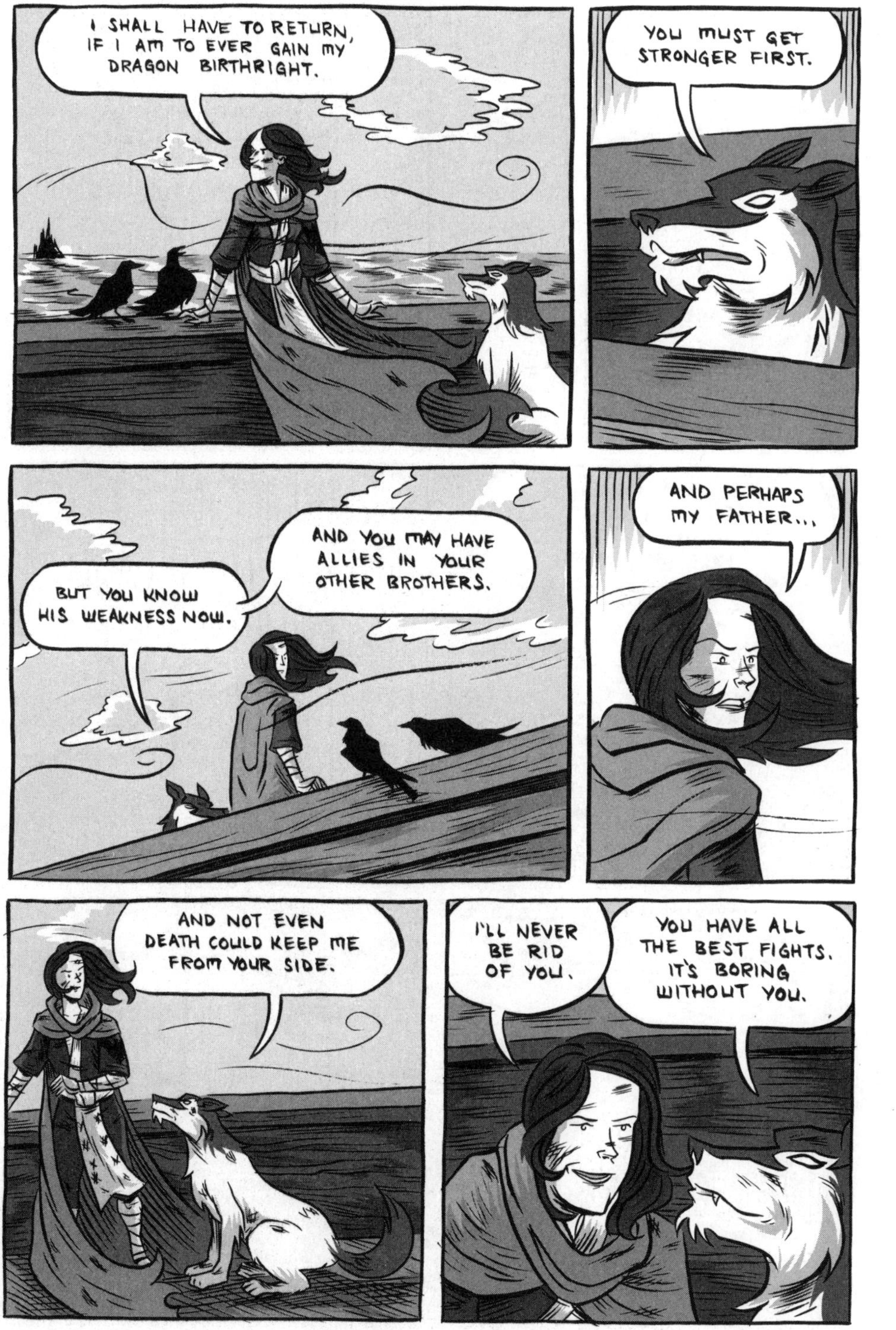
I SHALL HAVE TO RETURN, IF I AM TO EVER GAIN MY DRAGON BIRTHRIGHT.
YOU MUST GET STRONGER FIRST.
BUT YOU KNOW HIS WEAKNESS NOW.
AND YOU MAY HAVE ALLIES IN YOUR OTHER BROTHERS.
AND PERHAPS MY FATHER...
AND NOT EVEN DEATH COULD KEEP ME FROM YOUR SIDE.
I'LL NEVER BE RID OF YOU.
YOU HAVE ALL THE BEST FIGHTS. IT'S BORING WITHOUT YOU.

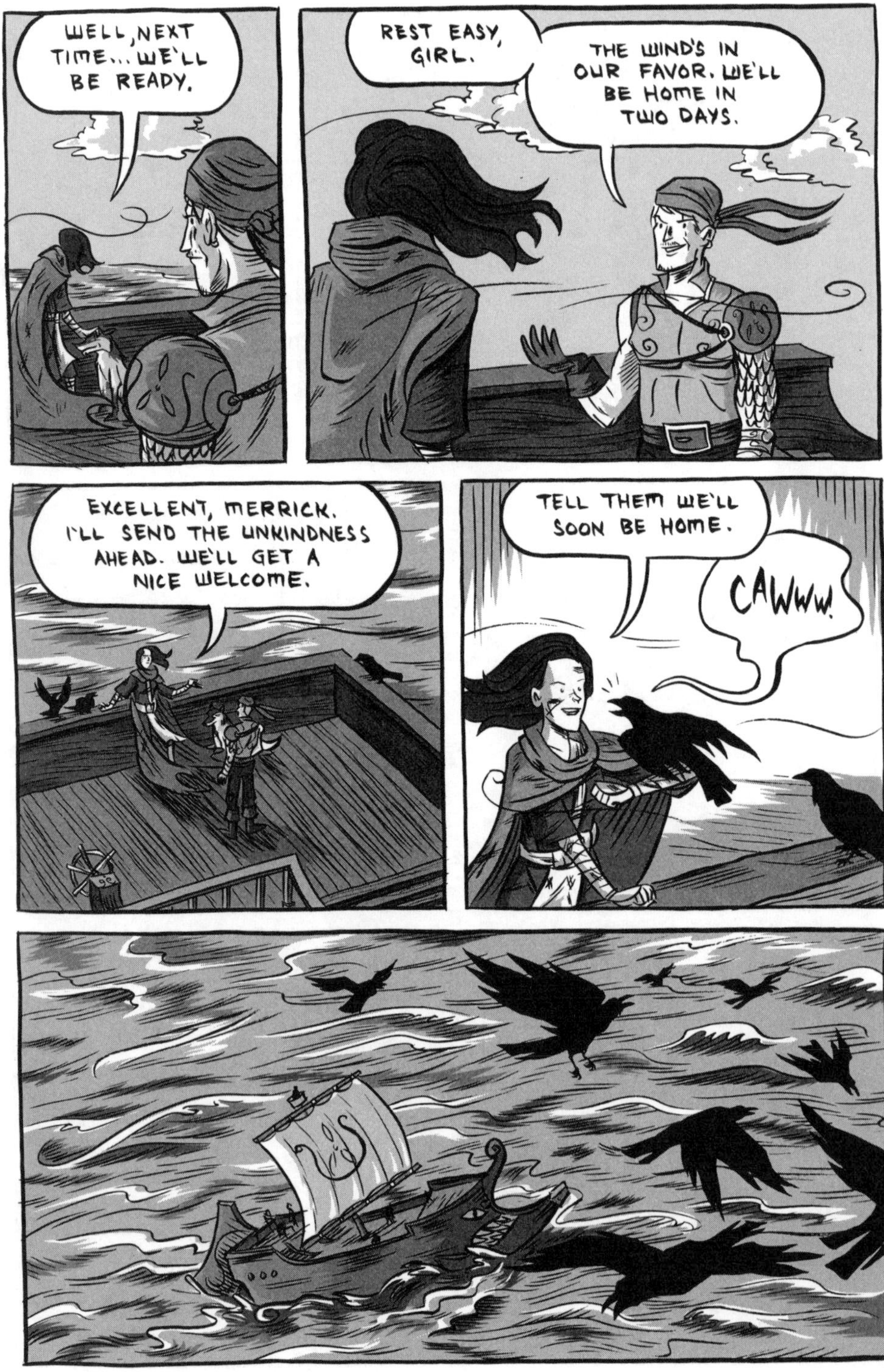
WELL, NEXT TIME... WE'LL BE READY.
REST EASY, GIRL.
THE WIND'S IN OUR FAVOR. WE'LL BE HOME IN TWO DAYS.
EXCELLENT, MERRICK. I'LL SEND THE UNKINDNESS AHEAD. WE'LL GET A NICE WELCOME.
TELL THEM WE'LL SOON BE HOME.
CAWWW!

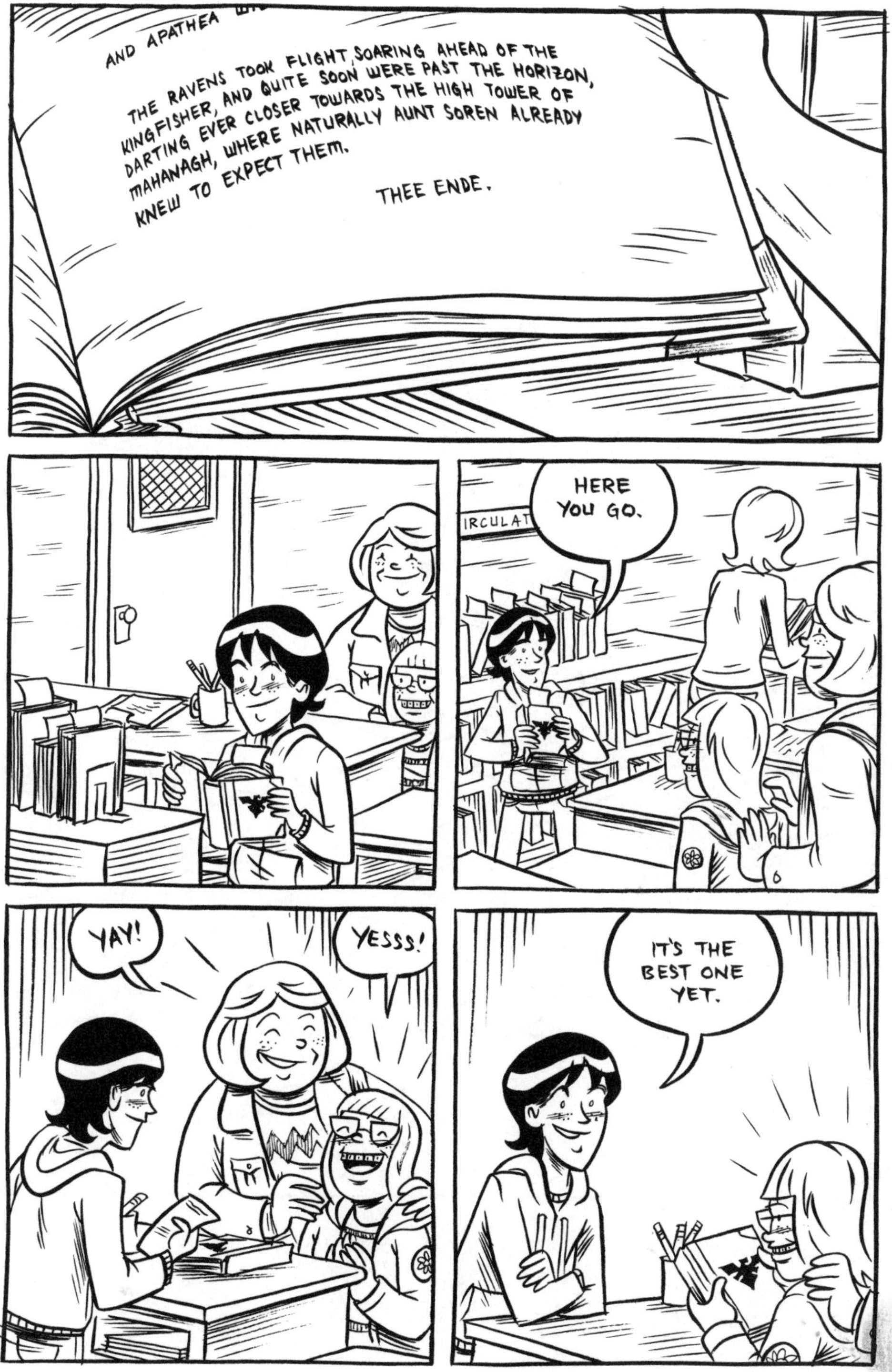
AND APATHEA
THE RAVENS TOOK FLIGHT, SOARING AHEAD OF THE KINGFISHER, AND QUITE SOON WERE PAST THE HORIZON, DARTING EVER CLOSER TOWARDS THE HIGH TOWER OF MAHANAGH, WHERE NATURALLY AUNT SOREN ALREADY KNEW TO EXPECT THEM.
THEE ENDE.
HERE YOU GO.
YAY!
YESSS!
IT'S THE BEST ONE YET.

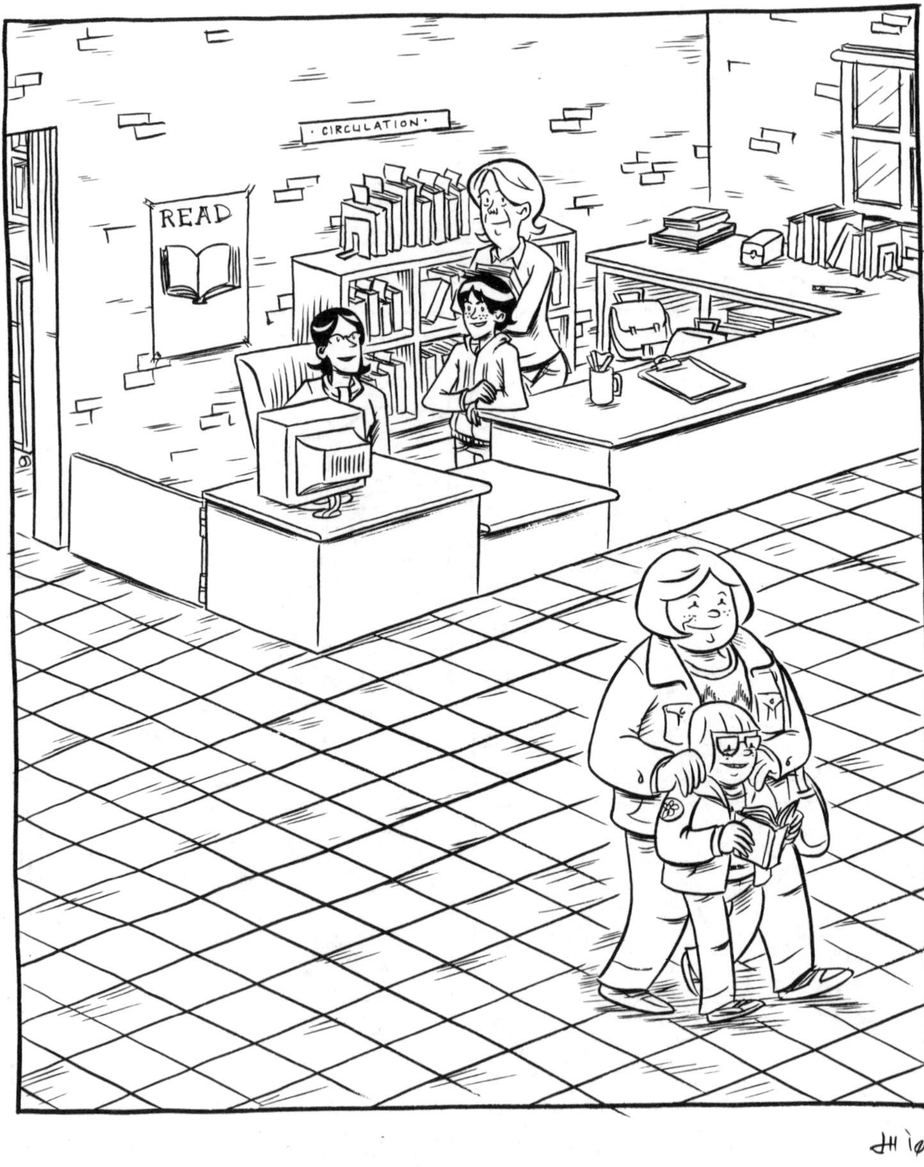

· CIRCULATION ·
READ

JH '10

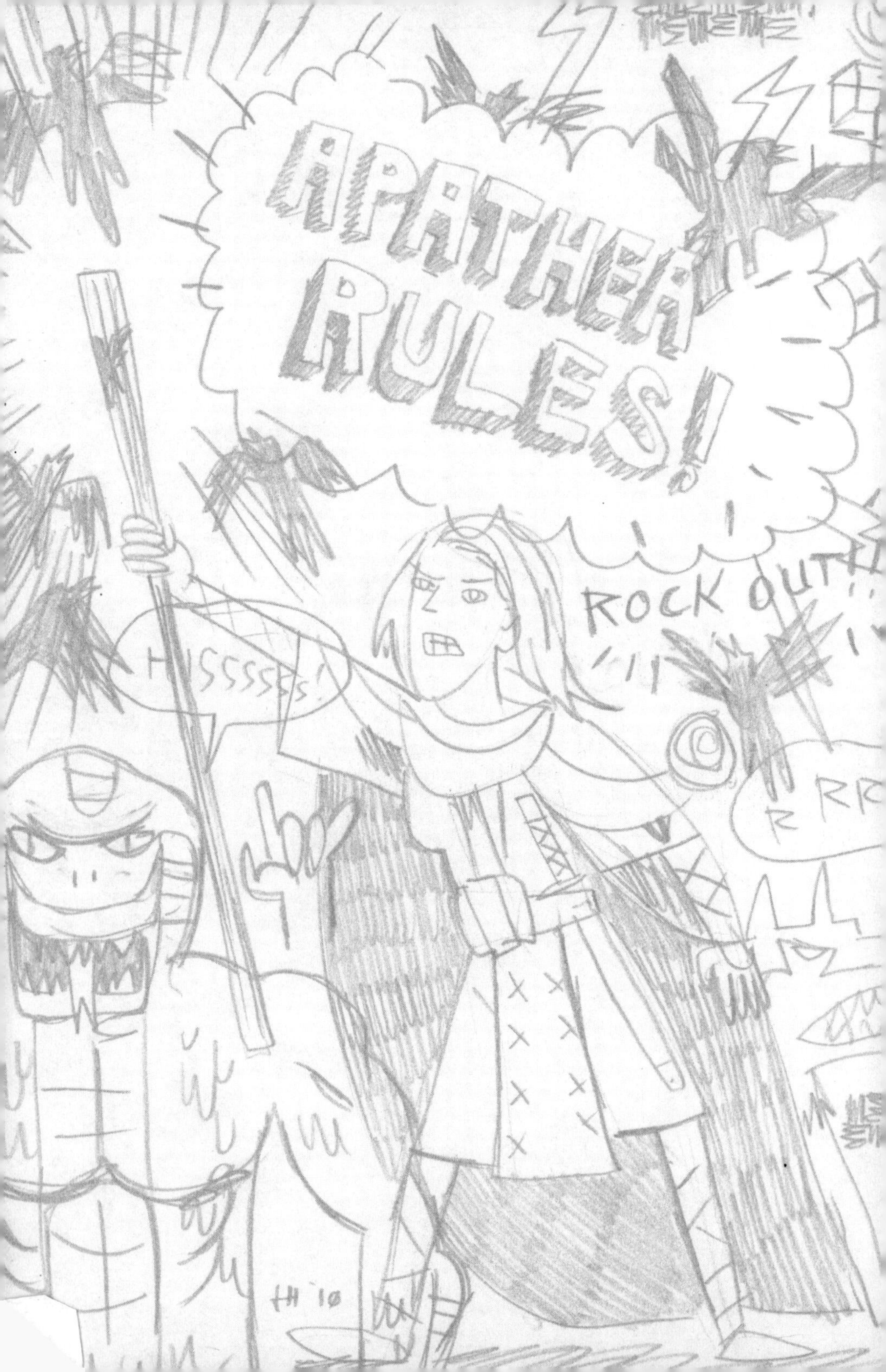
APATHER RULES!
ROCK OUT
HISSSSSS!
HH '10